Bewitched

Between

Hex After 40

BOOK 4

Paranormal Women's Fiction

SHELLEY DOREY

ISBN: 978-1-988913-80-3

Contents

One

Shannon

If Beth James actually believes she can drive us out of Wesley because we're Witches, she has another think coming." I link arms with Mary-Jane beside me as we stride down the street.

"We *are* freaking Witches, and we'll be damned if we're going to be ashamed of it." Libby, on my other side, blares.

"Yeah! Beth and her half-dozen lackeys can pound sand. We're not going to just own our nature; we're going to *lean* into it." Cynthia's battle-cry makes even *me* scared.

As we continue down the main street to face Beth and her mob—that conniving bitch—the sight ahead, stops me dead in my tracks.

Holy crap on a cracker. Is this for real?

"What the actual hell?" Mary-Jane gasps.

Sure, we expected Beth and her cronies, doing some kind of protest demonstration...But they're gaping—same way I am!—at the crowd of townspeople facing them. Their protest signs of 'Witches out of Wesley' wilt before them as they press back into the plate glass window of MJ's restaurant.

The citizens of Wesley form a half-circle facing Beth and her gang. But I've never...EVER seen anything like it!

Not the angry townspeople demanding we be burned at the stake. Nope. It's like someone dropped acid and decided to throw a supernatural Comic-Con convention.

"Are those... *Fairies*?" MJ points at a cluster of winged beings hovering at the back of the crowd. There're four, fully grown adults, with translucent wings whirring hover about ten feet off the ground. One of them leans to the other, points at us and starts giggling.

"I think the correct term is 'Fae,'" Libby whispers, her eyes almost popping out onto her cheekbones.

Yes, there are freaking Fairies floating above the crowd, watching the scene unfold below. Before them is a crowd of at least fifty people hemming in Beth and her group.

My gaze darts over the people facing off with Beth. Oh my good, goddess. Is that Wayne Silver? His normally clean-shaven face is sprouting hair faster than a Chia Pet. That's my boss? The distinguished newspaper editor's tweed jacket strains at the seams, buttons hanging on for dear life as muscles ripple beneath. He's at the forefront, his arms outstretched, trying to herd Beth and company, but of course, they stand frozen in place, gawking at him.

Wayne looks over at me and gives a small salute, before *his face begins to stretch...* into a *wolf's* muzzle! His forehead slopes back into a thick brow while his *eyes start to glow red*! And to top it off, his teeth grow, to become long ripping fangs.

The piercing scream of one of Beth's buddies hardly registers... my mind in shell-shock. She collapses, her knees folding in a dead faint, but like a cat, Wayne the Werewolf darts forward to catch her. I blink fast watching him lay her gently on the sidewalk.

"Smooth move, Wayne!" the mayor of our town calls out. "Couldn't have done better myself!"

After rising up to his hind feet... HIND FEET? Wayne shakes himself like a dog caught in the rain for a second or two, then blinks slowly, like things are back to normal. He gives the Mayor a look bordering on disgust. "You could have helped, y'know." Ending with a poke to Mayor Jefferies' round stomach like it's a party balloon.

"Oh, Wayne, my boy...coming out in broad daylight takes sooo much out of me!" Jefferies replies blithely. "However, in light of this wonderful moment..." He bends at the waist, letting out a series of grunts before straightening up to his full height.

Holy shit!

His face is flour white, his eyebrows jet black, and a set of fangs protrudes from his upper lip! "Satisfied?" he asks. "Like I said, it's not easy in daylight!"

Another one of Beth's compadres lets out a squeak. "You're...you're..." she says, pointing at him.

He steps over to her with a malevolent grin and snipes, "*Vampire* is the word you're looking for, my dear." Leaning over, he sniffs her neck. "Oh my..." his voice is a seductive growl, "*O-positive*...my favorite..."

"Easy, Mayor," Wayne says. "None of that now..."

Beth jumps in front of the mayor and shoves him in the chest, causing him to stumble back. "You cut that out, Mayor Sadler! She's not from here, and you know it!"

He wags his finger in her face, glaring at her. "And you're a damn blabbermouth, Beth! You took The Oath of Silence!" His mouth opens wide, advancing on her before Wayne speaks.

"That'll be enough of that, Jeff old buddy," Wayne steps forward and puts his arm around the mayor's shoulder, easing him back. "You need to take a breath, bud."

The mayor's head droops. "Damn normies..."

"C'mon, Jeffrey. Just switch back, okay? You're going overboard."

Mayor Sadler does that thing again—he curls at the waist, and with a series of guttural grunts, trembles for a moment before righting himself, and just like that, he's just another middle-aged balding man with a weight problem. Staring at Beth, his eyes narrow, "You've gone way, wayyy too far, Beth!"

Snapping my gaping mouth shut, I scan the rest of the crowd. Some look like regular people, but most of the others are...are *other beings*. There are a few more Fairies, one or two Werewolves, and a couple of other strange-looking people I can't figure out.

Mary-Jane lets out a whoosh of air. "What the actual, ever-loving hell is going on here?"

"We're gonna sure as hell find out!" I snap, before marching the last twenty feet up to the gaggle of townspeople. My coven is right behind me.

The instant our eyes meet, Beth elbows her way out of the crowd, "I've kept quiet about all of you my entire life! Now, those damned Witches are back and I won't stand for that!" She points at me. "Maeve was *supposed* to be the last Witch, and now this bitch shows up! NO! I WON'T STAND FOR IT!"

My blood reaches the boiling point. Getting right into the bossy bitch's face, "What is your damn problem?"

"*You're* my problem! It's one thing to share this place with Werewolves, Fae, Shifters, Druids and all the rest of them! They're born that way! But you? YOU'RE HUMAN!" she shrieks. "You're the worst! You are *traitors*!"

She spins around, confronting the crowd. With spittle flying from her mouth, she yells, "And if you don't get rid of them, I'll betray all of you! NO WITCHES IN WESLEY!"

"Betray us?" The mayor asks, his voice dripping with menace. The crowd behind him starts to rumble.

Mary-Jane edges herself between me and the shrieking Beth. "We need to dial it down here, hon." Her voice is soothing as she stares at the angry harridan.

"Up yours, MJ!" Beth snaps.

With a sigh, MJ lifts her hand. "Wait and watch as you will. But for now, you shall be still!"

And just like that, Beth's mouth clamps shut and she freezes. Her eyes move back and forth, but she doesn't make a sound.

I stare at MJ. "Where the hell did you come up with that?"

Mary-Jane blows on her knuckles before polishing them on her chest. "Just came to me, to be honest." She shrugs. "But it worked."

Before we can say another word, Devon's car careens onto the street, pulling into a parking slot with his tires squealing. All four doors pop open, and our guys pile out. MJ's husband Ray hustles over to his wife as Stan heads to Libby. Eric makes a beeline to Cynthia.

"Took you long enough," I smile as Devon approaches me.

Scanning the crowd, "Never a dull moment with you around, Shannon." His eyes are wide when he looks at me. "What the *hell's* going on?"

With Beth now as chilled as an ice sculpture, the rest of the crowd goes quiet when Mayor Sadler speaks.

"Well, Devon, I suppose, it's time you learned that not everything in Wesley is as it seems." He has the audacity to punctuate his words with a chuckle.

"You're a—" I stammer, one hand instinctively flying to my jugular.

"Vampire? Why yes!" Jeffrey beams, patting his enormous belly. He glances over at Beth's group, eyeing the woman he had just spoken to.

"Type O Positive is my jam," he says in a voice so seductive, I instantly have cringey thoughts about him. Whoa...talk about being ensorcelled by a vampire... I give my head a shake and my brain clears.

My gaze darts over to my boss, Wayne Silver. He's transformed back to his normal-looking self and I whisper, "Werewolf. My boss is a freaking *Werewolf.*" I blink fast, still trying to process this. "You knew? EVERYONE KNEW?!" My voice cracks as I gape at the crowd gathered. Citizens. Neighbours.

The mayor just shrugs at me with a sheepish smile.

"Shannon," Cynthia murmurs, tugging on my sleeve. "It looks like we're the last magical beings in Wesley to come out. I can't believe what I'm seeing!"

I startle at a familiar rub against my calf and look down to see Robert, my one-eared bobcat familiar, looking back up at me. *"Well, well, well. Looks like you got upstaged, witch."* Typical sarcasm from that fleabag.

All I can do is stare at the gala of mystical creatures—my neighbors, my boss. Robert's right. Our grand witch reveal has just been spectacularly upstaged.

Devon takes my hand. "Like I said," he repeats, "*what the hell's going on here*?"

The Mayor rubs his hands together. "Well, as long as you're here, Devon, it's high time you learned a little more about this town of ours. I'm sure you'll learn a thing or two as Shannon and I have a little confab."

Mayor Sadler sweeps his gaze over me and the rest of my friends. "Congratulations on *finally* embracing your power, ladies!" His eyes glint as he continues with a shit-eating grin. "You have no idea how difficult it's been, waiting for this moment. At long last—the Witches of Wesley!"

Turning to the crowd, he raises his pudgy arms, encouraging them to applaud like we're contestants on some twisted supernatural talent show, and a cheer comes up.

"Hang on! Just a *damn* minute!" Cynthia steps forward, chin jutting out. The cheers die faster than my houseplants.

I wince. Having been on the receiving end of Cynthia's wrath when we first started practicing, I know that tone. Someone's about to get verbally disemboweled.

"I've lived in Wesley my entire life, kept to myself practicing the craft, and only NOW I find out?" Her voice reaches a pitch that probably has every dog within a five-mile radius cowering. "Surrounded by Werewolves, Vampires and Fae—"

"And Shape-shifters too..." Eric says.

Cynthia spins to face him. "WHAAAT?"

"Don't forget shifters, babe," Eric's voice is low, dropping his chin in an attempt to look contrite. "Damn, it was so hard keeping that from you, but I had to."

There's a stunned expression on Cynthia's face for a moment.

Then she whips back to face the crowd, eyes narrowed in rage. "Unlike Shannon, Libby and MJ, I have ALWAYS been a witch! Yet you couldn't let ME in on the big secret? Werewolves and vampires sneaking around, probably laughing up your sleeves at me." Her nostrils flare like she's about to breathe fire.

Claire from the grocery store steps forward, her demure voice barely carrying. "Well, to be honest..."

My eyes nearly pop out of my skull when I see her incisors pinching into her lower lip and her sallow complexion. Another sucking vampire? The sweet-as-pie checkout lady who always reminds me about the two-for-one special, clipping my coupons, is a *bloodsucker*?

"You can't blame us," Claire continues, nervously twisting her name tag. "You're always so aloof, Cynthia. And...well, to be completely honest, you never were much of a Witch, were you?"

"What the hell is that supposed to mean!"

Claire tilts her head, and with a small smile, continues, "A spell here and there, but you lacked a *coven*." She bats her eyes at Cynthia. "It's *your kind* that needs other practitioners of your craft in order to come to fruition." She spreads her arms out. "But us? We, other Mysticals...well, we come into our own all by ourselves!"

Wayne, nods in agreement. "Yes, but that's what makes them special, Claire. For all intents and purposes, they're human."

"They're also Magical, Wayne," she replies.

He nods. "I know, I know. But unlike us, they're not born that way. They *become* Witches." He looks over at us as he explains, "They're able to draw their power from Mother Earth." After casting a glance above, at the sky, he adds, "We get our power from somewhere out there, I suppose." He cocks an eyebrow. "Like the moon. Both Werewolves and Vampires are governed by the moon, right?"

"Whatever, Wayne." Claire gives a dismissive wave of her hand. "We all know that Witches are *different.*" Crossing her arms in front of her chest, she smiles. "And I, for one am glad they're outed...finally. Lord knows, this town needs a Witch's touch, don't you think?"

Mayor Sadler looks like he just swallowed a lemon but doesn't want to show it. "Now, now," he says, "We've been through quite a bit since dear old Maeve Burke passed on, I'll admit that. But we've managed to hold everything together, haven't we?"

Robert lets out a series of low rumbles that nobody but me and Libby can understand. *'Sounds like the Mayor is concerned about his position, methinks!'*

I shoot a glance at Libby, as I shush him. "We'll discuss that later, fur-ball. You didn't say a word all this time, did you?"

'Hmph. Can you blame me? I wasn't sure your coven was going to last!'

Before I can feed some of Robert's snark back to him, Libby decides to sound off.

"And *this* isn't?" Libby explodes, marching forward to stand beside Cynthia. Her face is redder than any hot flash I've seen on her.

"I nursed you all when you were sick. Helped deliver half the town's babies and I'm only now seeing what you really are? And only because I came out as a Witch? *Come on*!"

This is so crazy, I know it's up to me to sort this out. As the coven leader and an outsider to Wesley, maybe...just maybe, I can be objective; the voice of sanity in this coup of creatures.

"Okay. Let me get this straight. So, not everyone in Wesley is a magical being. There *are* some normal people here, right?" I glance over at Stan and Ray, desperately hoping neither sprouts wings nor fangs in the next five seconds.

"Well, sort of..." The Mayor's grin falters. "Of course, there are what we call 'normies' here." His fingers quote "normies" like it's a slur. "The normies have a recessive gene, so becoming a Were', or Fae or Shifter never happens to them." He pauses for a moment. "Now, the *Druids* are a different breed altogether."

"What the hell is a Druid?" Libby snaps.

"All in good time, dear. Right now, let me give you ladies the broad strokes, alright?" He stares at each of us in turn. When we nod, he continues. "We're pretty sure that the water here plays a part in bringing on the change. And being a Magical just doesn't have to *happen* all at once, either."

He casts a look across the street. "Wayne didn't transition until he was in his thirties. Now he's a veritable role model teaching young werewolves the proper protocols of being a Magical for more than twenty years."

The Mayor clears his throat and raises his voice. "Now that you four—Shannon, Libby, Mary-Jane, and Cynthia—are officially out of the Magical closet, I suggest you get acquainted with your supernatural neighbors. They might surprise you! Let's reconvene in a few days to discuss your new community responsibilities."

Beth is still frozen in place, and her posse is still cowering by MJ's restaurant. I hold up my hand. "Okay, that's fine; I'll stop by your office. But for now..." I point at Beth the statue, and the other people with questions in my eyes.

"Okay. I see your point." Jefferies replies. He looks over at the gaggle of interlopers. "Back in the olden days, they'd be taken for a ride out of town. A *one-way* ride if you get my drift..."

"THAT'S NOT HAPPENING, MR MAYOR!" I yell, and the ground beneath our feet trembles.

"I know! I know! We stopped that ages ago!" Sadler tilts his head at us. "Back in the '80's some outsiders learned about us. It was during that whole paranormal hysteria that was going on. Your Aunt Mave did a simple spell on them that made them return home, go to bed and forget all, and I mean *all* about Wesley, New York. In fact, they'd get ill if they just passed the town on the highway." He leaned over to me. "How does that sound, Witch? Think you're up for it?"

Mary-Jane elbows me aside. "I got this, believe me."

"You sure?" I ask.

She just points at Beth, still as a statue, and gives me a look that screams, *'Duh!'*

"Okay, okay!"

MJ sashays over to the group of about six or seven people that had been Beth's coterie, the skirt of her black outfit swaying as she adjusts her pointed hat. "Good day, everyone! How are you doing?"

They're too terrified to make a peep. Mary-Jane extends her arms and gestures like she's smoothing out a tablecloth. I can't hear what she says clearly, but there is a patter, a rhythm to her cadence. She claps her hands, and the people in front of her startle. They all look at one another and make their way to the vehicles they came in and drive off, leaving just Beth.

"Well?" I say to the mayor. "What about Beth, blabbermouth in chief?"

"She's one of our own," Mayor Jefferies says in a grim voice. "We're not going to harm her, but we need to keep her apart from the world until she learns the error of her ways."

"You're going to *imprison* her?"

He holds up his hands, gesturing the opposite. "No, no, no! Think of it like we're going to...prevent her from doing any more damage to our fair town...or herself. The Fae will look after her. They've done this sort of thing before."

I don't like this one bit. On the other hand, Beth *has* been, and still is a threat to Wesley. And I don't have much sympathy for her after all she's put me through.

For some reason, I have the feeling that the Mayor needs my approval, though. "I don't want her harmed, Mr. Mayor."

He nods sagely as he puts his hand over his heart. "No harm will befall Beth, Shannon. You, as the leader of the Witches of Wesley, have my solemn word."

In that case...I turn to Mary-Jane. "Could you remove her spell now?"

MJ gives me a look. "You *do* know she's seen and heard everything, right?"

Mayor Jefferies makes a gesture. "Beth has spent her entire life in Wesley, Mary-Jane, just like you. Unlike you, she's known about the magical aspect of our community all her life. She's not a Magical, but her parents were. There seems to be something genetic about it; not everyone in a family becomes magical necessarily. Her brother Eric is, you know."

"Eric? Yeah, what was that thing he said about Shifters?" MJ and I turn to where Cynthia and Eric are. She looks at Eric too.

"Well," he says with a guilty shrug, "I've just kept it on the down low?"

"And you're okay with what the Mayor wants to do?"

He nods. "Yes, I trust the Fae, and Beth..." He looks over at his sister. "You need to straighten up. You're hurting a lot of people."

She just blinks at him.

I shrug. "In that case, MJ... could you..."

Mary-Jane makes a few gestures with her hands and whispers something, and Beth almost falls on her face.

"You'll never get away with this!" Beth screeches.

"Officer Grassley, could you and Ms. Ivy take her to where she belongs?"

They go up to Beth, each taking an arm. The back of the cop's uniform shirt rips open, displaying enormous dragon-fly type wings. Ivy has been prancing around in full Fae mode since we arrived, in an outfit inspired by Tinkerbell, right down to the slippers with the pom-poms.

Beth starts thrashing between Ivy and Officer Fairy Cop. "You're all freaks! I have video proof of their witchcraft and this whole ungodly sideshow! I'll expose every one of you if it's the last thing I do!"

The Fae's wings begin to whirr and buzz until they're just a blur. Holding her firmly, they rise and fly off and out of sight.

"I'll be stopping by your office, Mayor Jefferies," I say after they're gone.

"I look forward to it, Shannon."

Turning to MJ, I murmur, "If your bar is open, I could use a stiff drink." My nerves are shot to hell. "Like, the kind of drink that makes you temporarily forget you just discovered your grocery clerk might be secretly dining on your neighbors."

Libby turns to Stan, whose face has cycled through more colors than a kaleidoscope. "We all need alcohol. Immediately. And explanations. Lots of explanations." She places her palm on his cheek. "Nurse's orders."

Stan swallows hard. "God, yes."

"Drinks are absolutely on us after all that." Ray throws his arm around MJ's shoulders. "We're closing the restaurant for the day. Maybe the week. Maybe forever. Who the hell knows after today's shitshow?"

As we trudge toward Ray and Mary-Jane's place, he keeps muttering under his breath: "Wayne Silver. A Werewolf. Makes sense now why he's always got that five o'clock shadow by noon. Wonder if I could become one. Would he consider mentoring me? If I get to pick my supernatural flavor, I'd definitely go Werewolf. Better than being a blood-sucker or a freaking Fairy."

I glance over at Devon, hoping for some support from this dog's breakfast, but he looks shell-shocked. "You okay?" I ask.

"What's a Druid?" he says, his voice flat.

"I...I really don't know. Why?"

He points with his chin at Mary Morton, who owns the coffee shop *The Bear Claw.* She's almost naked, in just a sports bra and bicycle shorts. Her entire body is covered with woad and tattoos. "She said I come from a long, loooong line of Druids, and I should get some of her special ink to see if I'm one as well."

Mary must have a sixth sense. She had been chatting with Ida-Red-Car, but turns at the sound of her name. She gives Devon a wink and sashays away, locked arm in arm with Ida.

She's my age, and I hate her bubbly ass with the scorching heat of a thousand suns. "Oh, *really*?"

His expression is the contemplative one men get when considering a major life decision—like whether to buy the red or blue truck.

Except now he's contemplating joining the druid club.

At *Mary's* invitation.

Fantastic. Because what I really need right now, on top of discovering I live in Supernatural Central, is my boyfriend considering magical body art from Wesley's resident hot cougar waitress. Who also has a major crush on him.

Great. Just freaking great.

Two

Mary-Jane

My hand shakes a little as I pour Jack Daniels into the glasses Ray lined up on the bar. "Gee. You think you know someone and *BAM!* They're either a Werewolf, Vampire or some kind of Fairy." But a hand tremor is nothing compared to the way my brain is melting at this revelation, threatening to ooze out my ears. It makes me downright giddy.

"Don't forget *Shifters*," Eric adds with a grunt. "You'd think that being able to transform into any kind of being would get just a *little* recognition! I mean, of all the Mysticals, why are we always forgotten, when we're *clearly* superior?" Eric punctuates his comment with a slug of whisky.

Beside him, Cynthia extends her glass for me to fill with soda water. "Drinking for two now. But if ever there was a time for copious amounts of whisky, it would be now. Seven more months of sobriety, though."

"Got it." I smile at her as our fingers briefly touch. In just that small brush, the image I get is clear as a sonogram that her baby is a girl. It's still not evident whether Eric is the father, or if it's Steve's child. She had been under Steve's spell when he tried to take over our coven, and that union could have resulted in this pregnancy. Thank goodness she decided to just proceed as if Eric's the father and carry on with the pregnancy.

Libby thrums on the bar with her fingers as she stares at me. "I still can't believe they kept this from us all this time. I mean, *we grew up here, MJ!* I've seen these people at their best and their worst, when they got sick enough to go to the hospital. And how often did you serve them meals? This is insane..." She slaps the bar. "Damn it, it's devious."

Shannon's attention is fixed on Eric. "How is it that you're one of them—a Shifter—but your sister Beth isn't?"

Eric does an eye-roll before sitting back on the bar stool. "The Mayor really didn't explain things well, did he? For such a bloviating public official, he quite literally *sucks*."

He takes a breath before launching in. "The best theory we have is that it's about having a recessive gene. People who don't transition into a shifter or any other Magical being, have that particular *recessive* gene. No one knows if they have it. And won't know until they're older, and they transition. It makes normal people more accepting of us. I mean, it might happen to them, too. Or their sister or aunt. No one knows. It's like having blue eyes or brown eyes, except it's not as obvious."

Even though Eric smiles as if the issue is settled, Shannon isn't letting it go. "Okay, so Beth has the *recessive* gene. And she knew about you and...your parents. Along with the rest of the so-called normies. She went along with everything until we showed up, coming out as witches."

"Yeah, that was the last straw for her when you guys showed up. She never cared for the magical types, but she tolerated us." He drummed his fingers. "But when she discovered you four are witches, she cracked." He made a sad face. "She's really gone over the deep end though; she's obsessed with Magicals now, and the resentment that stems from being a normie focuses on you witches." He sighs. "She's pathological now."

"That's just a polite way of saying she's nuts, Eric," I say. He only shrugs.

"But she wasn't alone." Cynthia sighs. "There were about ten people with her when she confronted us. What's going to happen to them, or to Beth? Obviously, she can't keep spreading word on social media or... Damn! She could go to a newspaper or reporters, and then the world will descend on this town. It'll be like Area 51 in Nevada, with all kinds of crazies camped out!"

"What am I, chopped liver or something?" I say. "Don't you worry about Beth's squad, Cynthia. They're not going to remember a damn thing. Right now, all we have to worry about is Beth." I look over to Eric. "As the Magical member of *this* squad, any idea what's going to be done with your sister?"

Eric shrugs. "I really don't know; but I don't think the Fae will hurt her. This *has* happened before, but not during my lifetime." He gives Cynthia's hand a squeeze. "Don't you worry, babe. I won't let her hurt you or our baby."

Ray claps Stan on the shoulder. "Hey Stan! Cheer up, man." "It isn't the end of the world to have a girlfriend who's a Witch or to live in a town of Magical creatures." As he tops up Stan's glass with more whisky, he adds, "And maybe you don't even have to be born here to become a werewolf or druid or—"

"No way!" Stan's jaw tightens before he looks over at Libby. "I barely had my head around you being a Witch... Which is wonderful. Weird but wonderful. And now this? No one told me when I came here and took the job as fire chief that I'd be serving a bunch of...of *creatures*."

When Eric clears his throat, Stan quickly adds. "No offense, Eric. I guess your transforming into a bird to spot forest fires early-on *could* work out OK for us going forward, maybe... It's just... *a lot* to take in all at once."

Devon looks off to the side, musing quietly. "My mother was a Druid. How did I not know? But I guess, there were clues. She always had the best garden around for miles. She said it was because she talked to plants... and I guess she did. As well as chatting up rocks and trees and even the soil. And Mary Morton? She was Mom's *acolyte*?"

Shannon looks like she's ready to spit bullets watching him lost in wonder. After all they've been through, the whole enemies to lovers thing and now *this* curve ball? With Mary practically throwing herself at him? Hmmm... now that I think about it...Mary always gave Devon the biggest Bear Claw pastries and free up sizes on his coffees... Not only a love-sick waitress, but a *Druid* one. Or is the term Druidess? Shit this is a lot to process.

Shannon's gaze drifts over everyone. "It's weird that Mayor Sadler's a Vampire. He doesn't look like the type, right? I mean, aren't Vampires always portrayed as wickedly sexy, tall, dark and panty-melting? But Sadler's got the John Candy, *Uncle Buck* vibe. He looks like he'd rather suck *butter* than blood."

Eric chuckles. "Oh yeah, that's Jeffrey all right. He's kind of fringe with the undead set. But he serves their purpose, which is to keep an eye on things. It works with normies, but the Druids and Shifters are onto the Vamp game. We know why the blood bank is almost always empty."

"Oh, but he has one helluva seductive voice when he wants to, Eric," Shannon says. Did she just blush a bit?

"Shit!" Libby curses. "No wonder the hospital is always asking for people to donate. And the Vampires get *away* with robbing the clinic?"

Eric chuckles. "It helps when the administrator is also a Vamp. Been that way for years. But it slakes their appetite, so their numbers remain stable. I mean, do we really want *more* of the filthy, walking corpses? I absolutely agree with the damned Druids on that one." He nods, as if the reasoning in his statement is obvious. Which at this point, it totally isn't.

Ray frowns as he leans on the bar. "You make it sound like there's some kind of turf war or hierarchy among the Magicals. Where do Witches and Werewolves fit into that?"

"Witches are revered. Which is understandable when you look at my gorgeous fiancée—"

"Fiancée? You haven't even asked me, Eric! What makes you think I'll marry you?" Cynthia chides, although there was no mistaking the happiness that Eric's remark put on her face.

"Well, I'm asking *now,* babe! I thought it was a given, though. I mean, we're having a baby, and I adore you..."

Cynthia's arms fly around Eric's shoulders, and she kisses him. "Of course, I'll marry you! I just needed to be asked!"

"Congratulations!" A chorus goes up with glasses raised high.

As I look at her, it strikes me as strange how I could have disliked her before. Once you get past her aloof demeanor, she's actually pretty damn sweet. Well, more like a salty, caramel torte.

"And of course, I will cater your wedding. It'll be my gift to you, Cynthia."

"Thanks, MJ." Eric kisses Cynthia before turning to Ray. "As I was saying, witches are top of the heap. Sooner or later, we would have let Cynthia in on the town secret, but when Shannon arrived, we decided to see if Maeve's line would continue. We were all smoked when Libby and Mary-Jane took up the craft. And then to have Cynthia team up with them... We were thrilled!"

Shannon grins, "So, witches are the shit, huh? I like that. Who's next in the pecking order after us witches?"

Eric jerks back, frowning. "*Shifters,* of course. But we're more like equals rather than below you. Although the Druids contest that, like everything else, just being their Druid asshole selves. But both species—Shifters and

Druids—are evolved humans, adhering to the natural order, the same way witches do."

Grimacing, he looks over at Ray. "I hate to break it to you, buddy, but werewolves aren't ranked high. Neither are vampires. They're both an abomination of nature, feasting on blood. You might want to set your goals higher if you hope to transform."

Libby's face screws up, puzzled. "What about the Fae or are they Fairies? Still trying to get the terminology right. How do they rank?"

"You mean the *airheads*? That's what we think of them." Eric smiles. "Don't get me wrong. I like Amy and Suzanne, but we never count on them or any Fae. They're basically hippies— all they want to do is fly, get high and fu—"

"Hey! Language!" I say with a grin.

"Sorry. Anyway, I think they do too many mushrooms when they tend to the forest. Half the time, they're high as kites. But they do right by nature in their own way, I suppose."

Devon's eyebrows arch above a grin. "Sounds like the United Nations, but all here in our little town. Politics and rivalries. Glad our witches are in the top tier."

"No kidding." Shannon nods before saying, "So, I have to meet with the mayor to find out our *responsibilities?* What the heck does that even mean? What do they want with us?"

Eric shrugs again. "I really don't know what Jeff's up to about all that. I'm just a Shifter living my life. I've never really indulged in the politics among the different species."

"Species? You sound like a zookeeper. They're people, you know."

"Well, we're not different *races*, are we? We're not Asians or Black...you got a better term?"

Shannon shrugs. "Not off the top of my head, no. I'll think on it. Still, I'm not a fan of that term."

"Whatever. Enough of the woke terminology debates." I interrupt. "At the same time, we all want to make sure Beth doesn't spill the beans. If she had her way, half the planet would know about Wesley. Remember how she posted those horrible things about me and the other ladies in our coven on Facebook? And that had just been based on her speculation. Now she has video proof, threatening to show and tell the world."

How did things get this complicated, so fast? When we started the day, our main problem was admitting to being Witches. But now we find out the whole town is full of mythical creatures.

Eric interjects, going back to his earlier explanation. "In addition to it being something we think is genetic, there's also the water and the air in Wesley. Even the land itself is infused with magic. It's been going on for a very long time, and it had to start somewhere."

Shannon nods, "I guess that makes sense. It started for us at the well, after all."

I set my glass down and turn to her. "The water explains the *living* beings in town, but not the Vampires. Okay, they were once alive, but they're dead now. How does dying turn them into Vamps? What's the water got to do with *that*?"

"Exactly!" Eric slaps the bar before adding. "*Now* you're getting it. They drink blood, not water. Honestly, I don't know how Wesley got stuck having them here. It's high time a Witch got back in the saddle!"

"What's that supposed to mean?" I ask.

"Well, up until Mave passed away, it was always a Witch that assumed leadership of this town. Not these stinking undead ghouls."

Holy Hannah. We'd barely learned about these Magicals and Eric is sounding like we should start a riot or civil war... or a coup? Truth be told, I'm not crazy about this prejudicial side of him.

I look over at Shannon. "I think it'd be good if I went with you when you meet with Mayor Sadler. With my gift of telekinesis, I can get a reading on how truthful he's being."

Cynthia and Libby nod, before Libby jerks straight, interjecting.

"Wait. Your gift works for *living* people, MJ. We're dealing with the undead. I think *all of us*, the whole coven, needs to be there at the meeting. Remember the well and Alice Johnson? She always advised us to have each other's back, so things work for us."

"Absolutely." Cynthia smiles. "And maybe after that meeting, we can go to dinner so you can plan my wedding and baby shower. I'm all in on that!"

As I stare at Cynthia, I can hardly believe the change in her. Normally, she'd be second in command, advising Shannon about possible roadblocks, but now she's turned positively 'giddy girly'. Huh.

I watch Eric from the corner of my eye as he and Cynthia cuddle. He's a Shifter, but he's got a real chip on his shoulder about other Magicals in Wesley. A stab of apprehension goes through me when I realize that it's likely that *all* of the Magicals feel like this about the other...species. After all, he probably learned his prejudices as a child, right? That undercurrent of animosity is *not* a good thing.

We were never aware of that until today! Not only did we learn about all these other beings living here, but just now I see that they really don't get along all that well.

And from what Jeffery Sadler implied to Shannon, she's going to be the one to keep everyone in line.

Libby and I are going to have to up our game to cover Shannon's back during all this.

This was a whole new cadre of crazy we were dealing with.

Three

Libby

Stan only had the one drink, so he drives us back to my place. I look over at him, and you don't need to be a psychic to tell that he's preoccupied. Aside from the silence, his mouth's set in a straight line with his jaw working. Who could blame him, really? In just the last few days, he's learned that I'm a Witch, witnessed a magical battle when that nut job millionaire tried to dominate the entire coven, and now to learn that Wesley is populated by a host of Magical people… yeah, he's had a day.

'As have I!' I quickly brush that self pity aside. Damn it; I've been a nurse for decades—dealing with the wild and crazy of life is nothing new; this is just that sort of stuff dialed up to eleven! So, I'm going to hold it together for Stan; Lord knows it was a freaky experience for me when I first learned about Witches and Maeve's ghost.

Obviously, his brain's spinning a hell of a lot more than mine from the crazy carnival in the town square.

It's clear he's still in a state of shock. Placing my hand on his forearm, I focus, willing dopamine to flood through him. His muscles are taut, knuckles ivory gripping the steering wheel, but ease a bit under my touch. He actually manages a smile when he looks over at me.

Even so, finding out that people I'd known all my life are actually mythical beings—Werewolves, Vampires, Druids and Fae… Wow. Oh, and

Shape-Shifters. I sure as hell better remember them if I want to stay on Cynthia's boyfriend—correction, —soon to be *husband's,* good side.

Stan side-eyes me. "You're doing something to me, right? You know, that healing thing? If we could bottle that magic, we'd put liquor stores out of business, you know." He bobs his eyebrows. "And if we could bottle and sell *'Libby's Libations'* we'd be millionaires and retire to Tahiti!" His voice lacks conviction, even if some of the color has returned to his face.

"I just gave you a nudge of comfort, that's all. Think of it like a good hug from when you were a kid—all will be well, Stan. And no. Much as it might be nice to steal away to some South Pacific island, I've got the kids to think about. Kevin will be gone in the fall; Jack still has another year—if he ever gets serious with school to even get *into* college. And Dahlia is just starting high school."

"Yeah, and she wants to work with you at your vet clinic Patrick Doyle set up for you, right?"

I give my head a shake thinking of the vet clinic. Was it only last week that my dream had become a reality? I had really come into my full healing potential when I'd had to save Robert...and MJ. Wow. It's just been a *week*! No wonder my brain is fried.

And that was all before I learned about the mythical beings in my town. Yeah, it's been a week to remember.

As we approach my place, I ask, "Are you coming in? Stay for dinner and maybe the night?" It wasn't like the kids would be shocked at that. They loved Stan...almost as much as their father. Wow. Seven years that he'd been gone? Almost half of Dahlia's life.

Shaking his head, "No. Thanks, but I think I need to be alone tonight. It's a lot to process, Libby. And I'll be no help in talking to your kids about all this. Not when I can hardly get it straight myself. I'll come by tomorrow after work, maybe pick up a pizza."

Just as Stan wheels the truck into my driveway, Dahlia comes flying out the front door of our house. Yup. From the excitement lighting her face, this latest development has her firing on all cylinders in overdrive.

How am I supposed to keep her focused on her schoolwork when the town abounds with magic? I'd be lucky if she just focused on becoming a Witch! That seems almost *normal* now. And my sons? What's to become of them living here? Maybe Stan's right. Escape to some semblance of sanity for their sake.

Just before I get out, I lean over to give his cheek a kiss. All the while, I push out waves of calm healing. "I'll see you tomorrow." As I alight from his truck, I wonder how this will work for us. Will *he* leave Wesley? And would he be wrong?

"Mom! You just missed Chloe and Jack. They're getting together with a bunch of kids to talk about these magic beings!"

My eyes widen. "Word's gotten around that fast, huh?"

"Are you kidding me? We have a whole Facebook group set up!"

How the hell are we going to keep this quiet if the town's kids are all in on this? I sigh heavily. "What about trying to keep this on the down-low?"

"Well, Susie Griffin set it up. Her mother's a Shifter. She says that nobody will pay any attention; it's just a bunch of kids role-playing. She found out about *you* being a Witch and sent me an invite!" Dahlia does a squeal shudder. "This is sooo cool!" She takes my hand as we walk up to the front door. "They want to know how they can become one of these magical people. Jack wants to become a Werewolf, but I think Chloe's like me, wanting to be a member of the coven. A few others are interested in being Druids. I can't—"

"What about Kevin?" Of all my kids, Kevin is the most like Hank and as the oldest, always trying to fill his dad's shoes, be the man of the house. Jack might be a wild one, but the still waters running deep in my firstborn also worry me.

Dahlia's smile droops. "Kev won't talk about it. The only thing he said was, he can't wait to get the hell out of Wesley in the fall. He's okay with you being a Witch, but this other stuff...it's too out there for him. Not that he can change what just *is*, right?"

I'm worried that Stan feels the same as Kevin. I put my arm around my daughter, herding us up the walkway to the house. As soon as I step over the threshold, Mis Purdy Cat flounces in from the kitchen.

'Word is finally out, I guess.' The mangy cat yawns before proceeding to lick her paw. *'About time you came home to feed me. With all the talk about Mysticals, your daughter's head is in the clouds. She's totally self-absorbed today.'*

I scowl at the fat little feline. Despite my best efforts to keep her inside the house, she's probably carrying another litter of kittens. "Don't you dare slag Dahlia or I promise you, you'll be down to eight lives."

"Crap!" Dahlia bends to scoop the snippy cat into her arms. "I'm sorry, Miss Poor Purdy Cat! You're hungry, and here I am plotting with Jack and Chloe. I'll get you something to eat."

Yeah, her ability to communicate with animals is coming along. She's still not as proficient as I've become, but she can definitely feel that feline's vibe.

Shaking my head, I watch her carry the cat into the kitchen. With that taken care of, it's time to chat with *Number One* son. When I go up the stairs, his door is closed. I sense the waves of tension drifting in the air, even as my hand raises to tap the frame. "Kevin?"

"C'mon in, *Mom*."

When I enter, he's perched on the bed with his attention glued to his phone. The look on his face reminds me of Hank, a *pissed-off* Hank. "Hey Bud, how're you doing?" Taking a seat on the edge of the bed, I rub his jean-covered calf. Again, a part of me sinks at the bewilderment, and apprehension inside him, the same as Stan's, but stronger. He shouldn't have to deal with all this.

"How am I *doing*?" His grey eyes flash when they meet mine. "Things are just *peachy*, Mom. I've barely got my head around you and your friends being Witches, when I learn half the town is infested with...with *freaks*."

"Kevin. Please don't call them freaks. They're *people*, many of them our friends." Despite knowing how hard this is for him to process; it worries me how much he sounds like Beth James.

He stares at me open-mouthed for a second before saying, "Oh my God!" His eyes widen. "Was *Dad* one? Did he ever go howling at the full moon? Or was he a Fae or a Druid? What if *I'm* one?"

Shit. This is worse than I'd thought it would be, and it's happening so damn fast! I barely understand this and having to appear reasonable, the responsible parent, I keep my voice steady. "No. Hank never did anything other than be your father and a wonderful man. But..."

His attention is fully on me now.

"Your dad died in his late thirties. It might not have *happened* to him yet. I didn't become a Witch until this year, and I'm forty-six. And if it did happen, that you became a Druid or Shifter...well, Eric is fine and so is Mary Morton. I guess." Not really sure about Mary, with her fixation on Devon.

"MOM! Do you even *hear* yourself? I notice you didn't mention Werewolf or Fairy...and if you say *Vampire*, I'm gonna scream." He punches the bed, emphasizing his point.

"Not Vampire. Never that. But, honey...you might not have a choice. This might happen even if you don't want it to. I doubt very much that Duncan Moroni envisioned himself as a Druid, when he went to law school. But here he is, back in Wesley. He moved back after he transitioned in his 30s. He had a great law career in New York City, but came back here."

"Duncan Moroni the garbageman?" When I nod, Kevin shakes his head slowly. "He's a *lawyer* but now he's a *garbageman*?"

"Yes. I think he just wanted to be around people like him or something. From what I understand, Druids are even more nature lovers than the Fae."

"Our garbageman's some kind of Magical creature. Who used to be a hotshot New York City lawyer..." Kevin's voice drifts off in wonder. "I can't believe this, Mom."

God. Kevin's right. Can I even *hear* myself rationalizing the existence of Druids? Or Werewolves?

This is a conversation I *never* thought I'd have.

Kevin slaps the bedcovers. "I swear, if there's a chance that will happen to me, I'm never coming back after I graduate. But maybe... if I avoid the water here, it won't happen. From now on, it's bottled water for me, Mom. Didn't the mayor say something about the water in town? It's the water and some stupid recessive gene. I told Jessica to stay away, so this doesn't happen to her."

"Jessica?" My eyebrows bunch as I try to place that name. "I don't remember you mentioning a Jessica. Is she in your class?" Had someone new moved here while I was so fixated on my witchcraft and leaving that horrible *admin* job at the hospital?

"Jessica *Johnson*!" Shaking his head, his cheeks flush pink. You know her, Mom! She's *Shannon's* daughter."

Shit, that's right! Johnson was Shannon's married name! "What? I didn't know the two of you stayed in touch. I mean, you met her only once, when Shannon first moved here." Then it hits me.

Oh, my good goddess! Kevin told *Shannon's daughter* about *all this*? Shit! Shannon hadn't told Jess about being a Witch! And now all this about the other Magicals in town?

Kevin's face flushes darker. "Well... We kind of hit it off. But then she bailed on her plan to come to Wesley this summer. But we kept in touch."

His jaw tightens, and he meets my eye, not backing down. "With all that happened today, I had to tell *someone! A*nd when she called...Well, I spilled the whole shit-storm about this town."

My gut sinks. Worry about Shannon getting blind-sided jerks me to my feet. "I really wish you had talked to *me* instead of Jessica, Kevin. I think you just created a huge problem for Shannon. It should have been Shannon telling her daughter, not you."

He has the grace to look down and mumble a sorry, before once more defiance flares in his face. "She has a right to know, though. All of us do. To find out like this...it *sucks*, Mom."

I sigh, nodding in agreement. "Yeah. Well, it is what it is. I'd better give Shannon a call and give her a heads up that Jessica knows. For now, try to keep an open mind. These people are still our friends and neighbors. They just have an extra element of *specialness* about them."

To put it mildly.

Damn. Shannon is going to blow a gasket about Jessica finding out like this.

Four

Shannon

Since I moved to Wesley last year, one of the most rewarding aspects of my new life is sitting on my deck watching the sunset's effect on the small lake that borders the property Aunt Maeve left me in her will. Back when I was a young girl, spending every summer here, this was a blessed time of day for me. Just before setting, the golden sunlight brightly washes the world before turning into a red fading orb.

It's like a promise — *'Tomorrow's another day'* — that always leaves me feeling optimistic.

Devon is beside me; we're both comfy in Adirondack chairs (the *only* chair suitable for moments like these) as we watch a blue heron circle overhead before heading to its nest. Day is done...

He takes my hand. "Sure has been some day, huh?"

I nod. "That's putting it mildly."

We both startle at the howl behind us. "Damn it, Robert!" I gripe. I look behind us to see him sitting like an Egyptian statue with his head tilted. "What the hell is your problem!"

He lets out another series of growls, and soft snarls. *'If you're not too busy birdwatching, I haven't been fed ALL DAY!'*

"FINE!" I get to my feet.

"What's going on?" Devon asks.

"My Fleabag Familiar—"

'Fleabag! I'll have you know that I have excellent hygiene!' he grumbles back. *'And I'm so poorly taken care of by my Witch, no parasite would be bothered with poor me!'*

I stare at him. "Bobcats are predators, Robert. You're perfectly capable of finding something to eat."

Devon's head is ping-ponging between Robert and I. "I get such a kick out of you and Robert being able to communicate," he says in a wonder-filled tone.

I snort. "*Most* of Robert's communication with me revolves around his stomach, Devon."

Robert lets out a loud yowl and hops to his four feet. *'I'll be having the salmon tonight, Witch.'*

"Oh really? I'm thinking more along the lines of Friskies cat kibble!"

'You. Wouldn't. DARE! Why, that's...that's Familiar Abuse, Witch!'

"Don't push it, then." Naturally, I wouldn't. Robert, with all his high and mighty attitude, knows that he's got me wrapped around his front paw. After all the trials we've been through together this past year, I spend more on salmon for him than I do on steak for me.

But man, is he pushy.

A few minutes later, I'm putting his feeding dish on the kitchen floor for him. "More than you deserve, you hairball-hurling stinky-toes."

He shrugs. *'At least I don't have crow's feet, you middle-aged hormonal hexer,'* he says before tucking into his salmon fillet.

I can't help but chuckle. "Good one." I give him a scratch behind his remaining ear before heading back out to the deck with a couple of Bud Lights.

The sunlight is fading now, but the heron is still circling. I nudge Devon. "Poor thing is probably still looking for its dinner," I say.

He chuckles. "Maybe."

"Oh?"

He pops the cap off the bottle and takes a pull. "Well, after today's events, it could just as easily be a Shape-Shifter spying on us." He tilts his head to the side. "Why, that could be Ida Watkins up there right now, shifted into a bird checking up on you."

"Ida-Red-Car? She's a Shifter? I didn't know that." Ida was the first person I ever hexed. I didn't even know at the time I had magical powers, but when she stole a parking spot from me, my first day after moving in,

I wished something crappy would happen to her and her red convertible, and it did.

He nods. "Yeah. Mary Morton sent me a text and told me."

He looks a little sheepish right now, and that sparks my curiosity. "Now why would Mary Morton tell you about Ida being a Shifter?" I ask, trying to sound as innocent as possible.

Devon's sheepishness collapses into a downright furtive expression now. "Uhhh...well...."

"Devon..."

"Well, Mary's a Druid."

"Mary's an exhibitionist. Walking around this afternoon in nothing but short shorts and a sports bra! What's with all those tattoos?

"It's part of being a Druid. My mother was a Druid, right?"

"Well, that's what we've been told, yeah."

"So, Mary figures I'll probably come into being one...she sent me a bunch of texts telling me that if I have the gene, if she gives me a couple of Druid tattoos, then I could transform too."

"I *see*." I lower myself into my chair beside him. I'm actually seeing a bit of red. Devon's *my* guy, dammit; and I'm not going to tolerate anyone trying to move in on that! "So..." I ask in as light a voice as possible, "when are you planning on having her do this?" My eyes narrow. I wish I had MJ's ability to read minds right now, but now, I'm stuck with just being able to command Nature when I get pissed off.

And right this second, the wind picks up.

Devon looks at me with an even stare. "I definitely want to look into the whole Druid thing, Shannon."

"Oh?" A gust of wind whooshes through the trees.

"Yeah." He tilts his head at me with a sly grin. "Maybe I'll try out that whole 'magic ink' thing they've got going..."

"Oh, really..." The lake's surface starts to roil in whitecaps.

"Absolutely." When the wind and water dial up to another level, Devon puts up a hand. "But not with Mary Morton, that's for sure. I think I'll ask around; I think one of the garbagemen in Wesley's a Druid too. I'll touch base with him."

"Oh." I huff out a breath, and the wind and waves die down. "That might be interesting to find out, I suppose."

Devon's eyes shift to the left and right; he noticed the wind and waves. "Not that you're the jealous type or anything, right Shannon?" He barks a quick guffaw. Before I can snipe back a response, he holds up a hand. "I'm perfectly happy here with you; I'm not on the market, babe."

"Not even a little, huh?" Sorry, but my getting thrown under the bus after twenty years of marriage still stings, okay?

"Not a bit." He knits his hands behind his head and nestles back in his chair. "I know I'm supposed to say something really romantic and mushy right now, but I got nothin'; sorry."

"Don't be." I lean over and kiss him. A really, *really* good kiss.

Just as his hands start to wander, my phone rings with Libby's ringtone. Damnit.

"Hi Libby, what's up?"

"Are you sitting down, Shannon? I really need you to stay calm right now."

The hurried worry in Libby's voice has my skin tingling. Which is saying something after everything that happened that day.

"What's wrong?" It comes out louder and way sharper than I'd intended, judging by the look Robert and Devon shoot me.

"Did you know that my son Kevin and your daughter Jessica are friends? That they keep in touch with one another?"

"No." My forehead tightens. That news came out of left field, but why would I care? I mean, it's kind of sweet. "Jessica never mentioned it. And the last time I talked to her—"

"He told Jessica *everything*. About us being Witches and that the whole town is full of Mystical creatures. She knows! I'm so sorry, Shannon. I didn't know he kept in touch or that he'd tell her and..."

"Oh...*shit!*" My knees give out, and I sit down. "Oh, man..."

"What's wrong?" Devon grabs the phone from my numb hand and speaks to Libby. "What's going on, Libby? Shannon looks like her best friend just died."

I swallow hard, staring at the floor. The tempest of emotions swirling through me—fear that she'll be revolted, and guilt that I hadn't told her before this—consumes me.

I'm only mildly aware of the sudden breeze and the dark clouds scuttling across the sky, waves now frothing on the lake.

Robert jerks up and hops up on me, his paws on my shoulders. *'Easy, Shannon. Get a grip RIGHT NOW before the lake washes us and the house away!'*

I take a deep breath and close my eyes. Robert is right—my elemental power can be a nuisance sometimes.

I look in Robert's eyes while Devon's on the phone with Libby. "I thought I'd have more time to figure it out before telling the twins! I mean, she's all the way over in Boston at college, and Thomas is wayyy down in Texas..." I hit the armrest with my fist. "I'm not ready!"

'Oh, my dear Witch...we're NEVER ready. Fortune, with its whimsical hand, perpetually deals us the most surprising of turns.'

I stare at him. "Whaaaat?"

Robert hops down and shakes like a wet dog. *'Oh dear...let me put it in a way YOU'D understand...Life throws us curveballs; is that clear?'*

"Show off."

'Guilty.' He looks over at Devon, who ended the call with Libby. "Shannon?" His eyes show concern. "We'll get through this. Look, if I can accept that you're a Witch...and all the shit that's gone on here...

"She's going to freak out!"

"Well, I don't know Jessica all that well, but if she's anywhere near as kind, sweet and smart as you, she's still gonna love you. But..."

I look up into his eyes.

"You need to have this conversation in person. And I think that it needs to be here, not in Boston. And...he extends the phone to me. "You need to call her now. After you call Jessica, give Libby a call. She's beside herself about all this."

Robert weighs in before he eases back. *'Devon is right. Don't overthink this. Get it done now.'*

Taking a few deep breaths, I stare at the phone like it's a razor about to slit my throat. Then I pull up Jess's name and hit call. It rings a few times and it's sooooo tempting to chicken out and hang up. But then...

"Mom! I was just about to call you! You will never believe what Kevin Walker just told me. Does he do drugs? I mean, it's so out there that he has to be on some really strong mushrooms."

My eyes meet Devon's, which are inches from mine, as he crouches trying to eavesdrop. This is it. My out. Devon's eyes flare and he shakes his head; I don't need to be a mind reader to get his message— *'Shannon, don't you DARE lie to her!'*. Frig! Can *he* read my freaking mind?

"Jessica, I'm not sure about Kevin or what's up with him. But I need you to come here to Wesley. I haven't seen you in over two months, and it's time."

Ignoring the daggers Devon shoots me with his eyes, I continue. “I miss you. I need to see you. Book the bus to Albany and let me know what time you will arrive. Tomorrow’s Friday. “

“But Mom!”

“Jessica! This is *important*! Your mother needs you to be on the next bus to Albany!”

“Mom, now I’m worried...”

“There’s nothing to be afraid of,” I lie; I’m scared shitless right now. “This is very, very important, and I’m not saying another word until I see you in person. Text me your arrival time, dear.” And with that, I end the call.

“Whoaaa...hard ass Mom when you need to be, huh?” Devon says with a smile. “Good job. I was worried you were going to lie and say that Jack had been on drugs.” He rubs my shoulder.

Then why am I crying?

Five

Mary-Jane

As Ray finishes setting the clean glasses on the shelf behind the bar, I flip the sign on the door to show we're closed. No way will I be able to cook anything, not in the numbed shape I'm in after learning about the *beings* in Wesley.

Before I lock it, the door swings open, and I stumble back with my jaw dropping. Jane glides in— literally *glides* — with gossamer wings spreading from her shoulders, catching the afternoon light in a rainbow shimmer.

Holy shit. My kitchen helper of ten years has *wings*.

"Finally!" Jane stretches her translucent appendages wide. "You have no idea how cramped these get, folded up under normal clothes." She does a little twirl, her wings trailing stardust. "Summers are the worst; it's like wearing three sweaters in a sauna."

I'm transfixed by the sight before me. Her wings shimmer like the finest silk; translucent with a soft iridescent glow, rippling with hues of pale rose and lavender glistening where the light kisses the surface. The edges of her wings seem to dissolve in the air itself like a morning mist.

"They're beautiful, Jane," I say, my voice awed into a whisper. Then I notice her ears - pointed at the tips. How had I never noticed? I point at them. "Your ears, how...?"

Jane laughs lightly. "It's called 'magic' for a reason, hon. I didn't *want* you to notice my ears, and so you didn't." Her eyes narrow. "But so help me, if you call me 'Spock'..."

"What? You? Spock? Are you kidding me? You're the most un-Spock person I've ever met!" Still, I snicker. I hold up my hand, creating the 'V' of the Vulcan salute. "Live long and—"

Jane's eyes narrow. "Why I oughta..." and we both giggle. "You can be such a witch, Mary-Jane."

"Jane, we're actually closing early. Today's been too damn much, you know?" I gesture at the empty tables in the dining room. "But don't worry, we'll still pay you for the shift."

"Thanks, MJ." She settles onto a barstool and Ray wordlessly slides her a Diet Coke. "I know this must be overwhelming, but you'll get used to it. Wesley's special because of its people; all of us. The Vampires, the Werewolves, the Fae like me..." She takes a sip. "We're just your neighbors and friends, same as always. Just with a few extra...features."

My fingers itch to touch those wings, to see if they feel as delicate as they look. Also, to glimpse the emotions and memories stored in their ethereal strands through telekinesis, my witchy gift. But I keep my hands to myself, still processing that my reliable kitchen helper is actually a fairy tale come to life.

I settle onto a stool as Jane's wings flutter with excitement. "God, my life before I transformed... When I think about it, what a waste." She purses her lips. "You know my ex has a drinking problem, right?"

"Yeah, you mentioned that when you split up."

"Oh yeah. The last five years of our marriage, Tom would park himself in front of the TV every night, beer in hand, screaming at whatever game was on. By the time the game was over, he was three sheets to the wind." Her lips form a thin line. "And that was on *weeknights*. On the weekends, he'd start drinking right after breakfast. Try having a conversation? Might as well talk to the wall."

Her wings shimmer as she leans forward. "Then one morning, I woke up with this...*tingling*. Like champagne bubbles under my skin. Next thing I knew—wings!" She laughs. "Talk about having a 'change of life', huh?" Her face falls. "It completely freaked Tom out."

"Well, it must have been a shock."

"It sure was! None of my family were Fae growing up! I thought that I'd be a normie my entire life!"

"Kind of like me, huh?" I hold my hand out. "But Jane, I never knew about...I grew up here, Ray grew up here, and we never heard a single word about the Magicals. Did you?"

Jane nods. "Yeah...it was a surprise to me, let me tell you." Then her mouth quirks up to the side. "But it was *no* surprise to my ex. When I showed Tom my wings, he totally freaked out."

"Well, like you said, it was a shock."

She cuts the air with her hand, and her wings buzz for a moment. "No, it wasn't a shock *to him*! It turns out, his family comes from a whole line of Magicals! He's got an uncle who's a Shifter, and some cousins who are Druids! He knew all about the Magicals! But when my wings appeared, he got furious!"

"What? Why?"

"Because *he* wasn't a Magical! He knew about all this, but never, in fifteen years of marriage ever mentioned a word to me! And then when I transformed, he told me he wasn't going to spend his life with some winged freak..." her eyes teared up. "Not only did he move out, he went to live in freaking Alabama!"

I remember them splitting up a few years ago and Tom just disappearing. I thought Jane had taken the breakup pretty well; I didn't know she had been *dumped.*

Ray leans over and touches Jane's arm. "That guy is a piece of shit, Jane. I'm sorry that happened to you." He looks over at me. "Hon, it never crossed my mind when I found out you're a Witch." He turns back to Jane. "But like Mary-Jane said, we had no idea what was going on in Wesley about all this stuff."

Jane nods. "I'm pretty sure Shannon's aunt Maeve had something to do with that. Before she died, Maeve told me that she had some kind of spell to keep normal folk blind to the magical aspect of the town..."

"A *ward*? She cast a ward on the town?"

Jane shrugged. "I guess. But it had gotten weaker over time after she passed away. Now word's getting around like crazy after the shit Beth James started." She shudders. "After the Fae found out about me, they sort of adopted me to help me complete my transformation." She looks at both Ray and me. "We really hope we can put this toothpaste back in the tube. Normies don't take well to Magicals, Mary-Jane."

I nod. "I hope so too. They didn't treat Witches all that well back in Salem, right?"

"Well, it's on you gals to protect Wesley now, you know."

"Shannon's going to meet with Mayor Sadler; we'll figure something out."

Ray perks up from behind the bar, his eyes showing that familiar gleam when he gets an idea in his head. "So how exactly did your magic show up, Jane? You drink a lot of water? Everyone keeps talking about Wesley's water being special."

His eager tone makes my stomach tighten. The last thing I need is Ray trying to transform himself into a Werewolf. Being married to a Werewolf? Not sure I'd like that.

But then... If he channels his inner animal to our sex life, that could be...*fun*. I squirm a little picturing it. Beauty & The Beast... the PornHub version! I snicker.

Jane looks at me puzzled before replying to Ray, "I can't say one way or another how much the area's water has to do with the magicalness of Wesley. But then... they do say, 'water is life', right?" She drums her fingertips on the bar's surface. "Now, I don't know how it is for others, but *my* garden is something special; maybe the water has something to do with it, but I do know that after I transformed, it really changed for me."

"What do you mean?" I ask.

She practically floats off her stool, lost in her own world. "Oh, the *garden*! You should see it at sunrise when the dew catches the light. The flowers open just for *me*, and the vegetables—they practically jump into my basket. And the trees, each one with a different vibration, a unique song!"

Eric's earlier comment about the Fae being nature-obsessed airheads, springs to mind. Watching the rapture in Jane's eyes as she extolls on each of her tomato plants' personalities... He might have a point. Still, she's the same Jane who's had my back in the kitchen all these years. Wings or no wings, she's a friend.

Jane hops off the stool, her wings catching the light. "Well, since I've got the night off, might as well pop over to Amy and Suzanne's. They promised me some seedlings of their new cloned weed." Her eyes go wide, and she claps a hand over her mouth. "Oh! Please don't mention that to anyone who's not Fae. Especially not to Jonas Stone."

"Don't worry," I wave my hand, dismissing her worry. "I won't say anything, and especially not to the *police chief*."

"Oh, honey, I couldn't care less about that! But he's a *Werewolf*." Rolling her eyes dramatically, she snipes, "Weres are such tight-asses about everything. Rules this, regulations that. You should hear them at town meetings - 'proper protocols must be followed.'" She affects a stuffy, pompous voice. "Though I guess they loosen up during that *special* time of the month." With a wink, adding, "And I'm not talking PMS."

Ray snorts, nearly dropping the glass he was drying. I have to bite my lip to keep from laughing at the mental image of Jonas Stone, our stern police chief, on his haunches, howling at the moon. Though now that I think about it, it explains his monthly "fishing trips".

"Though, I have to admit," Jane continues, "the Weres do keep the vampires in check. Otherwise, we'd have blood bank robberies every other night instead of just once a month."

After Jane flutters out the door, Ray leans against the bar counter, a sheepish grin spreading across his face. "Maybe I'm not cut out to be a Werewolf. I can't see me being a stick in the mud with rules and stuff. I'm too easygoing for that."

I cross over to him, pressing myself against his chest. "There *could* be some advantages though," I nuzzle into his ear, whispering, "Going so primal in the bedroom."

His eyes darken, and he pulls me closer, his lips descending toward mine—

"Oh, my God! Get a room, you two!" Chloe's voice breaks the moment. Standing in the doorway with Jack, her face scrunches up in disgust. "Seriously, you act more like teenagers than an old married couple."

Jack grins, ignoring Chloe. "Just came from hanging out with some kids in the park." He rocks back and forth on his heels. "Everyone's stoked about this mystical stuff; they're so pumped about what they might turn into." His eyes light up. "Here, I thought Wesley was this boring podunk town, but now? No way I'm leaving, not even for college. Just hope when I transition, I'll be a Werewolf. They're totally ripped and badass. Base, man."

I watch Chloe inch closer to him, her eyes going all soft and dreamy. Poor girl has it bad.

"Hate to break it to you, Jack, but you don't really have the personality for it. You're more the shifter type, I think." I shoot Ray a look, and he stifles a laugh.

"When's the next coven meeting?" Chloe asks, twirling her hair with her finger. "Some of the other girls want in on it. Except Rachel Knowles; we definitely don't want that bitch in the coven club."

"She's not that bad," Jack protests. "You just don't like her 'cause she's a cheerleader. The guys on the team don't seem to mind her." His gaze shoots to Chloe before adding, "Not me though. I'm totally team Chloe."

I don't need my gift to sense the jealousy radiating off my daughter in waves. I nod at Chloe. "First off, it's not a club, honey. And second, any new members need to go through Shannon; Libby and Cynthia too." I pause and add, "As well as *me*." We're a proper coven, not some high school clique."

"Whatev..." Chloe's head falls back sarcastically before chiding. "But if Dahlia gets to go, then I'll be pissed if you don't get me in, Mom."

"Look. I'm still trying to figure out all these Mysticals in town. When I see how the coven fits in, we can talk about you and your friends joining us. Until then... just cool your jets, Chloe." Even as I scold her, I notice the stubborn streak in her. Damn. Just like the one I have.

Folding her arms across her chest, she glares at me. "Fine. So maybe we'll start our own coven. I'm going to buy some things from Amazon and at least *look* the part. What is it they always say? Fake it till you make it."

Finally, Ray weighs in. "You need to listen to your mother on this, Chloe. I'm no Witch, but it's more than just a costume, like it's Halloween or something. When it's time, your mother will handle your training. Until then..."

Chloe rolls her eyes so hard there's a chance they'll get stuck staring at her brain. "Aww Dad. Come on! You always side with her. It isn't fair." Turning to Jack, she grabs his hand. "Come on. Let's go see if anyone's still in the park."

As they head back out the door, I call out to her. "Be home at ten. It's still a school night."

I'm hardly aware of Ray behind me until his hands are on my tummy, pulling me into him. His breath is hot as he whispers. "Speaking of werewolves... Where were we before we were interrupted?"

Immediately, I know his thoughts, his hot fantasy, going all animal. Of course, I fall right into it. This might not be that bad...

I think back to Shannon's first spell, when she'd wished for me to shed the pounds my doctor had ordered. How accidentally she'd made exercise so pleasurable—hell, orgasmic—that I'd become addicted, dropping five dress sizes.

Was Ray's fantasy of going all animal that different from what had happened to me? The heat in my body was definitely telling me it wasn't.

I could get used to my husband going wolf, even if it was just once a month…

Six

Libby

I stare at the mess of ingredients on my kitchen counter. Usually, I'm not this scattered cooking dinner, but considering what today's been like I guess I can cut me some slack. The pot of water refusing to come to a boil looks like it's mocking me.

My Witch powers don't extend to making pasta cook faster, apparently. Dammit.

Kevin is pacing in the kitchen as I cook. "This is *insane*, Mom. The Mayor is a vampire who drinks blood. Like, actual blood?" He runs his hands through his hair. "And Wayne Silver can turn into a wolf? The same guy who wrote that article about my baseball team last spring?"

"Honey, I know it's a lot to process--"

"A lot to *process*? Half the town isn't even *human*!" He grabs his jacket from the chair. "I need some air. This is so whacked."

The door slams behind him, and I wince. How did life get so complicated? Kevin's almost as weirded out as Stan.

I'm tempted to give Shannon a call and see how she's doing. Kevin telling Jessica about all this magical business isn't good, but honestly, what teenager wouldn't spill *that* tea? It'd be easier to ask them to keep quiet about winning the lottery.

My phone sits there on the counter, taunting me. Shannon has every right to be upset. This isn't exactly how she'd planned on breaking the news to Jess. But if she *had* done that, this wouldn't be an issue!

"Mom, the sauce is burning." Dahlia appears at my elbow, reaching past me to stir the pan I'd completely forgotten about.

"Thanks, sweetie." I rescue the marinara and dump the pasta into the strainer, steam rises in clouds around my face. This day has been trying enough without burning my hands on top of everything else.

"Mom, it's not working." Dahlia's voice borders on being whiny. Sitting cross-legged on the floor, she has Ms. Purdy Cat curled in her lap. The cat's eyes are half-closed, that smug feline expression smirking that says she knows exactly what's going on and finds it amusing.

"What's not working?"

"I've been sitting here trying to hear what she's saying. All I get is the rumble of her purring."

I set the pot down and turn to face her. My daughter's face is scrunched up concentrating, her fingers buried in Ms. Purdy's grey fur.

"That's probably the problem. You're trying too hard." I wipe my hands on a dishtowel. "When it happened to me, I wasn't even thinking about it. Rocky Raccoon just started chatting away about how thirsty he was. Kept repeating 'water' and then a lot more, the little shit."

"But how?" Dahlia's lower lip juts out.

"Honestly? I don't know. Just don't rush it. It's still pretty awesome that animals can understand you when you talk to them, y'know? Pretty soon, you'll know what *they're* saying too."

But as I gaze at my daughter, I wonder how much the witching well had to do with me getting this power. How did Witches of Wesley pass the torch to the next generation? I should really check Shannon's Grimoire to see how it's done; when should the younger ones be taken to the well?

Ms. Purdy Cat stretches and yawns, showing off her perfect little teeth. For a moment, I catch a snippet of her thoughts - something about the tuna we'd had yesterday being subpar—but I keep that to myself. Dahlia needs to find her own way to this particular power.

A knock at the door makes Ms. Purdy Cat's ears twitch. Who could that be? When I open the door, Duncan Moroni stands on my porch, still in his dark green sanitation uniform. The setting sun cast long shadows across his tanned face, highlighting the stubble of dark beard growth. Although we'd been neighbors for years, our only exchange is just a friendly wave as we drive by. What the heck does he want?

"Evening, Libby." He shifts his weight, hands thrust deep in his pockets. The truck with *Wesley Sanitation* emblazoned on the side, sits idling at the curb behind him, its white bulk gleaming orange in the fading light.

"Duncan? Is everything okay?"

"I need to talk to you about something." His eyes dart past me into the house. "About the shifters."

"Shifters?"

"Ayyy-up."

I step out onto the porch. The spring evening air is cool against my skin, carrying the scent of blooming dogwoods from next door. The sense of the surreal hits me; I'm about to have a discussion with one of the town's garbagemen. Not about my recycling habits, or how to dispose of my grass clippings...no. I'm going to talk with the town garbageman about *Shapeshifters.* "What about the shifters?"

"There are things you should know about Eric James and his people." He takes a step back, propping his backside against the railing of my porch. "I know Eric seems like a stand-up guy," Duncan's voice drops lower, "but shifters play the long game. They've been positioning themselves against us Druids for decades."

Goosebumps ripple along my skin, and I cross my arms. But it's more than just the evening air; my defenses are up. Eric is not only engaged to Cynthia, but I also like and trust him. What is Duncan up to, casting shade on Eric?

"What does that have to do with me? Or our coven?"

"Everything! The shifters are trying to get you witches on their side. They act like they're above all the mystical politics, but they're the worst for stirring up trouble and pitting us against each other." He glances at his idling truck. "They've got half the town looking down on the Fae like they're just tree-hugging hippies."

My mind flashes to MJ's restaurant earlier, how Eric had made fun of the Fae, saying they did too many magic mushrooms.

"The Fae aren't what everyone thinks they are," Duncan continues. "Sure, they're easy-going nature freaks, but push them too far..." His voice fades, and then in an intense tone, he says, "They can get nasty, too." His eyes narrow, "Let's just say Jonas Stone and I keep tabs on the shifters for good reason."

The mention of Chief Stone's name takes me aback a little. Not weird enough to find out the town is full of these beings, but now to get caught up in the melodrama? Or paranoia? This is some kind of weird small-town politics. Keeping my voice even, I answer, "Okay, I get that you don't trust the Shifters, but... *Eric's* a good guy. Even Ida Watkins is basically a good person. Eccentric of course, but a decent person. Are you sure—"

"Look, I've lived here my whole life." Duncan straightens, pushing away from the railing. "Seen things most folks wouldn't believe. The Shifters are patient. They'll wait years to make their move to rule the roost."

Oh damn, not again! Just last week, me and the gals in the coven fought off a warlock who wanted to rule over the coven! What the hell is all this power-grab stuff? I stare at Duncan pointedly. "Why the hell would they want to 'rule the roost'?

He shrugs. "To get their own way about how things are done. For example, the Vampires would have a *regional* blood bank built in Wesley if given half the chance. The Fae would open marijuana stores and set up franchises is another example. Each of the groups of Magicals wants to do things their own way."

"Look, Duncan, we've been neighbors for what—eight years? We've hardly ever even spoken. I really don't get the sudden urgency that you're telling me this." Sheesh. Can I get my head around just one thing before you hit me with political intrigue?

Leaning against my front door, I study his face. He seems sincere, but something isn't adding up. Like he's just trying to make trouble? But why? What does he hope to gain?

He rubs the back of his neck, glancing away for a moment before saying in a slow, deliberate tone, "Well, for starters, all your life, you've just been a normie, Libby. A wonderful nurse, yes! Even gifted. But now..." he gestured at me. "You're a Witch, dammit. And it's your coven's *responsibility* to keep everyone in line in this town."

I fold my arms. "Even the Druids, Duncan."

He nods. "Ayyy-up. But my kind just keep to ourselves. We're happy with the way things are. We're not the ones to be worried about. We have traditions and rites that go back thousands of years." He tilts his head at me. "You and your coven are new players in town, and I have to warn you. The shifters are gonna try to use you."

"And the *Druids* won't?" The words came out sharp, but his sudden concern feels off. "Look, if the Shifters are such a problem, why doesn't Mayor Sadler step in?"

"The *Vampires*?" Duncan's laugh is bitter, like burned coffee. "They couldn't care less about maintaining order. They pretend to care, but let's face it. *Chaos* works in their favor." Leaning in, he adds, "Think about it—if things get messy, people panic. When people panic, the Vampires can feed more easily. More normals get turned and no one can do anything about it. *If* they even notice, that is."

"That's ridiculous. People would know. The Mayor—"

"Is just a *puppet*. The real power behind him, the *elite Vampires* want Wesley destabilized. Makes it easier for them to expand their numbers." Glancing back at his truck. "Look, I've probably said more than I should. Just... watch your back around the Shifters. *Especially* Eric James."

Duncan has never shown any interest in anyone before, let alone town politics, but now he's dropping bombshells about vampires and shifters on me?

"I appreciate the head's up." I don't bother hiding my skepticism. "But Eric is engaged to one of my best friends. If he were plotting something, don't you think we'd know?"

"Huh." Duncan's expression hardens. "They're *engaged* now? Great. This is worse than I'd thought." He's silent for a few beats, staring hard at me. "The *Witches* need to run this town."

Duncan's words hit me like a splash of cold water, but he doesn't seem to notice, when he continues. "The election's coming up in three months. Not only do I see everyone's garbage, I *know* everyone. Every faction in town. I can help manage your campaign."

Mouth gaping, I blink at him. "*My* campaign?"

"For Mayor!" Stepping even closer, his voice drops like we're co-conspirators, "Think about it, Libby. A Witch leading Wesley? Someone who understands both the normal and mystical world? You're *perfect* for it."

The porch light flickers on automatically as dusk deepens around us. Inside, I hear Dahlia talking to Ms. Purdy Cat, still trying to make that connection.

"Look, Shannon's our coven leader," I say. "Why aren't you taking this to her?"

"*Shannon Burke*?" Duncan's face twists, looking disgusted, like I'd offered him a shit sandwich. "The *Burkes* are part of the problem. That well of theirs—you know what they did? They tapped into one of the most powerful ley lines in the county. Just took it, like they *owned* it."

I shift my weight, narrowing my eyes as I stare at him. "The same well helped us discover our powers, Duncan."

"Proves my point *exactly*. The Burkes think they can just manipulate ancient forces without consequences. Most Druids can't stand them for that reason alone."

He doesn't back down one iota. "Look, I know politics. I know every player in this town, their strengths, their weaknesses. Let me help you run for mayor." He stares at me. "You know I wasn't *always* a garbageman, Libby."

"Yeah, you were a lawyer but came back here when you transitioned. I know that."

"And if there's one thing lawyers are good at, it's politics. I have some experience in that department. I can help you."

"Oh, for *Pete's* sake!" I look away for a beat, trying to remain calm. "I'm a nurse, Duncan. And I'll soon be running the vet clinic. So, way too busy to even consider your offer." Scoffing, I add, "Plus, I don't know the first thing about running a town, even if I wanted to."

"See? That's where I come in. Think about it - you're respected, level-headed. You understand both sides of Wesley. The normals trust you, and now you've got power of your own." His eyes gleam in the porch light. "And while you're considering it, maybe have a chat with Cynthia about Eric and warn her off."

Despite the anger bubbling up in my chest, I hold my tongue to see what else he'll say.

"I suggest you tell her that she should dig deeper into his past. Ask about that year he went away to university in Richmond. Why he never finished. There's more there than he's letting on." Duncan straightens up, adjusting his uniform shirt. "You don't have to decide about the mayor thing right now. But remember what I said about the Shifters. And Eric."

As I watch Duncan's garbage truck pull away, its taillights glowing like red eyes in the growing darkness, I scowl. The whole conversation leaves a sour taste in my mouth, like drinking orange juice after brushing your teeth. I thought Druids were supposed to be these wise, nature-connected beings, but Duncan comes off more like a conspiracy theorist with an axe to grind.

Mayor? Me? It's laughable. I have enough on my plate with the clinic opening, and three kids who seem to find new ways to give me gray hairs daily. Besides, the last thing Wesley needs is more division. If Duncan thinks he can use me as a wedge between the Mysticals, he has another think coming.

And Eric? Sure, he can be a smart-ass sometimes, but the way he looks at Cynthia—that's something you couldn't fake. The baby has him walking on air. No way am I going to mess with their happiness based on some vague warnings from a guy who spends his days picking up garbage, and his nights plotting political strategy.

Still, Duncan's visit illustrates that I need to be careful about taking anyone's word as gospel around here. Does every faction carry grudges and rivalries? Or is it mainly Duncan? And more importantly, do I even care to get involved? I wasn't kidding about having enough on my plate.

Movement at the end of the driveway catches my eye. Kevin and Jack approach, heads bent together in conversation. Whatever they're discussing has Kevin gesturing wildly while Jack nods along, hands stuffed in his pockets. The sight of my boys actually getting along instead of sniping at each other is enough to push thoughts of mystical politics aside.

"Boys!" I call out. "Dinner's ready!"

Seven

Shannon, the next day...

With Jessica in the back seat, I grip the door handle tight as Devon's jeep bounces along the winding mountain road. My stomach churns, but not from the motion. How am I going to explain to my daughter that everything Kevin told her on the phone is actually true? And that he only told her the tip of the iceberg? My inner voice is going nuts:

'That's right, honey, the decrepit home I inherited from my Aunt Maeve does in fact have a Witching Well on the property—yes, it's now disappeared, but its effects have remained. What effects? Well, for starters, your dear mother can whip up a thunderstorm at the drop of a hat, and if you really get her pissed off, she'll open up the earth right under your feet, how's that?

Oh, and that's only part of the legacy, you see. Guess what else? We're descended from a line of Witches and... Oh yeah, chances are it runs in your blood too, daughter dear. But don't sweat it; Witches are apparently the elite. We're way higher in the pecking order than Vampires, Werewolves, and Fae people, Shapeshifters & Druids. And no...I'm not really sure just what a Druid is, other than they have strange tattoos and one of them has the hots for my current boyfriend.'

In the back seat, Jess is oblivious to the hurricane in my head. She's prattling on about stuff at school. "And then Sarah said we should all go camping after finals, but I told her I'd have to check with you first." Jessica pauses for breath, and gives me a questioning look. "Mom? You're doing that thing with your face again."

"What thing?"

"That worried-mom scrunching between your eyebrows. The one you got when Thomas crashed Dad's car into the mailbox."

I force my features to relax. "Just thinking, honey."

"About why you called me home?" She shifts in her seat, her eyes searching my face. "I know you said you'd tell me when we get to your place, but we're just about there. Spill it, already."

The jeep rounds the last bend, and my home bathed in sunlight comes into view. The afternoon glow highlights the fresh paint on the wraparound porch, making it gleam.

"Well, here we are," Devon announces, breaking my spiral of anxiety.

Jessica leans forward. "Wow, Mom. The place looks amazing. Way better than the photos you sent."

I manage a weak smile. "Wait until you see inside. You won't know it with everything I've done."

But it isn't the renovated interior I need to reveal. Nope. Revealing that I'm a Witch is the thing causing my fingers to knot together. The magic hums beneath my skin like electricity; itches to come forth, even as I dread seeing her face when it does.

Devon parks the car close to the front steps. As Jessica grabs her overnight bag from the back, I catch his reassuring nod, as if to say 'you've got this'. I climb out of Devon's jeep, and before I can turn to help Jessica with her bag, she grabs my arm.

"Mom! There's a bobcat!" Her fingers dig into my sleeve, tugging me back into the safety of the vehicle. "Devon, do you have anything to scare it away?"

Of course, Robert would *have* to make an appearance, complicating things even more. Seriously? When I look over at him, his golden eyes slowly blink, casually perched on my front step. It's clear he relishes seeing me squirm.

Asshole.

"That mangy bobcat is Robert." I open the car door wider. "Don't worry. He won't attack you."

Jessica's jaw drops. Her eyes bulge as she watches Robert rise and pad over to where I stand. He bumps his head against my outstretched hand, a deep rumble of satisfaction vibrating through his thick fur.

"No. Way," she whispers.

When she slides out of the jeep, her movements are slow and careful. Robert stays put as she inches closer, her hand trembling as she reaches toward him.

"I never thought I'd get this close to a wildcat." Her fingers brush the top of his head, and a big grin lights her face. "Mom, this is incredible. You've actually tamed him?"

She scratches behind his ear, and Robert leans into her touch.

"Wow! Would you look at that." Jessica's laugh echoes across the yard. "You take 'crazy cat lady' to a whole new level, Mom."

If she only knew half of it. Robert's golden eyes meet mine again, and I swear I catch a glimmer of snark there. But really, this went better than I thought it would.

"Let Devon take your bag inside." I touch Jessica's arm as she reaches for her overnight bag. "There's something I want to show you first."

Robert pads alongside us toward the tree line. The May sunshine filters through the fresh spring leaves, casting dappled shadows across the path.

"I take it that whatever you want me to see, is why you insisted I come here. Am I right?" Jessica pulls her cardigan off and ties it around her waist. "Why the big mystery?"

"You'll see. It's not far." I lead her deeper into the woods, following the familiar trail that winds between ancient oaks and towering pines. My feet know this path by heart now—every root, every stone that marks the way to where the well once stood. The place is still hallowed ground to me, even without the numinous well.

Robert darts ahead, his tawny form weaving through the underbrush. The warmth has brought out the wild roses early this year, their sweet scent mixing with the earthy smell of the forest floor.

I decide I'll start at the beginning. "You know, when I was a teen, Aunt Maeve used to take me walking out here." I duck under a low-hanging branch. "She knew every inch of these woods."

"I remember you telling me about those times, how close you were." Jessica smiles. "She was the mother you never had, right? And that those summers spent here with her were some of your best memories."

I feel my throat constrict with emotion. "Yes, those summers were pretty damn special." I turn to her. "But there's even more to that story. My mother had her reasons—and they were pretty good ones, she thought—to keep moving around the country. But she wanted me to have someplace I could go back to that would always be there..."

"Like home." Jess says.

My eyes film with tears, and I nod. That was accurate, though the full story runs deeper. So many years I'd been angry at Mom for being so distant, dragging us back and forth across the country as if we were fugitives. Now I know her motives; she'd been trying to shield me from someone she wrongly believed meant us harm. In reality, that person was my own flesh and blood, a relative who'd simply wanted to connect with me. I stop at the edge of the glade, my hand reaching out to catch Jessica's arm. Robert sits at attention nearby, watching us.

"Before we go any further, I need to tell you about me, who I am." The words catch in my throat. "I'm not the same person who came here after the divorce."

Jessica's brow furrows. "Well, yeah. You seem happier. More... I don't know. Confident?" She eyes me up and down. "You're happier than when you were with Dad..."

"Yessss. But it's more than that." I squeeze her arm gently. "A lot more. When Kevin told you—"

"*Stoner* Kevin? Doing drugs and spewing all that crap?" She rolls her eyes before jerking back, gaping at me. "What he said was crazy." She pauses and looks at me strangely. "It was, right?"

"Not crazy." I draw in a deep breath, screwing up my courage. "I should have told you myself. I wanted to, but I needed time to understand it all first."

"Mom?" Her voice wavers. "You're starting to freak me out."

I meet her eyes; so like mine, like Aunt Maeve's. The same eyes that had watched over this land for generations. "I'm a Witch, Jess. We are descendants of a long line of Witches who settled here in Wesley."

There. I'd said it.

I watch my daughter's face, waiting for some reaction—shock, disbelief, anger. But she just stands there, her blue eyes fixed on me. The silence stretches between us, broken only by the rustle of leaves overhead.

Finally, her lips part. "A Witch? As in *Wiccan*?"

The tension in my shoulders eases a bit. At least she hasn't run screaming into the woods. I smile, grateful for her measured response.

"That's part of it. We honor nature as Wiccans do, but it's more than that. When I choose, the elements around me—air, water, earth and fire—bend to my will, doing what I command it to do. In short, when I use intention... *magic* happens."

Seeing the stunned look in her wide eyes, her mouth drifting open, it's clear she needs to see it to believe it. Closing my eyes, I will a stiff breeze, directing the flow of air over her with a sweep of my hand.

When I look, her hair swirls over her face, and she gasps, trying to scrape it back to stare at me.

"No. You're telling me you did that? Made that breeze? C'mon, Mom!" She steps back, frowning at me. "And I thought Kevin was doing drugs. It looks to me like he's not the only one."

I twirl my hand, willing the twigs on the path to rise in a whirlwind, following my fingers. When I look over at Jess, she shakes her head, gaping at the litter of grass, leaves and sticks still swirling.

"Holy shit." Her eyes are like dinner plates. "Make it go higher!"

With a laugh, I throw my hand up in the air, so that the debris rises and then rains down on the ground between us.

I grab her hand. "Now do you believe me? I want to show you where it all started — this magical spot where a witching well once stood."

Pulling her along, not daring to look at her and see skepticism there, I lift a branch higher, darting under it.

"Mom, hang on. We need to discuss this."

Stepping into the familiar glade, her words fade and I freeze mid-stride. My heart slams against my ribs, and for a moment, I can't breathe.

The well! Holy shit! The Well is back!

Black solid stone rising from the earth like it had never left. Sunlight glints on the moss-covered rocks, making them gleam with an otherworldly presence.

"Mom?" Jessica bumps into my back. "What's wrong?"

"It's back," I whisper, then louder, "I can't believe it! It's back!"

My hands fly to my mouth as pure joy surges up inside me. I bounce on my toes, unable to contain my excitement. The well that had started everything—my transformation, my understanding of who I really am—has returned!

Up ahead, Robert pads out from behind the ancient structure, his golden eyes fixed on me as he places his front paws on the high ledge. As he peers down into the depths, his stubby tail twitches.

"That's the witching well?" Jessica moves to stand beside me. "Doesn't look very...*magical* at all."

"It had disappeared and now it's back!" I grab her arm, squeezing perhaps a bit too hard. "It vanished right before... well, before Alice and Patrick found each other again."

"Alice? Patrick?" Jessica's eyebrows draw together. "Who are they?"

I stare at the well, memories of Alice—my ancestor inhabiting its depths for over a century—fill my mind. The day she and Patrick, the warlock who'd loved her, finally reunited still felt like a dream.

"That's a long story," I say, taking a step toward the well. "One I promise to tell you. But first..."

Robert's purr rumbles across the glade as I approach, my fingers tingling with the familiar surge of power emanating from the ancient stones.

I stop short, my hand flying to my forehead. "Damn! I forgot the Jack Daniels." The realization hits me and I bite my lower lip. "But how could I know? Alice will have to understand. I'll give her an offering the next time!"

I spin toward Jess, bouncing on my toes in joy. "Libby, Mary-Jane and Cynthia are going to be thrilled! This is so *exciting*, Jess!"

My daughter stands there, arms crossed, looking at me like I've sprouted a second head. "Okay? I guess I'm happy for you?"

Shit! Of course, she has no context for any of this; the well's significance, Alice's story, or why we'd need whiskey as an offering. Here I am, babbling about Jack Daniels and Alice while my poor kid is still processing the whole *'my mom's a Witch'* bombshell.

Taking a deep breath, I try to control my excitement. Robert rubs against my legs, his purr a reminder to slow down. My daughter needs time to absorb all this; I can't dump everything on her at once.

"Sorry, honey. I'm getting ahead of myself." I reach for her hand. "Let's start at the beginning. This well? It's where I first discovered who I really am. Who *we* are."

I sink down and prop my back against the solid stone wall of the well. When Jessica takes a seat next to me, I feel the strength, the power to tell her everything.

And that's what I do.

Eight

Mary-Jane, the next night...

I wipe sweat from my forehead with my sleeve as I chop vegetables for the dinner rush. The kitchen's heat wraps around me like a blanket, and the chef's coat is *not* helping. Beside me, Jane hums, her knife clicking against the cutting board like canastas.

A heavy knock echoes from the back door.

"Come in!" I call out, not looking up from the carrots.

When the door creaks open, Miguel Lopez's stocky frame fills the space, arms loaded with a big box. Something is different about him...

I give my eyes that off-center squint that I use when I want to see an aura, and Miguel's entire appearance changes. He's grown a thick, dark beard, and his hair is long, getting entangled with his facial growth. For a split second, his eyes flash red. Even if I didn't see the purple waves of his aura, it's plain as day that my delivery guy, someone I've known for years is a Werewolf.

A Werewolf.

"Where do you want these, Mrs. Matthews?" His voice carries a slight growl. Why in the world did I never notice that before?

"Just there by the prep table." My knife pauses mid-chop watching him. The way he moves is pure predator, controlled power in every step. Once you see it, you can't un-see it.

He makes two more trips, his long dark hair swinging loose instead of tied back like usual. The wolf in him shows through more than ever.

After setting down the last box, Miguel pulls a small jar from his jacket pocket. "Is Jane around? Got a little something for her."

"Here!" Jane steps out of the cooler with more veggies and immediately scowls, seeing that it's him.

"Found this at the farmer's market." Holding the jar of golden honey out, his voice almost purrs as he swoons at her. "Raw and unpasteurized, just like you, Jane." His hairy unibrow wiggles up and down a few times, and I swear there's drool on his lower lip.

Jane shoots me a scowl before stepping closer to the Were. "Thanks."

Miguel's smile reveals slightly pointed teeth. "Hard to forget anything about you." He holds the jar back from her hand and edges closer.

"My dearest Jane, so wild and free.
You put the buzz in meant to be!
This honey's sweet, but better shared.
With one like me, a guy who cares."

She snatches the honey jar from Miguel's grasp, her back stiff as she marches back to her workstation. "Not going to happen, Miguel. No matter how much honey or sweets you bring, I'll never go out with you."

Miguel's shoulders slump, his thick beard seems to droop with his mood. He casts me a look of such disappointment that inspires sympathy before slinking out the back door.

Poor guy. I turn on Jane. "Why're you always so mean to him? He's kind of sweet, bringing you gifts and stuff." Maybe he's not her type, but there's no need to be rude.

"Don't start, MJ." Jane's knife attacks the vegetables with more force. "You've nagged me about him before, and I'm sick of it."

"Only because it's so obvious that he adores you! And he's got that whole man-beast thing going—"

"The only thing he wants is sex." Her knife bangs against the cutting board.

"So?" Shrugging, I wipe my hands on my apron. "What's wrong with that? It's been years since your husband left, and surely...well, you must get *lonely,* Jane."

She grits her teeth before leaning closer, hissing at me. "Everyone knows the Werewolves are horrible lovers. Think only of themselves and it's over before it even *begins*."

A dreamy look transforms her face, and she smiles. "Now Duncan Moroni... That garbage-guy Druid? Mmmm... He can take out my trash anytime. Anywhere. And as often as he wants. I've got a thing for Druids, but especially *him*."

I nearly choke on my own spit. "Duncan?" Rail thin, with a weak jaw-line, and balding? Smells like rotting broccoli? What am I missing?

"Mmhmm." Jane's hips sway as she resumes chopping, with slow sensuous moves. "His hands lifting those heavy bins? Pure magic in those fingers, I'll bet. And he knows his way around trimming a hedge, if you catch my drift." She winks before giggling like a schoolgirl. "Or so I've been told..."

Totally not getting the attraction, but... No accounting for taste, right? All part of Wesley's rich tapestry of Mysticals. But if she's right about Werewolves being inconsiderate lovers, no way am I letting Ray go there. Maybe he ought to have a chat with Duncan, if he's such a lothario.

Jane dips her finger in the jar of honey and pops it in her mouth for a moment, closing her eyes as she licks the sweetness off. "MJ! I just had a *brilliant* idea." Her brown eyes sparkle when she stares at me, a big grin on her face. "Since you're a Witch, maybe you could help me out with a little *love spell*?"

"A love spell?" I set my knife down, gaping at the sparkle in her eye, the way her wings shimmy.

"For Duncan." Clasping her hands, she steps closer. "Just an itty-bitty spell to make him *notice* me. Even if it's just a temporary thing." She licks her lips, and her eyes roll up, fluttering her lashes. "Hot damn. Just one wild night with him."

My mind flashes back to the love spell I had cast on Shannon. It did not go well. At all. Good goddess, it had been *ridiculous* how she'd lost any filter on her mouth. She'd taken flirting and put it on crack, telling Devon how hot she was for him—in front of practically the whole town! Just thinking of how furious she'd been with me afterwards still makes me wince.

But hey! They're together now, aren't they? So, I HAD helped. Sometimes people just needed a little nudge...

"I don't know, Jane." My fingers twist together as I rethink this. "Love spells can be tricky. And Duncan's a Druid. It might backfire...that is, if it even *works*."

"Please?" Jane's lower lip juts out as she peers at me. "I'm not asking for a forever, till death do us part kind of thing. Just a little something to get his attention, to make him want me. My wings positively *quiver* at the thought!"

Oh shit. I try not to notice her obvious agitation, how she bends at the waist lost in her fantasy, twerking. Her wings start to vibrate and quiver in what I can only interpret as Fae arousal. Now that we know about the Mysticals, they flaunt their nature constantly, and it's getting to be a pain to deal with. There might be something to the old adage 'ignorance is bliss'. Now there're sparkles of fairy dust everywhere!

I grab her arm. "Stop that! Fine! I'll *think* about it. But don't get your hopes up. Druids with their connection to nature, have their own variety of magic. The spell might bounce right off him."

Jane let out an ear-shattering squeal before hugging me tight. "You're the best!"

"Yeah, yeah." The shrill ring of my cell phone breaks off the moment. When I pick it up, Shannon's name flashes on the screen.

"Hello—"

"It's back! The well is back!" Shannon blares through the speaker. I yank the phone away from my ear. "We're having a coven meeting tonight to visit it! Ten o'clock!"

My jaw opens so wide, it nearly hits my chest. "The *well*? But it vanished a week ago, taking Alice with it. "Are you *serious*?"

"Yes! Get your butt over here tonight. And bring whiskey!"

My heart is in overdrive as I lean against the table. "Oh my god! I'll be there. Do Cynthia and Libby know?"

"Just got off the phone with them. They're coming too!"

Like a souffle fresh from the oven deflates, so does my excitement. She'd called them *first*? I thought *I* was her best friend. "Oh. Great." I try to keep the disappointment out of my voice.

"What's wrong? I thought you'd be thrilled." Shannon asks.

"Just surprised. That's all." I force brightness into my tone. "I really thought the well was gone for good."

Inside, my stomach churns. I should have been the first to know about the well. I'd stood by Shannon through everything—the divorce, moving to Wesley, helping her relationship with Devon. Yet *again*, I'm last in getting the news.

"See you tonight!" Shannon chirps before ending the call.

As I set the phone down, my head swirls with emotions. The well is back—that should've been amazing news, but being dead last *again* on Shannon's call list bothers me.

Who am I kidding? It hurts.

"What's wrong, MJ?" Jane's voice cuts through my thoughts. "Not bad news, I hope."

"The well is back." I blurt, before immediately clapping my hand over my mouth. Damn. I probably shouldn't have said anything about the well. Do these Mysticals even *know* about it? They knew we were Witches...but...

Jane's eyes widen. "*The magical well*? I'd heard rumors about that well, but never believed them. I've covered every bit of forest in Wesley and never saw it. But you say it's back. So, it *was* true, then!"

"I shouldn't have told you that." I give her a stern look. "You can't tell *anyone.* Not a word, Jane."

"No worries, your secret's safe with me." Patting my hand, she coos, "Just don't forget about helping me with Duncan."

I pull away, but not before her emotions flood through me—determination, cunning, and a hint of malice that makes my neck muscles knot. The image of Duncan flashes in my mind, but it's a little twisted, seen from Jane's perspective. She doesn't just want him, she's *obsessed* with him. And now...now she has leverage over me.

"Jane, I—"

Cutting me off with a wave of her knife, her smile is sly. "You know, it's funny how secrets work in Wesley. One person tells another, who tells another..." Her wings shimmer with an unsettling gleam. "Sure would be a shame if word got out about that well."

My throat goes dry. "Sounds like you're threatening me. "

"No, no. Never." She scrapes chopped vegetables into a bowl, her movements precise and controlled. "We're friends, and friends help each other out, right? I know you'll help me with Duncan, *won't you*?"

The threat hangs in the air between us like a nasty fart. The Jane I knew—my friend—is nothing like the Fae standing before me now. She feels like a stranger. Someone I now see as clearly as recognizing Miguel as a horny werewolf.

I've been oblivious to the true nature of the people in town until now. I stare at Jane for a moment, because I'm not liking what I'm seeing right now. I make one slip of the tongue, and she's all over it, using it to bend me to her ends. I grip the edge of the prep table until my knuckles are white. I don't like this one bit.

Jane hums as she goes back to her prep work, but the tune is more like a warning than a melody. I had seen what she wanted in that brief touch just now—she wouldn't just tell people about the well, she'd use that information to get whatever else she wanted, too.

For now, I'll let this play out until I can figure out some kind of countermove. "Fine, I'll do the love spell." My stomach sinks as I say it though; famous last words. Been there. Done that. And the backlash really, really sucked.

But what can I do for now? Shannon will kill me if word gets out about the well's return.

Nine

Libby

Cursing under my breath at being the last to arrive, I wheel my car into Shannon's driveway. Dahlia had tried every trick in her arsenal—from puppy dog eyes to outright begging—to get me to bring her along. She knew it was a coven meeting, and she wanted in.

That kid is only 14, but she's a pro at wheedling for what she wants.

"Mom, please! I promise I'll just watch. I won't touch anything. I won't be in the way."

"You're grounded if you keep bugging me," I'd told her, pointing a stern finger. She'd flopped dramatically onto the couch, Ms. Purdy Cat curled in her lap. The cat had given me a look that said "*Really*?" clear as day.

My power that allows me to understand animals is both a blessing and a curse. Now even the household pets question my parenting.

The echo of her pleas still rings in my ears as I kill the engine. The forest around Shannon's house stands dark and quiet, but warm light spills from her windows. MJ's red Mazda and Cynthia's silver Prius are already parked out front.

I grab the bottle of Jack Daniel's from the passenger seat—Shannon had texted that we needed whiskey for Alice. The gravel crunches under my feet as I make my way to the front door.

Robert lounges on the porch, giving a wide yawn. *"Evening, Libby. You're late."*

"Tell that to my teenage daughter, who suddenly developed separation anxiety." I squat down to scratch behind his ear.

Robert's purr rumbles under my fingers as I scratch that sweet spot. *"Shannon's daughter took the news better than she'd expected,"* he says. *"Kevin spilling the proverbial beans might actually have helped in getting Jess to accept everything."*

"Really?" Relief washes through me. "She's not pissed with Kevin... or *me* by extension?"

Robert stretches, his claws extending. *"Nope. Jessica's now fascinated by everything magical. You should have seen her face when Shannon made a whirlwind for her."*

I straighten up from petting the bobcat as Shannon, MJ, and Cynthia emerge from the house, each carrying supplies for the ritual. The sweet scent of sage drifts from the bundle in MJ's hands, while Cynthia holds a batch of candles. Shannon clutches a worn leather sack that I recognize as her ritual pouch.

"Here." Shannon thrusts a dark bundle of fabric at me. "Join the club and put this on."

I shake out a black satin robe, similar to the ones they're wearing. "Really? We're doing the whole wardrobe thing, too?"

MJ winks, adjusting her own robe. "It adds some atmosphere, and this is a celebration! Am I right?"

The screen door creaks, and Jessica steps onto the porch, her eyes bright with excitement. She wears a robe too, though hers is blue instead of black.

"Jessica's coming with us," Shannon announces, beaming at her daughter. "She wants to learn everything about being a Witch."

My forehead tightens. Not that I have anything against Shannon's daughter, but this is a big step, bringing someone else into the coven. I can't help but think of Dahlia back home, desperate to be included.

"Shouldn't it just be just us?" MJ's voice carries an edge. "I mean, you *know* how prickly Alice can be. Shouldn't we make sure she'll be okay with us adding members?"

Shannon waves her hand dismissively. "Jess was with me this afternoon at the well. Even though Alice didn't speak, I'm sure it's fine. If I'd known the well was back, I would have brought a whisky offering."

My thoughts fly to Dahlia, sitting at home with a determined look on her face, trying to communicate with Ms. Purdy Cat. "Well, I wish you'd told me Jess was being included. I practically had to hog-tie Dahlia to keep her from coming with me."

Guilt gnaws at my stomach. My daughter has been working so hard, desperate to unlock her magical abilities. It doesn't seem fair that Jessica gets to waltz right in.

"Look. We all knew our membership would grow," Cynthia chides, adjusting her armload of candles. "And since Jess was already at the well, what's the big deal? Next meeting, bring Dahlia."

"Don't forget Chloe," MJ adds quickly. "She wants to be included too. And some of her friends as well."

I trudge behind Shannon, my new robe catching on brambles. The whiskey bottle, dangling from my fingers, bumps against my thigh with each step, and I couldn't care less. MJ keeps pace beside me, with an odd expression on her face.

"She could have at least warned us," I whisper, keeping my voice low enough that Shannon and the others wouldn't hear. "I practically had to peel Dahlia off me to leave. If she finds out Jessica got to come..."

"Tell me about it!" MJ pushes a branch out of her way. "Ray's been on my case about including Chloe. Says if we're teaching magic, his daughter deserves to learn too. I had to promise him we'd discuss it at the next meeting just to get him off my back."

"Things will work themselves out," Shannon calls over her shoulder, making me jump. Damn it; she heard us. "The well returning is a gift. Let's focus on that instead of arguing about who gets to join our coven."

"It's not about joining the coven," I mutter. "It's about fairness. And warning the coven members before making decisions that affect all of us."

Cynthia urges Jessica forward as the path narrows. "We'll see what Alice has to say. Although I agree with Shannon. Everything will be fine."

I catch MJ rolling her eyes before she looks away. We both know Shannon has already made up her mind, regardless of what Alice or anyone else thinks. Sometimes I wonder if she forgets we're *supposed to be* equals—not just her backup singers.

The crunch of leaves under our feet fills the silence as we follow the narrow path. My mind drifts back to Duncan's visit earlier that day, asking me to run for mayor of Wesley.

Keeping my voice low, I look over at MJ. "Duncan— the Druid garbage man— stopped by my house today. He had some interesting things to say about the Shifters, warning us not to trust them. And get this—he thinks I should run for mayor in the next election."

MJ stops dead in her tracks, nearly dropping her bundle of sage. "*You* as mayor?" After letting out a snort, she continues. "Don't get me wrong, but if any of us should be mayor, obviously, it should be me. But I think he's wrong about Shifters. Look at Eric. He's a nice guy. If anything, it's the sneaky Fae we should keep an eye on."

"Now just wait a minute!" I grab her arm, pulling her to a stop. Heat fills my cheeks. "Why wouldn't *I* be a good mayor? I've got administrative experience, and I'm good with people. Just ask any of my patients."

Shaking her head, MJ wiggles her fingers in front of my face. "These babies are why, Libs. I can *read* people. I know when they're lying and what their true motivations are. Of course, I'll give you a spot in my administration, but I should run it."

"Hmph." I take a deep breath, trying to keep my temper in check. "Not sure Shannon would agree with that."

The clearing opens before us, a sliver of moonlight spilling across the ancient well. Shannon's black robe swishes against the grass as she approaches and lights a thick white candle. Cynthia places crystals and herbs at the cardinal points around the well's perimeter; just like we'd done dozens of times before.

But tonight is different. Not only has the well mysteriously re-appeared but with a new member, everything feels off-kilter. A quick glance at MJ shows my own uncertainty reflected in her eyes.

I step toward my usual position at the eastern point, while MJ takes her place in the west. When Shannon guides Jessica to stand between us, breaking our usual circle, my stomach clenches.

"Here, take Libby's hand," Shannon instructs Jessica, who grips my fingers with sweaty palms. Excitement radiates from her in waves.

"Just watch and learn tonight, sweetie," Shannon says to Jessica. "No speaking during the ritual."

I let out a slow breath, satisfied that she's putting Jessica in her place as a neophyte. Still, how is Alice going to react? It really should have just been the four of us here tonight to welcome the well's return.

The candle flames dance in the night breeze, casting flickering shadows across our faces.

Shannon begins the ritual:

"Mother Gaia, I offer this soil.
A gift of life from sacred toil.
Our gratitude for the well re-
turning with Alice."

Cynthia steps forward next, her candle casting dancing shadows across her face. Her poem comes out smooth and practiced.

"Flame of truth and guiding
light,
Chase the shadows, break the
night.
With Alice near, our path is
bright.
The well returns, our souls ig-
nite."

MJ goes next. Holding out the bottle of whisky, pouring it into the water.

"Spirit strong, both bold and
true,
I pour this gift to honor you.
The well restored, our hearts
embrace,
With Alice near, in sacred
grace."

My stomach churns, seeing it's my turn. I fumble in my robe pocket for the white feather I'd grabbed from my craft supplies at home. Public speaking is bad enough, but poetry is my personal hell. I'll take a medical emergency any day over having to rhyme some words.

I step forward, the feather trembling in my fingers, feeling everyone's eyes burn into me, waiting.

"Uh..." I hold the feather out over the well, my mind completely blank. "Well, here's a feather. It's... air, y'know?"

My face burns hot enough to light another candle, when I add, "And air is... important. Like breathing. And stuff." Oh goddess, make this stop. "Anyway... thanks for Alice. And the well." I drop the feather, watching it drift down into the darkness. "Yeah... that's it. Thanks."

Stepping back into place, I notice MJ's stifling a laugh and Jessica's wide-eyed questioning look. Next time, I'm definitely writing something in advance. Or calling in sick. Or moving to Antarctica. Damn, I hate this part.

The well erupts without warning, sending a geyser of water high into the night sky. Sputtering, I wipe my face as the spray drenches us, my robe now clinging uncomfortably to my skin. Shannon laughs, pulling another bottle of Jack from somewhere in her robes.

"Alice sure likes her whisky," she calls out to Jessica, while tipping the bottle over the well's edge. "And it's been a while sooooo..."

"I'M NOT ALICE!"

The thunderous voice booming up from the depths, makes me jerk back. What the hell? My mouth drifts open as the voice keeps blaring.

"SINCE ONE OF US HAD TO ACCOMPANY THE WELL TO GUIDE YOU, WE DREW STRAWS. I LOST!" it roars.

"Oh, shit." Shannon's eyes flash wide, and the bottle slips from her fingers, clattering against the well's stone rim. "*Mom?* Is that you?"

"Obviously!" The voice sounds pissed. "And quit with the whisky. If you must offer anything, for Gaia's sake, make it champagne. And not the cheap shit."

I'm barely able to process that it's not our Alice, but Shannon's mother? Judith? A spirit who I'd only heard about and then witnessed a week ago at the showdown with Patrick!

Jessica breaks the connection of our hands, darting forward to peer over the edge. "Grandma? Oh, my God! I can't believe it. Finally, we meet! Kind of..."

"Meeting *you* is the only plus side of pulling the short straw. And of course, seeing Shannon... I guess." The voice had softened, addressing her granddaughter.

My eyes meet MJ's, seeing her shock, like mine. Alice had been replaced with Judith? Shannon's mother? As crusty as Alice had always been with us, compared to Judith, Alice would seem like Mother Teresa, judging by the stories Shannon told.

Now here she is, the new witch of our well. My stomach knots as I think of Dahlia and even Chloe. How will Judith react to their learning witchcraft? Would she even allow it? Obviously, she's totally cool with Jessica, her *granddaughter*.

Maybe it was a good thing Dahlia didn't come with me tonight. Better to see how this plays out before bringing my daughter into it. The look on Shannon's face shows that she isn't exactly overjoyed with this new twist either.

Mary-Jane whispers almost under her breath, but not quite. "Oh shit. Just when we thought we had it good, Judith Burke shows up."

Ten

Shannon

My legs turn to jelly and I barely catch myself, gripping the well's cool rim. Holy shit! Mom's here? *Not Alice?* Oh boy...

Sure, last week she was warm, caring and had my back when her spirit appeared during my battle with Patrick the Warlock, but acting that way was a side to her I had rarely experienced when she was alive. But now...the snarky, testy grump down in the well? Well, that's the Judith Burke I grew up with.

Wait, a damn minute! I grasp the edge of the well and peer down. "The only reason you're here is that *you lost a draw*?" My voice cracks as I stare down into the well's depths. "That's the *only* reason you're here? Of course, it wouldn't be to see me, your *only* child!"

Mom's voice echoes up from the depths. "Oh, Shannon, don't start with the drama. I thought that was all behind us, that you forgave me and understood why I did the things I did. Hell, you accepted my apology, so what more do you want? Think it was easy for me to leave your father to come here and be the Guardian of the well? *Someone* had to maintain the connection between the worlds. It was Aunt Maeve who suggested we draw straws, although I'm pretty sure she cheated."

My eyes close, fighting back the familiar ache that my mother always caused. She didn't want to spend time with me any more than when she'd raised me. Stupidly, I'd thought she'd changed, but nope, not Judith Burke.

"Grandma? This is freaking awesome! You're actually here, a spirit, and I can talk to you! Can you come up here so I can see you?" Jessica leans further over the edge. "Or are you trapped? What's it like down there?"

Her enthusiasm squeezes my heart. But at least Mom seems genuinely happy to meet her granddaughter finally. Better late than never, right?

"Down here in the watery depths?" Mom replies. "It's sufficient, I suppose. But the place needs work. It might have been fine for Alice, seeing as how she lived centuries ago, in a primitive cabin, but it's not up to 20th century standards, let alone the 21st. Needs better lighting for a start."

I can't help but snort, rolling my eyes. Trust Mom to critique the decor of a magical well.

MJ catches my eye and mouths, "You okay?" I give her a tight nod, but my stomach is a churning knot. Why did it have to be Mom in that well, and not Maeve or even Alice? But maybe, just maybe, we might manage to have a better relationship than when she was alive.

"Shannon?" Mom's voice softens. "I know we have much to discuss. But for now, let's focus on teaching Jessica about her heritage. She has the Burke gift, I can sense it, even from down here!" Her voice has a lilt of excited pleasure.

My throat tightens. She's right, of course. This isn't about us and our relationship—it's about Jessica. And despite everything, maybe my daughter will know her grandmother in a way I never could.

Cynthia joins me at the rim of the well and calls down, "So, Judith...What can you tell us about these magical beings? As in how we should deal with them, what they're about? How we fit in?"

"Ha!" Mom's harsh laugh bounces off the stone cylinder. "Good luck with that!"

"Whaaat?"

"Well...to be honest, I really was never here long enough to get to know *any* of them in any meaningful way. In fact, it was years before I learned of their existence." She let out a huff. "And of course, Maeve was no help on that front."

My chest tightens. Of course, she hadn't been here much—she'd been too busy running away from her responsibilities.

Running away from *me*.

"Look. All I can say is don't trust any of them until they have proven themselves worthy of it. Now that you know their true nature, they aren't your friends anymore. Even the humans who know and accept them can't be trusted."

The words are like ice water. What about Eric? He's been totally supportive of Cynthia. Or Devon, who's stood by me through everything. Even Mary from the diner, keeping her Druid nature hidden. Although on second thought, maybe not Mary. Not the way she threw herself at Devon.

"Don't you think that's a bit harsh, Mom? These people are our neighbors, our friends—"

"*Were* your friends," she cuts in. "You are witches, and everyone knows that now. They know you have power, and power changes everything, Shannon. *You* of all people should understand that."

"What the hell does that mean?"

"What I *mean* is that when circumstances change, people change, silly. Look what happened with your ex-husband when he started making oodles of money. It wasn't long before he started sniffing around for a younger model, isn't that true? Same thing here in Wesley with the Mysticals. The circumstances have changed."

My cheeks burn. Trust Mom to bring up David and twist the knife. Jessica shifts uncomfortably beside me, and I squeeze her hand.

"One thing I *do* know about the beings in Wesley is that the politics among them and between the groups is off the charts." Mom continues. "Alliances form and then shift like sand. One week the Vampires and Werewolves will be best buddies, but on the next full moon, they'll be at each other's throats! And don't get me started on how the Druids and Fae folk run so hot and cold." She snorted. "And the Shifters? Oh boy... Your Aunt Mave told me that keeping them in line is harder than herding cats." She paused. "And that's *your* job, Shannon. "Which is why you need to be pretty darn careful around all of them." She makes a disgusted sound. "But you'll see how suspicious they really are for yourselves."

"Suspicious? That's rich coming from you! Y'know Mom, Maeve lived among them, and she seemed to do okay. Maybe you're just being paranoid." I peer down the well. "What exactly should I be suspicious of?

"You'll find out soon enough."

Oh, damn it! Anger at her non-answers eggs me on. "Y'know, we need a little more than just to *suspect them all*. Aren't you supposed to guide us? The way Alice used to?" I shake my head. We all thought that Alice was prickly and obtuse in her answers sometimes. But she doesn't hold a candle to Mom's style. Annoying as anything, and not helpful at all.

The water ripples again, catching moonlight in the dark surface. For a moment, there's silence; the kind of loaded pause Mom was famous for, before delivering a cutting remark.

But before she can say anything, Jessica leans even further over the edge, her eyes all excited. "So, can you help me become a Witch, Grandma? I'd like to be like Mom, an elemental one. If these Mystical dudes turn out to be enemies, we'll need strong magic. Plus, it could be cool as hell to make it storm or cause an earthquake."

My stomach sinks hearing Jessica. The girl has so, so much to learn. She has yet to develop an appreciation that magic, that becoming a Witch, comes with a steep learning curve and can be dangerous. She's only seeing the glamour in doing spells like I did with the air just before; not the hard work involved, the intention, dedication. With magic, mistakes can be dangerous, and she's clueless about the downside.

And no help from Mom on that front. No, instead Judith's voice softens when she answers Jess. "Of course, I'll help. But you need to begin by reading the Grimoires. And then do some serious meditation. Magic will come to you in time, and you will be a strong Witch. Never fear about that, my dear."

Before I can comment, Mary-Jane rushes to the lip of the well.

"What about *my* daughter and Libby's? They want to be Witches too. Will you help them?"

A plume of water erupts, hitting MJ squarely in the face.

"What do you take me for?" Judith roars, "You toss in some whisky and expect me to grant wishes like a fountain in *Rome*? Your daughters will have to prove themselves worthy. I need to see pure intention before I'll commit to helping them."

Oh shit. Not too obvious that Mom's playing favorites! A look at MJ and Libby show their eyes narrowed, casting a glance between them. And it's not like my daughter has proven any pure intention; her strongest attribute is by accident of birth, making her a direct descendant.

Mom's voice echoes up from the well. "Let's focus, okay? You asked about dealing with the Mysticals and expect my help. You need to divide and conquer. Each of you should focus on one species and get all the information you can about them."

"Like what?" Jessica asks.

"Good question. Learn all you can about their powers. What are they actually capable of? And what limits to their powers are there?"

I cross my arms. That was exactly what I was going to suggest, so no big revelation from my mother. But I'd cut her some slack. Much like witchcraft, there might be a learning curve to being the Spirit of the Well. Worst-case scenario, I'll try to conjure a visit from Aunt Maeve to help us.

"Shannon, you take the Vampires. You've got that journalist's nosiness that might actually work with them. Plus, they respect power, and you're the strongest."

Great. Just great. Stuck dealing with Mayor Jeffrey and his bloodsucker friends. Though she has a point about my investigative skills.

"Mary-Jane, the Druids are yours. Your ability to read emotions will help navigate their rigid mindset."

MJ nods, but I catch her grimace. Not that I blame her. It seems like most of her work will involve Duncan the garbage man, not known for his personality or hygiene.

"Cynthia," Mom continues, her tone dripping with disapproval, "since you're clearly biased toward the Shifters—being engaged to one—you can handle the Werewolves. Maybe you'll learn something from digging into the Mysticals and their ilk that will make you reconsider your current...life choices...."

Cynthia's spine stiffens, but she says nothing. I want to defend her relationship with Eric, but Mom barrels on.

"And Libby, you get the Shifters. Your practical nature, the gift of communication with animals, might actually get through to them."

"What about the Fae?" Libby asks, frowning.

After a few beats, Judith speaks slowly. "What I know about the Fae is that they're gentle beings, rooted in nature and among all the Mysticals, they have the purest of intentions. Still, you must not trust them entirely. Jessica can lead Dahlia and Chloe in learning more about them, how they'll work with the coven."

My daughter actually does a happy dance, and I smile seeing it. But she's not ready for this. Plus, it may be dangerous. What my mother is telling us to do sounds a lot like spying on other members of the Mystical community; I don't think that would go over all that well if they were caught.

"Hold on," I raise my hand. "Jessica's just learning about all this herself. Maybe we should—"

"She has the *gift.*" Mom interrupts. "More importantly, she has fresh eyes. The Fae will respond better to youth and innocence than to... *established* perspectives."

The way she says 'established' makes it sound like a fault. Classic Mom.

"I won't let you down, Grandma!" Jessica bounces on her toes, reminding me of when she was little and got picked first for the soccer team. "When can I start?"

"Tomorrow," Mom replies. "You'll need to meet with Jane at the restaurant. She's Fae, and she can guide you."

My jaw drops. Jane? Sweet, quiet Jane, who works in MJ's kitchen? I'd never suspected...

"Wait!" MJ cuts in. "I'm not sure Jane's the best choice. Amy and Suzanne Smith would be better. Jane's got some issues that I'm dealing with. I'd feel more comfortable with my daughter studying Suzanne." She glares at Jessica. "And you better be damn careful about eating anything they offer you to eat."

"Huh?" Jess replies.

"Look, I've only found out about all these beings myself, okay? But already I've found out that simple foods from the Fae can pack a wallop—don't have *any* mushroom dish if it's offered...and absolutely don't eat any brownies they bake, if you catch my drift."

Wow. MJ had jumped in fast with that objection. What issues was she dealing with involving Jane? Plus, MJ avoids looking at any of us; since we were kids, that's her 'tell' when she's hiding something. There's more to this that I'll have to explore later, but for now, I'm still not comfortable with Jess diving in so quickly.

Turning to my daughter, I take a breath, hating that I'm about to rain on her parade. "Jess, you need to get back to college. Maybe after exams and the school year is over, you can return and help out. Until then, I'll help Dahlia and Chloe with the Fae."

Jessica's mouth drops open, scowling at me. "No! I can't go back, not now after learning all this." Looking away for a moment, she continues. "Look, I'll ask for an extension on my exams, tell the profs that there's a family emergency, which there kind of is. I'm sure they'll let me." Turning back to the well, staring down into the depths, she murmurs. "Maybe I'll drop out and live here."

My heart sinks at Jessica's words. She's ready to throw away everything she's worked for, her education, her future, all because magic seems more exciting right now.

"Absolutely not." I grab her arm and turn her to face me. "You're not dropping out of college. This isn't up for discussion."

"But Mom—"

"No." My voice comes out sharper than intended. "Magic isn't going anywhere. The well isn't going anywhere. Your education comes first."

Mom's voice drifts up from the well. "Let her stay, Shannon. She needs to learn about her heritage. And she's an adult now."

Of course, Mom would undermine me. Some things never change. "Her heritage will still be here after finals."

Jessica yanks her arm away. "You can't control everything. Grandma's right. I'm an adult. I can make my own choices." With that, she turns and storms off into the woods, on the path back to the house. The others are quiet, watching our confrontation. I catch Libby's sympathetic glance—she knows exactly what I'm going through.

Judith sends up a bubbling cauldron before her voice thunders. "This is becoming tiresome. Go now! Settle this and report back in three days."

Shit. Some things never change. Just when I could have used Mom's support, she not only bails on me, but cuts the legs out from under me in keeping my kid in line!

We gather up our items and follow Jessica down the pathway. Cynthia steps over and puts an arm around my waist. "Don't take this personally, Shann, but your mother's a bitch. She's wrong about Eric." She gives a small laugh. "Never thought I'd say this...but I miss Alice."

Me too.

Eleven

Mary-Jane, early the next morning...

I stare at the ingredients laid out on my prep table: rose petals, cinnamon, and vanilla beans. Beside my ingredients is a red candle positioned in a holder with a small brass pot suspended above it. I also have fresh lake water I brought home from Shannon's last night. The kitchen's quiet except for the hum of the industrial fridge. Ray won't show up for another hour, which gives me time to work this spell before anyone catches me.

"Got it!" Jane bursts through the back door, waving a hair comb like she's won an Oscar. "Swiped it right from his truck while he was collecting Mrs. Peterson's garbage."

"You broke into Duncan's truck?" My voice comes out as a squeak.

"It wasn't locked." Jane dumps a clump of dark hair onto my counter. "He really needs to trim more often. But hey, more hair means a stronger spell, right?"

I pick up a single strand between my fingers. "How do you know this is actually Duncan's? Could be Mrs. Peterson's for all we know."

"Trust me, I've been watching him long enough to know his hair." Jane's eyes get a dreamy look. "The way it falls across his forehead when he's lifting those garbage bins..."

"TMI, Jane." I separate out three strands and wrap them in a rose petal. "You realize if Shannon finds out about this, she'll kill me? Like, actual murder."

Jane looks at me, her face a question mark. "Why?"

I sigh. "Let's just say that love spells are tricky, and...well...I've had problems in the past."

"Who cares?" Jane shrugs. "She won't find out." Jane hops onto a stool, practically vibrating with excitement. "Besides, you owe me for keeping quiet about the well."

"That's blackmail."

"That's *insurance*." She grins. "Now come on, work your witchy magic. Get Duncan attracted to me!"

I light the candle and take a deep breath as I pour just a couple of tablespoons of lake water into it. The last love spell I cast went sideways fast—Shannon practically jumped Devon in public. But Jane's got me cornered.

"Fine. But if Duncan starts reciting poetry in the middle of garbage collection, that's on you."

I hold out my hand. "I need a few strands of your hair too. And..." I gesture vaguely at her back. "Maybe some sparkles from your wings."

She plucks a few strands of her dark hair, then shakes her shoulders. Tiny iridescent flecks drift down onto the counter. I sweep them into the mixture, watching it turn from murky brown to shimmering amber. The mixture already starts to bubble.

As I stir the bubbling concoction, I keep my tone casual. "You know, I've been meaning to ask; you're pretty tight with Amy and Suzanne from the Natural Foods shop, right? What are they really like? They've always seemed so sweet and gentle whenever I stop in."

Jane's expression shifts, just slightly. If I hadn't been watching for it, I might have missed it.

"They're... nice enough." She fiddles with a loose thread on her apron. "But you shouldn't judge Fae by how they seem on the surface."

"What do you mean?"

"Let's just focus on the spell." Jane leans over the pot, inhaling deeply. "Mmm, smells like summer rain and honey. Perfect for catching a Druid's attention."

I notice how quickly she changed the subject, but before I can press further, the mixture starts to bubble more, demanding my attention.

I close my eyes and grip the wooden spoon tighter, trying to focus on the spell. The mixture's scent of roses and cinnamon fills my nostrils as I begin to murmur the ancient words from the Grimoire I studied:

"By earth and air, by flame and sea, bring these two hearts together to be..."

Ugh. The mental image I need to conjure makes me want to gag. But Jane's standing right there, practically bouncing on her toes, and I've got no choice. I picture Duncan, his skinny frame and stringy hair, and Jane with her delicate features and those gossamer wings that catch the light.

My mind reluctantly paints them together on a bed of soft moss in some forest clearing, their bodies intertwined, her wings shimmering...

Oh God, I'm going to need brain bleach after this.

"Let passion bloom like spring's first flower, bind their hearts from this sacred hour..."

The mixture starts to glow with an eerie purple light. Steam rises in spirals, taking on shapes that make me blush. I stir three times clockwise, trying not to look too closely at what's forming in the vapor.

"As I will it, so mote it be!"

The purple glow intensifies, then suddenly snuffs out like someone flipped a switch. The remaining liquid looks innocuous now; just a slightly shimmery yellowish tea.

"Is that it?" Jane peers into the pot. "Did it work?"

I wipe sweat from my forehead with my sleeve. "We'll find out soon enough. Just... maybe don't tell me the details if it does?" Handing her the pot, "Put this in the walk-in, will you?"

I watch Jane practically skip to the walk-in cooler with the small pot. "Put it on the top shelf," I call after her. "Once it cools to syrup consistency, I'll mix it into a milkshake and deliver it to Duncan." Killing two birds with one stone, but she doesn't need to know that. The less this conniver knows, the better.

"Perfect!" Jane emerges from the cooler, her dark eyes sparkling. "I'd like people to think his attraction to me is natural, so I won't tell *anyone* about this."

"Speaking of which," I cross my arms, "about the well—"

"Oh, don't worry." She waves her hand dismissively. "Once this spell works, my lips are sealed forever about that."

Before I can respond, she's already crossing the floor, going to the back door. "Well, I better run home and change. Got to look my best for tonight!"

"Wait—what?" I gesture at the stack of vegetables waiting to be prepped. "You can't leave. I need help in the kitchen!"

Jane tosses her apron onto a hook. "Part of our deal, remember? I get some time off to enjoy myself with Duncan." She throws me a wink. "That's nonnegotiable."

"But—" The back door slams shut before I can finish protesting.

I slump against the counter, running my hands through my hair. What have I gotten myself into? First the well, now this; Jane's starting to show a side I never knew existed. If she keeps using this as leverage...

I grab my phone and dial Libby's number while keeping an eye on the walk-in where Jane's love potion sits cooling.

"Hey, MJ. You're up and about early today." Libby chirps.

"Things to do. People to meet. Like Duncan. I'm heading over to the Druid's house shortly."

Libby sighs, "I've got lunch with Ida Red Car at the Bear Claw today. Maybe she can give me a more unbiased perspective on Shifters. Although, I'd rather talk to Eric."

I lean against the prep counter, getting to why I really called her. "How are you handling this whole Judith situation?"

"Not great, to be honest."

"Judith as our spirit guide?" I shake my head. "Talk about drawing the short straw. We drew the short straw too."

"Tell me about it. After lunch, I'm checking on our daughters. Jessica is picking Dahlia and Chloe up around noon to visit Suzanne and Amy. After I'm finished with Ida, I might stop by to see how they're doing. Something about Jessica jumping into all this makes me nervous."

The timer dings, and I glance at the clock. The syrup should be cooled.

"Jessica's got no business leading these girls into anything," I say. "She just found out about all this yesterday, and now she's supposed to be their guide to the Fae? Shannon needs to put the brakes on this."

"Agreed. We need to talk to her. Soon." Libby pauses. "Since you're going to see him, I want you to know that Duncan popped by yesterday to talk about Shifters. He's no fan of theirs or Vampires. But it could just be him being paranoid. But keep me posted on how you get on with him, okay?"

"He's always struck me as being a bit strange. But whatever." After a beat, I add, "And Libby? Keep an eye on our girls, okay? This is moving way too fast."

After hanging up, I head into the walk-in cooler to get the potion. As I make the milkshakes, I wonder. Between Jane's blackmail, Judith's attitude, and this mess with the girls, I'm starting to think that well coming back might not be the blessing we thought it was.

I pull into Duncan's driveway with two milkshakes in the drink holder. The morning sun beats down on his modest ranch-style house with its perfectly manicured lawn. Not a single blade of grass out of place. I guess that's typical of Druids with their preoccupation with nature.

My hands shake slightly as I grab the drinks and head to his door. One's loaded with Jane's love potion; the other's just vanilla. I've chosen my favorite thermos, one showing Jason Mamoa's face, for mine. The last thing I need is to accidentally dose myself. Been there. Done that. Didn't work out so good when Devon became obsessed with me for a short period of time.

The doorbell chimes with a deep, earthy tone. Footsteps approach, and Duncan opens the door, his dark hair still damp from a shower. He's wearing cargo shorts, and a faded T-shirt with a tree design.

"Mary-Jane?" His eyebrows shoot up. "This is unexpected."

I hold up the drinks with what I hope is a winning smile. "Thought we could chat about Druids. You know, since you're basically the top of the Mystical food chain around here." Flattery never hurts, although he's not the best specimen of that species.

His expression shifts from surprise to what passes for friendliness. I guess. But before he can answer, something behind him catches my eye. There, prominently displayed on his living room wall, is a massive photo of Cynthia. She's wearing that knockout dress from her first date with Eric, her legs going on for miles as she struts down Main Street.

Duncan quickly steps outside, pulling the door almost shut behind him. But it's too late; I've already seen it. Suddenly, Jane's crush seems a lot more complicated. Unrequited love and all that crap.

Duncan's face blooms pinker as he tries to cover his embarrassment. He accepts the milkshake with a forced smile. "Thanks, that's... thoughtful of you to bring this."

Our fingers brush during the handoff, and whoa! Images flood my mind: Duncan watching Cynthia from afar, taking secret photos, following her and Eric on dates, plotting ways to break them up. The intensity of his obsession makes me dizzy. Almost as intense as Jane's is with him.

"No problem." I take a sip of my vanilla shake to steady myself. "So, tell me about being a Druid. Must be pretty powerful, having that connection to nature."

He leans against the porch railing, already halfway through the doctored shake. "Well, you Witches are at the top of the Mystical pecking order because you're both human and magical, and I accept that. But you should know that *we're* the original guardians of Wesley. Been here since before the town was founded." He takes another long gulp. "The ley lines, the ancient groves... we're really the guardians to protect all that."

"And what exactly can Druids do?" I watch him drain the last drops of the milkshake and try to hide my smile. One reason I'm here is done.

"We safeguard nature. Our relationship lets us command its elements." He gestures at a nearby oak tree. Its branches suddenly twist and dance like they're caught in a wind that isn't there. "Earth, plants, animals even; they all respond to us. Even the weather, to some degree."

Over the next hour, Duncan demonstrates more Druid abilities while I carefully steer the conversation away from Cynthia. He shows me how he can make flowers bloom instantly, speak with birds, and even cause small tremors in the ground.

The whole time, I'm tracking subtle changes in his demeanor—his pupils dilating, and his movements becoming more fluid. The spell is definitely having an effect.

When I finally stand to leave, he seems disappointed. "Thanks for stopping by, MJ. Tell Jane I said hello." He blinks, looking surprised at his own words.

I turn away to hide the grin as I head to my car.

Mission accomplished.

Twelve

Libby

After stepping into the Bear Claw Cafe, I freeze. Holy moly, it's a supernatural convention in here! Eve and that Fae cop are squeezed into a corner booth, their gossamer wings twitching as they whisper over their coffee. At the counter, a hulking Druid sips a cup of coffee sitting beside a Werewolf.

It's not just that it appears that everyone's showing their true nature; it's how blasé the 'normie' residents are about it all. I wonder...is Mave's ward still holding and they're not seeing this, or do they just not care with everyone now out of the proverbial closet, now and showing their true colors? Or species?

Well, I'm certainly not going to start asking around—if the normies can see them, no biggie, I guess. But if they can't and I ask, 'Excuse me, do you see Vampires in here?' They'll think I'm out of my mind.

I'll file this for later. For now, at least I know the players, right?

At the counter, Ed the editor stands next to some young Werewolf dude I don't recognize, giving Mary their order. I don't know which is more disconcerting, the excessive facial hair of the Werewolves or Mary's Druid sleeve of mystical tats.

"Libby! Over here, sugar!" Ida Red Car waves from her window booth, nearly knocking over her coffee cup. That pink leopard-skin top she's wearing should be illegal, especially paired with those black leggings. Well, modesty was never Ida's strong point.

I slide into the booth across from her, noting the spread of pastries she's already ordered. "Starting early with the sugar rush, I see."

"Well, I just had to celebrate that we're finally able to be ourselves." Ida leans forward, her red hair falling onto her face. "Do you know how hard it's been keeping this secret from you guys? Reminds me of when I first shifted...Frank thought I was having an affair when I showed up home with bite marks."

I nearly choke on the coffee I just swallowed. "Bite marks?"

"Oh, honey, when you become an animal, things can get a bit...rough. Although Robert is usually gentler than most." She winks at me.

My jaw drops. "You and Robert? Shannon's familiar Robert?"

Ida cackles. "That tom's got some fine whiskers, if you know what I mean."

Yuck. I'm never going to look at Shannon's bobcat the same way again. I change the subject to something less disturbing.

"Eric told me that Shifters rank pretty high among the Mysticals. Is that true?"

Ida's face lights up like she just won Publishers Clearing House. "You better believe it! What we can do is beyond special. Even you Witches, with all your fancy spells, can't transform like we can." She takes a sip of coffee, leaving a pink lipstick smear on the rim. "When my gift emerged, it was like hitting the supernatural jackpot."

Her expression shifts slightly, and a shadow crosses her features. "Course, it wasn't all moonlight and magic. Not at first. Poor Frank - he's had to make some... adjustments." She smiles. "We've come to what you might call an 'understanding' in our marriage."

Recalling Ida's nude sunbathing habits, this conversation needs a hard redirect. The last thing I want is details about her marital arrangements.

"How do shifters get along with the other Mysticals?" I ask, thinking about my conversation with Duncan. "Like the Druids, for instance?"

Ida's perfectly manicured nails drum against her coffee cup, and she rolls her eyes. "Druids? Please. They're about as flexible as petrified wood." She leans closer, lowering her voice despite the general bustle of the café. "They act all high and mighty, flaunting their 'special connection' to nature, but here's the thing—they can't come close to what we Shifters can do. Sure, they can make flowers grow, but can they turn into a honeybee one minute and a robin the next?" She shimmies. "I think not! And honey, that just burns their britches."

I take a sip of coffee. "So...what is it that Shifters want? I mean, that and what do you see in Wesley's future?"

Her face lights up; there's a wild glint in her eyes. "Freedom. Being able to choose who and what we want to be, without anyone's permission or judgment." Gesturing with her pastry fork, "Take me — I'm a proper lady having coffee one minute, and the next I'm racing through the woods on four paws. That's real, and it's freedom, baby!" She tilts her head at me. "I can feel the judgey-ness oozing off you right now, doll. And that's what I mean has to change."

"But there have to be some controls, some boundaries, right?" I press. Like not getting it on with another actually wild species. Thinking of you, Robert.

"Oh, absolutely. Certain beings should never just run wild." She dabs at her lips with a napkin. "The Weres, bless their hairy hearts, they've got a system. Full moon comes around, they either lock themselves away or go on organized hunts. It works for them thanks to Wayne."

Her expression darkens. "But the Vampires? Of course, we all know about the blood bank raids and their wild parties. But we don't trust them. The Werewolves are like puppies in comparison to the bloodsuckers."

I shiver, thinking about Mayor Sadler. He looks harmless enough, but maybe there's more to his portly, bloviating appearance than meets the eye.

"So, what about the Fae?" I ask, breaking off a bit of pastry. "They seem harmless. Are they?"

Ida snorts, "I've never had issues with them personally. But honey, the Druids and Weres never have a good word to say about them. Some Shifters as well. But my motto is live and let live."

"What do you mean?"

"Lots of Druids say there's a mean streak under all the Fae's flower-power facade. Cross them, and you'll wish you hadn't." Ida takes a delicate bite of her Danish. "I don't know. Maybe just best to leave them be. They seem happy enough, y'know; even if they're pretty ditzy."

"Need a warm-up?" Mary appears at our table with the coffeepot, and I jerk. She tops off our cups, then fixes her gaze on me. "So, Libby... Jack's coming over to my place tonight. Is that okay with you?"

My eyes flash wider. Jack meeting with Mary? News to me. I try to keep my voice steady. "Oh? He never mentioned it." Shit, she's old enough to be his mother, and I'd know, since I am. This better be innocent or Mary would be spelled into tomorrow.

"He's curious." Mary's eyes twinkle. "Between you and me, that boy would make one hell of a Druid. Might be just what he needs to get his act together. A little discipline and order in his life."

Before I can process that bombshell, she adds, "Oh, and Devon wants to chat with me too. But it'll be later, after I'm done with Jack. Wouldn't want any interruptions when I give him the skinny on being a Druid. I think he needs to come into his own, feel the...connection."

I don't need to read minds to get the attraction she has for Devon. My cheeks warm. That connection Mary swoons over won't impress Shannon. Not. One. Bit. Does she even know about this meeting later tonight?

Mary glides away to other tables, leaving me with a knot in my stomach. I turn back to Ida. "About Amy and Suzanne — just how bad can angry Fae be? They seem so... gentle."

Ida clucks her tongue before leaning in conspiratorially. "You know about Steve Murphy's divorce from Amy?"

"Yeah, of course. My coven took care of banishing him." I shift in my seat, remembering the horrible confrontation, how close he'd come to taking control of our coven.

"Suzanne played a bigger part in that mess than most folks know." Ida's voice drops to barely a whisper. "Story goes, when he came out to her as a Warlock, she not only left him for Suzanne, she learned how to screw with his power. I think it helped you Witches in the end."

I blink a few times, picturing sweet little Amy and how she could have done anything to disarm Steve. If it's true... The blood drains from my face. Dahlia is with Amy and Suzanne right now. "But they seem so..."

"Sweet? Gentle?" Ida's laugh has an edge to it. "Look, nobody shed a tear when your coven took care of Steve. Warlocks aren't welcome here. And Suzanne played her part in driving him from this town. She made sure everyone knew what he was."

I check my watch again. I need to get over there.

"Before you run off..." Ida leans across the table. "Have you considered running for mayor in the upcoming election?"

My coffee cup freezes halfway to my mouth. "What?" The same thing Duncan asked me to do.

"You'd be perfect! The town needs someone like you in charge. You're organized, and everyone likes you. You'd be a natural. Far better than the current mayor Jeffrey, the bloodsucker."

I set my cup down carefully. "Thanks for the vote of confidence, but I can't. The vet clinic will keep me too busy. At least that's my hope — I mean aside from helping sick or wounded animals."

Ida's smile fades. "Sugar, you didn't think that your gift just appeared out of nowhere, did you? It was me who helped you! I shifted into that scraggly raccoon, Rocky, and started chatting you up."

I stare at her dumbfounded.

Ida smiles at me. "I had to give your gift a little nudge."

I blink a few times, remembering that first conversation with Rocky — or rather, Ida — in my garage when I was nursing it back to health. It had floored me at first when he... or rather she kept saying 'water'. "But why?"

"We needed you to come into your power. You were on the way, of course; you had a bit of progress when you and a squirrel shared your lunch, but you weren't really progressing. And sometimes the universe needs a nudge." She leans forward again. "This gift, talking to animals? It might have taken months to develop naturally. I knew you had it in you. Just needed the right... catalyst."

I think about Dahlia trying so hard to talk to animals, failing every time. "So when my daughter tries to-"

"She's got the gift too," Ida interrupts. "But hers needs to develop naturally. Can't rush everything, honey."

She sits back, smoothing her leopard-print top. "So my asking you to run for mayor is the same sort of thing. Sometimes you need someone to give you a little push in the right direction. Think about it, Libby. Really think about it."

Later, I ease my car into Suzanne and Amy's driveway, my conversation with Ida still rattling in my brain. The neat Victorian house looks innocent enough with its gingerbread trim and cheerful yellow paint, but after what Ida told me about Suzanne's doing whatever mischief she did to Steve Murphy... well...I'm on the lookout now.

Laughter drifts from around the corner. I slip out of my car and follow the sound.

Pausing, I peek around the corner to see a garden that looks like it's been transplanted from a fairy tale. Suzanne and Amy hover above beds of poppies, their translucent wings catching the sunlight. With graceful gestures, they coax the red blooms to open and close like synchronized dancers.

Dahlia, Chloe, and Jessica sit cross-legged in the grass, completely entranced. My daughter's face glows with wonder as she watches the display, and my heart clenches. She looks so young, so vulnerable, not fourteen.

Movement catches my eye. Kevin's there too? He tosses a softball back and forth with Amy's son, Byron. But Kevin's attention keeps wandering to Jessica. Every few throws, his eyes drift over to Shannon's daughter, lingering just a bit too long before snapping back to the game.

The scene looks perfectly wholesome — exactly what you'd expect from two kindly Fae chatting with our young Witches-in-training. But Ida's words echo in my head: "There's a mean streak under all that gentle hearts and flowers facade."

I grip the corner of the house, wondering if I should interrupt this little garden party or let it play out. These women might have played a role in vanquishing Steve Murphy, but right now they're just showing my daughter how to appreciate nature's magic.

Something small and furry brushes against my ankle, and I nearly jump out of my skin. Looking down, there's a squirrel with familiar eyes peering up at me.

"Hi. Me again! Ida. Just had a feeling you were coming here after asking about Suzanne and Amy."

I ease back from the corner and squat down, keeping my voice low. "So, you read minds too? You never mentioned that when I asked about your powers."

The squirrel chatters, her tail twitching in what I swear is amusement. "Just women's intuition. There are some good things about being human after all. See? I told you, Suzanne and Amy are fine. In lots of ways, they're like me. Just want to be free and left alone. Which is why you need to become the mayor here. I'd trust a Witch way more than the bloodsuckers."

My patience wears thin with her political persistence. First at the café, now here as a squir,rel? "Again, I'll think about it. For now, I want to check on my daughter. And apparently my son, too!" I whisper at her.

Standing up straight, I plaster on my best mom smile and round the corner. Suzanne and Amy immediately stop their flower performance, their wings glinting in the sunlight as they touch down and hurry over.

"Libby! What a lovely surprise," Suzanne beams, offering me a plate. "Honey biscuits? And we have fresh lemonade."

Amy clasps her hands together, practically bouncing with enthusiasm. "We're just thrilled to have your daughter here with the other new Witches. And Kevin too, of course!"

I watch Kevin's face turn beet red when he spots me. "Mom! Uh, Jessica asked me to join them. Seemed like a good idea to keep an eye on Dahlia, you know?"

Sure, that's why; such brotherly concern. Right. I glance over at Shannon's daughter, who's sitting with Dahlia and Chloe, all three of them giggling like they're sharing the world's best secret. My nurse's instincts kick in, and I find myself scanning for signs of substance use. After all, the Fae are known for their "special" mushrooms and herbs.

"Mom! Mom!" Dahlia bounds over, her ponytail bouncing, thrusting a vibrant red poppy toward my face. "You have to smell this! It's amazing!"

I lean in, checking her pupils as I do. But all I see is pure joy dancing in her eyes; no dilated pupils, no glazed look. Just my daughter, glowing with wonder.

Behind her, Jessica drifts over to Kevin, slipping her hand into his. The gesture is so natural, so innocent, that I feel my earlier suspicions melting away. There's real magic happening in this garden, but not the kind I feared.

The poppy's scent hits my nose — sweet, fresh, with an undertone of something that makes my shoulders relax and my worries fade. Maybe I've been too quick to judge the Fae based on rumors and warnings.

Ida, now Red-Squirrel instead of Red-Car, scampers across the garden and perches next to Dahlia. "Well hello there, young lady!"

Dahlia's eyes go wide. "Mom! Mom! I can understand her! I really can!" She drops to her knees beside the squirrel, her face glowing with pure delight.

Looking at Suzanne and Amy now, their wings shimmering as they tend to their magical garden, I have to admit that of all the Mysticals I've met so far; they seem the most genuinely joyful.

Maybe that's its own kind of magic.

I hope.

THIRTEEN

SHANNON

As I cross the street to the town hall for my meeting with the mayor, my mind is a whirl of thoughts. There's so damn much going on, all at the same time.

Wesley, my new home is filled with all kinds of magical beings, and the vibe I'm getting is that they don't get along. The undercurrent of tension worries me; if it got out of control, what the hell could anyone, let alone a few middle-aged Witches do?

On top of that, my daughter wants to drop out of college, and my dead mother's spirit is just ducky with it.

On top of that whole mess, both Libby and Mary-Jane want their daughters to join our coven! Mary-Jane doesn't think Chloe's too young, and Libby's kid is only 14! High school kids? Learning magic? Good grief, they're too young to drive and they want to learn how to do magic? And if I freeze them out, Libby and Mary-Jane will be well and truly pissed off.

On top of all that, according to the scuttlebutt I've heard, it's up to us Witches to keep everyone in line.

Everything is in motion now. All of us—even Jessica—are meeting with a species of these Mysticals to see what they're all about.

On top of that dog's breakfast, I'm not sure how I feel about my mother being the new Spirit of the well. THAT totally blind-sided me. But time will tell; right now, I have a meeting with my mayor. Who happens to be a Vampire. Oh boy.

Yeah, my head's spinning, all right.

I push open the heavy glass doors of the entrance, determined to get some straight answers about what's simmering under the surface of our town.

A sleek brunette sits behind the reception desk, watching me with an almost condescending smile as I cross the foyer.

She looks about my age, but way better turned out. Her hair is jet black and sleek, hanging to her shoulders. I know she's a Vampire on sight; she has a pale, almost glowing, complexion, and her pale blue, almost silver eyes have me fixed with an intense gaze as I approach. Her blood-red lips are curled in a condescending smile.

I thought Cynthia was beautiful; this woman is stunning.

And yes, a part of me hates her on sight. Sue me.

The nameplate reads 'Sarah Stone'. Is she related to Jonas Stone, the police chief? It's obvious she's a Vampire while according to MJ, the police chief is a Werewolf. Can that happen, two different Mysticals from the same family? Seems odd, but maybe not in this town.

"I'm here to see the mayor," I say.

"Do you have an appointment?" Sarah's voice oozes condescension, in her tailored, burgundy pant suit (one that doesn't leave much to the imagination about her bust). She looks me up and down like she's reading my mind about how I envy her appearance and is enjoying herself.

"The mayor's expecting me." I start toward his office door.

Sarah moves faster than my eyes can track and is right in front of me. Yep, she's a Vamp. In a tone so phony sweet I'm getting a sugar rush, she says, "I'll need to check if he's available." Her red lips curl into a smirk.

Oh, hell no. I've dealt with enough power plays in the last few weeks; she's picked the wrong Witch to cross today. "Step aside, Sarah. This isn't a social call."

She bristles. "Listen here, Witch—"

I flick my fingers, and a blast of wind shoves her to the side. Nothing dramatic, just enough to make my point. Striding past her, I throw Mayor Jeffrey's door open wide and stride in.

I stop, staring at the spacious office; it's bigger than my living room, and a hella lot more tastefully appointed. Dark brown wainscotting all around, with a lighter oak paneling above. Original oil paintings—wait; is that a Rembrandt? I stand there open-mouthed, taking it all in.

"Shannon! Come in, come in." Jeffery—no, Mayor Sadler; you have an office like this, I'll call you Mayor—waves me over to an ornately carved oak desk with two wingback visitor chairs in front of it.

He watches me smiling as I take a seat. "Pretty sweet digs, huh?" I'm about to make a crack about my tax dollars, but he adds, "I paid for all the renovations out of pocket, Shannon."

Damn Vampires; they can read minds, I guess.

"On a Mayor's salary?"

He waves me off. "On my investment income."

"Investment income?"

He laughs. "For example, I bought Ford Motor Company for a dollar twenty-five a share over a hundred years ago." He leans back in his chair and clasps his hands behind his head. "I'm doing okay."

"You mean you're filthy rich, right?"

He bursts out laughing. "You're as direct as Maeve was, Shannon! Let's put it this way...the older the Vampire, the wealthier they are, how's that?"

"Ummm...how old *are* you?"

"Hmmm...let's just say I remember when the State of New York was a British colony."

Holy shit. My jaw drops. I collect myself and lean forward. "We need to talk about Wesley's power structure. I need to know more about the supernatural beings in this town so I can figure out where we fit in."

Sarah glides into the chair beside Jeffrey's desk, her movements fluid and predatory. "I'll be taking notes."

I shrug. "No skin off my nose." Besides, having two Vampires in this discussion couldn't hurt. "So, Mister Mayor, how do we Witches fit into Wesley?"

He tilts his head at me. "According to your Aunt Maeve from back in the day, isn't there a spirit in your Witching Well that can fill you in on all that?"

Whoa. "You know about my well?"

The mayor cuts through the air with a sharp wave of his hand. "Let's get something out of the way right off the bat. While I appreciate your respect, I'm not 'Mister Mayor', alright?" He leans forward across his desk. "Especially to you, Shannon. You're the head of the Wesley Coven, and it's the Witches all of us…" he slides a look over to Sarah, "what's that term the others use?"

"Mysticals," Sarah says with a sigh.

He nods. "Yes, that's right." Looking back at me, he says, "While I may not agree with it all the time, all of us 'Mysticals' look to you and your coven for leadership. So in that respect, please don't use my title when we speak. You're not asking for any title, and I certainly am not going to be dependent on such formalities, okay?"

He holds my gaze. It's not a friendly gaze, necessarily; it's more businesslike. "Fair enough, Jeffery. And just how are we Witches expected to lead then? I can't see myself arguing with people over trash pickups or parking regulations."

Jeffery laughs and points a finger at himself. "Nooo…that sort of thing is my job! As the leader of the Mysticals, you will be more concerned with mediating disputes amongst our kind." He glances over at Sarah. "Such as Fae interfering with Werewolves celebrating the full moon, for example."

Sarah rolls her eyes and sighs again. "That was a dilly."

"What are you talking about?"

"You're aware of how Weres pretty much cut loose on nights of a full moon, right?"

"Just what I've seen in movies."

"Okay. A Werewolf is a predator. That's their nature, and their human side is able to manage it rather well the vast majority of the time. But on the night of a full moon, their predatory nature becomes overwhelming. Many of them chain themselves in their basements or something like that out of consideration of their neighbors—"

"Or their neighbors' animals," Sarah interjects.

Jeffery nods. "But as well as having a killer instinct, that predatory nature can also manifest itself in more…more shall we say, 'sensual' urges." He leans back in his chair. "You've heard the expression 'A wolf on the prowl'?"

"Yeah, I've been to enough bars and dance clubs when I was younger."

"Exactly! And so they go on the prowl to fulfill their mating urges. It's usually in the forests where they…hook up. And from what I've been told—"

"And what I've witnessed having been married to a Were…" Sarah interjects.

Jeffery nods to her. "Yes." He turns back to me. "Those wooded areas are, well…rather…ummm…spicy."

"Huh?" I ask. Please Lord, don't let this go where I think it's going...

"Like out-of-control orgies, silly girl," Sarah says. "I've witnessed them, but since I'm not a Were myself, I didn't...ahem...participate. But as rowdy and licentious as you can imagine."

"Okay, so they had some kind of sex party," I say with minimal blushing.

"But!" Jeffery says, "The Fae also celebrates the full moon. And where the Weres had their soiree was where the Fae would gather for their own celebration."

"They call it a 'Moondance', I think," Sarah adds.

"Right. And let's just say that the two communities did not see eye to eye that night."

"To say the least," Sarah titters. "My now ex came home pretty banged up."

"Well, the Fae folk had their own share of bumps and bruises," Jeffery replies. He looks over to me and says, "It's that sort of disagreement you'll be mediating."

Well, that doesn't sound all that hard.

"It is complicated, you silly thing!" Sarah snaps at me.

I spin to her. "Will you please stop reading my damn mind?" Jeez Louise, at least MJ needs to touch someone to get a read! This beeyotch just waltzes right into my head like she owns the place!

"Ladies...please...." Jeffery holds his hands up in mock surrender. "I apologize on behalf of Sarah, Ms. Burke. She's only recently turned and isn't seasoned enough in her new...life to have the judgement she'll need to develop."

I roll my eyes.

He looks over at Sarah with a steely gaze. "Now, Sarah..." He points a finger at her.

She folds in on herself. "I'm sorry," she says in a plaintive voice.

"Sorry what?"

"Sorry...sir."

"Good girl. Now apologize sincerely to Ms. Burke."

What the hell is going on? Before I can say anything, Sarah gets to her feet and faces me, her hands clasped before her. "I apologize, Ms. Burke, for being so prying. It won't happen again," she says in a low voice, looking me in the eye. She looks from me over to Jeffery.

"That's very good, Sarah," he says. "You may be seated."

In a movement as graceful as a ballerina, she sits back down; back straight, knees clasped, staring straight ahead.

Holy shit, I'm watching Fifty Shades take place right in front of me. My damn jaw drops again as I look from one to the other.

Jeffery looks back at me. "As I was saying, it's the Witches that would mediate a dispute such as this. I've made attempts, but frankly my words don't carry as much significance as those of a Witch with the other Mysticals."

"Because?" Then it hits me. I study his face, trying to read between the lines, but there's nothing there—literally nothing. No aura, no energy signature, just... emptiness. The same void surrounds Sarah. "It's because you're not alive and they are."

"We use the term 'undead', but yes. I can't even play the 'wisdom borne of age' card, because a Fae, let alone a Druid is much, much older than I. And that's where you come in. They all listen to Witches with deep respect."

"Why?"

"Good question." He turns to Sarah. "Why do you think, Sarah?"

She instantly brightens at his including her back into the discussion. She looks off to the side for a moment and says, "I think it's because it's only the Witches who have been openly persecuted and have forgiven humans rather than taken vengeance."

"Precisely." He turns back to me. "Yes, we Vampires had been feared and hunted centuries ago, but back then we were rather murderous. We've been able to circumvent that now, but it came at a price. The other Mysticals haven't really had to deal with that other than Witches, and your good hearts are admired by all."

Sarah adds, "And while the Vampires were hunted because of our killing, Witches were hunted and killed because they were 'different'." She turns to me. "Your kind were innocent victims of ignorance, fear, and zealotry for hundreds of years. And yet, despite your formidable power, never took vengeance." She bows her head briefly to me. "Again, my apologies for lack of respect."

"We're good, Sarah. Sorry for the wind blast."

"Well, sure beats a broomstick to the heart, Shannon," she replies with a quick grin.

"This is wonderful, just wonderful." Jeffrey beams. "Now that you Witches know everything, we can all be ourselves! No more sneaking around." He taps the surface of his desk. "Wesley needs the ward fixed though. It's grown weaker ever since Maeve passed on, and more and more normies are noticing things they never did before. Our secret about our town is no longer safe. I must stress that your new position as leaders of the community comes with serious responsibilities." He sounds like he's reading from a script. "You must protect Wesley's magical secrets while promoting harmony between our... diverse population. As they say...diversity is our strength."

Jeffery continues. "But Wesley is like a powder keg right now. The Fae and Druids are often at odds, which is funny considering they're pretty much cousins. Family dynamics, right? And the Shifters barely tolerate being in the same room as Werewolves. Such drama. Makes me glad I'm a Vampire..."

He trails off as Sarah gazes at him with an expression of pure admiration. She leans forward. "Jeffrey has done an exceptional job maintaining order. His... diplomatic approach has prevented countless conflicts." She looks at him adoringly and whispers, "It's been an honor to assist him this past year, streamlining communications between all the factions."

I resist rolling my eyes at her obvious brown-nosing. "That's great, but what I really want to know is how Vampires fit into all this. The ley lines under Wesley promote life magic—they're literally rivers of life energy. So, how do the undead exist here? You're basically walking contradictions to the magic here."

Jeffrey lets out a belly laugh that makes his whole body shake. "Oh, it's quite simple, actually! We're not native to these shores at all. Pure European stock, to be precise." He puffs up with pride. "The first of our kind fled there when they were pursued by Van Helsig and his minions. Nasty hunters, all of them. As soon as we discovered the magical energy surrounding Wesley, we realized it could mask our presence."

Spreading his hands wide, he effuses, "The ley lines created the perfect hiding place. And since we came from noble European bloodlines, it was only natural that we would assume leadership of the town."

"Okay, that explains how you came to settle here," I say carefully, "but how many vampires are there in Wesley? Sarah doesn't look as though there's any European blood in her veins. If she has blood, that is." I lean forward, fixing Jeffrey with a hard stare. "So, your numbers, do they increase?"

"Now Shannon, that's a rather personal question, don't you think?" He fusses with the pens on his desk. "Every community has its ways of... sustaining itself."

"She has a right to know," Sarah cuts in, her voice sharp. "After all, I was human just last year. Jonas Stone's wife, actually."

My stomach falls through the chair. Good goddess. They're turning humans? Regular people? Willing ones maybe, but still, how many others have they "changed"? How many more are they planning to turn?

Jeffrey nods, folding his hands together over his paunch as he leans back. "There were only a handful of Vampires who came to Wesley. Since that time, our numbers have increased, yes; but only by a small number." He gestures at Sarah. "Dear Sarah's been the first human to be turned in Wesley in a long, long time."

My mind is racing. "They were all people who wanted eternal life?"

Jeffrey nods. "You could say that, yes. Even so, we're very selective and hesitant to do so. It's a real... 'departure' for a human to be turned, pardon the pun." Despite the reasonable sounding explanation, the thought makes my skin crawl.

"So, your powers..." I lean forward, "The incredible speed, strength... that's all true." But even as I say it, I recall how fast Sarah had been trying to block my entrance.

Jeffrey jiggles with laughter, his multiple chins wobbling as he pats his enormous belly. "You wouldn't know it by looking at me, but yes. I can run faster than a cheetah; I'm stronger than a bear."

I raise an eyebrow, finding it hard to picture this blob of a man doing anything athletic. The way Sarah moved earlier was impressive, but Jeffrey? He looks like he'd get winded walking to his car.

"I've heard rumors," I press on, "that you raid the hospital's blood banks. Is that how you all survive, or do you sometimes sample the odd animal... or human?"

Jeffery's face hardens. "I'm not crazy about what you're implying. Suffice it to say, we would never harm innocent humans! We have arrangements with legitimate suppliers, proper medical facilities." He sees the look of skepticism in my eyes. "As I said, we're fairly well off, and we purchase what we need." He slides a quick look at Sarah. "In most cases, anyway."

"And furthermore," Jeffrey continues, "you need not be too concerned about our behavior, Shannon. "It's the Werewolves you should be concerned about! Do you know what happens during full moons? The property damage alone! Not to mention the livestock incidents...We Vampires maintain our dignity and self-control at all times."

Sarah's shoulders tense at the mention of Werewolves. There's clearly some bad blood there—no pun intended—between her and her ex-husband's kind.

Sarah's phone chirps, and she turns away slightly to answer it, her voice dropping to a whisper.

"Shit!" Sarah barks before spinning to face Jeffrey, her perfect composure cracking, as she holds the phone out. "It's Jonas. Beth James escaped somehow. They've got roadblocks up but..." She swallows hard. "She managed to snatch her phone as she broke out."

Jeffrey's jovial mask slips completely. For the first time, I see the predator beneath his composed and bovine exterior. His eyes go flat and cold, like a shark's.

"When did this happen?"

"Twenty minutes, tops." Sarah's fingers slide to end the call. "Jonas has Werewolves searching the woods, and a roadblock on the highway, but if she's able to get away..."

"Or posts anything online," I add, my stomach clenching. Beth filmed us when we met with Patrick the Warlock...and my dead aunt and mother...and Alice. She has everything on her phone! If she posts it, it will go viral. Or one phone call to a news station, and Wesley's carefully maintained secrets would explode into the open.

The whole world would descend on our small town.

Jeffrey heaves himself up from his chair with surprising speed. "Get Peter Bond on this. He can track her phone signal." He turns to me, all pretense of the jolly mayor gone. "Shannon, we need you and your coven to help with this. Beth knows too much about all of us. If she exposes Wesley..."

"The town will become the next Area 51, with every sort of paranormal fan pouring in." Sarah cuts in. "Not to mention maybe scientists, or the military. They'd tear this town apart trying to study us or destroy us."

The door to Jeffrey's office crashes open so hard it bounces against the wall. When I spin around to see, Ivy Miller and Officer Alf hover in the doorway, their gossamer wings catching the fluorescent light. Stone cold expressions harden their features as they stare at the mayor.

Ivy's tiny frame somehow commands the entire room as she speaks. "We know where Beth is."

Fourteen

Shannon

I spring from my chair, relief flooding through me that Ivy and Alf know where that treacherous S.O.B. Beth is. "Thank god! So, where is she?" I demand. "We've got to find her before she does any damage to the town!" Visions of Men In Black, scientists in hazmat suits and soldiers fill my mind's eye. "We have to get hold of her before she gets the word out!"

"Not so fast, Witch," Officer Alf says. He's still hovering close to the mayor, fixing Jeffery with a stare that could freeze lava. "If you want us to help you, some things need to change around here." He looks back at Ivy, sharing a conspiratorial smile before returning his glare to Jeffrey. "We know what all of you think of us, Fae; treating us like we're idiotic airheads, never taking us seriously. We're sick and tired of your contempt for our kind."

Jeffrey's jaw drops. "This is not the time for your fragile ego to be stroked! The entire town is in danger from that woman!"

"It's exactly the time," Ivy cuts in, "For decades, we've been the brunt of every joke, every disparaging remark, every sideways smirk you and the other Mysticals toss out. When's the last time a Fae had a seat at the Council table, Mayor? When's the last time anyone asked what we want?"

I glance between them, feeling anger borne of resentment roll off Ivy in waves, her eyes narrow slits staring the Mayor down. She may look delicate with those gossamer wings, but there's steel in her spine.

Sarah hisses, turning on Ivy, "You ungrateful little—" Her face tightens into a snarl, exposing a pair of sharp fangs.

"Careful," Alf warns, his finger tapping the badge on his uniform. "I'm still a police officer."

"And I still know exactly where Beth is hiding," Ivy adds with a smirk. "And how much time there is until she goes live on TikTok, Insta and even Facebook with the Witch videos."

"How long?" My stomach drops. Dammit! "How the hell did she get away? Weren't they supposed to wipe her memories as well as her phone? When is she gonna post videos?"

"Tonight," Ivy says. "Just because we wanted to give enough time for the Mayor here to agree to our terms."

The only thing I'm concerned with right now is how perfectly crappy it will be if Beth exposes Wesley. Not just for the sake of the town, but my own son would not take it well at all. When he was last here to visit me, he sensed the town was different, telling me that it had a 'weird vibe'. Now? If this gets out, I have no idea how he'll react. He's been distant ever since I moved here, bugging me to return to the city.

"Can we deal with your demands later? AFTER we have Beth in custody again?" I yell at Ivy and Alf, desperation making me glare at her. "I promise I'll help you—"

"No!" Ivy's wings shed a layer of sparkles. She's so angry she's vibrating from head to toe, staring down the mayor. "If we give up Beth, we lose whatever leverage we have to change the way we're treated!" She turns to me, those ethereal eyes burning with rage, and jabs a finger. "And you just found out we exist, Shannon! You're the last person to have a say in all this." "That rotund bloodsucker has had things his way for too long. Along with the rest of them. Fae are every bit as worthy of respect as Druids are." She pauses, her voice dropping to something more personal, almost pleading. "You realize the Druids and Fae are cousins, right?"

I blink, momentarily thrown off balance. "Yeah, I just learned that." I glance between the Mayor and Ivy, and my mind races. The clock's ticking toward disaster, and we're stuck here in a standoff. "Look, time is running out. If Beth gets on social media or makes some phone calls, you will be exposed along with everyone else. Surely, you don't want that."

My heart pounds fast as I try to make Ivy and Alf see reason. The life of every single person in Wesley will be thrown into chaos because these two want to settle a score.

Sarah is flushed with anger. Glowering at Ivy and Alf like they're insects beneath her designer heels, she sneers, "You two aren't pushing us around. Typical Fae, you lack the intelligence to think things through. While it might be awkward to have the outside world descend on us, we will survive. It's basically Beth's word against practically the whole town."

Way to inflame the situation, Sarah.

Alf's wings vibrate with rage. Shaking his head, a cold smile forms on his lips. "Typical Vamp. Slipping and sliding, but this time you're wrong. Ivy and I will side with Beth and confirm everything she says. We're past caring at this point."

"Hang on!" I hold my hand up, stopping the argument before it gets any worse...if that's possible. "We can't let it get to that point. Beth has photographic evidence on her phone exposing me and my coven as witches. So—"

"Evidence about Witches, not the other Mysticals." Mayor Jeffrey interrupts, his voice chilling. My skin crawls as he leans back in his chair, fingers steepled beneath his fleshy chin. "As for Alf and Ivy, it'll be pretty hard to back your friend Beth... if you're dead."

The mortal threat hangs in the air. The temperature feels like it dropped to sub-zero in an instant. I glance between Ivy and Alf, seeing their wings flutter nervously despite their brave faces.

Sarah grins, her teeth gleaming unnaturally white against her bloodless lips. She takes a step closer to Ivy, eyes traveling up and down her slight frame like she's examining merchandise.

"Never sampled Fae blood. It could be fun to take a Fae." Her tongue darts out to wet her lips. "That is...if my IQ doesn't take a hit."

Her casual cruelty makes my stomach turn. So much for Jeffrey's claims about Vampires being peaceful or even trustworthy. They're willing to kill these two Fae and let us Witches swing in the breeze for the world to see.

"No one is turning anyone!" A loud masculine voice thunders.

I spin around and see Jonas Stone, the police chief, pushing his way into the room, his face twisted with fury. The tension in the air was already thick enough to cut, but it suddenly doubles.

When Jonas scowls at Sarah—his undead EX—his features twist with revulsion. "Not bad enough you became one of them, but now you're feeding on living creatures? You're disgusting."

Before I can even blink, Sarah is a blur of motion. One second she's standing near the desk, the next she's across the room, her fingernails raking across Jonas's face. Only his thick beard saves him from being slashed open. He grabs her wrist mid-strike, and they lock into a struggle.

"You never understood!" Sarah hisses, her face inches from his. "You were so content just to exist, day after day, nothing changing, nothing at all. Never thinking of me! What was I supposed to doooo?"

What the hell is that supposed to mean?

Jonas doesn't flinch, holding her at bay with what looks like considerable effort. "I understood perfectly. You wanted the party life. The thrill. You threw away twenty years of marriage for immortality and what? Blood and nightclubs?"

Their bodies strain with tension, locked in a duel that probably played out many times in their marriage. This isn't just about Vampires and Werewolves—it's about betrayal. And I thought I disliked my Ex. It's a love-fest compared to these two.

"You could have believed me," Sarah whispers, something almost vulnerable flickering across her face before hardening again. "But you were too self-righteous."

"The undead are an abomination!" Jonas growls back, looking at Jeffery with pure hatred.

I stand frozen, watching this marital drama play out against the backdrop of our supernatural crisis. Part of me wants to remind everyone about Beth and her ticking time bomb of exposure, but another part recognizes that what's happening between Jonas and Sarah is a microcosm of Wesley itself—creatures bound by history and resentment, unable to move forward.

I'm hardly aware of the mayor now at my side, roaring at...Oh shit! Ivy and Alf are gone! There's only shimmering dust on the floor where the Fae pair had hovered.

The Mayor's face looks like a festering boil, about to explode.

My attention snaps back to Sarah and Jonas, still locked in their toxic dance. I raise my hand and summon a blast of air that strikes them both, knocking them to the floor and apart.

"Stop fighting!" I yell, "Thanks to you two, they got away and they're now helping Beth!"

The Mayor helps Sarah to her feet, then he turns to me with a cold smile.

"This is your problem more than mine, or even any of the Mysticals." With a shrug he continues, "We'll have Witch fans and even some reporters nosing around, but we've lived for centuries undetected. You never knew. And you're supposedly gifted Witches."

His dismissive tone makes my blood boil. As if this isn't a crisis for everyone. As if my coven is somehow solely responsible for this shit-show. We just found out!

"As for those two Fae whack jobs," he straightens his tie and smirks, "it's up to the Fae community to deal with them." He looks over at Jonas Stone, the police chief. "Isn't that right, Chief?"

Jonas transforms before my eyes—his face elongating into a snout, thick hair sprouting across his skin, his uniform straining against newly bulging muscles. It's both terrifying and fascinating to witness.

"I'll get word out to the Cloister leadership to take care of it," he snarls, his voice deeper and rougher than before. "And if ..." his gaze sweeps over Sarah and Jeffery, "the Vampires are bowing out, I'm going to advise my pack to do the same then."

Sarah, rubbing her wrists where her ex-husband had manhandled her, shakes her head. "Typical. You are such a Were. I'm so glad to be done with you and your kind."

My blood boils. These people—these creatures—have been running this town into the ground with their feuds. And now, when we're facing exposure that could affect all our lives — and so not for the better! — they're still playing politics?

"You're kidding me," I mutter, my hands beginning to tingle with elemental energy. The air around me stirs, responding to my mounting frustration.

I've been pushed around enough in my life—by my ex-husband, by circumstances, by my own self-doubt. But I'm done with that. I'm a damn Witch now. I have power. Real power.

I raise both hands, feeling the air currents bend to my will. Papers on Jeffrey's desk begin to flutter.

"When I find Beth—and make no mistake, I will! — we are going to make some changes in how this town is run," I declare, my voice growing stronger with each word. "From what I've seen, Ivy and Alf have a good point. You guys totally suck, in more ways than one!"

With a forceful motion, I swirl my arms, channeling my fury into the elements. The air responds with explosive force, whipping into a miniature cyclone that tears through the Mayor's office. Furniture crashes against walls, papers and pens become dangerous projectiles, and the three of them stagger backward, fighting to stay upright in the magical windstorm I've unleashed.

Not waiting to see the aftermath. I turn and stride out, my rage carrying me forward. The coven is on its own, but that's nothing new. We've been figuring things out by ourselves from the beginning.

And we'll handle this too.

I slam my car door and punch in the group call, my hands still trembling with anger. The phone rings three times before Libby's voice comes through.

"Shannon? What's—"

"No time," I cut her off. "I need everyone at MJ's restaurant. Now."

Cynthia joins the call. "I'm with Eric. We were just—"

"Alone, Cyn. Just the coven." I grip the steering wheel tighter, watching a flock of birds scatter from a nearby tree. Did I do that? My emotions are making my magic leak out in unpredictable ways.

"Is everything okay?" MJ's voice breaks in, sounding concerned.

"Not even close. Beth James escaped custody." I pause to let that sink in. "And it gets worse. Ivy and Alf know where she is, but they're refusing to help. They're actually backing her up now."

"What?" Libby gasps.

"The Fae are helping Beth?" MJ sounds incredulous.

I pull into a parking spot behind MJ's restaurant, killing the engine. "Everyone meet me at MJ's restaurant as soon as you can get there."

"I'm already here," MJ says. "In the kitchen. Come around back."

"Twenty minutes," Libby promises.

"On my way," Cynthia confirms.

I end the call and rest my forehead against the steering wheel, taking a deep breath. The Vampires won't help us. The Werewolves have checked out. The Fae are actively working against us. And I just threatened the most powerful beings in town.

What a mess.

Robert appears from between two parked cars, padding silently toward me. His golden eyes lock with mine through the windshield, and I feel a small measure of calm return. At least I'm not completely alone.

I open the door and he jumps in, settling on the passenger seat.

"We've got trouble, Robert," I mutter, scratching behind his ears. "And I think I just made it worse."

He makes a low rumbling sound in his throat. "What else is new?"

I grab my phone and head for the back entrance to MJ's kitchen. Time to Witch up and fix this mess.

FIFTEEN

MARY-JANE

As I shove my phone in my pocket, Shannon's urgent message rings in my ears. Beth James escaped? We're on our own? Perfect. Just what I need after casting a questionable love spell on our garbage man Druid.

It's pretty quiet in the dining room, so I duck into the kitchen. The moment I push through the swinging kitchen doors, my jaw drops. What's Jane doing here? She leans against the prep table, her wings catching the fluorescent light, making sparkles dance across the stainless-steel surfaces. The dress she's wearing is painted on, with a neckline that plunges to places lingerie ads fear to go.

Barb, my assistant chef, slams down a knife mid-chop and glares at me. "When were you going to tell me she got the night off? I need help here, MJ!"

"I—" The words stick in my throat as Jane gives me a little finger wave, her grin screaming, 'I got what I wanted!'

"The love potion worked like a charm," Jane whispers, sidling up to me. "Duncan's picking me up in twenty minutes. I owe you one, my Witch bestie."

"Great," I mutter, feeling betwixt and between. Between Beth James on the loose, ready to blab to the world About us being Witches and Jane blackmailing me into casting spells, I'm about ready to turn someone into a toad.

If I knew how.

"MJ!" Barb waves a spatula at me. "Hello? Friday night dinner rush? Who's gonna help me?"

I take a deep breath, counting to five. "Call Anita or Whitney. I won't be around to help either."

"You've got to be kidding me!" Barb's face turns the color of the marinara bubbling on the stove. "On a Friday?"

"I'll double your wages for tonight," I snap, watching Jane prance toward the back door. "Triple, if you stop bitching."

I skedaddle and grab Jane's arm, hauling her to the side. "What do you know about Ivy and Alf? Beth James escaped, and apparently, Ivy and Alf are helping her."

"Oh, shit." Jane jerks back with a shocked look. "I never thought they'd do it."

My fingers tighten around her arm. "You knew they were planning something?"

"Not exactly." Jane's eyes dart toward the exit. "There's been talk among the Fae. Resentment's been building. Ivy's always yammering on about how we're treated like shit."

"And you didn't think to mention this?" My blood pressure rises so much that magic tingles in my fingertips. "While I'm making you a love potion?"

Her wings flutter quickly. "It was just talk!" Look, everyone gripes about their life, wanting more." She lowers her voice. "But Ivy's always been... extreme. Ivy and Beth were always chummy, even as kids! But recently, something changed. She started talking about leverage. Whatever that means."

I'm just about to throttle her for more information when the back door flies open with a bang.

"MJ!" Shannon bursts in, wild-eyed and crackling with energy. Little sparks dance at her fingers, and I can tell she's barely containing herself from unleashing holy hell.

"Shannon!" I release Jane, who immediately backs against the wall. "It seems that Jane knew something about Ivy and Alf's little rebellion."

Shannon's eyes narrow as she stalks toward the dolled-up Fae. "Talk. Now. Where the hell are they?"

Jane shakes her head. “No. I don’t have time.” “You know I have to meet up with Duncan, MJ! You made that love spell for me! How long does it even last?”

Shannon’s jaw drops before she glowers at me. “Don’t tell me you tried another love spell, Mary-Jane!”

Heat infuses my face as my gaze darts between them. “I had to! She was blackmailing me! Look, I’m sorry, but I accidentally mentioned the Well. She was going to blab it all over town.”

The kitchen door swings open again, and Libby walks in, catching the tail end of my confession. Great. Perfect timing.

“Hate to break it to you, but I think the Mysticals already know about the well,” Libby says, crossing her arms. “... according to Duncan, when I spoke to him yesterday.”

My stomach drops. “What? But... but that means...” I turn on Jane, who’s suddenly very interested in examining her glittery nail polish. “You played me! You knew the Well wasn’t a secret!”

“I needed that love spell, okay?” Jane bites her lower lip nervously. “And you weren’t exactly jumping in to help me. So—”

Grabbing the nearest wooden spoon, I point it at her, barely resisting the urge to swat her with it. “So, you manipulated me! Made me think I’d spilled some huge secret when everyone already knew!”

“Not everyone,” Jane protests, backing toward the door. “Just... most of the Mystical community.”

I glare at her. This manipulative little Fairy had played me like a fiddle. My supposed friend and kitchen helper. Before I can unleash my fury, Jane spins toward Libby.

“What were you doing with Duncan? I thought you and Stan were a thing! But not so much, now that you know Duncan’s a Druid, I guess. Hands off my Druid, Witch!”

The absurdity of it makes me laugh...almost. Jane’s claiming ownership of a guy she needed magic to attract, while accusing Libby of poaching. The irony is rich.

“Excuse me?” Libby’s mouth drops open. “I was just talking to him about—”

“Save it,” Jane snaps, her wings shedding even more sparkles across my clean kitchen floor. Great, more glitter to sweep up.

The kitchen door swings open again, and Cynthia walks in, looking like she’s just rolled out of bed. Her hair is a tousled mess, and she’s wearing baggy gray sweats that have definitely seen better days. Not exactly the polished look she usually presents to the world.

Shaking my head, it looks like the love triangle is triangulating even more, based on the poster I glimpsed in Duncan's house. He's got his own obsession with Cynthia. Poor Jane has no idea she's just a stopgap, that only a spell could accomplish. But there's no way I'm sharing that little tidbit right now. Jane's already furious enough, and we have bigger problems to deal with.

"So, what are we gonna do?" Cynthia asks, stifling a yawn. "You sounded so urgent, Shannon."

Jane's eyes narrow as she looks Cynthia up and down. "What happened to you? You look like something the cat dragged in."

Cynthia gives it right back, doing a once-over of Jane's skin-tight sheath. "Doing a photo shoot for Comic-Con or Stripper Weekly? Your wings need to be clipped, I'd say."

Great. A catfight on top of everything else. I, for one, totally don't need that high-school drama. I step between them. "That's enough, both of you. We've got a serious situation with Beth James escaping, and being helped by your friends, Jane. So, consider your date cancelled. You're joining us in the office while we try to figure this out." I grab Jane's arm before she can flutter off.

"No!" Jane tries to wrench free, but I've got a death grip on one arm while Shannon latches onto the other. Her wings beat frantically, shedding more glitter all over my frigging floor.

"Let me go!" Jane screeches as we drag her toward the back office. "Duncan will be here any minute! The spell—"

"Will have to wait," I snap. "You think I care about your love life when Beth James is out there? She'll expose all of us, including you and your Fae friends."

We frog-march her through the kitchen, past Barb, who's staring with her mouth hanging open. I'll have to come up with some explanation later, but right now, there's a bigger problem.

Ray looks up from the computer when we burst into the office, his eyes widening at the sight of us manhandling Beth in her too-tight dress.

"We have an emergency coven meeting," I tell him, jerking my head toward the door. "Will you call Stan, and Eric and Devon? Get them looking for Beth. She's escaped."

"But I was just about to—"

"Now, Ray!" I use my no-nonsense voice, the one that stopped working on him years ago until I became a Witch. Now he snaps to attention like a soldier.

"Right. I'll make the calls." He grabs his phone and heads for the door.

I push him the rest of the way out and close it firmly behind him. When I turn around, Jane is sitting in Ray's chair, wings drooping, while Shannon, Libby, and Cynthia stand in a semicircle around her, looking like judges about to render a sentence on her.

"Alright," I say, crossing my arms. "Start talking. What exactly are Ivy and Alf planning to do with Beth? And where are they?"

Jane sputters and tries a puppy-dog look, like it has a prayer of working. "I don't know where they are. Honestly, MJ."

My patience has worn thinner than baked phyllo dough. Her wings flutter nervously as I place my hand firmly on her shoulder, feeling the connection open between us like a faucet turning on. The moment our skin touches, her thoughts flood into me—resentment, jealousy, and a deep, burning desire to be taken seriously.

"That's not true," I say. "You know where they are and...you've even sided with them. You know a lot more than you're letting on."

Jane tries to squirm away, but Libby steps forward and places her hand on Jane's other shoulder, pinning her in place.

"Let me go!" Jane's eyes dart between us. "I told you, I don't know!"

But the truth hums beneath her skin. The lies taste bitter in my mind, like burnt coffee grounds. She knows, and I'm going to get it out of her.

"Jane," I tighten my grip slightly, "I can literally feel what you're thinking right now. The truth, please."

Her eyes widen with genuine fear. "You can read my thoughts? That's... that's not fair!"

"Neither is blackmailing me into making love potions," I counter. "Or helping Ivy and Alf expose all of us to the outside world."

Shannon crosses her arms, and it feels like a storm brewing. "You'd better tell us, Jane! Or so help me..."

"Fine!" Jane's shoulders slump. "Yes, I knew what they were planning. Ivy's been talking about it for a while now. Conspiring to do something, but I never thought she'd do it."

A flash of memory from her mind—Ivy and Alf in heated conversation at the edge of the forest, their wings vibrating with anger—enters my head.

"You were there when they decided to help Beth escape." I say. It's not a question.

I concentrate harder as she tries to mentally squirm away. Her thoughts are a jumbled mess of wings and garbage men and spite—so much spite. Behind all that, she desperately tries to block me by focusing on Duncan in various states of undress, that I really wish I could unsee.

"Stop fighting me," I mutter. "We're trying to help everyone here, including you."

"Get out of my head!" Jane hisses.

But I've gotten better at this. When I first discovered my ability to read thoughts through touch, it was overwhelming—like trying to drink from a fire hose. Now I can sift through the noise, searching for what matters.

There—behind the Duncan fantasies (ugh, on a bed of lichen? Really?), I catch glimpses of something else. Trees. Water. A dilapidated structure with peeling paint and broken windows. It's familiar somehow...

The image solidifies as Jane's attempt at blocking me slips: a small, weathered cabin perched on the edge of a lake. Overgrown weeds surround it, and moss on the roof. But it's clearly being used—I see fresh footprints in the dirt, a lantern glowing through a grimy window.

My eyes snap open wide, and I stare directly at Shannon. "That last cabin on your aunt's property—"

"I didn't..." Jane jerks away from me, her face paling beneath her fairy glow. "I didn't tell you that."

"That's it though, isn't it?" I sense the truth of it even as she tries to deny it. "They're hiding Beth at the abandoned cabin at the end of the lake."

Shannon's eyes narrow. "One of my aunt's? The one I've been putting off renovating — it's so bad? It's practically falling down."

"It makes sense," Cynthia steps closer. "It's isolated, nobody goes there anymore, and it's the last place anyone would think to look." She tips her head at Jane. "Hiding in plain sight. Clever."

"Plus," Libby adds, "it's technically on Burke family property. There might be some magical protections there that would make it hard for others to find."

"Well, my Aunt Maeve did ward the property..." Shannon says, thinking aloud. "Actually, it's a smart move."

I look at Jane, my mind racing with all the information I've gleaned from her thoughts. The pieces suddenly fit together in a way that makes my stomach sink.

"You were at that meeting. And so were Amy and Suzanne. You're all in on it."

Jane's face contorts with fury, her wings trying to escape from the chair back. "Why wouldn't we be?" she spits, tears welling in her eyes. "I've got nothing against you Witches, but the Weres and Vamps and Shifters...they treat us like dirt."

The raw emotion in her voice catches me off guard. Behind her indignation, I sense genuine pain—years of being dismissed, overlooked, treated as nothing more than pretty decorations with wings. For the first time, I truly see Jane—not just as my sometimes-annoying kitchen helper, but as someone who's been denied simple respect her entire life.

My anger deflates like bread being kneaded. I step back and nod to Libby, signaling her to release Jane's other arm.

"We're going to try to change that, Jane, I promise." My voice softens as I meet her tear-filled eyes. "But we have to stop Beth. If you promise me that you won't alert Ivy or Alf, you're free to go and enjoy your date with Duncan."

Jane blinks at me in surprise. "You're letting me go? Just like that?"

Sighing, I suddenly feel every one of my south-of-fifty years. "Look, I get it. I really do. For most of my life, I've been the chubby friend, the one people underestimate or never take seriously. It sucks feeling invisible or somehow less."

Shannon starts to protest, but I raise my hand. "I trust her. Even though she tried to blackmail me, she's sincere when she says she won't double-cross us."

Jane stands up, smoothing her dress and giving her wings a little shake. She shoots a glare at Libby. "Stay away from Duncan, okay?"

Libby rolls her eyes. "No problem. He's all yours."

I almost feel bad knowing what I know about Duncan's crush on Cynthia, but some lessons have to be learned the hard way. Besides, we've got Beth to deal with.

Shannon steps aside to let Jane out and then turns to us, her mouth set in a straight line. "We know what we have to do."

When we step outside the office, Ray is waiting, phone in hand. His worried expression makes my stomach clench.

"I got in touch with Eric and Stan," he says. "But Devon's phone just goes to voicemail."

"Oh, shit." Libby murmurs.

Shannon whips around. "What's wrong?"

"Earlier today, Mary told me Devon was meeting up with her about becoming a Druid," Libby explains, wincing as she stares at Shannon.

Shannon's eyes go wide, but she gives her head a little shake. "I'll deal with that later. For now, we need to stop Beth."

SIXTEEN

LIBBY

As I drive to Shannon's place, I glance over at Cynthia. She's slumped in the passenger seat, her normally vibrant red hair looking as limp as her shoulders.

"I'm sorry I'm not more help," she mumbles, rubbing her eyes. "I had no idea pregnancy would be like this. My back hurts, I'm sore every morning, and I can barely keep my thoughts straight these days. "

"It gets better, don't worry." I say, glancing over at her. "We've all gone through the first trimester; it's a real slog, but it gets better as you go forward. You'll be okay. Just hang in there."

Cynthia shakes her head. "This morning when I went to my hairdresser, I fell asleep in the chair! Poor Tina had to wake me up!" She shakes her head. "It was sooo embarrassing."

She's so wrung out and exhausted that my heart aches for her. The first trimester really sucks for a lot of people. I wheel the car to the side of the road and let it idle as I turn to her. "Let me help you."

"What can you do?"

I shift closer and place one hand on her head and the other on her chest. "You need a boost of energy, sweetie."

With Cynthia cradled in my hands, I close my eyes, calling upon the same restorative energy I had called forth to save Robert's life just a few months ago.

Oh! The intensity of the surge of healing vitality that blooms up in me is richly gratifying; like the opening chords of a favorite melody from long ago. Steady pulses fill me, a warm throbbing travels down my arms to my hands to emanate out into Cynthia, caressing her faded aura.

Cynthia inhales deeply and lets it out with a sighing 'yessss...'

Her eyes flutter open, and she stares into mine as I ease the revitalization into her. I can feel her entire being respond; her body goes from slack to attentive, her aura begins to shine, and the lines on her face fade, replaced by an expression of joy.

We silently commune for a few more minutes until I take my hands away and sit back. Even in the dim light, I see color has returned to her cheeks again, and her eyes look brighter when she grins. And yeah, her aura's revitalized too; its surface has gone from dull to shiny.

"Oh, wow..." she sighs. "That was...wow." It's like I just slept for a solid eight hours. Wow." She squeezes my hand. "Can you move in with me? My own personal recharging station."

"Anytime you need it, cupcake!" I shift over and put the car in gear. "You'll be fine in a few weeks; the second trimester's a lot easier; but until then...I'm glad to help." I chuckle. "I wish I had a me back when I was pregnant."

In a few more minutes, I wheel the car into Shannon's driveway. There's an SUV parked next to hers that I don't recognize. When I step out, Shannon and MJ are talking to the driver, while Robert watches from his position at Shannon's feet.

"Who's that?" Cynthia asks.

"I'm not sure..." I mutter, walking closer.

When I reach them, I recognize Miguel Lopez. He works as an Uber driver in town and makes deliveries to the hospital sometimes. Wow, no one is hiding their true natures anymore, judging by the rug of body hair, and the slightly elongated canines breaking through his smile. So, Miguel's a Were...my, my.

"Hey, Libby," he nods to me.

"What's going on?"

He scratches his beard before answering, "Your daughter and Mary Jane's daughter hired me to take them out here. I was waiting to see if they wanted a lift back when you ladies showed up."

My eyes widen, "Dahlia's here? She's supposed to be working on her science project."

"Yeah, well, they took off into the woods about ten minutes ago," Miguel continues, oblivious to my concern. "I couldn't help overhearing—" he taps his ear with a hairy finger "—Werewolf hearing, you know. Shannon's kid Jessica was all hyped up about showing the other two something special."

He chuckles, his eyes crinkling at the corners. "I didn't want to burst her bubble, but I know it has to be about the Well. Tempting as it was to follow them — I didn't." He stretches his stocky arms above his head and yawns.

"Wait. You know about the Well?"

"Sure. All the Mysticals in town do." He shrugs. "Not that it matters; Maeve has a ward around it, none of us could ever find it no matter how hard we tried. And..." he lets out a huff, "if any of us got too close, we'd get sicker than a dog." He drums his hands on the steering wheel. "So, I just stayed put here."

That was news to me. Not only a ward of concealment, but one of protection? I look over at Shannon. "Did you know about this ward?"

"Nope. But it sort of makes sense though, doesn't it? Especially knowing how much friction there is in town between the different Mysticals." She looks down the pathway to the Well. "The Well," Shannon grumbles. "Great. My mother is going to have a field day with this. She's not going to like being disturbed and, naturally, it'll be my fault."

"I guess your daughters won't need my services, so I'm going to skedaddle." Miguel perks up suddenly, looking over at MJ. "Hey, is Jane working tonight? Maybe I'll stop by the restaurant when I get back to town."

MJ looks down at her shoes, suddenly finding them fascinating. "Yeah, well...Jane was there earlier," she says carefully.

"Terrific!" Miguel beams, completely missing MJ's discomfort. "Maybe I'll surprise her with some flowers." Without another word, he pulls out and heads back to town.

Mary-Jane looks after him as his taillights head off. "It's a damn soap opera in this town..." she scoffs. "Miguel's hot for Jane, who's hot for Duncan Moroni, who's hot for..." she stops and glances at me and Cynthia. "Well...someone, I'm sure..." She shakes her head. "What a soap opera."

"We got bigger fish to fry than Mystical love-life drama," Shannon says.

And she is right about that! Our daughters are alone at the Well. It's not wild animals I worry about as much as how Judith will react. That might be a disaster waiting to happen. I speak up. "One of us should go get the girls from the Well while the others go deal with Beth. What the hell! They're not even Witches..."

Shannon sighs heavily. "And at this rate, Jessica might never become one. I'm definitely grounding her for taking Chloe and Dahlia there without clearing it with me. Especially with everything that's going on now."

MJ nods in agreement. "Yeah. What the hell were they thinking?"

"I'll go get them." I say, already stepping off the porch. "Damn it. Dahlia is only fourteen. She's too young to be there on her own."

Shannon nods. "Okay. MJ and I will take the trail along the lake and deal with Beth. The sooner we shut her down, the better. Then we'll deal with the girls." She shakes her head and grumbles, "Frigging Jess, showing off!"

I watch as Shannon, MJ and Robert hustle down the trail that winds alongside the lake, heading to the last cabin. Cynthia follows them, giving me a wave before she disappears.

I follow the wooded pathway to the well. The late afternoon sun filters through the trees, casting dappled shadows across the path. Birds call overhead, preparing to roost for the night as I make my way.

"Dahlia!" I call out, pushing aside a low-hanging branch. "Jessica! Chloe!"

No answer. Great. I press on, my heart pounding with each step. I doubt very much Judith will be welcoming to them; she sure didn't give me that impression at our first meeting with her. Even though Jess is her granddaughter, I doubt she'll be kicking into 'Nana' mode.

Gosh. For some reason, the path to the well seems longer today, as if the forest is trying to slow me down. Finally, I reach the edge of the clearing and stop, hidden in the shadows of the trees.

My eyes widen watching them. The three of them, Chloe, Dahlia and Jess are standing at the Well's stone wall, their hands resting on the surface as they peer over the side. A candle flickers on the wall of the well, and Jessica lifts a bottle—is that wine?—and pours it into the dark depths.

"Grandma?" Jessica calls, peeping over the edge of the well. "We brought you wine. Are you there? Talk to us if you are."

I half expect Judith's acerbic voice to roar, but nothing happens. The well remains silent.

My eyes narrow and I smile. Good. Maybe this will teach them not to go off on their own, thinking they can become witches this easily. Shannon's going to ream Jessica out over this stunt.

Movement at the edge of the clearing catches my eye. A family of skunks—a mother and three babies—waddles across the open space, their black and white tails held high.

Dahlia sees them first, and her eyes go wide. "Look!" she whispers. She steps away from the well and moves toward the small animals.

"Dahlia, wait!" Jessica hisses, but my daughter is completely focused on the skunks.

She crouches down a few feet from the animals, and her head tilts to one side, like she's listening. She's trying to communicate with them.

Bless her heart, but this could raise a stink. Literally.

Mama skunk freezes in place, watching Dahlia closely. Uh-oh.

Stepping out from the trees, I speak softly, "Easy there, my little furry friends. No need to get your backs or your tails up."

Dahlia whirls around, and grins when she sees me. "Mom!" They're so cute! I just wanted to say hello to see if I could understand them."

Ignoring her, I'm focused instead on the mother skunk, who is zeroed in watching us. I bend down. "Thank you for not spraying my kid, Mama Skunk."

The skunk sits back on her haunches, whiskers twitching. "When are you going to get that critter clinic going? We've been waiting."

Smiling, "Soon. And you'll be welcome there, anytime you need medical help." I pause. "Is there anything wrong right now?"

The mother skunk's nose sniffs as she considers this. "There are a few critters who could use your attention now. Maybe you can follow me and—"

"What's wrong? Is it an emergency?"

"Well...nooo....one of the squirrels fell off a tree and hurt his leg."

"Is he able to walk on it?"

"Ummm...yes. But then there's an otter who lives on the lake who has a cold."

Okay, nothing very serious. "Sorry." I shake my head, noticing that Jessica and Chloe have joined us. No time right now, but I can come tomorrow."

Dahlia looks between me and the skunk. "Can I come too? I want to help."

The skunk's dark eyes gleam in the fading light as she turns to Dahlia. "We're counting on it."

Dahlia lets out a squeal, bouncing up and down on her toes. "Yes! I can understand her!" She drops to her knees, looking directly at the skunk. "I mean you. For sure, I'll be here!"

The mother skunk gives what almost looks like a nod before waddling away, her babies following in a neat line behind her.

I turn to face the three girls, folding my arms over my chest. "You should have waited for us to bring you here, girls," My tone brooks no argument. "And you, Jessica, should have known better. Being a Witch takes work, and you haven't even begun that."

Jessica tosses her hair back, scoffing, "Doesn't seem to work that way for Dahlia!"

My cheeks heat up, but I force myself to stay calm. Teenagers. Always thinking they know everything. "That's because Dahlia has been working at it with me for quite some time, Jessica." There's no need to let Jessica know that Dahlia's gift might have got a boost from Ida, like mine did. I turn and start walking back toward the path. "Your mother is going to have a word with you. She's not happy you came here without us."

Chloe hurries to catch up with me, her face anxious. "Don't tell my mom, please, Libby."

I glance back at her with a sad smile. "She already knows. She's with Shannon. Not cool, Chloe."

The girls fall into step behind me, whispering among themselves. As we walk, I realize someone's missing.

"What happened to Kevin?" I ask, looking back at the girls. "I'm pretty surprised he didn't come along with you, Jess."

Dahlia quickens her pace to walk beside me. "We told him no boys allowed. Witches are female." Her face brightens suddenly. "Hey! Now we can catch a ride with you."

"Yeah," Chloe adds, wrinkling her nose. "Miguel kind of smells, y'know? We had to keep the windows open. Maybe because he's a werewolf?"

Poor Miguel. "I guess that's a werewolf thing." I hold a branch aside for the girls to pass. "Maybe they don't know that humans—and witches—don't care for earthy smells. Besides, he's already heading back to town once we showed up. Probably didn't care for your smell, either."

Jessica laughs, but I know she's nervous about facing her mother. She should be.

"Mom's going to kill me, isn't she?" she mutters.

"Not kill," I say, nudging her shoulder. "Just maim a little."

Before Jessica can respond, Shannon, MJ, and Robert come tearing around the side of the house, breathless and wide-eyed. Shannon skids to a stop when she sees us, her eyes darting between the girls and me.

"Did you see them? Beth and Ivy weren't there when we got to the cabin. But the light bulb was still hot, so they must have just left."

They're gone?" My stomach sinks. "Shit. We just got here, and we didn't see anyone."

MJ's hands ball into fists at her sides. "I'm going to kill that Jane! She must have warned Ivy and Alf we were coming. That's twice she's pulled the wool over my eyes!"

Cynthia comes up from the lake pathway and joins us. "So back to square one, right?"

Headlights cut through the gathering dusk, coming down Shannon's driveway. When it gets closer, I see that it's Ray in their van.

Ray is barely out of the vehicle before a dark shape plummets from the sky. Instinctively, I jerk back as the bird—a hawk, I think—transforms just above the ground and Eric lands gracefully on his feet, his human form materializing in a fluid motion that bedazzles me. He's done this trick before, no doubt about it; he landed like an Olympic gymnast.

"Oh, my God!" Jessica pushes forward. "Did I just see that? This is crazy! That bird...now some guy?" She clasps her hands over her mouth.

"Guess you're new here." Eric lets out a laugh before going over to Cynthia and pulling her into a hug. "So, Ray told us about Beth. I take it she gave you the slip."

"Did you tell Stan as well, Ray?" I ask.

"He didn't answer his phone, but I left him a voicemail to get out here."

"Oh."

But he's not here. That must mean Stan is sidestepping all this, unable to deal with it. It's understandable, but still... But dammit, if it was important enough for both Ray and Eric to get here as quick as they could...Stan couldn't even answer the phone? And he sure as hell hasn't tried to call me.

Not gonna lie—it stings. I turn away from the others for a moment to collect myself. Maybe this magical aspect of our life is too much for him.

Shit.

Dahlia comes over and whispers, "What's going on, Mom? Who got away? Maybe we can help."

And Dahlia isn't the only one of the girls wondering about that. Jessica asks the same of her mother.

Shannon turns to Jessica, and her voice is sharp. "I'll explain later. And no, you can't help. You're grounded until further notice, young lady."

Jessica's shoulders slump. "Sorry, Mom. And just so you know, Grandma never even showed herself. Not a word."

"Why am I not surprised?" Shannon punctuates with an eye-roll.

Cynthia clears her throat before speaking. "Can we deal with grounding your daughters later? We need to keep looking for Beth."

"Should we keep searching the roads?" Ray shifts his weight from one foot to the other. "What if she went into the woods?"

Eric says, "I think I'm the best one to cover the forest. Maybe as an owl this time." He gives a small shrug. "Haven't done that one in a while." Turning and looking down at Robert, he asks, "Maybe you can pick up their scent? It'd be great if you covered the ground."

Robert looks less than impressed taking orders from Eric, mumbling a growl at Shannon, "If you agree, I will."

"Yeah. Sounds good." Shannon runs her fingers through her hair. "The rest of us will check out the roads and streets in town. This could be an all-nighter."

"Shit!" MJ blurts out. "I just tried Miguel, and he's not answering. I think maybe Beth and her friends hitched a ride with him."

She turns to Ray, gesturing toward town. "Can you check the restaurant to close up for the night? I'm sticking with Shannon to find Beth." Her eyes narrow. "But keep an eye out for Miguel's beige SUV when you go."

Ray nods. "Yeah, sure. This magical stuff's really not up my alley, is it?"

"Thanks, hon. Doesn't mean you're not needed, babe."

I'm still miffed at Stan. Sure, Ray's just going to close up their restaurant; he's not getting directly involved in this kerfuffle with Beth James directly...but at least Ray showed up, dammit. I look over at Shannon, MJ and Cynthia. It'll be up to us to find Beth; I just know it. As for Stan... I can't count on him in this.

Dammit. I wish this damned town weren't full of these weird creatures. This is really getting complicated. Maybe Stan's right about moving to an island somewhere away from here.

But to be honest, right now, I don't know if I'd want to go with him.

Dammit.

SEVENTEEN

SHANNON

I watch Ray's van carrying Dahlia and Chloe go down my driveway headed back to town, and I sigh. My life was supposed to get simpler when I moved to Wesley, not turn into a supernatural Jerry Springer episode. I have to laugh. 'Supernatural Smackdown! Magical Melee in the Moonlight!'

"What's so funny?" Libby asks. When I try to wave her off, she says, "I could really use a laugh."

"I was just thinking that everything going on is like an episode of Jerry Springer."

She nods and grins. "Yeah, I can see the title card now — 'Chaos In The Enchanted Forest!'."

Her face falls though, and I don't need to be a mind reader to know what's bothering her. "Yeah, Stan didn't show up," I say. "Sorry about that."

She looks into my eyes. "Neither did Devon; I'm sorry too, Shannon."

"Let's go inside," I say, nudging Jessica toward the house and putting my arm around Libby. "Coffee. I need industrial-strength coffee if I'm going to be out searching all night."

MJ and Cynthia follow us in, and I head right to the kitchen. Jessica frumps down at the kitchen table with a pout that gets on my last nerve as

I prep the coffee. While it brews, I grab cups and stuff, setting up on the table. Jess lets out a sigh. Oh, man...she's in college, and yet still acts like such a kid sometimes.

"So much for my perfect small-town life," I mutter, waiting for the brewing to finish. "Just wanted to run a small summer resort, maybe date a nice guy. Instead, I've got Fae rebellions, Vampire politics, and a daughter who thinks sneaking off to a magical Well is cool."

Jessica rolls her eyes. "Mom, it's not that big of a deal."

Before I have a chance to answer, MJ speaks, "Not a big deal? Listen up, sweetie. Magic can go haywire real fast and without warning, and that's if you have a clue what you're doing!" Her eyes are fiery as she jabs a finger at Jess. "And you don't."

I let MJ go to town; she's absolutely right, and Jess won't sass nor dismiss another woman as quickly as she would her own mother.

"Oh, come on! What could have happened?"

"ANYTHING!" Mary Jane yells. "Your own mother got pissed off and a twenty-foot canyon opened up right in this house's backyard! And that's after her studying the Grimoire and practicing for weeks!"

Jess' mouth drops open, and she looks at me. I just nod.

But MJ's not done yet. "You say a spell wrong, or with wrong intent and you can do some serious damage to someone's life!" She looks at me. "Right, Shannon?"

"Oh, yeah." I'm not sure if she's referring to my screwup trying to help MJ lose weight, or her 'revenge spell' on me that caused my mouth to run off like I was insane.

MJ sits right across from Jess. "And you started messing around with Magic, and brought my daughter and Libby's kid along! It's like you decided to start playing with guns!"

"Or worse," Libby chimes in.

It hits home. Jess' eyes go as big as coat buttons, and she looks from one of us to the others. "I...I just wanted..."

When her chin starts to quiver, I shoot MJ and Libby a nod and take her hand. "Look, you didn't know, but now you do, okay? You have to realize that there's a hell of a lot going on that can really hurt me, Mary-Jane, Cynthia, and Libby...the whole town, frankly. We've got a woman on the loose with evidence that could expose us all, the mayor is totally useless, and the Fae are staging some kind of uprising. It's a big frikkin' deal, Jess."

Cynthia weighs in next. "Today was definitely not the time to play Witch tour guide, sweetie."

"Look, Jess, I'm sorry for the way things are going right now." I bring the coffeepot over and fill the cups. "It wasn't supposed to be this way. But you have to promise me you won't go to the Well without me being there."

Jessica nods glumly. "It's not like Grandma even answered me. But sure, I promise."

"Well, that's my mother in a nutshell."

"More like in a well," MJ quips, breaking the tension.

I nod in agreement. God, I love these women. "Listen Jess, you need to read the Grimoires, and then you and I will start with some small spells, okay?"

She grins, leaning forward on her elbows. "I'm a fast reader. Had to master that in college."

"Good luck with that shit, kid," Cynthia says. "They're hand written, and are really, really old." Jess' face falls, and Cynthia adds, "But when you do, I'll show you how to..." She steps up to Jess, puts her hand in front of her eyes and snaps her fingers. A bright flame dances just above her fingertips.

"Ohmygod! That's sooo cool!" Jess squeals, her own hands covering her mouth.

"So, you'll listen up to us old gals then?" Cynthia asks. Jess nods yes furiously in reply. "Good girl."

While Cynthia and Jess are bonding like the cool aunt and niece, I look over at Libby. She still looks like she's lost her best friend as she sips her cup. Yeah, Stan not showing up really bothers her. Our eyes meet in disappointment, and we both nod.

MJ sidles up closer to Jess and puts her hand on her shoulder. "Look honey, we have to go soon, but you can't come with us. Much as you'd like to help and be one of us, you aren't. Not yet. Like your mom said, this is not a good time. We need to know you're safe here at home."

Cynthia downs the glass of OJ she got from the fridge. "I feel like this is my fault...this crap with Beth. If I wasn't with Erik then—"

"Don't say that." Libby steps over and tilts Cynthia's chin up. "Beth isn't a nice person. If it wasn't you, it would just be someone or something else. But it's time we stop her before she brings the world down on our heads." She smiles, "Erik's a good guy. I'm glad he's with you."

Which only underscores Devon's absence. I grab my phone and hit the icon to call him. Again, it goes to voicemail, just like when I'd tried to call him earlier on the ride out. Could he still be with Mary? What the hell are those two really up to?

Jessica looks over at me. "Ray and Eric were here, but where's Devon? Shouldn't he be here helping?" Whatever vibes she picks up on coming from me, she adds, with narrow eyes. "Where is he, Mom?"

I take a deep breath. "He's meeting with a woman to see about becoming a Druid." From the corner of my eye, I notice MJ and Cynthia share a look, but I try to ignore it. Their pity is the last thing I need, or I'll lose my shit and start crying. Dammit.

Jessica watches me closely as I take a sip of coffee. "Is he pulling the same dickwad move that Dad did? Please tell me he's not because you really don't need that, Mom. You deserve better."

Which of course, triggers thoughts of David... My Ex's betrayal flashes through my mind—the texts I found, the late nights at "work," the way he looked at me like I was an inconvenience. That familiar knot of worry and anger twists my stomach.

"Let's not jump to conclusions, ladies." Cynthia cautions, "Devon loves Shannon, which is obvious to anyone with eyes. So what if he's exploring becoming a Druid? Stan isn't here either, but..." She looks over at Libby. "Oops. I'm sure there's a good reason he's not here, so..."

I stand up and drain the last of my coffee, pretending to be stronger than I feel. "We've got to get started. Enough worrying about freaking men! We have each other, and that's what Alice always preached, right?"

MJ and Cynthia stand and step over to me. "Totally." After a beat or two, Libby smiles and gets up.

"This is what we do, right? We stick together, whether it's facing down a Warlock or cleaning up after a spell goes off the rails." Her eyebrows bob high when she looks over at Jessica. "That happens a lot, Jess. This witching business goes wonky sometimes. At least, when you're starting out."

"I can't wait!" Jessica sits back and smiles. "I'm proud of you, Mom. But really, you need to get your asses out there and find this Beth. Thomas won't be nearly as understanding as your favorite child is."

I go over and hug her. The smell of her coconut shampoo, so familiar from my days living with her, is balm to my soul. "You're both my favorites. But you're right that we need to get going. Lock the door, and if your great Aunt Maeve shows up—always a possibility—try not to freak out."

When I pull back, Jess's eyes are huge. "This place is haunted, too?" Shaking her head, she grins. "Shit, does it get any better?"

As we leave, I wonder if she'll ever go back to Boston to finish her school year. She'd better. But I can't think of that right now. When we step onto the porch, "MJ, you come with me. Libby, can you cover the north side of town with Cynthia?"

Libby nods. "We'll be right behind you. But first, I'm going to see if there are critters around to get the word out about Beth, or Ivy and Alf. It's all hands-on deck in this, even if the Vampires and Werewolves are sitting this one out."

MJ lets out a loud huff. "And the freaking Fae! When I get my hands on Jane, I'm going to give her wings a good clipping!" She turns to me. "We need to check on Suzanne and Amy and see what they know. Maybe Beth is hiding out there. If the Fae are all in cahoots in this, it's a good place to start."

"That was my thought, too. Work smarter, not harder." I get in the car and start it up, trying to ignore the ache in my heart. Devon should be here with me, but he's not. He chose to be with Mary just when I needed him here.

That hurts waaay more than I'd like.

Eighteen

Mary-Jane

Gripping the steering wheel, I glance over at Shannon to see her staring out the passenger window, silent as a tomb. This night's been a real shit show—Beth on the loose, our daughters going rogue visiting the Well, and now Devon's spending time with Mary, getting tatted up, or whatever those Druids do. I hope he's just getting some ink. Shannon's face is all hard angles in the dashboard light, her jaw clenched tight enough to crack walnuts.

"You okay?" I ask, which is probably the dumbest question ever. Anyone with eyes could see she wasn't, no special powers needed.

She doesn't answer, just keeps staring out the window, trying to hold herself together. Or maybe she's plotting Devon's slow, painful death. Hard to tell.

I reach over and squeeze her hand. It's cold as ice. "You don't have to put on a brave front for me, Shannon. I know it hurts that Devon isn't here. But honestly? I really don't think you have anything to worry about. He's nuts about you."

Her fingers twitch under mine before she pulls away.

"Hey! I've been down this road before," she says finally, "and I survived. If he's stupid enough to take up with Mary, it's his loss, right?"

The harsh laugh that follows tightens something in my chest. I've known her long enough to know when she's putting up a brave front.

"Look, men can be complete assholes." I tap my fingers on the wheel. "But Devon doesn't strike me as a cheater. Even if he got a tattoo, it probably means nothing."

"Just that he wants to be a Druid," Shannon snaps. "and sneaking away to do it. With Mary, who's made it pretty explicit how she feels about him."

"Maybe he wanted to surprise you? Like when Ray bought me that stupid vacuum for our anniversary. He thought he was being romantic because it was self-emptying."

That gets a tiny snort from Shannon, which I count as progress.

From that brief touch on her hand, the depth of her hurt is like a raw wound—familiar territory for her after what she went through with her ex. If Devon's really screwing around with Mary, I swear I'll turn him into the ugliest toad Wesley's ever seen. He'll be catching flies with his tongue while Shannon moves on to someone who deserves her.

She gives me a wan smile. "So help me, MJ, if he's wearing a tattoo when I see him..."

I barely catch her words as something catches my eye up ahead. Someone is walking along the roadside, shining a flashlight into the woods. My heart leaps—could we actually get lucky? That it's Beth or even Ivy?

Slowing the car, I lean forward, squinting through the windshield as we get closer. In the headlights, a slender guy in a plaid sports jacket and dockers, tries to shield his eyes.

When I get closer, "Duncan?" It sure looks like the Druid garbage man. "What's he doing out here?"

I pull over and kill the engine. Shannon and I exchange a quick glance before climbing out of the car. The night air hits my face, cool and damp with the promise of rain later.

"Duncan?" I call out as we walk closer.

His flashlight beam momentarily blinds us before he points it down.

What's he doing out here, like he's searching? The love spell should have him pining after Jane, not wandering along the woods alone. Maybe the spell didn't work, or it wore off.

"What are you doing out here at this time of night?" I ask.

"Looking for those two jerks—Ivy and Alf." He snaps back. "I heard about the Fae uprising. Someone's got to do something since our so-called leaders are less than useless."

I move closer, searching his face for any sign of Jane's love spell. Nothing. No dreamy expression, no lovelorn gaze—just the usual Duncan intensity with a generous side of annoyance.

"Did you see Jane tonight?" I ask, trying to sound casual while my mind races. The spell should have worked. I did everything right—the hair, the rose petals, the candle, the whole enchilada.

Duncan rolls his eyes so hard I'm surprised they don't fall out of his head. "I don't know what came over me asking her out. But it doesn't matter—she was a no-show, which is for the best." He waves his flashlight toward the woods. "Then I heard about the Fae and Beth. This is ridiculous! And that suck-ass mayor and the Weres are doing nothing!"

"So, the Druids are on our side?" Shannon asks, "Including Mary?"

Duncan shakes his head, running a hand through his thinning hair. "I tried calling her, but she didn't answer her phone. Must have a hot date."

Oh, shit, buddy! I swallow hard and sneak another peek at Shannon. Her face is a storm cloud in the dim light, eyes narrowed to slits. The temperature around us seems to drop several degrees, and a stiff gust blows.

"Jane's in on it too," I say. Better to change the subject before Shannon unleashes a lightning bolt of fury. "She told us where Beth and Ivy were hiding, but then she warned them before we could get there."

The Druid's expression darkens. "I thought I might hear something in the woods, so I parked my truck about a mile back. But even the forest has gone still. Not a whisper from the trees." He kicks at the dirt. "When we catch those Fae, I think they need to be banished. This is just nonsense what they're trying to do." He shakes his head. "I mean, okay, the Fae have been treated disdainfully, I'll admit it. But to get behind exposing Wesley to the world? That's pure garbage!"

I nod. He'd know garbage... Even though Jane betrayed us—after me helping her with that stupid love spell—I kind of understand why the Fae feel so angry. The other Mysticals have been pretty shitty to them from what I've gathered.

Duncan goes back to scanning the woods with his flashlight, and I ask. "What's the plan if you do find them? You going to take on Beth, Ivy, and Alf single-handedly?"

Duncan's shoulders straighten like I've questioned his manhood. "I'm a Druid. We have ways."

"Right." I roll my eyes. Men and their egos, Mystical or not.

"What about the rest of your coven?" Duncan asks, lowering his flashlight. "Where are they?"

His eyes light up, and it's not hard to guess who he's really asking about. His crush on Cynthia is about as subtle as a brick through a window.

"Libby and Cynthia are looking in the west part of town."

"Cynthia's out there?" His voice pitches higher. "With that Shifter boyfriend of hers?"

Shannon throws me a look that says 'really?' but keeps quiet.

After clearing his throat, Duncan asks, "Could I get a lift back to my truck? Save some time? I think we need to coordinate our search."

"Sure," I say, though Shannon's glare could melt steel. "Hop in."

The moment Duncan slides into the backseat, I'm hit by a wall of cologne so strong my eyes water. I roll down all the windows despite the cool night air. Holy hell, did he bathe in the stuff? I catch a glimpse of him in the rear-view mirror—he's clean shaven, and that jacket looks new.

Shannon keeps her eyes fixed on the road ahead, but Duncan keeps leaning forward between us, asking questions about Cynthia. I deflect with vague answers, peering ahead for any sign of his truck. Finally, I see it.

"Thanks for the lift," he says, climbing out. "I'll head toward the west side of town. Maybe I'll run into Cynthia—I mean, the others."

I nod and pull away before he can say anything else.

"That was weird," Shannon mutters once we're back on the main road.

She stares out the window for a few minutes, and I'm about to ask if she wants to check downtown before we head to Suzanne's place, when she suddenly blurts, "When the mayor first heard Beth had escaped, he said to call some Bond guy. He's some expert at tracking cell phone signals or something."

"Bond?" My eyes narrow, trying to place who she means. I tap the steering wheel, mentally flipping through Wesley's residents. "The only Bond I know is that weird ex-military guy—Peter Bond. Lives out at that old hunting camp near the reservoir. Total recluse. Ray mentioned him once—said the guy orders takeout from us but never comes in. And when we deliver, he always has Miguel leave it on the porch."

Shannon perks up. "That could be him. Call Ray—maybe he knows how to reach this guy."

I pull over and grab my phone, putting it on speaker as Ray picks up.

"Hey, hon," Ray's voice crackles through. "Any luck finding Beth?"

"No, but we might have a lead. Shannon says the mayor mentioned someone named Bond who can track cell signals. Is it Peter Bond, the guy who orders takeout sometimes?"

"Yeah, that's him. Ex-military intelligence or something. Why?"

"We need him to track Beth's phone. Any idea how to reach him?"

"Funny timing—Ida Watkins just walked in looking for you. She overheard Eric talking about the Beth situation."

There's a rustling sound, then Ida's voice comes through. "MJ? I'm here with Ray."

"Hey, Ida," I say. "We're trying to find Peter Bond. He might be able to track Beth's phone."

"I know Peter," Ida says, her voice brightening. "He's... an old friend. Total tech genius but doesn't like people much. I can fly out there right now and talk to him."

"You will? That'd save time." Shannon says, leaning toward the phone.

"Of course. We can't let Beth expose Wesley. The Fae are upset, and they have reason to be, but this isn't the way to handle it." Ida's voice lowers. "I'll get Peter on this. If Beth's phone is on, he'll find her. Just sit tight."

"Thanks, Ida." At least we have the shifters on our side, which is a relief.

"Don't worry," Ida replies. "We'll find Beth and those rebellious Fae before they can get stuff out to the outside world. I'll call as soon as I know something."

I tap the button on the steering wheel, ending the call, wishing I had half of Ida's confidence.

"Well, that's something at least," Shannon mutters beside me. "If this Peter guy can track Beth's phone, we might actually get ahead of them for once."

"Yeah," but my voice lacks conviction. "If her phone's even on."

As we head toward Amy and Suzanne's place, the whole time, my mind keeps churning through everything that's happened.

"Can we trust Ida?" Shannon says suddenly, breaking the silence.

"What? Why wouldn't we?"

Shannon shrugs. "Just a feeling. After being stone-walled by the Mayor and the police chief, I'm not sure who to trust. She seemed pretty eager to help us."

"I think she just wants this mess resolved like the rest of us."

"Maybe."

We fall silent again as I turn onto the street where Amy and Suzanne live. Their home sits back from the road, nestled among flowering shrubs and ancient oaks. Usually, the place is lit up like Christmas—the Fae aren't big on conserving electricity—but tonight it's completely dark.

I pull into the driveway and kill the engine. "That's weird. They always leave the lights on."

"They're gone," Shannon says flatly. "Probably helping Ivy and Alf."

I squint at the darkened house. "Or they could be hiding inside, the whole bunch of them."

We sit in the car, staring at the house. No movement, no lights, nothing.

"Should we knock?" I ask.

Shannon opens her door. "Might as well. Though I doubt anyone's home."

We approach the front door cautiously. The garden, usually so vibrant with magical blooms that glow in the moonlight, seems subdued tonight. Even the plants know something's wrong.

I knock firmly on the door. No answer.

Shannon tries the knob. Locked.

"Shit!" I mutter, peering through a window but see nothing moving. "Again, the Fae seem to be one step ahead of us."

Nineteen

Libby

I stumble out of the forest, brushing pine needles from my hair while Willy the fox walks beside me. His copper coat gleams in the moonlight, and he's showing off his newly healed paw with every prancing step.

"Remember our deal," he yips softly. "My whole family gets priority appointments when your clinic opens."

"Yeah, yeah. You drive a hard bargain for someone who couldn't even walk two weeks ago." I shake my head as he disappears into the underbrush with a flick of his bushy tail.

Cynthia's leaning against my Explorer, arms crossed and looking more alert than I've seen her in weeks. My healing touch did the trick. At least something's going right tonight.

"Any luck?" she asks, pushing herself off the hood.

"Actually, yes." I pull twigs from my sweater. "Just ran into a fox I treated a week ago. He had an infected paw. Turns out the woodland gossip network is better than Facebook or Twitter."

"They know about Beth?"

"And then some." I unlock the car doors with a click. "According to the fox, Beth and the Fae rebels have been moving between three different locations. They're at an abandoned hunting cabin a few miles from here."

Cynthia's eyes widen. "That's huge, Libby!"

"Yeah, well... It's gonna cost me." I slide into the driver's seat with a groan. "I just promised priority vet care to sixteen fox kits and their extended family. That little bastard negotiated like a Wall Street broker."

"It'll be worth it." Cynthia buckles her seatbelt. "Should we call Shannon?"

"Already texted her the news." I start the engine. "But I'd like to get there first. Those crafty foxes may not be reliable snitches."

"Why are you saying that?"

I roll my eyes at her. "Ever hear the saying 'crafty like a fox'? I mean, it is a lead, yeah; but I wouldn't bet the ranch on it."

Just as I start the car, my phone rings. Dahlia's face flashes on the screen, and my finger flies to answer. "Dahlia? What's wrong?"

"Mom! Jack's gone!" Panic and tears come through loud and clear.

"What do you mean, gone?" My heart ratchets up into my throat. With everything that's going on, he should be home, safe with Kevin and Dahlia. My frigging rebellious middle kid. Shit.

"We were just about to make popcorn when he heard something outside. He went to check and—" her voice breaks. "There was a shout, and when I looked out, he disappeared into the forest!"

My heart almost stops. "Are you alone? Where's Kevin?" Oh god. Can this day get any worse?

"I don't know where Kev is! I thought he went back to Shannon's to see Jessica, but I don't know. Mom, I'm scared. Please come home. Now!"

"Lock all the doors and stay inside. I'm on my way." I end the call and floor the gas pedal, my hands shaking. This town is crazy. What the hell is going on here? Now my kids are in danger.

"What's going on?" Cynthia grips the dashboard as I wheel the car up Shannon's driveway.

"Jack's missing. Dahlia saw him disappear into the forest." I stomp on the gas. "Those damn Fae must have taken him. I'll murder them if they hurt my kid."

Cynthia immediately pulls out her phone. "I'll call Shannon."

I catch fragments of their conversation as I navigate the winding mountain roads, my mind racing. Beside me, Cynthia's voice is as urgent as the spike of adrenaline surging through me. Closing in on a sluggish car, I mutter. "C'mon, C'mon." I wheel around it and keep accelerating.

"Shannon, is Kevin with Jessica?... Can you find out?... We think Jack's been taken... Yeah, we're headed there now... Libby's worried that it might be the Fae..."

She hangs up and turns to me. "Shannon thinks they might be targeting our kids for leverage. She's calling Jessica to see if Kevin's there. She's heading to your place."

"Try Eric," I say through gritted teeth.

Cynthia dials, waits, then sighs. "Voicemail." She leaves a message: "Eric, it's Cynthia. We think Libby's son, Jack's been kidnapped by the Fae. If you get this, go to Libby's house right away. We're heading there too."

I push the Explorer faster than I've ever driven it, taking corners too sharply. All I can think about is Jack—my wild, beautiful son—out there somewhere. Taken. My ability to talk to animals or move objects won't help me find him if the Fae have him hidden.

"Don't worry, Libby, we'll find him," Cynthia tries to be encouraging.

And she's wasting her breath. Jack!

Every nerve in my body is electric with fear. Jack's face flashes through my mind—not the sullen teenager who's been giving me grief lately, but my little boy with skinned knees and a gap-toothed smile.

"I remember when he was six." I say to Cynthia, my voice tight. "He climbed that massive oak in our backyard and refused to come down. Sat up there for three hours reading comics until Hank had to bribe him with ice cream."

My throat closes up at the memory. Jack perched on that branch, fearless and wild, dark hair whipping in the wind. Even then, he'd been testing boundaries, pushing limits.

"He's going to be okay, Libby," Cynthia says, but her words sound hollow against the roar in my ears.

I swipe a tear from my eye and grip the steering wheel tighter. "If those Fae hurt him, I swear to God, I'll make them regret it. They think they've been treated badly? They haven't seen what a mother can do when her child is threatened."

Witches can be tough.

The familiar curves of my neighborhood appear, and I take the final turn with tires squealing. As I pull into my driveway, headlights illuminate Stan's truck parked haphazardly near the front steps.

"Stan?" I whisper, confused.

Before I can even shut off the engine, he comes out from the side of the house, running to us. I fumble with my seatbelt and practically fall out of the car into his arms.

"I got here as fast as I could," he says, holding me tight against his chest. "Dahlia called me in tears. I've been checking the perimeter of your property."

I pull back to look at his face, finding comfort in his steady blue eyes. "Did you see anything? Any sign of Jack?"

Stan shakes his head. "Nothing yet, but I've got the guys from the station on alert. We'll find him, Libby."

His arms around me feel like the only solid thing in a world that's suddenly gone liquid with fear. For a moment, I let myself lean into his strength.

"Thank you for coming," I whisper against his shirt. "I don't think I could handle this alone." Tears form in my eyes as I pull away and race to the backyard.

"Jack!" My heart hammers fast as I scream. "Jack, where are you?"

The beam of my cell phone's flashlight bounces wildly as I crash through the underbrush, branches clawing at my face and arms. I don't care. All I can think about is my son somewhere out in these woods, maybe hurt, maybe—no, I can't even consider worse possibilities.

"Jack!" I scream again, my voice cracking.

Something scurries toward me, and I swing my flashlight down to see a raccoon standing on his hind legs.

"Get out of here!" he chatters urgently. "There's something wild out there—growling and howling like a bear gone mad!"

"My son is out there!" I push past him, ignoring his warnings.

"It's not safe! Whatever it is, it's tearing up the forest!"

I don't slow down. Jack facing a deranged bear or those crazy Fae rebels is exactly why I need to move faster, not retreat.

Then I hear it—deep, guttural growls punctuated by the snap and crash of breaking tree limbs. The sound freezes my blood, but I force myself forward, screeching Jack's name, desperation making me ignore my fear.

A cry answers me—faint but unmistakable. "Mom! Help!"

Jack's voice. My body responds before my mind can process, feet pounding fast as I race toward the sound. I'm hardly aware that it's started to rain.

Behind me, Stan's voice, then Cynthia's and Shannon's, all of them calling out to me, but I don't stop. My son needs me.

Another growl erupts, so close it seems to vibrate through my bones. I dart sideways instinctively, stumbling through a dense patch of ferns, and then stop short, my flashlight beam illuminating...Oh, my good goddess.

A Werewolf—massive, wild, with a thick coat of dark fur—stands there, snarling. Each of massive paws clutches a struggling Fae. Ivy dangles from one hand, her wings crumpled, while Alf twists helplessly in the other.

The beast's clothes hang in tatters, but I catch sight of something familiar—the Wesley High insignia on a scrap of shirt pocket flapping against his chest.

"Mom! He got them! Kevin got them!" Jack darts out from behind a tree, his face flushed with a big grin. "One got away, but Kevin got these two here. They had me, but he got them. Kevin got them!"

Kevin? My brain struggles to process what my eyes are seeing. I stare harder at the werewolf, and suddenly I see it—Kevin's eyes, Kevin's jawline beneath all that hair. My responsible, level-headed firstborn has transformed into something wild and primal. "Jack, get back," I manage, my voice barely a whisper.

But Jack bounces on his toes, circling his brother like he's a superhero. "Isn't this the coolest thing? Kevin is totally base! I can't wait till it happens to me!"

"What?" I gasp, and I sway a little from the shock of it. My son. My oldest son, a Werewolf?

Kevin growls, shaking the Fae like rag dolls. Ivy whimpers, her wings drooping pathetically, while Alf tries to pry Kevin's hairy paws away.

"I heard something outside. Then someone called out to me. When I got to the forest, it happened...so fast." Jack explains, his face full of wonder. "Then those two grabbed me. They dragged me into the woods for a bit and then started to flap their wings and fly away, but then Kev showed up!" He's gasping in excitement. "You shoulda' seen it! He just... changed! Right in front of me! It was freaking awesome! They dropped me right away and started running to take off, but Kevin chased them down. One of them got away—Beth James, I think—but Kevin caught these two!"

I step closer, my heart thudding fast against my ribs. "Kevin?" I whisper, looking up and searching for my son in the creature's eyes. This can't be happening. Not to Kevin.

The Werewolf's fierce gaze meets mine, and for a moment, I see it, the familiar deep set of his eyes that... Oh god. The confusion in his expression is a knife in my heart. This is as much of a shock to him as it is to me. And for this to happen to him, when he'd vowed to escape this madness. My poor son, now trapped by his genes and this town's mystical powers...

Flashlight beams illuminate the scene as Shannon and Cynthia rush up behind me. Kevin towers before us in werewolf form, his hairy paws still clutching the squirming Fae, Ivy now crying while Alf lets out a stream of curses. He's got to be seven, eight feet tall!

"Holy hairy shit." Shannon murmurs as she grips my forearm. "That's Kevin? Kevin?" Her voice breaks on the last word.

I can only nod, my throat too tight for words to escape. This is my boy—the responsible one, the one who makes his bed every morning and helps with dinner without being asked. Now he's a tower of muscle and fur, with fangs that could tear through bone.

"Kevin," I finally find my voice, stepping forward with my palm outstretched. "It's Mom. Can you understand me? I'm here to help you, sweetie."

The werewolf's ears twitch at the sound of my voice. His golden eyes—Kevin's eyes, somehow—lock onto mine. A rumble starts deep in his chest, but it's not threatening. It's a moan of anguish, maybe even shock.

"Put them down, honey," I say, my voice steadier than I feel. "Just set them on the ground, honey. Mommy's here...it's gonna be okay, baby."

"Mom, no!" Jack protests. "They were trying to kidnap me! They're working with that Beth woman!"

I shoot Jack my 'pissed off serious Mom' look. "We are going to handle this, don't you worry, but not like this. My first concern is your brother."

Kevin's massive form shifts, muscles rippling beneath dark fur. With a growl that vibrates through the clearing, he drops both Fae unceremoniously to the ground. Ivy crumples into a heap, her wings bent at unnatural angles. Alf lands on his feet but immediately stumbles backward, his face pale with terror.

"Don't you dare move," Shannon orders the Fae, summoning a ball of crackling energy onto her palm. "Or I'll make what the werewolf did look like a picnic."

I approach Kevin slowly, fighting every maternal instinct screaming at me to run to him, to hold him. His breathing is labored, his massive chest heaving.

"It's okay, Kevin. It's weird as hell, but it's going to be okay," I whisper, reaching out to touch his arm. The fur is coarse beneath my fingers, but warm—alive. "We'll figure this out."

Kevin makes a sound—half growl, half whimper—and I feel my heart crack open. Whatever's happening to him, he's still my son, still the little boy who used to climb into my lap during thunderstorms.

Good grief. How can this be happening to him?

TWENTY

SHANNON

Both Cynthia and I freeze in place watching Libby and her eldest son, stunned by what's happening right in front of us. 'Kevin's a Werewolf?' blasts in my mind; it's one thing to find out about so many people in town are Mysticals, but now? Seeing it happen to one of our own is a thunderbolt.

A powerful downdraft churns the air between Cynthia and me, whipping our hair as a great owl lands beside us. It shakes and trembles for a moment, and then Eric materializes.

He's as astonished as we are. His jaw gapes open as he stares at Kevin, the hairy behemoth, a mass of muscle holding the two struggling Fae like they're nothing more than rag dolls. Hard to believe it's Kevin, the sweet, low-key teen who helped me move in and cut my grass when I first arrived in this crazy town. "Holy shit," Eric gasps. "This only happens during a full moon!" His eyes widen as he leans forward. "That's Kevin, Libby's kid, right? He caught Ivy and Alf?"

Cynthia's whispers "Yes." Reaching to keep Eric back, at a safe distance. "They tried to abduct Jack and Kevin and caught those two hooligans."

Alf scrambles to his feet, looking around wildly.

Just as he bends his knees to jump up to take off, I yell, "Don't even think about it, Alf!" I raise the fireball floating above my hand. "I'll crisp your wings before you can get airborne!" When he stares at me, I make the fireball the size of a basketball. "Now sit down!"

He plops onto the ground beside Ivy, and I dial my fireball back down. Jeezuz! Like my brain's not fried enough? My thoughts are totally scrambled—Kevin's a Werewolf, Libby's about to have a stroke because of Jack, Cynthia's having a baby with a guy who can become an owl at will, and here I am playing 'inflate the fireball' with a couple of Fae thugs.

I need a drink.

Glancing quickly over, I see Kevin's clothes in tatters around his now massive, Incredible Hulk-sized frame. The acne he had on his face has been replaced with a coat of short fur; his perfect teeth are now a wolf's snarling fangs, glittering as he stands enraged at the two Fae on the ground.

Hard to believe, I can still see Kevin underneath this towering, threatening beast. His paws are flexing as he growls at them.

Libby looks like she's been hit by a truck. Can't blame her—finding out her son's a Werewolf was never on her bingo card.

"Mom!" Jack is beside himself, vibrating in excitement, completely unfazed by his Werewolf brother. "Kevin totally caught them! I came out back because I heard them prowling in the backyard, and they grabbed me! I yelled out, and Kevin came blasting out the back door! You shoulda' seen it! He's running at them as they're trying to fly away and changing at the same time! Omygod Mom! He musta' jumped fifteen feet in the air and grabbed them out of mid-air!"

The rain that began as a drizzle is turning into a downpour, soaking us all, but nobody moves. Kevin growls again—an actual, honest-to-God growl, and the two Fae stare at him in wide-eyed terror. Between my fireball and Kevin's beastly presence, they're well and truly terrified.

Good.

Stan steps forward gently. In a soothing voice he says, "Son? You okay in there?"

Kevin nods, his voice guttural and raspy. "I think so... But this fur..."

I glance at Libby, who's ghostly white. "Did you know?" I ask.

She shakes her head slowly. "Not a clue. Not even a hint."

The rain streams down my face as I try to make sense of this latest supernatural curveball. Just when I thought I'd seen everything, the universe throws Werewolf Kevin at us.

MJ comes up beside me, shaking her head in disbelief. "I would have bet that this would happen to Jack, not Kevin. But..."

Eric steps away from our group, pulling out his phone. I watch him dial and turn his back to us, speaking in hushed tones. Even with the rain and wind, I catch fragments—"Wayne... Kevin Walker... tonight. We... now."

I stand frozen in the rain, watching this unbelievable scene unfold. Libby's hands tremble as she reaches up to touch Kevin's face. Despite how fierce he looks, he stays perfectly still, allowing his mother to stroke the thick fur covering his cheeks. A quiet mewl comes out of him at his mother's touch. The tenderness of the moment catches in my throat.

I should do something, say something. But what? I don't even know if Kevin transforming is a good thing or a bad thing! No question, it's off the charts for bizarre. I keep quiet, holding my fireball and pay attention to the Fae.

Ivy's not going anywhere with a crumpled wing, but I don't trust Alf one bit. MJ shifts, nudging me. "Good job with the fireball, but should we grab them? Tie 'em up or something?" Before I can answer, Eric returns to our huddle, his phone call completed.

"Wayne Silver's on his way." Water drips from his hair, and he brushes it away before adding. "He's the go-to guy when it comes to new Werewolves. He'll know what to do." Eric steps toward Kevin, hands raised in a calming gesture. "Kevin, you did great, but we're going to take those two now, okay? You've done your part."

His only response is a rumbling snarl as Eric grabs the two Fae and begins to move them back from Kevin.

Dahlia comes out from behind us and inches forward toward her brothers and mother, her steps hesitant. It's hard to tell if she's more fearful or fascinated by the change in her older brother.

I place my free hand on her shoulder. "It'll be okay. Help is on the way, Dahlia."

She looks up at me with wide eyes, rain coating her lashes. "Is Kevin still... Kevin in there?"

I nod. "Yes, honey. He's still your brother."

As Eric goes off with the Fae, Stan steps up to Kevin. "Okay buddy, you need to let your mother help you. Eric's got those Fae. You're doing great, Kev." For a tense moment, it looks like Kevin might refuse, but slowly, reluctantly, he steps closer to Libby, his paws circling her and landing on her back.

I have no idea where he got it, but Stan's holding a coil of rope. He goes over to Eric, and working together, they tie Alf and Ivy's hands behind them.

"Careful with the wings!" Alf snaps as Stan pulls him aside. "That monster broke Ivy's wing!"

Anger bubbles up as I stride over to them. "You're lucky they're still attached!" I get right in Ivy's face. "Where's Beth?"

MJ appears at my side, her expression just as fierce. "And what were you planning to do with Jack?"

Ivy tosses her wet hair, sending droplets flying. Despite being captured, and despite her tear-streaked face, she smirks. "Beth's gone! She's probably in Albany by now. If she doesn't hear from us in an hour, she'll start posting her photos and doing interviews with reporters."

My stomach drops. Albany. That's more than an hour away. Even if we left now...

"The damn things people will do for money," MJ gripes. "She must have some deal with one of those gossip channels."

"Money?" Ivy shrieks. "You think Beth wants money? Oh lord, Mary-Jane, you really are as stupid as she says you are!" She looks over at me. "How about you, Shannon? What's your idea? Or is there one rattling around in that silly head of yours?"

MJ and I stare at one another; we're both stunned.

MJ finds her voice first. "You bitch." She shakes Ivy until the Fae cries out. "You just tried to abduct a child! Who the hell do you think you are!"

"Well, look at that! Finally got your attention, huh?" Ivy spits on the ground. "Took you long enough!"

"You tried to kidnap a kid?" My voice comes out low and dangerous. "To force our hand?"

Alf bursts out with a laugh. "One kid? You're as stupid as Mary-Jane, Shannon. Do you think Jack was the only kid we targeted tonight? Pretty sure Suzanne and Amy are at your house by now!"

The world tilts beneath my feet. Jessica. Oh shit. Alone in my house.

"You son of a bitch," I snarl. I'm just about to blast him with the fireball, but MJ catches my arm, snuffing it out.

"Shannon! No! You've got to call Jess and see if she's okay!"

Her words jolt me back to reality. My fingers fumble with my phone as I punch my daughter's number. My heart is going a mile a minute, and my fingers shake, gripping the phone to my ear.

"Pick up, pick up, pick up," I whisper, the words a desperate prayer.

The line clicks. "Mom?"

"Jess! Are you okay?" I can barely breathe.

"I was just about to call you, Mom!" Her voice is shaky, fighting tears. "There are lights outside, and someone is trying to get in! And your aunt... the dead one? She's here, telling me I'll be okay. What the hell, Mom?" She sounds terrified.

"Stay put. Keep the doors locked and—"

"Wait!" Jessica blares. "There's a car coming down the drive."

Holding my breath, I hold the phone in a death-grip.

"Oh God, it's Devon!" She shouts. Adding after a pregnant beat, "And some skinny guy in a sports jacket. Devon is walking to the house, but the other guy is doing some weird dance out there. What do I do, Mom?"

My mind races. Relief that Devon is there, but why? What's he doing at my place? And who's the dancing weirdo?

Eric steps closer, his clothes soaked through. He must have overheard Jessica because he nods reassuringly. "That's likely Duncan doing his druid thing. I saw Devon with Duncan earlier."

My forehead knots in confusion. But Devon was with Mary. He was also with Duncan? Jeeze. Now what the hell is going on?

"It's okay," I tell Jessica, trying to keep my voice steady despite the emotional whiplash. "Let Devon in."

I'm about to say more when MJ ends her call beside me, tucking her phone back into her pocket.

"Chloe is fine." She lets out a sigh, along with a faint smile. "She's with Ray at home." "That damn Beth!" I snap, turning back to Ivy, who still wears that insufferable smirk. "You'd better tell us where she is!"

"Or else, what?" Ivy replies. "You're not in the catbird seat now, Witch. How does that feel?"

"What the hell is that supposed to mean?"

Ivy and Alf exchange a look of disgust. Shaking her head, she turns back to us. "You don't seem to be too happy with other people doing whatever the hell they want, do you?"

"If Beth puts those photos out there, it's going to rip Wesley apart!"

Alf clears his throat. "So? So what? We don't give a damn."

Ivy nods in agreement. "Not with how things stand now, anyway."

Mary-Jane shakes her head. "What the hell is up with you?"

"What's wrong with us, huh? Can't handle people sticking up for themselves, Witch?"

I look at MJ's confusion, which matches my own. I hold my hand up. "Wait a damn minute. I just moved to Wesley recently. I didn't even know you existed until yesterday!"

"Me too!" MJ says. "What the hell do you mean by sticking up for yourselves?"

Alf leans over to Ivy. "They do have a point. They might be Witches In Full and all that jazz, but they don't know squat about Wesley, Ivy."

Ivy smirks. "Yeah, right. As. If these two are Witches In Full..." She turns back to me. "Okay, dim-wit, I'll speak really slow and make sure I use small words so you can understand, OK?"

I bristle. "You're the one tied up, Ivy. Watch your mouth."

She shrugs. I actually have to respect this wretch's chutzpah. I could toast her with a fireball in a New York minute, and she's still sassy.

"Alf has a point—you Witches are new to this." Her eyes narrow. "But your oh so sweet Auntie Maeve sure knew. And she didn't do a damn thing either."

"Knew what? Enough of the half-baked digs, okay? What the hell is your freaking problem?"

Ivy stands up straight. "The Fae folk have been part of this land from the beginning of time. They might say differently, but the Druids are our descendants, not the other way around. We were here before a single Vampire existed, before any human learned how to Shapeshift, and well before any Werewolf got moon-poisoned."

MJ scoffs. "Okay, you're the OG Mysticals. Got it."

Ivy shakes her head. "So, so nouveau Mystical, Mary-Jane. Just your style." She turns back to me. "We've been here for hundreds—no, thousands of years." She looks around. "We were here even before the Mohawks showed up." A small smile appears. "Why do you think they wear feathers today?"

"Okay, you made your point," I say. "What's your problem?"

Ivy sighs. "The ley lines around Wesley drew the others. And we welcomed them all. Even the Vampires." When MJ lets out a sigh of disgust, she says, "They've come a long, long way, Mary-Jane; you'd be surprised." She turns back to me. "And ages ago, they decided that they'd form a council of Mysticals."

"So?"

Ivy leans into me face-first. "So, the Druids, our very descendants, the Werewolves, the Shapeshifters and even the Vampires all got together to work out how to live among humans. When you Witches showed up back in the 1600's, it was decided that you'd be the bridge between them."

"Thanks for the history lesson. What's your point?"

"My point is we were never asked to join! My point is that for hundreds of years, we've been outcasts in any decisions about Wesley and the Mysticals! My point, Shannon, is that we don't count, and WE'RE SICK OF IT!"

Mary-Jane and I are taken aback by her vehemence.

"And ever since Maeve's been gone, the other Mysticals give even less of a damn about the Fae. They want to sell off the woodlands where we have our Moon Dances? They go right ahead and tell us to find someplace else! A Druid decides that he has the right to our magical herb gardens, well ain't that just too bad! A freaking Vampire decides that he's going to re-route the stream that feeds our gardens, well; we just have to pay him for water we've used for generations!" She catches her breath. "I can go on and on. But my point is that we're not going to take it anymore."

I look over at MJ. "You have any idea about this going on?"

MJ sighs. "Shannon, I didn't even know these guys existed!"

Ivy interrupts. "Promise that you'll get us a seat on the Council of Mysticals and make sure people start respecting us!" Her wings trying to flutter are now soaked as well as being bent. "Even if you have to spell them, make it happen. "

My fists clench, and it's so tempting to blast this manipulative fairy into next week. Who does she think she is, making demands after she tried to kidnap Jack?

"Shannon." Cynthia's voice cuts through my rage as she steps closer, her red hair plastered to her face. "We need to work with them." She turns to Ivy. "Call Beth. Tell her we'll make sure things change."

I take a deep breath, trying to rein in my temper. As much as I hate to admit it, Cynthia's right. Beth is far away with evidence that could destroy everything. Our personal feelings don't matter right now.

"She's right," MJ whispers beside me. "What choice do we have?"

Ivy's eyes narrow as she peers at Cynthia and me, water dripping from her pointy little chin. "You promise? Swear it on that precious Witching Well you have."

Her request sends a chill through me. The Well is sacred, powerful. Swearing on it isn't something to be taken lightly. Locking eyes with Ivy, I nod. "We swear. Call Beth and tell her not to release the photos. We'll do whatever she wants, but she can't post them online."

Ivy fumbles with her wings, wincing as she tries to straighten the delicate structures. The rain has made them like soggy tissue paper. She pulls out a phone that's miraculously dry—some kind of Fae magic, I suppose.

"Wait a minute!" I say. "You were tied up!"

Ivy looks at me with an expression of amused pity. "Yes, I was, wasn't I" My jaw is tight watching her tap an icon. Her eyes lock with mine as the phone rings.

"Beth?" Ivy says when the call connects. "They agree to our terms. You can delete the photos and come back."

Holding my breath, I strain to hear Beth's response, but the pounding rain drowns out any chance of that. All I can do is watch Ivy's face for clues.

And what I see makes my blood run cold.

Ivy's eyes widen and her mouth falls open, both filled with horror. "No!" she blurts, "That wasn't the deal. Don't do it, Beth. You promised!"

Oh shit. Whatever Beth is saying, it's clear their plan is imploding.

I grab the phone from Ivy, shouting into it. "Listen bitch! I don't know what deal you made with the Fae, but you'd better not cross me."

Beth lets out a cackle. "Or what? Your quiet life is gone, Witch. Too bad Jerry Springer isn't still on TV, cause you'd be his number one guest. But maybe Jimmy Fallon will do. Everyone will know what a freak you are!"

Her words are like a physical blow, but I refuse to let her hear my fear. "You think this is just about me?" I hiss with clenched teeth. "You're exposing an entire town of people, your neighbors and friends. People you've lived peacefully with, who never harmed you."

"Peacefully?" Beth scoffs. "Is that what you call it? Hardly."

"Where are you?" I demand, struggling to keep my voice level.

"Wouldn't you like to know?" she taunts. "I'm somewhere safe, uploading everything as we speak. By morning, Wesley will be crawling with reporters and paranormal investigators. Your little magical kingdom is about to become a shitshow for freaks."

My mind zaps to Thomas, and my heart squeezes tight. My son—who has no idea about any of this. Who still thinks his mom is just regular, boring Shannon Burke, divorced and running a resort in the mountains.

The thought of him seeing those photos, watching his mother go viral... He may never speak to me again!

The fight plummets out of me in an instant. I can't let that happen to him.

"What do you want, Beth?" My voice is softer now, defeated. The rain falls harder, matching my sinking spirit. "Name your price and I'll meet it. Please don't do this."

Water streams down my face—rain or tears, I can't even tell anymore. Everyone around me is silent, watching my desperate negotiation.

"Think of your brother if nothing else," I add, a final plea.

Beth's breath catches slightly at the mention of Eric. For all her hatred toward me, she cares about her brother. It's my last hope—that her love of Eric is stronger than her hatred of us.

Before she can answer, Eric lunges and snatches the phone from me. His face is lined with worry as he presses it to his ear.

"Please sis...don't," he pleads in a soft voice. "Think of me, of our parents."

The silence stretches for one heartbeat, two. Then the line goes dead.

I close my eyes, feeling the rain wash over me. I've failed. The coven, the town and, most importantly...my relationship with my son.

Twenty-One

Mary-Jane

"Shit," I mutter, watching Eric stare at the phone. "She's really going to do it." I can't comprehend the feeling of betrayal Eric must be feeling right now; his own sister is hell-bent on turning his life, and the lives of everyone in Wesley, inside out!

Shannon looks like she might throw up or throw lightning—possibly both. Cynthia closes her eyes, and her lips move with a string of profanity. None of us will be unaffected once Beth starts spreading her juicy gossip.

A wail of sirens makes me jerk before seeing red lights flash through the trees. I make out a police cruiser and an SUV barreling down the street. "Who called the cops?" I ask out loud.

"When I called Wayne, he said he was going to see if he could get hold of Chief Stone," Eric says. "First transformations are always kind of touch and go, even when they happen when they're supposed to."

"You mean a full moon."

"Yeah." He tilts his head over to where Libby and Kevin are. "With what's happened here, it's better to be safe than sorry.

I stare at Kevin—sweet, nerdy Kevin, who now looks like he could audition for the lead role in a horror movie. "Is he dangerous?"

"First transformation is unpredictable," Eric replies. "Wayne knows what he's doing, and he'll help him through it."

The sirens stop, and Chief Stone rounds the corner of the house, with Wayne right on his heels. Wayne puts his hand on the chief's shoulder. "I got this, Chief," and comes over to us. "Ladies," Wayne nods at us, then steps over to Kevin. "First time, son? Bad timing with the moon not even full, but shit happens."

Kevin growls, and his lips curl, showing long canines. "They tried to take my kid brotherrrrr...."

"Probably triggered by emotion," Wayne observes. "Protective instinct kicked in..." he eyes Kevin. "Protecting the pack, right?"

"Yeahhhhh"

"Good job, son." He turns to the two Fae. "You two have nooo idea how lucky you are. He could have ripped each of you apart without breaking a sweat...and who could blame him?" He turns back to Kevin. "You should be proud of yourself, young cub; I sure am."

Stepping closer to Shannon, I whisper, "We're so screwed if Beth posts those photos."

"I know," Shannon hisses back.

Stepping closer to Kevin, Wayne says, "I'm going to help you shift back, son. It's going to feel strange, but you need to trust me."

Kevin's eyes widen. "Hurt...meeee?"

"No, not really. It's just going to feel different. You ever workout with weights?" When Kevin nods, he says, "It'll be like you just finished a hell of a workout and jumped into a swimming pool, okay?"

The editor's calmness is impressive—I'd be freaking out if my body suddenly sprouted that much hair without a waxing appointment in sight.

Chief Stone approaches us, notepad in hand. "So, these Fae—"

"Tried to kidnap Jack! Not only did they help Beth, but this?" Shannon spits out. "You're going to arrest them, right?"

The Chief nods sharply. "Yep. We'll convene the Council and have them pass judgement."

"See?" Ivy sputters. "The oh-so-important Council! That doesn't have a single Fae on it!" She starts to struggle.

"IVY!" Shannon bellows. The wind picks up. "Not. One more. Word!"

Ivy shuts up, but the daggers in her eyes do her talking for her.

The Chief actually looks down for a moment before stepping over to where Stan is holding them. With a deep sigh, he says, "So disappointed in you, Alf."

As the Chief slips handcuffs on Alf, Ivy turns on Shannon. "You promised to help us!"

Cynthia answers. "We are and we will. Count yourself lucky that Shannon didn't torch you."

My patience is completely shot watching the chippy little Fae. "She still might, so count yourself lucky you'll be safe in jail. You can't just get away with trying to snatch one of our kids."

Ivy's wings flutter pathetically as she tries to look intimidating. "But what about our deal? What about getting us a seat on the Council?"

I cross my arms, remembering how Jane had played me earlier. These Fae and their manipulation tactics are really too much. "Are you kidding me? You kidnap Jack, threaten our families, and you expect us to put you on the Council?" I don't have a clue what this 'Council' is, yet, but I know it's a thing.

Alf puffs up his chest. "We deserve respect! All the Mysticals treat us like we're nothing!"

"Maybe because you act like idiots?" I snap, "Look around you! There's a new Werewolf who could have torn you to shreds, a coven of Witches who could turn you into fireflies, and the police chief standing right here. On top of that, Beth's still publishing all her stuff about Wesley! And you have the nerve to make demands?"

Ivy and Alf look a bit sheepish but still keep pushing. "You Witches made a promise. Even swearing on your stupid Well!"

I take a deep breath. Ray always says my temper will be the death of me someday. "Here's the deal. You're going to jail tonight. We'll talk about your status after we clean up this mess with Beth. But if she posts those photos, all bets are off."

Chief Stone steps forward, handcuffs ready. "You're finished with the force, Alf."

My phone buzzes in my pocket, and I fish it out. What now? Ray's name appears on the screen with a notification that sends my stomach plummeting. No words, just a link.

"Please don't be what I think it is," I mutter, tapping the link.

The screen loads, and there it is—Beth's first post online. It's a Facebook post showing Shannon in full Witch regalia, bending down to pet Robert, her familiar bobcat with his distinctive one-ear. The caption reads: "Head Witch of Wesley, New York. Now accepting spell requests at a magical discount."

My throat goes dry. The image is crystal clear—no Photoshop, no tricks. Just the raw truth in all its supernatural glory.

"Guys," I hold my phone up for Shannon and Cynthia to see. "It's started."

Shannon's mouth falls open as she stares at the screen. "Oh shit. Thomas is going to see this."

Cynthia leans in, her expression hardening as she reads the caption. "And so it begins," she mutters. "She certainly didn't waste any time."

I refresh the page, my heart sinking further as I watch the numbers climb. Twenty-seven shares already. Thirty-two comments. People tagging news outlets.

"This is just the first," I say quietly. "She's going to drip-feed posts online to keep the attention coming."

I look at the Fae still in handcuffs, and a wave of anger rushes through me. Their ill-timed rebellion just exposed us all. Jane's betrayal, Beth's vindictiveness—it's all converging into a perfect storm that's about to wash away our peaceful life. And what's going to be left after? I have no idea; but it won't be good.

As Chief Stone handcuffs Ivy and Alf, I snap, "Just make sure those two don't get away, like Beth."

Alf's wings droop as Jonas secures his hands. "Chief, please," he pleads, desperation creeping into his voice. "You know things have to change! The Fae deserve better treatment. I had to help Ivy and Beth!"

Jonas doesn't respond as he secures a band around Alf's chest, effectively binding his wings. He does the same to Ivy, who stares daggers at me the entire time.

"This isn't over," she hisses as the Chief leads them toward his cruiser.

I watch them go, my stomach churning with worry about what comes next.

My phone rings again, and I roll my eyes. Glancing at the screen, a flicker of hope surges when I see Ida's name.

"Ida? Please tell me you have good news," I answer, stepping away from the others for a moment of quiet.

"I do, actually." Ida's voice sounds triumphant. "Remember, I told you about my friend Peter Bond? The tech guy? Well, he got a line on Beth's phone. It's pinging from a place just north of Albany."

I let out a long breath. "Thank God. How far north of Albany?"

"He's got coordinates. So, we've got a window of opportunity," Ida explains. "Is Eric there with you?"

I glance over at the shifter who's talking with Cynthia. "Yeah, he's here."

"Put him on. I need to talk to him."

I walk over to Eric and hold out my phone. "It's Ida. She says Peter Bond has a line on Beth's location."

Eric's eyebrows shoot up as he takes my phone. "Ida? Yeah, it's me."

I watch as he listens, his forehead furrowing. He nods several times before handing the phone back to me.

"Okay, what's up?" I ask.

"Ida and I are going to fly there, following Peter's instructions. We can move faster than anyone else."

"Fly?" I ask stupidly, before realizing. "Oh, right. Bird form."

"Exactly." Eric nods.

"What about Beth's phone? If she posts more photos while you're en route..."

Eric shakes his head. "We can't stop that. But we'll be able to stop her from doing interviews or going to the media in person. That's what would really blow this town wide open."

"No way am I missing this. Can Ray send me Peter's address so I can pick him up?" Shannon's getting ready to leave when I grab her arm. "Hang on. You're not going anywhere."

"What? Of course I am!" Shannon pulls away, scowling at me. "I need to stop her before she does more damage."

"No, you need to go home," I say firmly. "Jessica and Devon are there. Your daughter needs you right now."

Shannon's frowns, "But Beth—"

"Eric and Ida will handle Beth." I insist. "And Cynthia and I are going to pick up Peter Bond and head out to Beth's place too. Shannon, right now, Jessica is scared. And you need to talk to Devon."

I can feel Shannon's conflict, her fingers clenching and unclenching at her sides. "I should be the one to confront Beth. This is my fight."

"It's all of our fight," I remind her, squeezing her shoulder. "We've got your back."

Cynthia steps up beside me, nodding. "MJ's right. Go home, Shann. We'll take care of Beth."

"But—"

"No buts," I cut her off. "Think about it. What if more Fae show up at your place while Jessica is there?" I look over at the Chiefs police car with the two Fae in the back. "What if those two aren't the only ones grabbing our kids? Your daughter needs protection, and she needs her mom."

Shannon looks over at Libby, who's crouched beside Kevin. Wayne has his hands on the boy's shoulders, speaking quietly. I watch dumbfounded as his pelt of fur begins to fade right before my eyes. I'm not the only one awestruck; Jack and Dahlia watch with wide eyes, both fascinated and terrified.

"Fine," Shannon finally sighs, and her shoulders slump. "But you call me the second you have Beth, understand? And if she posts anything else—"

"We'll handle it," I promise. "Go home. Make sure Jessica is okay. Talk to Devon. "

Shannon nods, "Call me. I mean it."

"We will," Cynthia assures her.

I'm not wasting any time and breaking every speed limit as I drive out to Peter Bond's place. What a shit-show this night's become. Beside me, Cynthia stares out the window, her profile highlighted in the dashboard lights.

"You okay?" I ask.

She nods but doesn't look at me. "Just thinking about Beth."

I grip the steering wheel tighter. "We'll stop her. We're almost at Peter's house, and I'll punch it to get to Albany. "

"Good," Cynthia says quietly. Then, after a pause: "When we get to Beth, I will handle her, okay? This started because of her resenting me, so I want to be the one to end it."

Something in her tone makes my skin prickle. I glance over and see her eyes—hard and cold like I've never seen before.

"What will you do?" I ask carefully. "Even though we're Witches, murder is kinda' against the law, you know." I smile to show I'm kidding, but the look on her face stops me cold.

"Not murder, don't worry." Cynthia shakes her head. "But she'll wish she was dead. She'll never know what hit her... or anything else after that. She'll live out her days in the asylum next to Steve."

My stomach drops. I've known Cynthia for years, but I've never heard her sound so... ruthless. The way she said it—so matter-of-fact, like she's discussing what to make for dinner—chills me to the bone.

"Cynthia..." I start, not sure what to say.

"Don't," she cuts me off. "Beth is trying to destroy everything. Our lives. Our town." Jabbing a finger behind us, "She just tried to have a child kidnapped! She's threatening our families." Her hand rests protectively over her stomach. "I won't let her."

She rubs her belly and continues, her voice level. "I'm pushing forty damn years old, Mary-Jane. I never thought I'd ever, ever meet 'the one guy', y'know?" She lets out a deep sigh. "I really thought Steve might be, but there was always something in the back of my head about him." She throws me a look. "And oh, boy was there ever, huh?"

"Yeah, he was some piece of work, alright."

"Damn right...Then Eric...I knew him somewhat for years...but...once we got together, I found my soulmate. I'm happy to bear his child!" She cuts through the air with her hand. "No, I'm honored to!" She snorts a giggle. "In fact, I'm even willing to overlook how he held back about being a Mystical!"

"Yeah...you'll make him pay for that indiscretion, won't ya?" I say with a grin.

"Damn right! But now? Our town's going to be turned upside down and inside out because of Beth's vendetta...against ME! I can feel her hatred towards me! I mean, it'll be one thing if we just become a tourist destination like Salem Massachusetts...but..." her voice fades and she looks off into space, afraid.

"But what?"

In a small voice, Cynthia says, "What if the Men in Black get interested? All those secret government agencies? What's going to happen then?" She looks over at me. "You KNOW they'll want to weaponize our magic Mary-Jane! Can you imagine a battalion of soldiers that are shapeshifters? They can fly into enemy territory, get behind the front lines, or line up like pigeons on the power lines right outside the window of the leadership, and it's game over! We think Navy SEALS are tough guys, right? What if there's Navy SEALS who are dolphins? What the hell kind of havoc could they do?"

She's not letting up as she continues. "And don't get me started on what a Druid could do on a battlefield! Make earthquakes in the middle of your enemy? You won't even have to bomb anyone! Just...hell, I don't know how they do it, but I've been told they can command earthquakes. So, they just clap their hands, and poof, your enemy's buried. No nuclear explosion, just poof, gone."

A chill goes through me. "I wonder how China would react to something like that..." I say.

"I guarantee you that they won't be sending congratulations!" Cynthia replies. Her voice takes on a bitter tone. "Up until tonight, I had everything I ever let myself dream of. And this...this bitch Beth has ruined it! Just to be spiteful."

She's not yelling. Her voice is more frightening because of the resolute tone.

I understand her anger—God knows I feel it too—but something about her coldness frightens me. We're Witches, not monsters. There has to be another way to handle this.

I wheel the car down an old logging road, wincing as branches scrape against the sides of my SUV. Ray's going to have a fit when he sees the paint job tomorrow, but that's tomorrow's problem. Right now, we've got bigger fish to fry.

"This can't be right," Cynthia mutters, squinting at her phone's GPS. "We're in the middle of nowhere."

"That's the point," I say, navigating around a fallen log. "The word I got is that Peter Bond values his privacy."

After another while of teeth-rattling bumps, the trees thin out and we emerge into a small clearing. A rustic log cabin sits in the center, but what catches my eye is the array of antenna towers staggered around it, stretching up at least a hundred feet; two of which are enormous satellite dishes.

"Wow," Cynthia whispers. "Someone probably has the mother of all cable TV setups, huh?"

"Not to mention the internet."

As soon as I shut off the engine, the cabin door flies open and a man storms out. He's elderly—probably in his late sixties—but moves with the energy of someone half his age. What's most striking is his bare chest, completely covered in tattoos. Intricate swirls and symbols that resemble Mary's mark every inch of visible skin.

Oh shit. "Of course he would be a Druid," I mutter, putting the car in park. "Just what we need. Not."

"What's your beef with Druids? You didn't even know they existed a few days ago."

I roll my eyes. "And since then, they've been in the restaurant in all their glory, tats up the wazoo. Let's just say they like to give orders, you'll see."

As Peter turns to lock his cabin door and grab a battered suitcase from the porch, I glance at Cynthia with a smirk.

"At least he's in better shape than Duncan Moroni," I whisper, noting the old man's surprisingly muscular physique. I can't help adding, "Duncan, who has a huge crush on you, by the way."

Cynthia's head whips toward me, her eyes wide. "What? The skinny garbage man with the comb-over? That old guy? No, he doesn't."

"Oh, honey," I laugh, "he absolutely does. I saw a poster-sized photo of you in his house. From that night you got all dolled up to meet Eric."

Cynthia looks like she's ready to hurl yesterday's breakfast at that news. Her face goes pale, and she presses a hand to her mouth. "I'm going to straighten Duncan right the hell out as soon as all this is over, don't you worry. Duncan? Ugh!"

Before I can reply, the back door of my SUV flies open. Peter Bond clambers in without so much as a hello, snapping his seatbelt with military precision. He's wearing an enormous headset, complete with a boom microphone. Has he been on the line with ET or something?

"Drive," he barks, fiddling with dials on a device connected to his headphones. "Northeast. I'll direct you."

I share a look with Cynthia, raising my eyebrows. It's going to be a long night.

"Nice to meet you too," I mutter, putting the car in reverse. "I'm Mary-Jane, and this is—"

"Cynthia," he interrupts without looking up from his equipment. "Witch. Specializes in the Elementals, similar to, but not as powerful as your coven leader Shannon. Been practicing The Craft for years. Currently gestating. Father uncertain."

My jaw drops. I glance at Cynthia, who looks equally stunned.

"How did you—" she starts.

"I know everyone in Wesley," Peter cuts her off. "Even the ones who think I don't know them. Especially them and their secrets."

I ease the car back onto the logging road, wincing as more branches scrape against the paint. Peter sounds like he might already be part of the deep state, one of those Men in Black types. Keeping my voice calm, I ask, "So, you've been tracking Beth's phone?"

"Tracking everything," he corrects, adjusting a dial. "Her phone. Her social media. Her email. The woman's digital footprint is like a herd of elephants trampling through mud."

"Is that... legal?" I ask, navigating around a particularly nasty pothole.

Peter snorts. "Legal. Illegal. These are constructs of a society that doesn't understand what we are."

Great. He's one of those Druids; always thinking they're so very special and cliquish. Kind of like Duncan, now that I think of it.

We head out, and for the next forty minutes or so I pin my speedometer at a hundred miles an hour. If we get pulled over, I'll spell the cop or something.

After we blow through Albany and continue north, Peter taps my shoulder. "Take the next exit."

I come off the exit, and he says, "Okay, slow down, Geronimo." When I do, he says, "Take a right at the fork," he instructs. "She's stopped moving. Holed up in a motel just beyond the bend."

TWENTY-TWO

MEANWHILE, BACK AT LIBBY'S HOME...

I didn't even say goodbye to Cynthia and Mary-Jane when they took off to stop Beth. Instead, I'm holding my eldest child, who had mutated into a monster and is now, with the help of the elderly Wayne Silver, trying to transform back into a human being.

Oh Kevin...

It's torture for him! As a Werewolf, he's an enormous beast—probably seven feet tall, with the build of an NFL linebacker. His muscles, bones and very skin had stretched and grown as he transformed. But now, as he regains his human form, his entire body is spasming in agony as he collapses back into his teenage form.

His head hangs, snot and spit drooling from his face as his snout and fangs begin to condense and shrink back to human forms.

"Oh, Mommm..." he grunts, "It hu-huh-huurrrrts!"

"Baby..." I take him in my arms, feel his entire frame spasm and quake. I close my eyes, willing my power of healing to infuse into my boy.

Suddenly I'm yanked back from Kevin and spun around to face Wayne Silver. He has my arm in an iron grip.

"He must endure this, Libby!" he says sternly. "It's part of the process! He has to transform back on his own! If you help him now, you could kill him!"

I hear the crack of bones breaking, and shove Wayne in the chest and spin back to Kevin. "He's my son!" I cry. Kevin is bent at the waist in pain, howling.

Before I can get to him, Wayne grabs me again, this time lifting me off my feet and tossing me back, so I land on my ass. He shudders from the effort. "You'll kill the boy!" he roars, his voice a deep growl.

I stare up at Wayne. His own face has elongated, his hands are now dangerous claws. "Stay back!"

Struggling to my feet, Stan grips my shoulders. "I think Wayne knows what he's doing here, Libby. Give him space to do what he can."

"No!" I wrestle out of his grip, but Stan puts me in a bearhug. He lifts me off my feet and steps backwards. I kick at his shins with all my might and throw my head back into his face, feeling his nose squish against the back of my skull.

"No, Libby!" he says, his teeth clenched tight.

He has me completely trapped and enveloped as I watch my son fall to his hands and knees on the ground. Wayne, now halfway transformed drops beside him. He puts a paw across Kevin's shoulders hugging him close, and his head is beside Kevin's.

"HAARRRRD!" Wayne growls, his voice blaring. "IS HAARRRD!" He sways from side to side, holding Kevin to keep him from collapsing to the ground. "IS HAARRRD!"

"HUH-HUH-HUNHHH" Kevin replies.

"Stay with it, laddie! Is HAAARRD!"

"Hard!"

"NO! HAAARRRRD!"

"HARD!"

"Again Kevin! Hard!"

"HAARRD!"

"AGAIN!"

"AHHH-WOOOOO!" Kevin keens into the night air. "AHHH-WOOOO! IS HAAAARRRRD!"

"Good!" Wayne then responds with an 'Aawooo' of his own. Still grasping Kevin's shoulder, he continues swaying both of them side to side, howling and baying in the night.

And it's over.

Kevin is back in his teenage form, and Wayne has reverted back into the elderly gray-haired editor of the local paper. Both of them now gasp for air, their heads dropped in exhaustion.

Stan releases me. "I'll look after Wayne."

Like I give a shit. I fly to Kevin's side. He pants, his back heaving with each breath. His shirt and pants are in tatters around him, rags hanging from his limbs.

"Kevin? Kevin?" My voice is a terrified hush.

"Hey Mom..." he whispers and begins to stand. I jump up to help, and he brushes me off. "Gotta get up on my own," he says. "Wayne tol' me." Finally, he's on his feet, wobbling like a punch-drunk boxer. Taking a deep breath, he lets it out and turns to Wayne.

"Thanks, Mister Silver." He shakes his head slowly. "Is it gonna be like that every time?"

"No. Just the first, son. Actually, you'll enjoy it pretty quickly. The explosion of power and strength in you is going to be a real rush, Kevin."

"No way!"

"Yeah...way. You'll see." Wayne looks over at Stan. "You probably saved this kid's life."

"Whaaat?" we all say together. Me, Kevin and Stan stare at Wayne.

He points a finger at me. "You almost killed him, Libby." When my jaw drops, he continues. "Had you done that healing spell, you would have stopped his transformation cold in its tracks. And so his body, trapped between Mystical and human would have failed." His face is stern. "He would have died instantly." When he sees the expression of horror on my face, he adds, "I saw it happen once, years and years ago. There was no way I was going to let you make that same mistake."

He looks past me to Stan. "You got great instincts, Stan. If you didn't hold Libby back..." he looks at Kevin, then back at me. "I might have died, too."

He's serious. And my gut tells me that he's telling the absolute truth. "I...I'm..."

Wayne slices the air with his hand. "Nothing to be sorry for, Libby. You were doing what you thought best. And thank God, Stan was here, and thank God your boy listened to me."

"I—"

Wayne shakes his head. "Nope. All's well that ends well." Turning to Kevin, "Now, Were-cub, you go take a long hot shower, y'hear?" When Kevin nods, Wayne looks at me. "You have any red meat in the house?" I nod and he adds, "He's going to need two rare steaks, understand? And I mean rare."

"Yessir."

"Good. Then I'll be on my way." He collects himself and starts to head towards the house. When he staggers a few steps, Stan rushes to help him.

"Hey, old-timer, let's head out together." Stan wraps his arm around him.

"Don't leave, Stan," I call out. He turns to look at me for a second, and a big smile lights his face. "I'm gonna need you here." Oh god...he has a bloody nose from struggling with me!

He nods. "I'll just make sure Wayne gets home okay. See ya in a bit." They round the back of the house to the driveway.

Putting my arm around Kevin's shoulders, "Let's get you inside, honey."

I startle when my other hand is grasped and tugged. Jack looks at me wide-eyed. "Is Kevin okay?" His face is lined with worry as he whispers.

Kevin snorts. "I'm standing right here, squirt!" He holds out his arm. "Gimme a hand, will ya?"

Jack flies to Kevin's other side. He tucks into his big brother, wrapping his arm around his waist and leans into him. "You gonna be okay?"

Kevin drops his arm across Jack's back. "Yeah. But man, I'm starved!"

"You smell like crap."

"I smell like youuu." They both laugh.

It takes all my self-control to keep from sinking into a puddle of tears.

I watch them enter the house and shake my head, trying to reclaim my strength. My hands still tremble as I pull out my phone and call Shannon.

"Hey," I say when she answers, my voice cracking slightly. "What happened while I was dealing with Kevin?"

Shannon sighs heavily on the other end. "Beth's already posting photos online. She's getting likes and comments. Eric and Ida are going to fly to Albany to track her down." Her voice sounds exhausted. "I'm almost home now. I need to check on Jessica. Devon's there too, with Duncan."

"Devon and Duncan?" I ask, confused by that pairing.

"Long story," Shannon mutters. "How's Kevin doing?"

I've made my way inside, and I glance toward the bathroom where the shower has just stopped running. "He's okay now. I hope." My voice catches. "Wayne helped him change back. I've never seen anything like it, Shannon. One minute he's this huge, hairy... thing, and the next he's my boy again."

"Jesus," Shannon whispers. "This town just keeps getting weirder."

"I'm going to check on MJ and Cynthia after I get Kevin settled," I tell her.

"Good idea. Keep me posted."

I dial MJ's number, but it's Cynthia who answers.

"Hey Libby," she says, road noise in the background. "We're on our way to find Beth with Peter Bond. He's tracking her phone signal."

"Any luck?"

"Yeah, he's got a line on her. How's Kevin doing?"

I lean my head back against the wall. "He's shaken up but otherwise okay, thanks to Wayne. I still can't believe what I saw."

"I can only imagine," Cynthia says softly. "Listen, go look after your kid. We'll call as soon as we have Beth."

"Thanks, Cyn. Be careful."

I hang up and close my eyes for a moment, trying to gather my strength. My son needs me to be strong right now, not falling apart.

I hang up the phone and hear Stan's heavy footsteps coming up the stairs. When I look up, his eyes meet mine—steady, concerned, a lifeline in this storm of chaos.

His nose is bruised, but he swiped off most of the blood from my head bashing him. Something inside me breaks. I've been holding it together for Kevin, for Jack, for Dahlia—but seeing Stan's face, his unwavering strength when everything else is spinning out of control, my defenses crumble.

The tears I've been fighting back spill over, hot and fast down my cheeks.

"Thanks for coming," I whisper, my voice cracking. "I don't know what would have happened if you weren't here."

Stan slides down the wall to sit beside me. He wraps his arm around me and pulls me into a hug. I collapse against his chest, breathing in his familiar scent—wood smoke and that spicy aftershave he always wears.

"I'm glad I was here, babe." He sighs. "It's where I should have been all along. I'm sorry for backing off earlier." His hand rubs gentle circles on my back. "This is a lot, but we're more. Much more, Libby."

I let myself lean into him, just for a moment. My son is a Werewolf. Beth is exposing our secret to the world. Everything is falling apart, but Stan's arms around me feel like the one solid thing I can hold on to.

"I never thought—" My voice catches. "Kevin was supposed to have a normal life. College, career, family. Not this."

Stan's chest rises and falls with a deep breath. "Normal is overrated. I've been a normie all my life. And who knows? Maybe he can still have all those things. Wayne does, right? He runs the paper; he has a wife, kids and grand-kids. From the looks of it, he's happy."

I look up from Stan's shoulder as the front door opens downstairs.

"Mom?" Jack's voice echoes through the house.

"We're up here," I call back, quickly wiping the tears from my face. Stan gives my hand a quick squeeze before we both stand up.

Jack bounds up the stairs two at a time, his face flushed with excitement. His eyes are wild, practically sparkling, and I feel a knot form in my stomach. I know that look. It's the same one he gets before doing something reckless.

"What were you doing outside?" Good grief, the boy had just been snatched by Fairies!

He looks at me baffled. "Whaddya mean? Dahlia needed some help with her cat, and we were looking at the stars."

I shake my head. The resilience of kids.

Jack is so pumped up. "Before he left, Wayne took a swab of my DNA," he announces breathlessly. "He's gonna test if I have the Werewolf gene! He's pretty sure that if Kevin was able to transform into a Werewolf, it's likely I will too!"

He says this like he's announcing he made the varsity team. Like it's the best news in the world.

Stan and I exchange a look—his concerned, mine horrified. I try to keep my voice steady.

"I think one Werewolf in this family is enough, but..."

"I totally want this," Jack interrupts, practically bouncing on his toes. "To be like Kev would be so, so cool! Dahlia's becoming a Witch, Kevin's already a Werewolf...oh man, I hope I do too!"

My heart sinks. Of course he does. Jack has always wanted whatever his older brother had—only more extreme. Where Kevin was cautious, Jack would dive in headfirst. Where Kevin followed rules, Jack broke them for the excitement.

Oh boy.

"Jack, honey," I begin, trying to find the right words. "This isn't like getting a tattoo or piercing your ear. This is serious. Kevin didn't choose this."

"But it's awesome!" Jack insists. "You saw him yourself! He was huge and powerful, and those fairy things were totally freaking out!"

The bathroom door opens with a rush of steam, and Kevin steps out in his bathrobe. I study him anxiously, my eyes traveling down to his legs. The hair on his calves looks normal—thank goodness. No sign of the beast that he had been.

"You okay, honey?" I ask, my voice steadier than I feel.

Kevin runs a hand through his damp hair. "I'm starving. Like, I've never been this hungry before. It's like there's this... hole inside me."

I swallow hard, trying not to react to the raw hunger in his voice. This is my son—my level-headed boy—but something has awakened in him that I don't understand.

I stand up and wrap my arms around him, feeling his solid warmth against me. He's still Kevin. Still my son, no matter what else he might be now.

"I have some steaks. Let me get them on," I say, squeezing him tight before letting go.

Jack watches this exchange with that same dangerous excitement in his eyes. "See? Already getting a Werewolf appetite!" he says with undisguised envy.

Kevin looks down at his younger brother, his expression suddenly serious. "Cool your jets, squirt; it was a bitch."

"Aaahhhh...I could handle it!"

"Then handle this!" Kevin grabs Jack in a headlock. "Noogie! Noogie! Noogie!"

"Why I oughta!" They're both laughing as Stan and I head to the kitchen.

Stan chuckles beside me, his hand warm on my lower back. "Reminds me of when I was a teenager. My mom used to say I had a hollow leg."

"Yeah, but you weren't literally turning into a wolf," I mutter, though I'm grateful for his attempt to normalize this insanity.

Behind us, Jack is peppering Kevin with questions. "Did it hurt when you changed?"

"Like a sonofabitch, Jack. Worse than the dentist."

"Could you still think like a human? How strong were you? I bet you could bench press a car!"

"Jack, give your brother some space," I say, my nurse voice slipping out automatically.

"It's okay, Ma," Kevin says. "Look buddy, I still need to process this. And I don't know when it's gonna happen again—"

"Full moon in two weeks! I checked!"

"Oh maaan! Lighten up a little, will ya? I'm beat to a snot and starving."

When we reach the kitchen, Dahlia is sitting at the table, her face illuminated by the blue glow of her tablet. She looks up as we enter, her eyes wide with worry.

"Mom," she says, holding out the tablet. "She posted this half an hour ago."

My stomach drops as I take the device from her. The screen shows a photo of the four of us—Shannon, Mary-Jane, Cynthia, and me—standing on that old logging road when we confronted Patrick. The image is slightly blurry but unmistakable. Even worse, the ghostly forms of Maeve and Judith are visible behind Shannon, their translucent outlines impossible to explain away as camera tricks.

The caption reads: "The Witches of Wesley aren't just playing dress-up. Real magic, real ghosts. #WitchesExist #HauntedWesley #CovenCentral"

I scroll down to see the comments and shares. Hundreds of them already, some skeptical but many excited. The post has been shared over two thousand times.

"It's been reported and shared tons of times," Dahlia confirms, watching my face. "People are asking if it's real or some kind of publicity stunt for a movie."

I sink down into a kitchen chair, the tablet heavy in my hands. This is exactly what we were trying to prevent.

Stan squeezes my shoulder before moving to the refrigerator. "I'll get those steaks on for Kevin," he says quietly.

I set the tablet down on the kitchen table, unable to look at those comments anymore. Each new notification feels like another nail in the coffin of our quiet life in Wesley.

Tomorrow is going to come all too soon. It won't matter if they get Beth. The damage is done.

Twenty-Three

Shannon

My brain is a hot mess as I speed back to my place. At least Jess isn't alone; Devon's with her, and from what I gathered, he showed up with someone else.

Still, there's powerful magic afoot, and I'm not going to relax until I know my daughter's safe and sound.

Period.

'Yeah, then you can handle the Thomas problem!' Shit. The thought of my straitlaced son finding out about his mother being a Witch fills me with dread. He's always been so quick to judge people; it's his biggest fault, and he reminds me so much of my Ass-Hat ex-husband when he does that it makes me...

'Scared. Admit it.' No! My inner voice is being a super pain in the ass right now. Except...it's true.

I'm scared of my own kid judging me and finding me wanting.

Damn it.

How the hell is he going to take it? Seeing Stan's response earlier today—how he pulled back from Libby—really unnerved me.

"One disaster at a time!" I yell to myself. I'm just about home—let me make sure Jess is okay, and then I'll worry about my son. Hard to believe how different Jess and Thomas are, despite being twins!

I snort in frustration as I wheel into my driveway.

And what a sight welcomes me home.

At the end of my driveway stands Duncan Moroni, our Druid sanitation worker. He's naked from the waist up, his entire torso covered in whorls of woad and tattoos.

And they're freaking moving! They pulse and glow on his chest, rippling up and out across his arms in shapes of glowing colors. It's like some kind of light show. He has one hand on his hip, and his other hand has Jane the Fae by the scruff of the neck.

And pacing around them in a circle is my familiar, Robert. His eyes are riveted on Jane as he circles her, his back spiked in hackles. He's hissing at her, showing one angry set of fangs.

Good boy!

I hop out of the car. "Where's my daughter?" Funny thing is, Jane doesn't look bothered one bit. In fact, she's smiling. SMILING! My blood pressure shoots to the stratosphere as I stomp over.

"You double-crossed us, Jane! And then you try to kidnap my kid?" I raise my hand, feeling heat gather in my palm. A fireball forms—again!—and I'm ready to toast this traitorous fairy.

"No!" Robert leaps between us, shielding Jane. "Shannon, stop!"

I freeze, the fire still sizzling in my hand. "Move, Robert. She betrayed us."

I step closer, trying to push Robert aside, but he's planted like cement there.

"Hey! It's my job to protect you," he snarls. "Which includes stopping you from making a big mistake."

"I've got her." Duncan says, giving Jane a little shake. "She's not going to hurt anyone, so calm down."

Jane's wings flutter as she stares at me. "I wasn't going to do anything to your daughter. I did my part, and now it's over." She shimmies her shoulders. "Beth's getting the word out, and there's not a damn thing you can do about it."

"You try to kidnap my kid the same way Ivy and Alf grabbed Jack!"

"Got you out here, didn't I?" She smiles sweetly back. "You stupid Witches aren't so tough when you're all split up."

My jaw drops. How the hell does this Fae know about the power of three? I let that slide. "Just so you can completely screw up our town?

Thanks to you, Beth is posting up a storm on social media. Now the world knows about us and Wesley."

"Focus, Shannon." Robert chides, "First we need to counteract Beth's story. Jane's a small fish who will be dealt with later."

As I look down at him, my breath is ragged, and I try to get it under control. Shit. He's right. Another fact he'll crow about later. Beth's posts are already spreading across social media like a grassfire. I extinguish the fireball with a flick of my wrist, though the urge to torch something still itches.

Duncan gives Jane a small shake and says to me, "Go check on your kid, Shannon. I have this under control."

Jane shimmies again. "There's a lot more I can do under you, lover boy!"

He rolls his eyes. "Would you cut that out!" He nods to my house, and I head inside.

Just as I get to the porch, Devon swings the door open. He grins when he spots me, but no way, pal. He's got some explaining to do.

"Boy, am I glad I decided to stop by, Shannon. Jessica was kind of freaked out with your Aunt Maeve appearing and then the Fae trying to get in." He looks at me. "You should have told her about Maeve's ghost, hon; it scared the hell out of her."

My eyes catch the dark mark on Devon's wrist, and my stomach twists. An infinity symbol. Freshly inked in royal blue. I grab his hand, yanking it up between us.

"So, you did get together with Mary!" I hold his wrist higher, shaking it so he knows exactly what I'm looking at. "She did this, and what else did she do with you?"

That tattoo proves he saw her. My throat tightens as I wait for him to answer, despising how much I care about what he'll say.

"No!" Devon's eyebrows shoot up. He looks away for a moment, then back at me. "Okay, I was at her place. But just for a little while. When it became clear what she really wanted, I got the hell out of there."

He looks past me over at Duncan and says, "Tell her, will you?"

"That's my work, all right." The Druid preens, "Mary could only dream of doing such fine detail, never mind how quick I am."

I blink, gawking at Duncan. "Your work? You did it?"

"Yeah," Devon says, "I went to Mary's to talk about Druids, but when I got there, she started coming on to me. I left and ran into Duncan outside. We got to talking, and..."

"I was waiting for him," Duncan says. "I had a pretty good suspicion as to what Mary's real plans were, and I knew Devon to be a loyal man." He blows on his knuckles and polishes them on his chest. "I'm an excellent judge of character, if I say so myself."

"Really?" I say, my voice a squeak. I turn to Devon. "No messing around?" He shakes his head and crosses his heart like we're a pair of eight-year-olds.

From the driveway, Duncan adds, "And I suggested he might have druid potential." He points at Devon's wrist. "The mark is a test. If it fades within a week, he's not meant for our path. If it stays..." He shrugs.

My anger weakens as I stare into Devon's eyes. His aura is pure blue, actually more striking than it usually is. While I marvel at how the blue of his aura matches the blue of his tattoo, I also know that the color only appears when someone's speaking the truth. I shake my head; I give up. Maybe he's becoming a Druid. For sure, he's telling the truth. The knot in my stomach begins to unravel.

"And as soon as Duncan finished, I came out here," Devon says. "Duncan came along too."

"Damn fine thing I did!" Duncan adds, giving Jane another shake.

She bobs her eyebrows at him. "I've been a bad, bad girl, Duncan!"

"Cut that out!" he replies. "I told you, this isn't the place nor time for that stuff." He pokes her in the chest. "Especially with you harassing Shannon's daughter."

Sidling up to him, Jane says, "I know, I know... I've been naughty. And naughty girls should be given a—"

"STOP IT, JANE!" he roars. He makes a gesture, and she falls silent. Duncan glances over at us. "Sorry about that," he says sheepishly. "She's a real firecracker, isn't she?"

"Well, you liked it last night!" Jane replies.

"You weren't trying to kidnap kids."

I lean past Devon. "Duncan? Can you keep Jane out here for a bit? I need to check on my daughter, but I will want to have a chat with her."

He nods. "No problem." He turns to Jane with an evil smile. "Let's play a little game, sweetie." He takes Jane by her arm and pulls her to a nearby tree. He taps it a few times with his palm. The earth trembles slightly, and roots suddenly erupt from the ground, snaking around Jane's ankles, locking her in place. Wow.

But it doesn't stop there. The druid murmurs something under his breath—words I can't catch—and the branches above us stir to life. Vines drop down, wrapping around Jane's torso in a tight embrace, pinning her wings flat against her back.

His display of magical power is impressive. There's more to these druids than I thought. Can't say as I blame Devon for wanting that.

"So that's what you're into?" Jane, restrained like some botanical mummy, manages to flash a seductive smirk at Duncan. "Bondage? I could get with that."

I turn back to Devon. "I'm sorry," I whisper, letting go of his wrist. "I guess I jumped to conclusions."

"Okay, if everyone is finished admiring the tattoo, can we focus?" Robert growls, his one ear flattened against his head.

"Mom!" Jessica races from the house over to me. "Thomas called about ten times."

"What did your brother have to say?"

"I let it go to voicemail, but he's seen the posts of you and your friends. And Aunt Maeve and Grandma? Holy shit. What are you gonna do?"

My stomach drops like a stone. Thomas. My beautiful, ambitious, and judgmental son, who's avoided my calls for weeks. Of course, he's seen the posts. Of course, this is how he finds out.

I close my eyes for a moment. What am I going to do? The question echoes in my head, bouncing off the walls of my skull with absolutely no answer.

"Everyone inside." My voice is steadier than I feel. "I'll make coffee, and we'll figure this out."

Devon falls into step beside me. His hand brushes mine—a silent offering of support that touches me.

When Robert and Duncan walk away from Jane, she calls out, "Hang on! You can't just leave me like this! I can help."

Duncan answers, "We can, and we are. Don't worry. I'll deal with you later."

"Promise?" Jane purrs.

I nearly gag. When Duncan joins us, I notice his face looks flushed and there's a small smile on his lips. Devon and I share a look, while Jessica scrunches her face up.

"Eeeew," she mutters, echoing my exact thoughts.

Jessica immediately heads for the kitchen and starts the coffee maker. The familiar domestic sound feels bizarrely normal amid the shitstorm. Yeah. My son has seen the posts; Beth is spreading our secrets across social media, and the Fae are in some kind of rebellion. Yet here we are, making coffee. Like any other Tuesday night.

Devon slips his arms around my waist, pulling me against his chest. His breath is warm against my ear as he whispers, "You were actually jealous. I can't believe the witchiest Witch in Wesley was jealous of Mary."

I give his chest a push. "Shut up. I wasn't jealous."

But Devon holds me tight, refusing to let me go. His blue eyes twinkle as he smiles down at me. "Were too. But that's okay, cause it shows how much you care."

My cheeks warm, hating that he reads me so well. After David, I swore I'd never let myself be vulnerable again. Yet here I am, melting into Devon's arms like some lovesick teenager instead of a forty-something witch. I take a deep breath and murmur, "Of course, I care. Now can you let me go so we can figure this out? The world is falling in on us, and you get all romantic?"

He releases me reluctantly, his hands lingering on my waist a moment longer than necessary. There's a flutter in my chest, but I push it down. No time for that now.

Duncan leans down to pet Robert. "Never thought I'd be thanking a witch's familiar, but you did good, bud!"

Robert's one ear twitches, his version of preening. "Just doing my job."

Grabbing cookies from the cabinet, I look over at Jess. "So, Maeve was here? How'd that go?" I watch her carefully, remembering my first ghostly encounter with my aunt. How she'd appeared in my bedroom and proceeded to give me unsolicited advice about my love life.

Jessica blows out a long breath. "Well...not nearly as scary as I would have thought."

"Really?"

She nods. "Yeah. I think it's because I talked to Grandma at the Well? I wasn't all that scared when Aunt Maeve appeared, even though I never met her before." She looks around the room. "In just a few days, I found out my own mother's a Witch who can call up a windstorm as easy as ordering an Uber, Fairies are legit, and there's a ghost in our well. So...seeing another ghost here?" She shrugs. "Just another day. It was kinda scary at first, but she's awesome. Once you get to know her. She vanished as soon as Devon walked in."

Devon snorts. "She scared the hell out of me the first time we met."

I set the cookies on the table. "Yeah, Maeve's cool. I wish she'd got the short straw, and it was her in the Well. Kind of." It's not just my mother's snarkiness, but Maeve has a way of making everything feel less dire, even when the world is falling apart.

"So, what now?" Duncan blurts. "It's not a big deal for us Druids, but I think you Witches are on the hot seat if this town fills up with lookey-loos."

"What's that supposed to mean?"

"Mean's I'm a Druid. If I don't want to be seen, I won't be. Simple as that." He points a finger at me. "You, on the other hand, are human through and through. Yes, you're a Witch, but they'll be able to find and track you down in no time."

Devon shakes his head. "I think you're overconfident, Duncan. Every freaking tech-bro in the world is going to be interested in all the Mysticals, especially the Vampires and Druids because you people are immortal. They'll move heaven and earth to get their hands on you, buddy."

Duncan's eyes widen. "I didn't think of that..."

Devon nods. "Yep. Every Bill Gates wannabe will hire an army of doctors and scientists to figure out how to get your immortality into their bodies, believe me." He leans into Duncan. "And they won't play fair—to them, it'll be a matter of life and death."

Duncan shakes his head slowly. "I didn't think about that." He looks up at me. "We're going to have to fix this, then. All of us."

"Thanks, Duncan." I take a sip of my coffee, letting the warmth spread through me. "Right now, the only people I actually trust are sitting in this room. Well, along with my coven, that is."

"Speaking of my coven," I continue, "I wonder how Cynthia and MJ are making out with Beth."

I check my phone again—nothing. Worry gnaws at me. What if Beth has managed to elude them? What if more photos are being posted even as we sit here drinking coffee like everything's normal?

Jessica sets down her mug. "Mom, what's the plan for tomorrow? There's going to be tons of people showing up, right? Looking for the Witch of Wesley?"

Damn. By morning, curiosity seekers will swoop down on our little town like vultures. Reporters. Paranormal enthusiasts. Skeptics looking to debunk us. And Thomas... Good grief, I need to call him.

I meet Devon's eyes across the table. "First thing tomorrow, before we face whatever's coming, I need to get to the Well with the coven."

If we're going to weather this storm, we need every advantage. My mother may be super-bitch, but she's powerful. And right now, we need all the power we can get.

Once we figure out what to do. And that scares me.

Because I don't have the slightest idea.

Twenty-Four

Mary-Jane

"How much farther?" I glance in the rear-view mirror.

Peter Bond doesn't look up from whatever contraption he's fiddling with in the back seat. The blue tattoos covering his bare chest shimmer in the dim light of his tracking device.

"Take exit 21B," he grunts, adjusting those ridiculous airplane headphones. "Then three miles east after the exit."

Beside me, Cynthia's head lolls against the window, soft snores escaping her slightly parted lips. Poor thing. Pregnancy, magical battles, and now this midnight road trip to catch the town's biggest blabbermouth. But what if I need her?

"You think we should wake her?" I whisper to Peter.

"Your Witch-friend needs rest," he mutters, returning to his beeping gadget. "Baby witches need it even more."

Wait. How did this tattooed Druid know Cynthia's pregnant? I shoot him another glance in the mirror. "You some kind of psychic Druid?"

He snorts. "Don't need magic to see what's obvious. Her aura is split. You didn't notice?"

"Of course, I did. Just didn't know you see auras." Insufferable jerk. Another Mystical who can see auras? Damn, that kind of sucks not having a monopoly on that ability. Sure, it's a petty way to feel; sue me.

Cynthia stirs beside me, rubbing her eyes. "Are we there yet?" She yawns, stretching her arms forward like a cat waking from a nap.

"Almost. How are you feeling?"

"Like I could eat an entire cow," she mumbles, patting her stomach.

When I reach over to touch Cynthia's arm, it's like touching a battery that's down to its last spark. The energy coming off her is weaker than my willpower at an all-you-can-eat buffet.

"You okay there, Mama Witch?" I ask, keeping my voice light while my insides twist with worry.

She forces a smile that wouldn't convince a blind man. "I'm fine. Just tired."

"Bullshit. I can literally feel how not fine you are." I tap my fingers. "These babies don't lie."

"Yeah." Cynthia sighs, "Whatever Libby did earlier helped, but..."

"But it's worn off." Another glance in the rear-view at Peter, who is pretending not to listen while obviously hanging on every word. "Look, when we get to Beth, I'm taking the lead."

"But—"

"No buts, except yours...staying in the car." I squeeze her hand. "You need to think about the baby. This stress isn't exactly what the doctor ordered." I want to slap myself, then Shannon upside the head; Cynthia shouldn't be here; she should be home getting her feet massaged.

"I can handle it," she protests, but her voice lacks its usual fire.

"Sure, you can. And I can resist fudge brownies. We both know that's a lie." I merge into the exit lane. "Seriously, Cynthia. Let me handle Beth. You've got enough going on in there." I nod toward her stomach.

Cynthia just nods and leans back against the headrest. What really freaks me out is that she doesn't argue back.

"Fine," she whispers. "Just make Beth delete everything when we get to her."

Peter Bond grunts from the backseat. "A mile ahead. Motel on the right."

I tighten my grip on the wheel. "Time to crash Beth's little social media party."

I pull up to the curb as the Knight's Inn sign flickers above us. The neon "Vacancy" blinks like a warning sign.

"Thank God this is almost over," I sigh, drumming my fingers on the steering wheel. "Just one social media influencer to throttle and we can all go home."

Peter Bond's tracking device lets out one final beep before he switches it off. "Room 14. First floor."

"How specific. And here I thought we'd have to knock on every door asking if they've seen our town's favorite attention-seeking psycho," I mutter, scanning the parking lot.

That's when I spot them—Ida and Eric standing under the motel's buzzing sign like they're posing for the world's most awkward album cover. They both reverted back to their human forms, which is smart. Giant birds of prey would attract more attention than we need right now.

I kill the engine and pop the door open, the humid night air hitting me like a wet blanket. My feet ache as they hit the pavement—these were not the right shoes for a midnight manhunt.

"Let's get this over with," Cynthia says, pushing her door open. "I need a bathroom and a bed. "

"Wait, Cynthia—you're supposed to—"

She steps out of the car, takes two wobbly steps forward, and suddenly doubles over with a cry that makes my blood freeze. Then she's against the side of the car.

"Cynthia!" I rush around the hood, catching her as she slides toward the pavement.

Her face has gone chalk white, her spray of freckles standing out like they've been drawn on with marker. "Something's wrong," she gasps, clutching her abdomen. "It hurts—God, it hurts so bad!"

Eric sprints across the parking lot with Ida on his heels.

"What's wrong?" Eric asks. "Cynthia? What's happening?"

"I don't know! She just collapsed!" My voice sounds shrill even to my own ears.

The sensation sparking from Cynthia is like touching a live wire—pain, fear, and something else... something darker that makes my stomach twist into knots.

"We need to get her to a hospital," I say, looking up at Eric's worried face. "Now."

He scoops her up and settles Cynthia into the car in a flash. Without a word to us, he jumps behind the wheel and they're speeding off into the night, burning rubber. Please let them both be okay. I'll give up chocolate for a month. Two months. Hell, I'll eat kale for breakfast if that helps.

"This wasn't part of the plan," Peter Bond snipes behind me, fiddling with his tracking device. "We're wasting time while Beth could be—"

I whirl around so fast my neck cracks. "It wasn't part of Cynthia's plan either, so put a lid on it! My friend might be losing her baby while we stand in a crappy motel parking lot."

Peter looks like I slapped him with a wet fish, but honestly, I couldn't care less. Ida steps between us.

"Mary-Jane's right," she says. "But we still need to handle Beth."

I take a deep breath and look at Room 14. The curtains are drawn, but there's light seeping through the edges. She's in there, probably posting more magical exposé while I'm out here having a meltdown.

"How the hell did she even get here?" I mutter, scanning the parking lot. "There's no car."

Ida snorts. "No doubt her accomplices brought her. Damned Fae are strong; they could have easily flown her here."

I straighten my shoulders and face the door. It's just me, Ida, and Peter with his magic tracking box. The 'A-team' we are not. An oversexed Shifter, an obnoxious Druid...

"I can do this," I tell myself, not believing it for a second. Yeah, practicing making brownies float across the kitchen and reading Ray's thoughts about my ass. Not exactly high-stakes witch work.

Peter's device beeps loudly. "She's definitely in there."

I take another deep breath. Shannon would know exactly what to do. Libby would have a clever plan. Cynthia would just kick the freaking door down.

But they're not here. It's just me. Can I do this?

I square my shoulders, take a deep breath, and march toward Room 14 like I'm heading into battle—which, let's be honest, I kind of am. My hand rises to knock, but then I pause.

What am I, an idiot? I'm a freaking Witch!

With a smirk, I flick my fingers at the door, channeling all my irritation into my hand. The lock clicks, and the door flies open so hard it bangs against the wall.

Beth James jerks up from sitting cross-legged on the sagging motel bed, her laptop balanced on her knees. A junk food graveyard—empty Doritos bags, candy wrappers, and enough soda bottles to give a dentist nightmares—surrounds her. Her hair is frizzed out, and she's wearing the same clothes from three days ago.

Her eyes widen like a cartoon character. For one beautiful second, pure shock shows on her face—but then it's gone, replaced by narrowed eyes and a sneer that would make the Grinch proud.

"Well, well, well," she cackles, typing something with dramatic flair. "If it isn't Betty Crocker, the Kitchen Witch. Come to whip up a spell to save your sorry asses?"

I step further into the room, Ida and Peter flanking me like we're some kind of supernatural SEAL team.

"Game's over, Beth. Delete the posts."

She throws her head back and laughs—an actual "mwahahaha" villain laugh that would be comical if I weren't so damn tired.

"You're too late!" She gestures to her screen like she's Vanna White revealing a prize. "The world knows all about you and your witch pals. It's not just people who'll be going to Wesley, but T.V. reporters too. You and your friends are finished."

I march over and plant myself right in her face, close enough to smell the stale Doritos on her breath. My nostrils flare. If looks could kill, she'd be six feet under with a tombstone reading, "Here lies Beth James: She fucked around and found out."

"Listen here, you vindictive harpy," I snarl, jabbing a finger at her chest. "You think you're so damn clever with your little social media campaign? Congratulations on being the biggest attention whore in three counties."

Beth flinches but manages to scoff. "Back off, Kitchen Witch, before I livestream this harassment. I bet your restaurant health inspection would get a shock seeing what's really cooking in your cauldron."

I laugh—a humorless bark that makes even Peter Bond take a step back.

"Oh, honey, you have no idea who you're messing with." I press my palm against her arm, and holy shit—the hatred pouring off this woman makes me want to take a bleach bath. But beneath it, I feel something else... A sad, pathetic need to matter.

When I lock eyes with her, the smug satisfaction on her face makes me want to turn her into something slimy with warts. Maybe later.

"You think you've won?" I press my fingers harder against her arm, feeling the pulse of her thoughts—petty, vindictive, and pathetic. "Let me tell you something about real power, Beth. It isn't posting grainy photos on Facebook for a few likes."

She yanks her arm away. "Don't touch me, Witch! My posts have gone viral. Everyone's coming to see the freak show in Wesley."

From the corner of my eye, I see Peter sit on the bed and grab the laptop. He immediately begins typing, his tattooed fingers flying across the keyboard like he's Elton John.

He lets out a hoot of laughter. "I'm in!"

Beth turns on him, lunging across the bed. "Don't you dare! That's my laptop!"

Ida grabs her by the shoulders, her red-painted nails digging into Beth's blouse. For a middle-aged shifter, Ida's got the grip strength of a professional arm wrestler.

"It's over, Beth," I say, watching Peter work his magic—the keyboard-clacking kind. "Your posts will be updated to show this was all a giant prank. A desperate cry for attention from Wesley's most pathetic resident."

"Child's play to fix this," Peter laughs, not even looking up from the screen.

Beth shrugs out of Ida's grip and slumps onto the bed, her shoulders sagging like a deflated cake. "It doesn't matter. People will still come to Wesley. Everyone will know. It doesn't matter what that old geezer writes."

Peter mutters, "Old geezer who's crushing your ass on social media."

I stare at Beth's crumpled form on the bed, and damn it all, a twinge of pity goes through me. She's like a deflated balloon animal—all the hot air gone, leaving nothing but sad, wrinkled rubber.

"Why?" I ask, softening my tone. "This can't be just about your brother being with Cynthia."

Beth's eyes fill with tears, and one escapes to track a mascara-stained path down her cheek. "Isn't that enough? It wasn't bad enough that my brother is one of you, a freak of nature, but then he takes up with a skanky Witch? A witch who's slept with every guy in Wesley."

Peter looks up from the laptop with an expression of disappointment. "Not me. Looks like I missed that window of opportunity."

Ida and I exchange a look that could only be described as the universal female "men are idiots" glance. I turn back to Beth, crossing my arms.

"Cynthia only dated single guys. Guys her own age," I say firmly. "And right now, she might be losing her baby because of this little stunt you pulled."

Beth's head snaps up. "Baby? Is she losing the baby?"

"Yeah, Eric's baby," I say, watching her face carefully, trying to see if she's happy or sad at this news. "Your brother is going to be a father, and right now he's rushing his pregnant girlfriend to the hospital because the stress of your revenge tour might have caused her to miscarry."

TWENTY-FIVE

MARY-JANE

Beth's face is vacant as we stare at each other. "Don't you give a damn?" I bark at her.

Ida shifts uncomfortably beside me, and Peter stops typing, the room suddenly quiet except for the hum of the ancient motel air conditioner.

Finally, I get a response. "I didn't... I never..." Her shoulders slump.

"Never what?" Now she won't look me in the eye; her eyes dart around like a housefly on meth. "Why?" I ask, stepping closer to Beth. "Why did you do all this? Try to hurt so many people? What the hell were you trying to accomplish?"

From the bed, Peter grunts, "Great question."

Beth gapes at me, her eyes brimming with tears. Finally, it's sinking in. I think. "I...I don't know..."

"BULLSHIT!" My hands start to actually tingle. I hold one up to look at it. Oh boy...this must be how Shannon feels when she gets ready to throw fireballs, because there's a blue-white orb of energy floating over my palm.

Beth jumps away from me. "Don't do it! Please don't hurt me!"

'Calm down, Mary-Jane,' the adult voice says in my head. 'Don't let this get out of hand.' I take a deep breath and give my hand a shake. That blue-white ball of rage fades away. I look over at Beth. "Nobody's going to hurt you. But you've got some serious, and I mean serious 'splaining to do. Why the hell did you start all this shit?"

Her voice cracks as she speaks. "I didn't know. All of this was never my intention. Especially not the baby, not Eric's kid." She sobs, covering her face with her hands.

Shit. Now what? I look over at Ida, who just shrugs at me. I glance over at Peter, who rolls his eyes and goes back to the laptop with a sigh. Great.

Beth is standing there, shoulders heaving as she wails into her hands. I take her by the shoulders and guide her to the vacant bed in the room. "Sit down, Beth," I say. She shuffles over and sits on the bed. I look over at Ida, and touch my schnozz. She gets the message, hops into the bathroom and comes back with a box of tissues.

Beth's still honking and bawling. I gently take her hands away from her face—whoa! Her mascara is leaving runny streaks on her cheeks Alice Cooper would envy. I hand her a wad of tissues and she wipes her face. I stay silent, waiting for her to speak.

"I must look a mess," she says.

"Oh yeah," Pete pipes up. Men!

"Why, Beth?"

Her lips form a thin line. "It's your fault."

"What? Are you freaking kidding me? What the hell did I ever do to you? I barely know you!"

She shakes her hand at me. "Not just you...all of you! But you and your cool girls' club was the last damn straw."

She looks over at me. "It was hard enough to be the only member of my family who wasn't a Mystical, Mary-Jane. I mean, I didn't even find out they existed until Eric changed when I was twenty! He was fourteen, and the puberty train arrived."

"What?"

"He came screaming out of the bathroom!"

Peter lets out a short laugh and looks up from his work. "Fourteen-year-old boy and in the bathroom? Oh, yeah..."

"Shut the hell up, Peter," Ida says. "You have a dirty mind."

Beth looks at both of them and back at me. "He was screaming because he was..." her eyes went wide. "He...he was some weird thing! His arms were like...half wings, and he had this huge beak where his mouth was supposed to be! Shit, it was terrifying! I screamed too!"

I stare at her. "It was the first time he shifted?"

"Well, YEAH! But I didn't know that! I didn't know anything! I didn't know about Shape-Shifters or Druids! I was all like 'What's happening to you!' I thought he had done so weird drugs or something! So, he's standing in the living room, thrashing around..."

And in a tiny voice, she says, "...and my baby brother turned into a humongous bald eagle! He's flapping these enormous wings, blowing pictures off the walls, flinging stuff off shelves and toppling lamps!"

"Wow," Ida says. "I only turned into a freaking cat! A regular-sized house cat!"

"Not Eric! So I'm in the living room, screaming blue murder, Eric's screaming blue murder—then he starts that eagle cawing!" She covers her ears at the memory. "It could break glass!" She's breathing raggedly, reliving the moment. "I start yelling for our Dad—he was in the garage or something."

Beth takes a deep breath. "My father comes running in and he wasn't scared or anything. Eric's wings are flapping like flags in a tornado, and Dad just walks right up to him. He grabs one wing and steps into Eric. He cups Eric's...face, I guess; but it wasn't a face anymore—it was an eagle's head!" She looks around the room. "My brother turned into a freaking eagle!"

"Wow, Beth. Then what?"

Dad guides him out of the living room, to the patio doors out back. He yanks them open, says something to Eric, and he flies away!"

Beth starts crying again. "I'm hysterical in the living room. Sitting on the floor which looks like a bomb went off." She shakes her head slowly. "Dad comes back in and says something like 'We need to talk' or some shit like that."

"Ya think!" Ida says. "At least my parents told me it would happen!"

Beth's face knots in rage. "They didn't tell us ANYTHING! It came right out of the blue!" Her face turns to stone. "And then it began..."

"What began?" I ask.

She looks at me. "That was more than twenty years ago, you know. I was working at the Furniture Mart..." she scoffs. "I'm still there, by the way; really tearing up the world, right?" She lets out a sigh. "What began was all about how special Eric was. How he was a Shifter, and all that crap about 'The Mysticals of Wesley' and all that shit."

She flings her wad of tissue away. "And how my parents are Shifters too!" In a disgusted voice, she goes on. "But Beth? First-born child? Nuthin'.

Not a Shifter, not a Fae." She shoots a look at Peter. "Not even a lousy, stinking Druid!"

"Hey!" he yells back. "I'll have you know—"

"Not now, Peter. Get back to work," I say. He grunts, and I turn back to Beth. "So...?"

"So, nothing! I'm just a normie. I find out about how there's all these freaks in town, and how we have to keep it secret. But once word got out that I did know, you freaking Mysticals rubbed my face in it all the freaking time!" She shoots a look that could kill at Ida. "Right, Ida?"

"It was a joke!" she says.

"Some joke! A freaking BOA CONSTRICTOR in the woods?"

Ida snorts. "It was kinda funny, you have to admit that."

"I PEED MY PANTS!" Beth jumps to her feet.

"Ida..." I say.

"Yeah...okay... Sorry, Beth. I was just trying to be funny. My bad."

Beth reels around on me, jabbing a finger at Ida. "That's been my freaking life for the last twenty damn years! Because I wasn't a 'full normie' and had Mysticals in my family, they pulled shit like that all the time!" She jabs another finger at Ida. "Because they knew I couldn't do a damn thing about it!"

"Hey..." Ida says, stepping over to Beth. "I didn't realize that. I'm genuinely sorry, Beth." She tries to put her hand on Beth's shoulder, but it's knocked away. "I'm sorry." She goes back and sits on the other bed beside Peter.

"Too little, and too late, Ida." She wheels onto me now. "I put up with all the teasing, and being left out of the so-called Council for twenty damn years. But then...you and your friends show up! A freaking full-blood normie one day, and the next freaking day a god-damned Witch!"

"Uh...it really wasn't quite like that, Beth."

"Who the hell gives a damn!" She throws her arms open wide. "So now you and your girls are the head of the Council, and I have to watch!" She points a finger at me. "The only ones who gave a damn about me are the Fae."

"Why the Fae?"

"Because Ivy Miller and I had been friends since the first grade. She transitioned when she was twelve. She didn't tell me until Eric transitioned and word got around. And as soon as she found out, she told me the truth." Beth crossed her arms across her chest, staring at Ida. "No Fae ever, and I mean ever pulled stupid pranks on me. Not like the Shifters, or Werewolves or the rest of you." She turns to me. "They were kind to me, Mary-Jane. You have any idea what that word means?"

"Hey! I didn't do anything to you!"

"Screw you, bitch. You stood right there in the middle of town with your thumb up your ass when they imprisoned me." She pointed all around the room. "It wasn't until I was a threat to your super-duper secret that any of you gave a shit." She leaned into me, putting her streaked face right up to mine. "And it's only now that you bother to ask me 'why'. Screw you, MJ."

She's right. Now it's my turn to feel like shit. I don't say a word. What the hell can I say? I hang my head.

Beth continues. "I wanted things to be different. If not for me, at least for the Fae. You Mysticals treat them like shit." Her voice cracks. "But...I didn't want my brother's baby to suffer for it!"

I put my hand on her shoulder, and the wall hits me. Holy crap, she's actually sincere. What floods into me is loneliness. Bone-deep, soul-crushing isolation. And beneath that, a desperate need to matter.

I take a deep breath, trying to fight the wave of sympathy that rolls through me, but failing miserably. It's like trying not to eat the last cookie when you're on a diet—technically possible but against all laws of nature. "We all want to matter, Beth," I say in a low voice.

"Yeah; I'm such a big deal now, aren't I? Every Mystical in town is on my case, all scared of me for a change." She takes a deep breath. "And now I'm killing my brother's kid!" She covers her face again.

"What are you going to do to me?" she whispers, and for the first time, I see fear.

Peter looks up from the laptop, his bushy eyebrows raised like two caterpillars. "Almost done here."

"We're not monsters," I tell her.

"Some of you suck blood to stay alive, MJ."

I put my hand on Beth's arm again, and this time she doesn't pull away. As I hold her arm, another image filters through—Ivy, sitting with Beth at a coffee shop, both of them laughing. Beth's guard down, her smile genuine.

"Except for Ivy," I say with a small smile. "You and Ivy are friends. The only person you let your guard down with and let her see who you are."

Ida steps forward, her blue eyes soft with understanding. "We've all experienced being outsiders, Beth. I didn't transform until I was much, older. When my change happened, when I became a Shifter, my marriage almost ended. I felt alone for a very long time, until we could reconcile our differences. But we did."

Ida smooths her slightly wrinkled blouse, a nervous habit I've noticed. "Lowell thought I was cheating when I'd disappear at night. He had no idea I was running through the woods as a bobcat. Or slithering like a snake..."

Ida shrugs. "Yeah...like I said, sorry about that."

"Even Peter over there is alone," I add, gesturing toward our grouchy companion. "His choice, he says, but I wonder..."

He looks up from the laptop, his face hardening like cement. "Don't drag me into your Hallmark moment," he growls. "I live the way I do by choice. After putting up with all the horseshit in the army, I wanted nothing to do with anyone again. Hell, I can hardly stomach sitting here listening to you three."

He taps a few buttons and grins, "Done! I've made memes and tried to undo everything she posted." He snaps the laptop shut and looks over at us. "We'll see if it worked tomorrow, I suppose."

My fingers tremble slightly as I pull out my phone. I've got to see if Cynthia's okay. I punch in her number and hold my breath. The seconds it takes for someone to answer feel like hours.

"Hello?" It's Eric, not Cynthia. My stomach drops.

"Eric! What's going on? Is she okay?" The words tumble out of me.

"She's been admitted. They're giving her intravenous right now and are monitoring her and the baby," Eric says, relief coming through in his tone.

Closing my eyes, I let out a long breath, leaning against the wall to steady myself. "That's great news," I try to keep my voice from cracking. "We've got Beth, and we're doing what we can to undo the damage."

Beth's been watching me, and I notice something shift in her expression. Her eyes soften just a fraction, and she reaches toward me with a hesitant hand.

"Can I talk to him?" she asks quietly.

I hesitate, studying her face. The vindictive Beth from earlier seems to have retreated, replaced by someone who looks... remorseful? I hand her the phone, watching her carefully.

"Eric? It's Beth." She pauses, listening. "I'm sorry. I really am." Her voice hitches a little. "I hope Cynthia is okay, and the baby too."

When I take in Beth's mascara-streaked face and puffy eyes, it's hard to stay angry. Sure, she created a tsunami of crap for all of us, but honestly? I can't help but feel for her.

"You okay?" I ask, taking my phone back after she ends the call with Eric.

She doesn't answer. I nudge her. "You know, Ida apologized to you. And I did too. Did your brother forgive you?"

"He said don't worry about it—the baby's fine." A small sob escapes.

"So, he forgave you. Maybe you should work on forgiving others."

She just nods. A strange warmth spreads through my chest. Wow. I handled this. Me. Mary-Jane Matthews. Not Shannon with her dramatic weather control, not Libby with her healing touch, not Cynthia with her fireballs. Just me, with a bit of Witchcraft and a lot of empathy.

Peter stands up, stretching his back with a series of alarming cracks. "Well, this has been real special, but I'd like to get home sometime this century. How much longer is your bird-boy gonna be with the car?"

"Eric's at the hospital with Cynthia," I remind him, narrowing my eyes. "They're a bit busy right now."

"Great," he huffs, "so I'm stuck in a fleabag motel with you three. Perfect end to a perfect day."

Ida rolls her eyes. "Always the charmer, Pete."

I pull out my phone and open the Uber app. "We'll call an Uber to get us home. There's no point in waiting around."

Looking over at Beth, I make a decision that surprises even me. "You're coming with me to my house."

Beth's head snaps up. "What?"

"You heard me. I can't promise you that everyone is going to understand and not want to punish you, but I'll help you as much as I can."

For a moment, I can hardly believe what I'm saying. Am I actually forgiving this woman? After everything she's done?

But I am. And that's oddly liberating.

"Why would you do that for me?" Beth asks, suspicion clouding her face.

I shrug. "Because everyone deserves a second chance. Even you."

Twenty-Six

Libby

Every nerve in my body begs for rest, but I pry my eyelids open. I fumble for my phone to check the time. Damn, 7:30 a.m. Feels more like death-thirty.

Stan snores beside me, blissfully unaware that my world has tilted on its axis. My son is a Werewolf. A freaking Werewolf. Not exactly what I had in mind when I worried about his college applications.

The phone shows MJ's message from 2:40 a.m. Damn Stan and his "let's turn off notifications so you can sleep" logic! I read the text:

> Cynthia is in the hospital, but she and baby OK. We found Beth and she's at my house. Peter added to FB posts saying it was all a prank. Call when you wake up.
>
> P.S. Hope you aren't too freaked out about Kevin's furry situation.
>
> ~~It'll be okay.~~

I bolt upright, my heart hammering against my ribs. Cynthia's in the hospital? And MJ has Beth? Oh man, this is gonna be some day...

"Stan," I hiss, nudging his shoulder. "Wake up."

He grunts something that sounds suspiciously like “five more minutes” and rolls over.

I jerk at the sound of paws scratching at my bedroom door, followed by what can only be described as that snippy cat cursing at me.

“Hey Witch! Open up! We got a situation out here!”

Great. Add Ms. Purdy cat first thing in the morning to this day. Because apparently, my life isn’t complicated enough with one son sprouting fur and fangs, another hoping to join him, and a daughter who thinks talking to skunks is her ticket to fame.

“Coming!” I call, throwing back the covers. “If you don’t stop scratching my door, you’re going to be one life short.”

“Whatever. Just hurry up. There’re reporters setting up cameras on our front lawn, and unless you want Kevin’s first full moon broadcast on the six o’clock news, you better get your Witch ass moving!”

REPORTERS? I stumble to the window and peek through the curtains. Sure enough, there’s a news van parked at the curb.

Oh, for the love of Mike.

My phone rings, nearly vibrating itself off the nightstand, and I grab it. It’s Shannon.

“Stan! Get up! There are reporters swarming the house like a god-damn SWAT team!” I screech, jabbing him with my elbow while jamming the phone to my ear."Shannon? Please tell me the world hasn’t completely gone to shit in the last four hours," I gasp."MJ’s on the call, too," Shannon says. “I just talked to Eric. Cynthia’s resting and seems okay.”

“That’s great. But what do I do about CNN camping out on my front lawn? There’s a guy with a microphone who looks like he’s auditioning for America’s Next Top Newscaster, and I’m pretty sure that’s someone from Fox News is trying to peek through my bathroom window!”

“Oh my god, us too!” MJ’s voice cuts in. “Ray just came back inside from putting the garbage out, and now they’re going through it! Like, literally digging through our trash looking for...oh hell, I don’t know what.”

Stan stumbles to the window, parts the curtain, and turns as white as my grandmother’s antique porcelain.

“No news crew here,” Shannon sighs with relief. “A blessing of living in the boondocks, I guess.”

“So, what do we do?” I ask, watching a woman with perfect hair arrange lighting equipment next to my hydrangeas. “Cause whatever that druid did to Beth's social media sure didn't work! Peter might be a tech genius in his own mind, but he's about as effective as a screen door on a submarine!"

I clench my teeth watching a TV news reporter in my front yard, hair shellacked into perfect submission, chase a raccoon around my bird bath, with a microphone clenched in its teeth. Could that be Ida?

"Stan, get dressed," I toss his jeans at him. Damn. Talk about a rude awakening this morning. I'll be lucky if I don't have a coronary.

My phone squawks with Shannon's voice. "Damn. I'd hoped we could all go to the Well to get some pointers on all this from Judith, but I guess we have to wing it."

"Wing it?" I sputter. "How's that gonna work when the entire world knows we're Witches?" Winging it has never been my strength.

"Get away from that window, Beth!" MJ's voice blares over the phone. "Ray! Take care of her, will you?"

My bedroom door flies open with a bang that makes me jump. Jack and Dahlia tumble in, talking over each other at warp speed, which makes my ears hurt.

"Mom! There's like twenty people outside—"

"—and some lady tried to give me fifty bucks for a lock of your hair—"

"—and some dude asked if we could turn him into a newt—"

"—and there's a raccoon biting ankles and now someone's chasing it with a microphone—"

"STOP." I hold up my hand like a traffic cop. "Both of you. Go check on your brother and make sure he isn't going into Werewolf mode. The last thing we need is Kevin going full tilt hairy on the six o'clock news."

They bolt from the room, arguing about whether Kevin's transformation would get more YouTube views than Dahlia's skunk whispering.

I press the phone back to my ear where Shannon is mid-sentence.

"—just need to present a united front and—"

"What? You'll have to repeat that as it's bedlam here," I cut in, watching Stan hop around trying to get his pants on. "What are we going to do?"

Stan pulls his shirt on inside-out while trying to peer through the blinds without being spotted. The circus outside is getting louder by the minute.

"We are on our own with this, as the Mayor made perfectly clear," Shannon says. "We tried to pass Beth's posts off as pranks, but the media's not buying it. So we have to stand together and prove to them this is a prank."

"Like what?" Mary-Jane asks.

"Maybe a publicity stunt for some...some movie or theatrical thing?"

"That's a great idea! Like Into the Woods!" MJ squeals, like she's mainlining Red Bull. "Remember when the high school drama class did that play in our restaurant? But this time, we've got actual Werewolves, Fairies and Druids for the parts."

A lightbulb flares in my brain, remembering. Jack and Chloe had been amazing in that play last year. Who knew at the time that my other son could actually be the Werewolf in that play now?

"It could work," I say, dodging as Stan nearly trips over his own feet trying to put on socks. "But we need to get the town in on it to pull this off."

"The park!" MJ practically shrieks. "This thing's too big for the restaurant. It can be hyped as a spring festival, welcoming summer. I'll make some calls to the high school to get costumes and everything."

"Dahlia can design posters and flyers," I say, warming to the idea. "Jack and Chloe can star again, and we can write some more Witch parts in."

Stan gives me a thumbs-up from across the room, finally dressed but with his shirt still inside out and backward. Good enough.

"I'll talk to the mayor and Duncan and Ida," Shannon adds. "If the Fae help us do this, it will earn them some respect. I'll find Jane and get the ball rolling while you guys deal with the reporters."

I glance at the window where I can see a woman edging closer to Ida the raccoon, who's now sitting on my birdbath looking smug.

"Deal with reporters. Right." I take a deep breath. "How hard can it be?"

"What about Beth?" MJ's voice is blessedly lower.

"She needs to get onside with this." Shannon answers, "Make her the play's manager and PR point person if we have to. You need to handle that, MJ. As for Cynthia, we leave her out of it."

My eyes narrow at the thought. "Yeah. Letting Beth play boss might actually be the perfect punishment. Nothing worse than having to clean up your own mess."

"We'll touch base at four to see how things are going," Shannon says before hanging up.

The bedroom door flies open again, and all three of my children crowd in. Kevin looks blessedly normal—no fur, no fangs, no claws. Just my college-bound son with bags under his eyes and serious bedhead.

"Oh thank heavens," I breathe, "You're not wolfing out."

"Not yet, no." Kevin runs a hand through his hair. "Wayne said it'll only happen with intense emotion or the full moon until I learn control."

"Intense like watching your mom hold a press conference on the front lawn?" Jack asks, grinning like this is the best day of his life.

"Or learning you'd give anything to become a Werewolf, too?" Dahlia adds, elbowing Jack.

I sigh, looking at my kids—one reluctant Werewolf, one wannabe Werewolf, and one wannabe Witch. Only a month ago, my biggest worries were Jack's detention record and Kevin's college applications.

"So, what's the plan, Mom?" Kevin asks, folding his arms. "Because there's a guy out there now offering five hundred bucks for a lock of your hair, and Jack was seriously considering the business opportunity."

Twenty-Seven

Shannon

I hang up the phone and toss it on the counter. "Well, this is just freaking perfect, isn't it?"

Devon looks up from where he's flipping pancakes, spatula suspended mid-air. "What's wrong now? Did someone else grow fur or sprout wings?"

"Worse." I grab a mug and pour coffee, gulping it black even though it scalds my throat. "The media has descended. They're camped outside MJ's and Libby's houses like vultures on roadkill."

Jessica pauses with a forkful of pancake halfway to her mouth. "So, Peter Bond's social media cleanup didn't work, huh?"

"Bingo." I slump against the counter. "We're officially screwed. Beth's posts went viral, and now every paranormal enthusiast and tabloid reporter in the country is converging on Wesley."

Robert stretches on the kitchen floor. "Another day, another catastrophe?" He yawns, showing impressive fangs. "Should I start practicing my circus cat routine for the cameras?"

I give him a dirty look. "You've never done tricks for me."

He stretches. "You never asked."

True, but still... I let out a sigh. "We're going with Plan Desperate." I take another hit of coffee. "We're telling everyone it's all publicity for a theatrical production of 'Into the Woods' that the town's putting on. Just one big marketing stunt."

Devon's eyebrows shoot up as he slides a pancake onto a plate. "That's... actually... not terrible. A theatrical cover story could work."

"It better," I mutter. "Otherwise, we'll be the star attraction at the Salem Witch Trials: The Sequel." Or worse, if The Men In Black show up; but I keep that quiet.

Jessica snorts milk through her nose. "Oh my god, Mom. You're going to turn the whole town into a Broadway production overnight? That's insane."

"Welcome to my life." I gesture wildly with my coffee mug. "Where insane is Tuesday's breakfast special."

I set my mug down with a thunk that makes Robert's ear twitch. "Okay, so we've got a plan. Not a great plan, but it's the only one we've got. We'll need everyone to pull this off—Druids, Shifters, Werewolves, the whole supernatural shebang."

Jessica pokes at her pancakes, her earlier enthusiasm suddenly fading. She won't meet my eyes.

"What?" I ask, that maternal sixth sense tingling. "What's with the doom face?"

She takes a deep breath. "Thomas sent me a text." Her voice drops so low I have to lean in. "He's coming to Wesley tomorrow to talk to you, Mom."

"Oh?"

She bites her lower lip. "Dad's bringing him."

The floor seems to drop out from under me, along with my stomach. "Your father?" I croak. "David? Asshat is coming here?"

"Tomorrow," Jessica confirms, wincing.

"Fan-fucking-tastic!" I slam my palm against the counter. "Because dealing with the media circus, rogue fairies, and exposing our entire magical community wasn't enough of a shit sandwich. The universe just had to add my ex-husband as the cherry on top."

Devon walks over and squeezes my shoulder. "Hey, we'll handle it. One catastrophe at a time."

I take a deep breath, forcing my brain to compartmentalize. "Right. Tomorrow's problems can wait until tomorrow. Today we've got a theatrical production to fake."

I grab his hand. "I need you to visit Duncan. Tell him what's going on with this whole theater charade. Then—and this is the big one—I need you to get a work crew together and build a stage in the park. With curtains, lights, the whole enchilada."

Instead of the expected groan, Devon drains his coffee in one gulp and heads for the door. He pauses, popping his head back in. "You need this by when?"

"Tomorrow." I wince, hearing how impossible it sounds. "If you can manage it."

I reconsider as I see his eyes widen. "Actually, scratch that. You'd better manage it. Or we're all going to be the next reality TV sensation: 'Real Witches of Wesley.'"

Devon salutes and disappears, the door slamming behind him.

"Jessica," I say, whirling around to face my daughter, who's still picking at her pancakes. "Get back to your brother and tell him we have something really special happening and he won't want to miss it."

She looks up, eyes wide. "What am I supposed to tell him exactly? 'Hey bro, Mom's a Witch and the town is full of supernatural creatures, but don't worry—we're pretending it's all fake so we don't end up as government lab rats?'"

"Just tell him we're putting on the theatrical event of the century and we need his engineering brain to help with special effects." I gulp down the rest of my coffee, wincing as the bitter dregs hit my tongue. "Nothing brings a family together like staging a fake play to hide real magic."

"Riiiight." Jessica rolls her eyes. "Because Thomas is totally going to buy that."

"He'll buy it a hell of a lot easier than the truth." I slam my mug into the sink. "Now grab your witch cloak."

"My what?"

"Your witch cloak. The blue one I gave you the other day. Shit! That was just the other day. Feels like a lifetime ago."

"Why? Am I starring in this fake play?"

I throw my hands up. "We need you in costume, handing out waybills for the play to everyone downtown. I'll drop you at Libby's. We'll have you work on this with Dahlia."

"You want me to parade around town dressed like a Witch?" Jessica stares at me like I've sprouted a second head. "After actual photos of actual Witches just went viral?"

"That's exactly the point." I grab my car keys. "Hide in plain sight. It's so obvious, it's brilliant."

"So obvious, it's insane," she mutters, but she's already following me to the door.

Robert stretches and pads after us. "Should I come along? I could do some cute tricks, really sell this whole theatrical angle."

"No," Jessica and I say in unison, although she shrugs as she has no idea what he said..

"A wild bobcat doing circus tricks might be a tad suspicious," I add, scratching behind his ear. "Stay here and guard the house from reporters. If any show up, just... look menacing but don't eat anyone."

I push through the crowd outside City Hall like Moses parting the Red Sea. As I wade through the scrum, reporters shove microphones in my face while witch-fans wave homemade "Hex Me!" signs.

"Are you the head Witch?" A sweaty man in a 'Wiccan Power' t-shirt blocks my path.

"No, I'm the head of the Wesley Community Theater." I flash my fakest smile. "Come see our production tomorrow!"

I duck under a boom mic and sidestep a woman trying to hand me crystals "for protection."

If only she knew I could conjure a lightning bolt with my pinky finger.

Mayor Sadler's receptionist, Sarah, gives me a bright smile as I burst through the door. "The Mayor's expecting you."

Of course he is. Vampires have excellent hearing.

When I enter his office, Jeffrey Sadler is peering through the blinds like a kid watching an ice cream truck pull up.

"Shannon! Our town savior!" He turns with a grin that's entirely too enthusiastic. "Tell me more about your theatrical plan."

I explain our idea for the fake production while he nods vigorously.

"Brilliant! Simply brilliant!" He rubs his hands together. "We'll set up a beer tent, food vendors, music—think of the revenue!"

Narrowing my eyes, "You're pretty damned excited about this. What happened to culpable deniability? That we witches are on our own?"

"My dear," he chuckles, "humans are so delightfully gullible. They'll believe anything if you charge admission. Besides," he taps his temple, "Vampiric suggestion works wonders on skeptics."

"So, you'll help?"

"The town council will provide full support." He winks. "And a few of us will be on hand for crowd control of the… mental variety."

Wow. Totally didn't expect that. As I leave his office, my phone rings and Devon's name flashes on the screen.

"Hey, how'd it go with Duncan?" I ask.

"Well…" His voice drops to a whisper. "Let's just say I should have knocked louder."

"What do you mean?"

"I walked in on Duncan and Jane. They were, uh… 'experimenting' with some magical vines."

"Eww! Stop right there." I grimace. "I do not need those mental images."

Devon laughs. "Let's just say Druids really know how to use nature magic creatively." He chuckles. "And what that man was doing with ferns would—"

"I'm hanging up now."

"Wait! The stage crew is already working. We'll have everything ready by tomorrow."

"That's the best news I've heard all day."

I stumble out of City Hall feeling like I've entered the Twilight Zone.

The street looks like Woodstock for the magically curious. People in pointy hats, crystal necklaces, and t-shirts with slogans like *'Witch, Please'* mill around taking selfies in front of Wesley's quaint buildings.

"For fuck's sake," I mutter, watching a man in a pentagram cape trying to levitate a mailbox with jazz hands.

My phone buzzes with a text from MJ:

How'd it go with Mayor Bloodsucker?

I type back:

Surprisingly well. He's all for it. Probably sees dollar signs instead of blood bags.

Stan's pickup pulls to the curb across the street, and out tumble Dahlia and Jessica in full witch regalia—pointy hats, flowing black capes, and matching satchels bulging with flyers. Wow. They even have striped hosiery and buckled shoes!

"Holy crap," I say, squinting at the enormous stacks of paper they're hauling. "How'd you manage that?"

Jessica grins. "Dahlia designed them, and then MJ worked her magic getting copies."

Before I get a chance to ask more, an RV rumbles down Main Street. On its side, the phrase "Magical Mystery Tour" is emblazoned in bright colors. Two middle-aged women are in the front seat, staring at me. Just great. More weirdos.

"You've got to be kidding me," I groan. "What next? Reporters, Witch-crazed people, and now tourists doing a magical mystery tour?"

"Cool!" Jessica says, waving at the RV. "They're totally buying it!"

"This isn't Disney World," I hiss, pulling her arm down. "And stop encouraging them!"

The RV honks twice, and someone yells, "You go, girl!" out the window.

"Right." I mutter. "How about magically making their tires flatten."

I spot the news van parked across the street, emblazoned with Channel 6 News on the side. A blousy blonde with hair that defies both gravity and taste is standing beside it, frantically waving at her cameraman.

"Oh shit," I mutter, grabbing Jessica's arm. "That's Lindsey Wright from Albany. She does those ridiculous 'Weird New York' segments."

The woman's eyes lock with mine, and her face lights up like she just won the lottery.

"There she is!" she shrieks, pointing at me with a manicured talon. "That's the witch from the video!"

Before I can teleport myself to Fiji—which sadly isn't one of my powers yet—she's charging toward me like a rhinoceros in pumps, dragging her poor cameraman behind her.

"It's Shannon Burke, right?" She pants, shoving a microphone in my face. "Lindsey Wright, Channel 6 News. Care to comment on your magical abilities? That video shows you clearly conjuring, doing magic. Is Wesley a haven for Witches?"

My mouth goes dry. My brain short-circuits. I'm about to either vomit or accidentally summon a tornado—both equally disastrous for PR purposes.

I stare at her wild-eyed, my mouth opening and closing, but nothing's coming out. I'm having a complete brain-lock. On camera. Shit!

Then something weird happens. A warm, tingling sensation washes over me, starting at my scalp and flowing down to my toes. It's like someone poured liquid confidence directly into my veins.

I recognize this feeling—magic. But not mine.

Someone's spelling me!

Suddenly, I'm grinning like I've practiced this interview for weeks.

"Lindsey! So glad you made it to Wesley!" I laugh, touching her arm familiarly. "I was hoping the video would draw attention to our little publicity stunt."

"Publicity... stunt?" She repeats, blinking rapidly.

"Yes! For our community theater!" I turn and look into the camera. "'Into the Woods' opens tomorrow. The whole town's involved—special effects, costumes, the works." I wink at the camera. "We're going for immersive theater. Everyone plays a part, even visitors."

Lindsey's eyes glaze over slightly. "Into the Woods... the musical?"

"With a Wesley twist. We've got a very talented special effects team. Those videos? Just teasers." I flip my hair dramatically. "You should see what we can do when we're properly set up!"

The reporter's expression goes vacant, like someone wiped her brain with a magic eraser. She lowers her microphone.

"I... think I have everything I need," she mumbles, turning away. "Good luck with your... play."

I watch in disbelief as she wanders back to her van, shooing away her confused cameraman.

"What the hell just happened?" I whisper, glancing around frantically.

That wasn't me. Someone just magically bailed my ass out of this disaster. But who?

TWENTY-EIGHT

MARY-JANE, THAT EVENING...

I shake my head as I stand with Shannon, Libby and Cynthia in the park watching the last of the makeshift stage being set up. A temporary fence cordons it off, and outside the theatre area, many people and a few reporters lounge in the park. Hoots of laughter and music almost drown out the four of us talking.

"Want something done? Ask a busy woman," I say with just enough smug to feel good.

Shannon replies, "You did a great job."

Cynthia adds, "I can't believe you got all this together so quickly. And it looks like you'll pull it off."

I blow on my fingertips. "Just good business acumen and, of course, a little magic to motivate everyone. The high school was only too happy to do a repeat of the performance."

A crowd swarms the park, buzzing like sugar-high bees around our makeshift stage. If someone had told me a week ago I'd be orchestrating a fake theatrical production to cover up our witchy asses, I'd have laughed myself into a hernia. Yet here I am, clipboard in hand, barking orders like a deranged theater mom.

"The banner needs to be higher!" I yell at Stan, who's balancing on a ladder, shooting a scowl at me. "People in the back can't see 'Into the Woods' when it's hanging at crotch level!"

"I'm doing my best, MJ," he growls. "Unless you want me to levitate, which—news flash—I can't do."

"Need I remind you whose brilliant idea saved us from becoming Salem 2.0?" I tap my clipboard. "Details matter."

Shannon sidles up beside me, looking surprisingly calm for someone whose ex-husband and estranged son are arriving tomorrow. "The mayor just called. He's bringing the entire town council to 'support the arts.'"

"A little late to the party, but whatever." I mutter. "Now that we're saving the town, no doubt he wants to take credit."

Libby takes a deep breath before she asks, "What about Beth? I saw her earlier with Ivy and Alf. I can't believe you just let her go, as if nothing happened."

I wink at her, adjusting my clipboard. "Mary helped with that. A little Druidy thing to make her less tense and erase some of her memories. She's helping Ivy hand out special brownies and some Fae candy to help people have fun."

Shannon rolls her eyes. "In other words, they're all stoned. But whatever works, right? When this is all over, we have to do some serious warding around this town. We definitely don't want a repeat of this. Still, I'm glad that the Mysticals are helping pull this off."

I smile, watching Beth hand a glittery paper bag to an elderly tourist. Pointing at the bag, she whispers in his ear, and he breaks into a grin so wide I worry his dentures might fly out. "It took a bit of arm-twisting and threats to make sure the kids avoid anything Ivy offers."

Truth be told, I didn't just twist arms—I practically dislocated shoulders getting everyone on board. Druids don't exactly hand out memory-altering spells like party favors. Mary agreed only after I promised her exclusive catering rights to the next three town events and a date with Duncan. Suddenly, he's a hot commodity? Go figure.

"The Fae are surprisingly good at crowd control," I watch Suzanne gently redirect a nosy reporter away from Mary, who's dolled up in her Wonder Woman outfit flashing her tats. "Who knew all it would take to get them respect was the crisis they helped create?"

I scan the park with a critical eye, making mental notes of what still needs doing. We've somehow turned this dumpster fire into a community event that might—just might—save us from becoming national news. Cynthia hovers beside me, looking better than she did yesterday, but still with dark circles under her eyes.

"Is there anything I can do to help?" she asks, watching me check items off my list with manic precision.

"Honey, the only thing you need to do is keep that baby happy and your feet up," I tell her, patting her arm. "The last thing we need is another hospital trip. Just relax and enjoy the show tomorrow—from a comfortable chair that I will personally enchant to feel like a cloud."

"But I feel useless," she protests.

"You're growing an entirely new human. That's enough productivity for one person." I adjust a crooked sign. "Besides, someone needs to stay sober enough to remember this disaster for posterity."

Devon and Stan swagger over, both looking pleased with themselves after finishing the stage. Devon's got that look men get when they think they've just saved the day by hammering four boards together.

"Ladies," Devon grins, "there's quite a party starting by the pond. Some of the Fae brought instruments, and I think I just saw the mayor attempting to dance. Care to join in?"

I check my watch and frown. "Much as I'd love to watch Jeffrey attempt the Electric Slide, Ray's at the restaurant dealing with a packed house. Every tourist and reporter needs to eat somewhere, and apparently 'Witch-owned establishment' is the new five-star rating."

"Go," Shannon nudges me. "We've got things covered here."

"You sure?" I ask, already backing away. "Because if one more thing goes wrong—"

"We'll handle it," Libby promises. "Besides, you've earned a break."

"A break?" I laugh, gathering my purse. "I'm trading one chaos for another. The only difference is one pays the bills." I wave goodbye, heading toward my car. "Don't let the Vampires near the punch bowl!" Sorry, but I just don't trust people who suck blood of complete strangers.

I barrel through the restaurant entrance like a Witch on a mission—which, let's face it, I am. The place is so packed with tourists and reporters that I can practically feel my bank account getting fatter with each step.

"Excuse me... coming through... move it or lose it!" I shoulder past a woman wearing a T-shirt that says *'I BELIEVE'* with a cartoon witch on a broomstick. She gasps and asks for my autograph. I keep moving.

The bar is three-deep with customers, Ray and Kevin are working in perfect sync behind the bar. Ray's face is flushed, his hair sticking up at odd angles, but he's grinning wider than I've seen in years.

"Kitchen! Now!" Ray yells when he spots me, gesturing wildly with a cocktail shaker. "We're drowning back there!"

I flash him a thumbs-up and push through the swinging doors into my domain. The kitchen is a hurricane of activity—Barb flipping steaks, Karen plating salads, and Jane... Jane is practically floating as she garnishes desserts, her wings shedding sparkles all over my clean floor.

"Jane!" I bark. "You gotta keep those wings out of sight! We're moving heaven and earth to sell this as a publicity stunt!"

She backs up for a second before Barb chimes in. "About time!" Barb shouts, sweat beading on her forehead. "Table seven's been waiting twenty minutes for their special!" Jabbing her finger at Jane, she says, "She's fine! Everyone is sooo amazed at her 'costume'!"

Hmmm...okay... I tie on my apron and grab an order ticket. "What's the special anyway?"

"Witch's Brew Stew," Karen deadpans. "Ray renamed half the menu this morning."

"Of course he did." I roll my eyes and get to work, falling into the familiar rhythm of chopping, stirring, and barking orders.

Jane sidles up beside me, her grin so wide it almost splits her face in half. "MJ, I can't thank you enough for that spell on Duncan." She leans in, voice dropping to a conspiratorial whisper. "That man has talents I never imagined. I'm lucky I can walk today, let alone work."

I nearly drop my knife. "Okay, TMI about the garbage man's bedroom skills."

Jane giggles, "Seriously, I owe you."

"We're square now," I point my spatula at her. "No more favors, except helping with the play tomorrow. And keep your sex life details to yourself—I have to look Duncan in the eye when he picks up our trash."

Jane's wings flutter as she arranges a perfect whipped cream swirl. "It will be so much fun! I hope there are no hard feelings between us."

I stare at her happy face, and the weirdest feeling washes over me. Instead of wanting to strangle her for all the trouble she's caused, I actually... don't mind her? What the actual hell?

"You okay, MJ? You look confused." Jane snaps her fingers in front of my face.

"I'm fine. Just..." I narrow my eyes at her. "Did you slip something in my coffee earlier? Some special Fae mushroom juice or something?"

Her mouth falls open. "No! I wouldn't!" Then she smirks. "Well, not without asking first."

I should be pissed. I should be holding a grudge the size of Ray's ego. But instead, I'm standing here feeling... forgiving? First Beth with her sad-sack story, and now Jane. What's happening to me?

"I think my magic's evolving," I mutter, mostly to myself. "Either that or I've pole-vaulted middle age, landing in full-on dementia."

"What?" Jane leans closer, nearly dipping her wing in the béarnaise.

"Nothing. Just—we're good, okay? All is forgiven." The words taste strange in my mouth, but not bad. "As long as you help us pull off this ridiculous theatrical deception tomorrow. And no more Fae rebellion crap."

Jane's eyes widen, and she literally rises a few inches off the floor in excitement. "Really? You forgive me? Just like that?"

"Don't make me regret it," I warn, wagging my finger. "And if you ever try to blackmail me again, I'll turn you into a fruit fly and put you on Duncan's compost heap."

Jane squeals and throws her arms around me, her wings vibrating. "You won't regret it! I'll make the most beautiful fairy illusions for the play tomorrow. No one will question anything!"

I awkwardly pat her back. "Great. Now get your sparkly ass back to those desserts before Barb has a meltdown."

As Jane floats away, I shake my head. Maybe this is what growing as a Witch feels like—finding compassion where there was anger. Or maybe I'm just getting soft in my old age.

Either way, I've got a restaurant full of Witch-fans to feed and a town-wide deception to pull off tomorrow. No time to question my sudden personality upgrade.

TWENTY-NINE

LIBBY

I wrap my arms around Stan's waist as we sway to the music, watching the surreal spectacle unfold around us. My head feels like it's stuffed with cotton candy after the day we've had, but somehow, we're here, pretending everything's normal while half the town shows their supernatural sides to unsuspecting visitors who think it's all theatrical makeup.

Stan's breath is warm against my ear. "Kevin's doing surprisingly well. When Ray called to ask him to help out at the bar, he never hesitated. Maybe that's a good thing though."

"Yeah, werewolf by night, bartender helper by day. I think the pep talk he got from Wayne Silver helped." But truthfully, there wasn't time for anyone to dwell on Kevin's new status. Not if we hoped to pull this off.

Stan chuckles, "You're handling this better than I would. But that's you, being a strong woman."

"Oh, I'm screaming inside, my heart galloping with nerves until this is all over. Can't you hear it?"

Devon twirls Shannon across the makeshift dance floor, her head thrown back in laughter. The Tiki torches surrounding the pond cast everyone in a golden glow that makes everything seem magical—which of course, it actually is.

"Look at Mary," I whisper, nodding toward the diner's server, who practically drags Duncan onto the dance floor.

The skinny garbage man looks terrified as Mary, all six feet of Druid power, yanks him into what might generously be called dancing but more closely resembles a hostage situation. Poor guy probably wishes he was back with Jane's kinky fairy dust.

"Ten bucks says he makes a break for it in the next song," Stan murmurs.

"Twenty says Mary tackles him if he tries."

The music shifts to something with more bass, and several Fae couples take to the center of the dance area. They've hidden their wings under jackets and shawls, but there's no disguising that ethereal grace. They move like water, like wind—like creatures who aren't bound by the same laws of physics as the rest of us.

"Holy crap," Stan whispers. "They're actually floating."

"Shh. It's just really good choreography," I say, winking at him.

A commotion breaks out near the refreshment table, and I spot Ida in a leopard-print top trying to organize a conga line with her husband Frank reluctantly at the back. She's shouting "CHA-CHA-CHA!" with each hip bump while Frank looks like he's calculating how many golf tournaments he could be watching instead.

"Should we join?" Stan asks.

"And miss the spectacle from here? Not a chance."

Something nudges my leg, and I look down to see Robert, Shannon's one-eared bobcat familiar, weaving between people's legs like he's not a wild predator at a public gathering.

"Holy shit," I mutter, bending down quickly. I pretend to fix my shoe while whispering, "Robert, what the hell? There are reporters everywhere!"

"Trouble brewing," he growls low. "Big trouble."

My stomach drops. For Robert to risk exposing himself like this—walking through a crowd of normals, supernatural tourists, and freaking news crews—something must be seriously wrong.

"What kind of trouble?" I ask, trying to shield him with my body. A woman with a press badge gives me a curious look, and I flash her a smile that probably looks more like a grimace.

"The mayor. Vampires. Feeding. The forest back of the beer tent."

"Jesus Christ." My heart hammers so hard I'm surprised it doesn't burst through my chest Alien-style. "Stay here."

I spot Shannon across the dance floor, laughing at something Devon said. I catch her eye and make the universal "get your ass over here now" face, complete with wide eyes and subtle head jerking.

She excuses herself and makes her way over; her smile dropping when she sees my expression.

"What's wrong?" she asks.

I point down at Robert. "We've got a situation."

We slip behind a large oak, my heart thumping so hard it could power a small city. Robert doesn't waste any time. "The Vampires are up to something," he growls. "A few of them wandered off into the stand of trees with some of these tourist types. You need to check it out."

Shannon and I exchange an "oh shit" look that perfectly communicates the dread churning in my stomach. Because nothing says "successful cover-up" like tourists becoming vampire juice boxes.

"Lead the way," Shannon whispers.

We follow Robert deeper into the trees, leaving the music and laughter behind. The temperature seems to drop with each step. The forest gets darker, and I'm about to suggest we use our phones for light when Shannon grabs my arm so hard, I'll probably have fingerprint bruises tomorrow.

"Listen," she hisses.

I strain my ears and catch it—hushed voices, a nervous giggle. Robert drops into a hunter's crouch, every muscle tense. His single ear swivels toward the sound, and he slithers forward through the underbrush with a grace I can only dream about.

We creep closer, and I spot them—three figures huddled against a massive pine tree. Two standing, one slumped between them. Even in the darkness, I can see the glint of too-sharp teeth.

A muffled scream cuts through the night, high and terrified, before it's quickly silenced.

"Oh, hell no." Shannon tenses, and before I can stop her, she's charging forward like an avenging Valkyrie on a mission."

"Shannon, wait!" I hiss, but she's already gone full Witch-zilla, her hands glowing with barely contained elemental fury. Something rustles in the bushes to my left, and I whip around so fast I nearly give myself whiplash.

What I see freezes my blood.

Mayor Jeffrey Sadler—our supposedly harmless, bumbling town leader—has a middle-aged woman in a floral maxi dress pinned against a tree. Her phone has fallen to the ground, the flashlight app illuminating the forest floor like some twisted horror movie spotlight.

I grab it and aim the beam at them. "Hey!"

The Mayor turns, and holy mother of—

Blood drips from his fangs. Actual, honest-to-goddess blood, thick and dark against his pale chin. The woman hangs limp in his arms, her head lolled to the side, exposing the raw puncture wounds on her neck.

He drops her like she's yesterday's garbage, and she crumples to the ground in a heap of floral polyester.

"Libby, dear," he says, his voice silky and hypnotic. "Why don't you go back to the party? Nothing to see here. Just helping a tourist who had too much to drink."

My skin prickles as I feel his vampire mojo trying to cloud my mind. It's like someone's pouring warm honey into my brain, urging me to nod and smile and walk away.

"Bullshit," I manage, throwing up my arm to block his gaze. "You're feeding on tourists! In the middle of our damage control operation!"

The Mayor steps toward me, blood still glistening on his chin. "You misunderstand. This is just a little... refreshment. She won't remember a thing."

"Neither will you when I'm done with you," I snarl, summoning my magic. The earth beneath my feet trembles slightly as I prepare to send this bloodsucker flying.

But before I can unleash my Witchy wrath, a blur of fur and fury shoots past me. Robert slams into the Mayor's midsection with the force of a furry freight train. The Vampire stumbles backward, his hypnotic spell breaking as he flails his pudgy arms.

"You mangy little—" he sputters, trying to regain his balance.

Seeing him try to take a swing at Robert, rage bursts from my fingertips—a jagged bolt of lightning that zaps the Mayor right in his expensive suit jacket. The crack of electricity echoes through the trees as his fine-wool blend ignites.

Mayor Jeffrey bats at the flames dancing across his chest, looking more amused than alarmed. His laughter sends chills down my spine as he casually extinguishes the fire with his pudgy hands.

"That tickles, Libby dear. Is that the best you've got? A little static electricity?" He grins, blood still staining his teeth. "I've been around since before your great-grandmother's great-grandmother was in diapers. You can't stop me."

"Wanna bet, Dracula?" I snarl, surprising myself with my own bravado. I'm a middle-aged nurse with three kids and a talking cat problem—not exactly Buffy material.

Robert latches onto Jeffrey's calf with razor-sharp teeth, growling and tearing at the expensive fabric of his pants. The Mayor howls, trying to shake him off like a toddler with a determined chihuahua attached to his ankle.

I seize the moment, raising both hands and focusing every ounce of my power. I picture a massive wall of energy—like the invisible weight of a thousand disappointed mom-stares—pressing him down to the forest floor.

"Get... down... and... stay... down!" I grunt, sweat beading on my forehead as I force him flat against the dirt.

"I've got this bloodsucker!" a voice bellows behind me. "Help the woman!"

I glance back to see Mary the Druid and Duncan rushing toward us. Mary's face is contorted in concentration as she and Duncan begin chanting in what sounds like really angry Welsh.

Vines burst from the ground, writhing like something from a horror movie before wrapping around Jeffrey's limbs and torso, pinning him more securely than my magic alone could manage.

"The woman—help her!" Duncan shouts, his skinny arms trembling with effort.

I rush to the tourist's side, kneeling beside her crumpled form. Her pulse is thready; her skin is clammy. The puncture wounds on her neck look angry and inflamed, oozing something that's definitely not just blood.

"Shit, shit, shit," I mutter, placing my hand over the wound. I close my eyes and focus, calling on my healing powers. "Come on, get out of her system. Whatever Vampire crap he pumped into her, get OUT."

My palm heats up, and I feel something moving beneath my fingers. When I open my eyes, I nearly lose my dinner. Phosphorescent green goo bubbles up from the wound, dripping onto the forest floor where it sizzles like acid.

"What in the actual hell?" I gag, fighting the urge to yank my hand away.

Behind me, I hear the mayor's desperate pleas.

"Mary, be reasonable," he wheedles. "Let me go, and I'll make you head of the town council. Duncan, I'll triple your garbage collection budget!"

"Shut your blood-sucking pie hole," Mary growls, tightening the vines with a flick of her wrist.

The green ooze finally stops, followed by a rush of normal, healthy red blood. I press my hand more firmly against the wound, picturing clean, healthy tissue knitting together beneath my fingers.

The woman's eyelids flutter open, revealing confused brown eyes that dart around like a trapped squirrel. Her hand flies to her neck, where my healing touch just extracted vampire venom.

"What... happened?" she croaks.

"You tripped and fainted," I say, smiling like I'm offering her a cookie instead of a massive lie. "Must've been all that special punch they're serving at the festival. Between us, I think someone spiked it."

She tries to sit up, wobbling like a newborn deer. "But I felt... teeth?"

"Nope! Just a nasty fall against this tree root." I point to a conveniently placed root. "You hit your neck pretty hard. Good thing I'm a nurse."

The woman touches her neck again, frowning. "It feels wet."

"I put some of my special herbal ointment on it. All natural! Organic! Locally sourced!" I'm babbling like a QVC host on speed. "Works wonders on... tree-root-neck-injuries."

Behind me, I hear the muffled cursing of our esteemed mayor as Mary and Duncan continue their Druid restraint therapy. Robert sits nearby, looking entirely too pleased with himself as he licks blood—Vampire blood—from his paws.

Shannon bursts through the bushes, wild-eyed and breathless, and there's a twig stuck in her hair.

"Libby! Need you. Now!" She grabs my arm, yanking me to my feet. "Two more down. Worse than this one."

"Excuse me," I tell the dazed tourist, patting her hand. "Festival emergency. You just sit tight. Maybe don't Instagram this moment, okay?"

I follow Shannon through the underbrush, tripping over roots and dodging low-hanging branches. She's moving like her ass is on fire, which makes me wonder if she actually set someone's ass on fire. With Shannon, it's always a possibility.

"What happened?" I pant, trying to keep up.

"Sarah and her bloodsucking buddy decided to have an all-you-can-eat buffet."

We break through the trees into a small clearing, and I skid to a stop so fast I nearly face-plant. Where there should be solid ground, there's a massive hole—like someone took a giant ice cream scoop to the earth.

I creep closer and peer down. Thirty feet below, Sarah Stone is sprawled in an undignified heap of designer clothes and fury. Beside her is—holy crap—Gerry the butcher from the grocery store. Mild-mannered Gerry, who always gives my kids extra slices of cheese at the deli counter. Except now his face is transformed into something monstrous, fangs fully extended and dripping with what is definitely not A1 sauce.

"What the actual hell?" I gasp. "Gerry's a vampire? The guy who makes those cute little meat animals for kids' birthday parties?"

Shannon points to a man and woman sprawled on the ground nearby. They're pale as ghosts, with matching puncture wounds on their necks that look like they've been attacked by staple guns.

"Can you fix them?" Shannon asks, her voice tight.

"I'm a nurse, not Dr. Frankenstein," I grumble, but I'm already moving toward them.

I kneel beside the first victim—a balding guy with a "Witch Way to Salem?" t-shirt that would be funny if he weren't half-drained of blood. His pulse is weak, and like the other one, his skin is clammy. Typical signs of blood loss and, oh yeah, Vampire spit in his system.

"This is getting old real fast," I mutter, placing my hands on his clammy forehead. I close my eyes and focus, picturing his blood cells multiplying, the vampire toxin burning away like morning fog. Heat flows from my palms into his body, and he jerks beneath my touch.

Behind me, Shannon is going full-on Witch rage at the pit-trapped vampires.

"You backstabbing bloodsuckers!" she shouts. "We had a DEAL! The whole point of this festival charade was to fix this mess, not create an all-you-can-eat tourist buffet!"

Sarah's voice floats up from the pit. "Oh please! These tourists don't matter. What's a few crazies? No one will miss them."

"We just wanted something warm and alive for once," Gerry whines. "Do you know how disgusting cold blood bank bags are? It's like drinking refrigerated ketchup through a sippy cup!"

I tune them out, focusing on the woman now. Her skin is even clammier, her breathing shallow. I press my hands to her neck, right over the puncture wounds, and channel every ounce of healing energy I can muster.

"Come on, lady. Don't die at a fake festival in a town full of supernatural freaks. That's just embarrassing for everyone involved."

Color slowly returns to her cheeks. Her eyes flutter open, confused and disoriented.

"What happened?" the man asks, sitting up slowly.

"Special effects accident," I say smoothly. "For the play tomorrow. You two wandered into our test zone."

"But... my neck feels weird," the woman says, touching the spot where, moments ago, two puncture wounds were leaking vampire-poisoned blood.

"Makeup residue," I explain, helping them both to their feet. "You might feel a little dizzy—that's just the fog machine chemicals. Totally safe, FDA approved, even."

They wobble unsteadily, still looking confused but apparently buying my bullshit explanation.

"The party's that way," I say, pointing toward the music. "There's free cotton candy at the blue tent. Tell them Libby sent you for the special batch."

They nod dumbly and shuffle off toward the lights and music, occasionally touching their necks in confusion.

I step over to Shannon. "What are we going to do with them?" I jerk my thumb toward the pit where Sarah and Gerry are still trapped. "Duncan and Mary helped me with the Mayor, but what about them?"

Shannon looks like she's about to suggest we fill the hole with cement and call it a day when Robert trots up, his one ear twitching with excitement. He's followed by three people I've never seen before—two middle-aged women and a handsome older guy who looks like he might have stepped off the cover of 'Silver Fox Monthly.'

"I may have solved our problem," Robert announces. "I've been feeling some strange magic in town—an unfamiliar signature. It was these three."

The tall blonde steps forward, exuding confidence like it's her personal fragrance. She's maybe late forties, with an easy smile and the kind of relaxed posture that says she's comfortable in her own skin.

"We saw the Facebook posts and thought we'd check it out," she says, extending her hand to Shannon. "I'm Kara West."

When their hands connect, Shannon's eyes go wide as dinner plates. She practically jumps back like she's been shocked.

"You!" Shannon gasps, pointing an accusing finger. "It was you who helped me handle that reporter! Your magic!"

The blonde—Kara—grins, "Figured you could use a little boost with the press."

I stare at Shannon like she's grown a second head. What the hell is she talking about? The blonde woman—Kara—just offered her hand, not a kidney.

"What do you mean 'it was you'?" I ask, but Shannon's already in full-on girl-crush mode, pointing and sputtering.

The shorter woman beside Kara sighs dramatically and flicks her fingers toward the pit where our vampire problems are still trapped. A shower of silver sparks erupts from her fingertips, raining down like the Fourth of July gone wrong.

Sarah's outraged shriek echoes up from the hole. "What is that? It burns! STOP IT!"

My jaw drops so hard I'm surprised it doesn't dislocate. Holy crap on a cracker.

"You're Witches," I blurt out, stating the obvious like it's some profound revelation. "You're not tourists. You're actual Witches."

Kara grins, looking way too amused. "Guilty as charged. We were passing through on our RV trip when we saw the posts. Figured we'd stop by and see if you needed help."

"Wait—" I hold up my hand. "You travel around in an RV? Like Witch nomads?"

"It's better than a broom," the shorter woman says with a straight face. "More cupholders."

Oh. My. Good. Goddess. There are more of us out there. Witches who weren't born in Wesley.

Thirty

Shannon

My mind races faster than a Werewolf with his tail on fire as I stare at the witches in front of us. Finally—FINALLY—some actual good news in this dumpster fire of a week.

"You're Witches," I state the obvious because apparently that's what I do now. "Like, real Witches."

The tall blonde—Kara—smiles. "Not always. It only happened a year ago, but that's a story I need a few drinks to tell."

The dark-haired man steps forward, and holy hell. He's Mediterranean gorgeous with cheekbones that could cut glass.

"I'm Mike," he says, looking down into the pit where Sarah and Gerry are still hissing like cats in a bathtub. "I'm glad these two decided to check this out. I hate it when my kind go full-on Vampire. They give us a bad name. These ones will be held accountable. I'll see that they're taken before our council to stand trial."

Libby's jaw drops. "A trial? Never knew Vampires were actually real until a week ago, and now, I'm learning there's a council and that there are more around? Outside of Wesley?"

The younger of the two women speaks, tossing her brunette hair over her shoulder. "Well, yeah. We've run into a ton of Vampires, Druids, Werewolves and Fae all over this country. Hate to break it to you, but Wesley isn't all that special. Although there is something in the air here. I thought it was just the mountains, but apparently not." She chews her lower lip. "I have a special place in my heart for the Fae, to be honest."

I let that last comment go because I feel like my brain just short-circuited. "Wait, wait, wait. You're telling me that Mysticals are EVERYWHERE? Not just in our little town?"

Mike nods, his dark eyes gleaming with amusement. "Did you think you were living in some kind of supernatural Brigadoon?"

"Kind of, yeah!" I throw my hands up. "That's what everyone here implied!"

The dark-haired Witch lets out a snort. "It looks like even the supernatural can be provincial. I'm Maren, the younger and smarter sister in this travelling road show."

I look down at Robert, who's suspiciously avoiding eye contact. "Did YOU know about this?"

My familiar suddenly finds the dirt extremely fascinating. "I may have heard rumors."

"Rumors?" I sputter. "RUMORS?"

I shake my head, turning to the two Witches. "Well, I'm glad you came, if for nothing else than to take care of these bloodsuckers. Wow. I guess I owe you one. Maybe drinks at my friend's restaurant?"

My mind is still reeling from the bombshell that Mysticals aren't just confined to our little Podunk town. All this time we've been acting like we're some special magical snowflake, when apparently the supernatural is as common as Starbucks across America.

At the sound of even more footsteps approaching, I turn to see Stan and Devon walking into the forest to join us. Devon's hair is tousled from dancing, and I feel a flutter in my chest that I immediately squash. We still have Vampires to deal with before I can think about making up properly.

Devon peers over the edge of the massive crack I'd opened in the earth and whistles low. "Your handiwork?" His eyes meet mine with a mix of pride and amusement. "Remind me never to piss you off."

He leans further over the edge, spotting Sarah and Gerry who glare up at us like angry cats trapped in a well. "So, those two down there were up to no good?"

I sigh, running a hand through my hair. "The Vampires took advantage of everything that happened. It wouldn't surprise me if they were behind everything, from riling up the Fae to helping Beth get away. Seems they wanted some fresh hemoglobin."

"Divide and conquer," Mike nods. "Classic Vampire strategy. Create chaos, then feed while everyone's distracted."

"Screw you!" Sarah shouts from the pit, her fangs still glistening with blood. "We have rights!"

"Yeah," I call back, "the right to remain silent would be a good one to exercise right about now."

I'm staring at these three Mystical strangers like they're unicorns who just waltzed into a petting zoo. My brain is still trying to process it all when Libby takes Stan's hand and nods toward our unexpected visitors.

"Beth's posts attracted other Witches and a Vampire. This is Kara and Maren and Mike."

Stan takes a deep breath, his eyes ballooning. "More Witches? And a Vampire? From the outside?" He looks like he's having a hard time processing this, which makes two of us.

"Welcome to my existential crisis," I mutter, gesturing to the chaos around us.

Mike peers down at Sarah and Gerry, who are still hissing and spitting from their dirt prison. "These two need proper containment. Not just a hole in the ground."

"Well, excuse me for improvising," I say, hands on my hips. "Next time I'll bring Vampire handcuffs and a portable dungeon."

Kara laughs, her blonde hair catching the moonlight. "Girl, I like your style. We should compare notes sometime. The shit I've seen this past year would curl your hair."

"It's already curly," I deadpan. "Any curlier and I'll look like I stuck my finger in an electrical socket."

Devon steps closer to me, his shoulder brushing mine in a way that sends little sparks through my body. "So, what's the plan with these two? And the Mayor? We can't exactly call the police since their boss is probably still tied up with vines."

Robert sits at my feet, his one good ear twitching. "We could always leave them there until they learn some manners. Might take a century or two."

"Tempting," I say, "but I don't think the park service would appreciate a Vampire pit in the middle of their forest."

Mike steps forward, radiating that casual Vampire confidence that screams, "I've seen some shit in my five centuries."

"You guys go on, and I'll join you after I take care of these two and that fat little fucker," he offers, nodding toward where the Mayor is trussed up like a Christmas turkey in Druid vines.

Libby smiles, her eyes twinkling with mischief. "Yeah, that just about sums up the mayor."

I snort. "'Fat little fucker' is practically a compliment for Jeffrey. I was thinking more along the lines of 'blood-sucking parasite with the leadership skills of a concussed goldfish'."

As if summoned by our trash-talking, Mary and Duncan appear through the trees, holding hands like high schoolers who just discovered hormones. Their fingers are intertwined so tightly I'm surprised they haven't fused together. Mary's got that freshly kissed glow, and Duncan's sporting a goofy smile that makes him look slightly less like he lives in a garbage can.

Well, would you look at that? My petty jealousy of Devon evaporates like morning dew. Mary and Duncan are a match made in Druid heaven—or whatever nature-worshipping afterlife they believe in.

"You two look cozy," I say, fighting the urge to make gagging noises.

Mary blushes, but Duncan puffs up like a proud rooster. "We've been talking about what happens next," he says, giving Mary's hand a squeeze. "The town will definitely need an election now that the mayor has revealed his true... appetites."

"An election?" I look from the druids to our three new Mystical visitors, my brain connecting dots. "Wait. We're actually going to do this democratically? Not just, I don't know, have a magical duel or something?"

"This isn't Hogwarts," Mary says with a laugh.

"Could've fooled me," I mutter, thinking of the chaos of the past week. "So, what—we put up campaign signs? Hold debates? Have the Werewolves form a PAC?" I get no response. "PAC, get it? Pack?" They look at me as if I'm losing it. I sigh. "Skip it."

Devon's hand finds the small of my back, warm and steady. "I guess, it's just like regular politics, but with more actual bloodsuckers."

I walk away from the vampire pit with Libby and our new Witch friends, my head still spinning. Mike's staying behind to deal with our fanged problem children, which is fine by me. I've had enough Vampire drama to last a lifetime.

"So, you're telling me there are Mysticals all over the country?" I ask Kara and Maren, still trying to wrap my brain around this bombshell. "This whole time we thought we were special."

"Sorry to break your bubble." Maren says with a laugh. "Nope. We've met covens in at least six states so far."

"Well, shit." I run my hand through my hair. "That changes everything."

"So, what happens next?" Libby asks, voicing the question bouncing around my brain. "With the Mayor gone, who's in charge?"

I feel a weight settle on my shoulders. Whether I like it or not, I'm going to have to step up. My coven, my responsibility. And if there's one thing I've learned in the past year, it's that running away from problems just gives them time to grow bigger teeth.

"We'll need to talk to the remaining Vampires," I say. "Find out how deep this goes. If they were all in on it or if it was just Jeffrey's conspiracy."

Kara walks beside me. She looks over with a smile that reminds me of MJ—practical but with a hint of mischief.

"I can't wait to see this play tomorrow," she says. "Whoever came up with that idea is brilliant."

I laugh, feeling a genuine smile break through my stress for the first time today. "Wish I could claim credit, but that's Mary-Jane. You'll meet her soon. And she'll be the one to help out, questioning the other Vampires in town about Jeffery's plot we just foiled. One touch from her, and she'll know the truth.

As we walk back toward the lights and music of the festival, I think about how much Libby and MJ have done during this crisis. MJ turning Beth from enemy to ally. Libby healing those tourists without a second thought. My coven isn't just holding it together—they're thriving.

We're not just witches anymore. We're leaders. And tomorrow, after this play charade is over, we're going to have to decide what kind of leaders we want to be.

Thirty-One

Mary-Jane

I wipe my forehead with the back of my hand, leaving what I'm sure is a streak of flour and sauce behind. The kitchen looks like a food bomb went off, but at least we've survived the dinner rush from hell.

"I'm heading out," I tell Jane and Barb. "You two can handle cleanup, right?"

Jane nods, still wearing that ridiculous post-coital glow that makes me want to both congratulate and throttle her. Whatever Duncan did to her has turned her into a walking advertisement for Druid sex.

"Got it covered, boss," Barb says, already attacking a pile of pots with industrial determination.

I push through the swinging doors into the dining room and stop dead. Shannon and Libby have just walked in with two women I've never seen before. One's a tall blonde who looks like she stepped off a Viking longship, and the other's a shorter brunette with sharp eyes that miss nothing.

But it's not their looks that freeze me in place. It's their auras—deep purple with silver threads weaving through them like electrical currents. Holy shit. They're Witches. Powerful ones.

Ray glances up from loading glasses into the dishwasher behind the bar and gives me a look that says, "More weird shit happening?"

"MJ! Cynthia!" Shannon calls out, waving us over to where Cynthia and Eric are sitting. "Beth's post not only brought reporters and witch fans but also the cavalry. As in fellow Witches."

I walk over, wiping my hands on my apron. "You're Witches?" I ask, not bothering with subtlety. My filter disappeared somewhere between the fiftieth order of fries and Jane's graphic description of Duncan's "magical staff."

The blonde extends her hand. "Kara West. And this is my baby sister Maren."

A quick glance at Maren shows me a very well-practiced eye-roll.

After five hours of cooking for tourists and reporters with the munchies, I look like I've been through a food processor. My feet hurt, my back aches, and I'm pretty sure I've got garlic powder in places garlic powder should never be.

When Kara reaches out to shake my hand, I expect the usual polite handshake. What I get is a jolt of electricity shooting up my arm like I've stuck my finger in a light socket. Holy crap on a cracker! Along with the zap comes a crystal-clear image of a roomy RV parked somewhere with two women drinking wine on lawn chairs.

"So, you're the one who thought up this play to divert everyone's attention?" Kara grins, still holding my hand. "Nice work."

My cheeks heat faster than my four-burner stove. Someone's actually giving me credit? Usually, I'm just the crazy chef in the background while Shannon gets to throw lightning bolts and look fierce.

"Well, I mean, it just seemed logical," I stammer, trying not to look too pleased with myself and failing miserably. "When life gives you lemons, make a theatrical production."

I watch Cynthia shake hands with both witches, her eyes flashing with recognition before her face splits into a grin wider than the Grand Canyon. Whatever she's picking up from them, it's something good.

Libby steps closer, lowering her voice. "Stan and Devon are with Mike, taking care of the Vampires."

"The Vampires?" I blink rapidly, looking between them. "What Vampires? Did I miss something while I was elbow-deep in bearnaise? Because if there was a Vampire throw down and nobody told me, I'm going to be seriously pissed."

Shannon takes a seat, pulling out two chairs for Kara and Maren to join Cynthia and Eric at the table. "Yeah, the mayor and a couple other

Vampires got the munchies and started sampling the tourists and reporters. Robert alerted us, so Libby and I took care of them. Apparently, there's a Vampire council of some sort that Maren's boyfriend Mike—also a Vampire—will ensure they stand before to face punishment."

I slam my palm on the table, making the silverware jump. "Are you kidding me? Jeffrey Sadler—the man who once got his tie caught in the cotton candy machine at the Fourth of July picnic—is out there treating humans like popsicles to suck on?"

"The mosquito was surprisingly quick," Libby adds, taking a sip of water. "But Robert knocked him down before he could ensorcel me."

"Wait," I hold up both hands. "You're telling me that I've been slaving over a hot stove while you guys were having a Vampire smack down? Not fair!" I grump. I knew I should've left Barb in charge earlier.

Kara snorts. "If it makes you feel better, they weren't very impressive Vampires. I've seen stronger ones a bunch of times. "

"Mike says the Council will deal with them," Maren adds. "They take unauthorized feeding very seriously these days."

"There's authorized feeding?" I ask, my voice climbing an octave.

Ray slides a glass of wine in front of me without a word. God bless that man. I squeeze in next to Cynthia, telling her, "And don't you feel bad about sitting that one out," I tell her, giving her arm a reassuring squeeze. "You've got a coven and strong Witches to deal with stuff."

Cynthia gives me a grateful smile, though I can still see the guilt swimming in her eyes. She's always been the one ready to throw down, not the one on the sidelines.

I turn my attention back to our new friends, still trying to wrap my head around the fact that Beth's social media temper tantrum actually attracted legitimate help instead of just looky-loos and reporters hoping to catch us flying on broomsticks.

"So, what's with the RV?" I blurt out, my curiosity overriding my manners. "That came through loud and clear when we shook. Like IMAX-level clear."

Kara's eyebrows shoot up. "You saw that, huh? Impressive." She takes a sip of the drink Ray delivered. "The Magical Mystery Tour mobile? Or as I call her, Betsy." She glances over at her sister. "Our lives changed forever when we set out on our cross-country adventure. It's how we found magic and became witches."

Holy doodle on a cracker with extra cheese! These two found their magic on a road trip? And here I thought our Witchy awakening via Shannon's haunted well was bizarre.

"Wait—you became Witches while road-tripping?" I lean forward. "Like, what—you stopped at a Gas-N-Go and picked up some hocus pocus between the beef jerky and pine tree air fresheners?"

Shannon laughs. "Oh, my goodness. I found a well which enabled us to become Witches."

"Not me," Cynthia holds up her hand. "I was a Witch for years before that."

Libby nods. "True. But when we started exercising power, you decided to join us." She looks over at Kara. "I hope you didn't have the mishaps we had when we were learning. It almost broke our friendship when we ended up hexing each other."

I snort. "Mishaps? Is that what we're calling it when I accidentally made Ray's dick glow in the dark for a week? Or when Shannon's rain spell flooded half the town? Or when Libby had that entire conversation with Ms. Purdy Cat about her sex life?"

Ray shoots me a death glare from behind the bar. I blow him a kiss. Whatever. The glow-in-the-dark incident actually spiced things up for us. Nothing says romance like a husband who doubles as a nightlight.

Maren rolls her eyes. "We've had to go through a learning curve too. But things fell into place, and here we are."

"Learning curve?" I laugh so hard I snort Chardonnay up my nose. "Honey, what we went through wasn't a curve—it was a full-on magical Tilt-A-Whirl with no seatbelts and a drunk operator."

I take a big gulp of my drink, watching Kara and Maren trade stories about their magical mishaps. Something about a Werewolf community in Florida and a cursed forest. Just when I think I've heard it all.

The door swings open and in walk Devon, Stan, and an older, damn sexy stranger who's got "Vampire" written all over his aura. The moment his eyes land on Maren, his whole face transforms. Not into fangs and glowy eyes, but something even more terrifying: a man completely, utterly smitten.

"Mike!" Maren squeals, jumping up from her chair.

So, this is the Vampire boyfriend. I don't need my magic touch to read the look on his face. The guy's aura practically screams, "I'd walk through fire, stake myself, and bathe in holy water for this woman." It's both nauseating and adorable.

Kara holds up a bottle of Jack Daniels. "We saved you some, don't worry. But considering this is a restaurant, I think there's plenty more where this came from. My treat this time." She gives me a smile. "I've had some luck and come into some serious cash this past year."

Ray sidles up behind me, his hands settling on my shoulders as he leans down to whisper in my ear. "See? We could sell this place and retire if you used magic to beef up the bank account."

I elbow him in the ribs. "We're fine. We'd miss this place and seeing everyone in town."

And I mean it. Despite the chaos, the endless hours, and the occasional Mystical crisis, I love this restaurant. I love feeding people, watching them enjoy my food. I love knowing everyone's favorite dish and their life story. Even if half those life stories now involve centuries of existence or monthly fur transformations.

At the sound of footsteps, I turn to see Jane burst through the kitchen doors in full Fae glory—wings extended and fluttering, shedding sparkles all over my clean floor. Great. That's going to be hell to vacuum up. I'm going to have to get her a net for her wings!

Simultaneously, the front door opens again, and Mary and Duncan stroll in, fingers interlaced like teenagers after prom night. Oh, shit on a stick. Jane is going to be heartbroken.

I watch Jane's eyes land on Duncan and Mary's clasped hands, waiting for the inevitable meltdown. Instead, she smiles—actually smiles—and turns to reveal Marcus Lopez standing behind her, his hairy Werewolf arm sliding around her waist like it belongs there.

What. The. Actual. Hell?

Jane catches my jaw-dropped expression and winks, leaning in close as she passes. "I'll explain later," she whispers, her wings fluttering against my cheek and leaving a trail of glitter on my shirt. Great. Now I need a clothes brush.

"But the love potion—" I sputter, too confused to form complete sentences. "Duncan—you—what?"

Jane giggles and pats my arm. "Your spell worked perfectly. Cured my Druid crush, and now? I might have been wrong about Werewolves."

I'm still trying to process this supernatural love triangle...well, more like a square really, when Maren lets out a hearty laugh from our table. "This is so cool," she exclaims, gesturing around the restaurant with her glass. "It's like the United Nations of Supernaturals in here. Druids, Fae, and Shifters." She takes another sip. "The only thing missing is a Werewolf."

Kevin steps out from behind the bar where he'd been helping Ray put away glasses. Even in the dim lighting, I can see the five o'clock shadow that's more like a midnight shadow creeping across his jawline. He's not in full wolf mode, but there's definitely something wild lurking just beneath the surface.

He raises his hand as if he's in class. "A Werewolf is present and accounted for." His voice cracks slightly. "Not my first choice, but it seems I didn't have the luxury of having a say."

Libby smiles at him with that mixture of pride and worry that only a mother can pull off. "That's my boy," she says, reaching over to squeeze his arm. "I thought he'd go away to college and be an engineer, but I'm not sure how that's going to work now that he's transitioned."

I watch Kara's brow furrow like she's trying to solve a particularly difficult crossword puzzle. "Wait. He wasn't born that way? A Werewolf with a Witch mother. That's odd."

My hand automatically reaches for my drink. Nothing about this week has been normal, but at least alcohol still works exactly as advertised.

"It's the water and the elements in Wesley," Eric explains, leaning forward with that professor-like tone he gets when sharing Mystical knowledge. "You can be a normal human for years, and then it just happens. You become a Mystical."

"Or you can take the initiative and nudge it along," Devon mutters, examining the tattoo on his wrist like it's a winning lottery ticket.

Duncan steps closer, looking down at it with the pride of an artist admiring his handiwork. "Looks promising, Devon."

The look that Shannon shoots him could curdle milk at twenty paces. Obviously not her first choice either.

Maren's jaw drops open before she says, "I take what I said back. Wesley is pretty special," she leans forward. "We've run into all kinds of Mystical beings, and they were always born into it. But here, it can happen to anyone, it seems."

Kara's eyes light up like she's won the magical lottery. "So, the whole town is basically a supernatural incubator? That's fascinating!"

"More like a Mystical pressure cooker," I reply. "I went from making souffles to making fireballs in less time than it takes most people to learn TikTok dances."

The conversation explodes into a magical show-and-tell that would make any normal person run screaming for the hills. Good thing we left normal in the rear-view mirror weeks ago.

"You think that's bad?" Kara cackles, slapping her knee. "I once accidentally turned a state trooper's ticket book into butterflies. He nearly shit himself."

I'm doubled over laughing when Ray slides me another glass of whisky. "Tell them about the aphrodisiac cookies," he murmurs with a wink.

"Oh God," I groan, covering my face. "I was trying to make cookies that would help Ray's... performance issues."

"I did NOT have performance issues," Ray interjects, his face turning the color of my spaghetti sauce.

"Fine, stamina issues," I correct, ignoring his glare. "Anyway, I accidentally brought them to the PTA bake sale."

Maren snorts wine through her nose. "No!"

"Oh yes. The principal and the gym teacher were caught in the supply closet. Three couples filed for divorce the next week. And Mrs. Henderson—the eighty-year-old librarian—propositioned the entire school board."

By midnight, we're all wheezing with laughter, my mascara's halfway down my face, and I've forgotten every ache and pain from my marathon cooking session.

Cynthia stands up, steadying herself against Eric's shoulder. "I hate to break up this magical confessional, but this baby and I need sleep."

Shannon glances at her watch and gasps. "Holy crap, it's almost midnight! We've got a play to fake tomorrow."

She turns to Kara, Maren and Mike. "You guys want to park that RV at my place? I've got plenty of room."

I shoo everyone out the door around 1 AM, practically pushing Kara and Maren's witch asses across the threshold. Love them already, but Mama needs sleep.

"Thanks for coming!" I chirp, slapping the CLOSED sign against the glass. "See you tomorrow for our totally legitimate theatrical production that is definitely not a hastily concocted cover-up for an accidental magical revelation!"

Ray starts gathering glasses, his shoulders slumped with exhaustion. Poor guy's been running interference between horny Fae, hungry reporters, and drunken Mysticals all night.

"Leave it," I tell him, snatching the dish towel from his hands.

He blinks at me like I've grown a second head. "But the health inspector—"

"Will have to deal with my magical wrath if he shows up tomorrow morning." I toss the towel onto the bar. "Ray Matthews, I've seen you scrub crusty marinara off plates until 3 AM. I've watched you alphabetize the spice rack. Hell, I once caught you lint-rolling the baseboards. But tonight? We're walking away from this disaster zone."

His eye twitches as he surveys the glittery carnage. Fae dust covers every surface like a strip club exploded in here. Half-empty glasses form a boozy obstacle course across the tables. There's even what appears to be werewolf hair clogging the sink drain.

"But—"

"No buts except yours heading home to bed." I grab his hand and pull him toward the door. "Tomorrow we're staging an entire Broadway-caliber production with zero rehearsal time, a cast of supernatural creatures who can't act, and a town full of reporters looking for Witches. We need sleep more than we need a clean floor."

Ray's gaze lingers on a particularly offensive puddle of something sticky.

"I promise it'll still be disgusting tomorrow," I assure him, flipping off the lights.

He sighs, finally, surrendering. "Fine. But I'm setting the alarm for 5 AM."

"6:30," I counter.

"5:45."

"6:15 and I'll do that thing with my tongue you like."

His eyebrows shoot up. "Deal."

As we step out into the night, I glance back at my restaurant—my beautiful, chaotic, glitter-bombed restaurant—and feel a surge of affection. Just yesterday I was worried about inventory and menu specials. Now I'm orchestrating a fake theatrical production to cover up the fact that my friends and I are Witches.

And honestly? I wouldn't trade it for anything.

Thirty-Two

Libby

Standing in front of my bathroom mirror, it takes everything not to stab myself in the eyes, applying mascara. Today's the day. My poor frazzled nerves, and I haven't even made it to the park yet. The whole town is buzzing like a hornet's nest that's been whacked with a stick, and somehow...somehow, we hope to convince a bunch of reporters, tourists and social media influencers that we're just quirky theater enthusiasts, and not actual Witches.

Thank God the focus is on us; what the hell would happen if they got wind that there's also Druids, Shapeshifters and Fae? And...real, honest to goodness, not sparkly at all Vampires?

"Mom! I'm missing the baker's white jacket of my costume. I've got the pants and the cap, but where the hell did the jacket go?" Jack shouts from downstairs.

I cap the mascara tube. "Check under your bed! That's where everything else ends up!"

"Got it!" Dahlia calls back before Jack can respond. "I noticed a stain on it and threw it in the laundry last night."

"Ever think that maybe the baker's coat should have some stains? But thanks, I guess." Jack replies.

When I come downstairs, Kevin's sprawled on the couch looking surprisingly normal after his Werewolf debut. No excess hair, no fangs—just my son, scrolling through his phone.

"Kevin! It's all hands-on deck today. You don't get to sit this one out. It doesn't matter that you aren't a Werewolf today; there's a costume at the set and you're going to be the wolf."

My dear firstborn rolls his eyes and sighs. When he shoots me a scowl, I add, "You DO know that Jess has agreed to be Red Riding Hood, right?"

That gets his attention faster than a cattle prod. I hide a smile as he gets to his feet. When he asks, "What happened to Iris Clarke? I thought she was playing Red."

"Change of plans. This is damage control, and we all agreed that Jess would be better to pull this off." From the look on his face, that secret crush on Jess might even bring about his transformation. Oh well… Not the worst thing that could happen today, all things considered.

Stan appears from the kitchen with two travel mugs of coffee. "Liquid courage, milady," he says, handing me one.

I take a grateful sip. "You're a lifesaver."

"I know." He kisses my cheek. "Ray just called. The reporters are already setting up in the park. He said it's a circus out there."

"Perfect," I mutter. "Just what we need."

My phone buzzes with a text from Shannon:

Where are you? MJ's about to have a coronary.

I text back:

On my way. Bringing reinforcements and coffee.

"Let's roll, troops!" I call to my kids. "Kevin—no howling at the moon, Dahlia, don't you even THINK of trying to talk to any animals, and Jack, not a word about anything, got it? We gotta nail this show, or we'll be dodging pitchforks instead of applause!"

The park is absolute bedlam when we arrive. Devon's crew did a good job with the makeshift stage, sitting on the elevated section. People mill around everywhere—tourists with 'Life's a Bitch' with the 'Bitch' crossed out and replaced with 'Witch', other wannabes wearing pointy hats and capes, with reporters and 'influencers' milling around the edge of the crowd with cameras and microphones like hyenas stalking a herd of prey.

And the locals are all locals trying to look like all of this is normal. Mysticals rubbing shoulders with normies, all going about the business of preserving Wesley as a haven.

I never loved this town more.

I spot MJ near the refreshment stand directing helpers like they're in her kitchen. Her face is flushed as she points to the spot where coolers of drinks and food are to be placed.

I jerk when my shoulder is grabbed from behind. I spin around to see Shannon. She looks surprisingly put together with her long cape and hood, in full witch outfit for the play. She nods at me and the kids. "I was beginning to worry that you'd skipped town. Not that I would blame you."

"And miss all this?" I gesture around us. "Never." I see Cynthia in the crowd, and she waves frantically at us. We make our way over to her, and she practically pounces on us. "Finally! Libby, I need you to check on the costumes. Make sure everything showed up and make any adjustments needed." She looks behind me, where Kevin and Jack are, before adding. "So, no full-on wolf today for Kevin?"

"Are you kidding? You do not want that to happen, believe me."

She looks off for a moment. "Yeah. Got it. No problem; we've got a costume that will fit him."

Cynthia gestures at Shannon. "Shannon, there are reporters who want to talk to you. They think you're the ringleader of this whole Witch thing in town thanks to Beth's posts that got out before we could track her down." She looks Shannon up and down with an approving smile. "Nice outfit, by the way. Better than the costume the high school sent."

Shannon rolls her eyes. "Like you haven't seen it a million times. I thought being in the play would give me a pass with those reporters." She looks around. "Where's my new Witch friend, Kara? We might need her and her sister on this caper."

"Just stick to the script," MJ reminds her. "We have to sell these people that this is all Beth's brilliant marketing campaign for our annual community theater production. And isn't it brilliant? Worked like a charm to get everyone here."

Speaking of Beth, I spot her across the park, handing out programs with Ivy and Alf. She looks surprisingly cooperative, though I suspect that has something to do with the Druid magic Mary used on her. She catches my eye and gives me a hesitant wave. That I return. MJ says she's seen the light; I sure hope so.

"I still can't believe this is working," I mutter.

MJ follows my gaze. "Don't jinx it. We've got a few hours before the play starts, and a million things could go wrong before then."

"Like what?" I ask immediately regretting the question.

As if on cue, a loud crash from behind the stage, followed by a string of curses that would make a sailor blush.

MJ closes her eyes. "Kind of like that."

"I'll handle the costumes; you handle... whatever that was." I can't help but shudder at the commotion.

"Deal," she says, already marching towards the stage.

Before I join MJ, I turn to Shannon. "Ready to face the press?"

"No, but I have to, right?" She takes a deep breath, squaring her shoulders.

As we part ways, I catch sight of Kara and Maren near the food trucks, looking amused by the whole spectacle. Mike stands behind them, sunglasses and a hat shielding him from the sun. Our backup witches, observing the chaos from a safe distance.

I take a deep breath and head toward the costume tent. It's going to be a long day in Wesley, and we're just getting started.

⁂

The afternoon passes without any more incident. Shielding my eyes from the sun, I squint at the crowd that's packed into the park, waiting for the curtain to rise. It's almost like we're hosting a rock concert instead of a last-minute thrown-together community theater production.

"Places, everyone!" MJ screeches through a megaphone that I swear wasn't there two seconds ago. "And remember—we're all just normal people putting on a normal play that we do every year! It's small-town theater at its finest!"

I snort. Subtle.

"This is actually going to work, isn't it?" I whisper to MJ as she drops into the chair beside me.

"It better," she mutters. "I've threatened the high school drama teacher with eternal boils if anything goes wrong."

"You can't actually do that."

She grins at me. "He doesn't know that."

The orchestra—which consists of three teenagers with keyboards and Mr. Peterson with his accordion—strikes up the overture. The curtain rises to reveal Jack in full baker regalia, looking surprisingly comfortable on stage. His chef's jacket is dusted with flour, and he's wearing a chef's hat at a jaunty angle. My heart swells with pride.

"I wish..." Jack begins, his voice carrying across the park.

I lean forward, watching my son perform. Never in a million years did I think I'd be sitting in a park full of reporters, watching my kids in a play designed to hoodwink the world.

Chloe joins Jack on stage as his wife, and I have to admit they have chemistry. Somewhere behind me, I hear Ray muttering about keeping an eye on those two.

Dahlia appears as Cinderella, and I'm once again blindsided by how grown-up she looks. When did my tomboy turn into this poised young woman?

"Wish in one hand, shit in the other—see which fills up first!" someone shouts from the audience.

I whip around to see an elderly woman in the third-row cackling. Great. The town's resident loon, Mrs. Cooper, decided to attend.

"Ignore her," MJ hisses. "Focus on the play."

Shannon makes her entrance as the Witch, and the crowd actually gasps. She's applied green face paint, donned a wild gray wig, walking with a hunched back, nailing the part.

"You wish to have a child?" She cackles at Jack and Chloe. "I'll grant your wish, but only if you bring me these items..."

A movement at the edge of the crowd catches my eye. Ida Watkins sidles up and takes the empty seat next to me.

"It's working," she whispers. "I've been mingling. The reporters are buying it."

"How are you so sure?" I hiss.

She snickers. "Because they're all whining! They're bitching up a storm about this being such a waste of time, and it's hours on the road back to New York City!

"Thank God," I murmur, watching Kevin stride on stage as the Wolf. He's wearing the costume, but I swear he might also be transitioning with some of his actual werewolf features showing through. Damn. It looks impressive. I've heard of 'method' acting, but this is a whole new level!

"I heard what happened last night," Ida continues. "With the mayor and those other Vampires."

I nod, arching my eyebrows. "They won't be coming back to Wesley for a very long time."

On stage, Jessica prances around in a red cape, looking adorably clueless as Little Red Riding Hood while Kevin stalks her. The audience is completely engrossed.

"Who are they?" I ask Ida, nodding toward a group wearing dark clothes and sunglasses clustered under a maple tree. "They look familiar, but I can't place them."

Ida snorts. "The rest of the Vampires in Wesley. They're not too happy either about Jeffrey and Sarah's pranks last night."

I'm about to respond when the audience erupts in applause. Duncan has made his entrance as the Giant, towering over everyone thanks to some clever staging that has him standing on a platform behind the set. His booming voice echoes through the park.

"Fee-fi-fo-fum!" he roars, and I swear the ground actually trembles. Show-off Druids.

"Once this is over and the town is back to so-called normal," I tell Ida, "we need to have a town hall meeting. Some things in this town need to change. What happened in the last few days with the mayor and his friends can never be allowed to happen again."

"Agreed," Ida says, narrowing her eyes.

Something at the park entrance catches my attention, and my stomach drops. Two guys walk in—one in his early twenties with an expression like he's smelled something bad, and an older man who radiates smugness even from this distance.

Thomas and David. Shannon's son and ex-husband.

"Oh no," I breathe.

"What?" Ida follows my gaze. "Who are they?"

"Shannon's worst nightmare," I say, "and they've picked the absolute worst time to show up."

Thirty-Three

Shannon

From backstage, I watch as the curtain drops for intermission, and I lean against a wooden prop tree. Sweat trickles down my back under this ridiculous black costume, but holy hell—we're actually pulling this off.

"Shannon, you're killing it out there!" MJ rushes over, her face flushed with excitement. "The crowd's eating this up, and the reporters are buying it!"

I grin, allowing myself a moment of pride. "Not too shabby for a woman who spent twenty years thinking her biggest talent was making grocery lists."

"Water?" Devon appears at my side, handing me a bottle. His druid tattoo peeks out from his sleeve as he reaches toward me. I'm getting used to it, I guess.

I take a long gulp, savoring the cool liquid. "Thanks. The crowd seems to be buying it, right?"

"Buying it? A reporter from the New York Times told me she's going to write an article about *'The Small Town That Hoodwinked The Internet!'* If they go in that direction, everyone else will follow." He chuckled. "Even so, they're practically throwing money at the concession stand for those 'magical' cookies Jane's selling." He laughs lightly. "They think that there's some funny stuff in them, but I'm pretty sure they're just Oreos with edible glitter."

Before I can respond, Libby rushes over, her face pale, with a look in her eyes that makes my stomach clench.

"Shannon, you need to know—" she starts.

"What? Did another Vampire decide to snack on a reporter?"

Libby shakes her head. "David's here. With Thomas."

The water bottle slips from my fingers, splashing across my witch boots. "What? Where?"

"Third row, left side," she whispers. "They got here about ten minutes ago."

I stumble to the edge of the curtain, heart hammering in my chest as I peek through the gap. There they are—David looking smug as ever in his designer Polo, and Thomas... my beautiful boy, arms crossed, expression tight with disapproval.

Jessica appears beside me, her Little Red Riding Hood cape swishing as she squeezes in to look.

"Dad and Thomas. Shit. What are you gonna do, Mom?"

I stare at my ex-husband and son, feeling my magic stir restlessly under my skin. The last thing I need is to accidentally turn David into the toad he truly is in front of two hundred reporters and tourists with cell phones.

My throat tightens as I watch Thomas's stony face. My brilliant, logical son, who'd never believe his mother turned into a witch overnight. The son who'd run screaming back to Texas if he knew half of what's happened.

"I don't know," I admit, my voice cracking. "But I can't think of it now. We still have the last act to get through."

Even as the words leave my mouth, I wonder if it will also be the final act with Thomas. The thought sends an ache through my chest worse than any spell backfire. Ever since his father walked out on me, Thomas has kept me at arm's length.

Jessica squeezes my hand. "He might surprise you, Mom."

"Right. And Mayor Sadler is going to change his drink of choice to Clamato cocktails." I take a deep breath, trying to steady myself. "Your brother thinks magic is for children and fools. You know that."

Devon steps up behind me, his presence solid and reassuring. "I'm right here, babe. Anything I can do? Want me to 'accidentally' spill some beer on your ex?"

Despite everything, I snort. "Tempting. But no."

"Five minutes, people!" MJ calls out, clapping her hands. "Places for Act Two!"

I straighten my witch's hat and smooth down my costume. "Well...as they say, the show must go on. Even if my son looks like he's attending my funeral rather than my theatrical debut."

"Mom," Jessica whispers, "just be you. The real you."

"The real me might send him running for the hills." I glance back at Thomas one more time. "Or worse—straight to a psychiatrist to have me committed."

The stage manager waves frantically, and I force my feet to move toward my mark. Witch or mom. Truth or lies. Either way, I'm about to put on the performance of my life.

I plaster on my best witchy smile as I sign the last waybill, my hand cramping from scribbling "Blessed Be" and my name for the past thirty minutes. Who knew playing a Witch in a hastily organized community play would attract actual autograph seekers?

"You were magnificent!" gushes a middle-aged woman with crystal earrings the size of golf balls. "Do you do private readings?"

"Only of bedtime stories," I quip, passing her signed program back.

The line finally dwindles, and I'm fantasizing about kicking off these pinchy witch boots when I look up to see the next person in line.

Thomas. Time freezes.

My son stands before me, all six feet of him rigid with disapproval, his sandy blonde hair—so like his father's—neatly combed, his blue eyes—mine—coolly assessing.

In a heartbeat, I'm transported back—Thomas as a chubby baby with dimpled hands reaching for my face. Thomas at three, solemnly explaining why dinosaurs were better than trucks. Thomas at seven, his science fair volcano erupting all over our kitchen. Thomas at sixteen, awkwardly straightening his tie before prom. Thomas at graduation, already looking beyond me toward his future.

My brilliant, logical, ambitious son sees the world in black and white, while his sister embraces all the colors.

"Mom?" His voice breaks the spell. "I saw the posts that woman made. She's saying that you think you're some kind of Witch now?"

I could laugh it off. Blame Beth. Say it was all marketing for this ridiculous play. Keep my son.

But something in me rebels at the thought. I've spent too many years being less than I am. Come hell or high water, I'm totally done with hiding who I am for the sake of other people's opinions. I am what I am, take me or leave me. I'm absolutely done with selling a lie of me.

Even if it shatters my heart.

"Come with me," I whisper, grabbing his arm and steering him away from curious ears.

We end up at a bench by the duck pond, far enough from the crowd that no one will hear us. A family of mallards paddles by, oblivious to my impending maternal doom.

"A lot of things changed for me when I came to Wesley, Thomas. Things that you might find hard to understand and accept."

I stare at my son's handsome face, now twisted with judgment and concern. My heart pounds as if I've chugged three espressos. This moment—this is what I've been dreading since Beth's posts went viral.

"You know what? Screw it." I stand up, hands on my hips. "I am a Witch, Thomas. Not the broomstick-riding, wart-on-the-nose Halloween cliché—though the flying part would be handy with gas prices these days."

Thomas's eyes narrow in anger. "I think the stress of being on your own has gotten to you, Mom. I don't know what you were doing, how you created that video to pretend you're something you're not, but it has to stop. And Jessica? She's throwing away a year of college, trying to look after you. You actually think you've changed? I think you're having some kind of mental breakdown. And this ridiculous play? What the hell, Mom?"

I swallow hard, fighting the anger rising in my throat. The words Thomas used, his dismissive tone, pregnant with judgement, is so much like David's it's eerie—like watching a ventriloquist's dummy mouthing someone else's words. But this is my son, and I love him, despite everything.

"That video? It wasn't something I cooked up. I didn't know Beth was there filming us. It's real. As real as my love for you. I'm...I'm—"

"No!" Thomas shakes his head. "I refuse to support your delusion. You need help, Mom. These women you've become friends with? I don't think they're doing you any favors. This whole idea of coming to this shitty town was bat-shit crazy. You need to—"

"No!" It's my turn to shut him down. "My friends are good people! They've been great friends to me for longer than you've been alive! And who do you think you are to say anything about Wesley? This place is my home now. I'm not delusional, Thomas. What you saw on Facebook was the real me. I've come into some strange but wonderful power since I moved here." I put my hands on my waist and lean into him. "As in magic. As in witchcraft."

I watch my son's face harden into a mask of rebuke that's so painfully familiar it might as well have David's signature stamped across it. Thomas rolls his eyes and starts to get up, muttering something about how he tried, but I'm beyond hope.

Oh, hell no. Not today, sonny.

A white-hot surge of maternal frustration bubbles up inside me. Twenty-one years of diaper changes, fever nights, and college tuition checks, and this kid thinks he can dismiss me like yesterday's leftovers?

I flick my wrist before I can stop myself.

The wind comes instantly—not a gentle breeze, but a focused cyclone that whips around Thomas's ankles, yanking him back onto the bench with a surprised "oomph!"

"What the—" His eyes widen as dirt, leaves, and grass swirl in a perfect circle around our feet.

I'm not done. I point at the duck pond, and the previously calm water churns into whitecaps. The mallards squawk in protest, paddling frantically as miniature waves crash against the shore.

The sun that had been beaming cheerfully overhead disappears behind a cloud that materializes out of nowhere, casting us in dramatic shadow.

Thomas's mouth opens and closes like he's auditioning for a fish food commercial.

I snap my fingers, and everything stops. The wind dies. The water settles. The cloud dissipates. The ducks give me the stink-eye before resuming their paddling.

"Wait. What the hell?" Thomas's voice cracks like it did when he was thirteen.

I grab his hand, squeezing it between mine. His fingers are cold with shock.

"Now do you see? I did that. With just a thought. I am a Witch, Thomas." My voice breaks as tears flood my eyes. "It doesn't change the fact that I love you. I'm also still your Mom."

The silence between us stretches so long I can hear a squirrel chattering in a nearby oak tree. My heart pounds against my ribs like it's trying to escape.

Jessica appears out of nowhere, sliding onto the bench on Thomas's other side. She must have been watching us.

"You can't tell anyone about Mom," she says urgently, grabbing his arm. "Please, Tommy, give her a chance." Her voice drops to a whisper. "I met our grandmother, Judith."

I watch my son's face shift through a kaleidoscope of emotions—shock, disbelief, anger, and something else. Fear? Of me? My heart cracks a little.

"I can't... I can't deal with this." Thomas stands abruptly, looking around wildly. "Where's Dad? I gotta get out of here."

"Thomas, please." I reach for his arm, but he jerks away. "Stay a few days. It's a lot to take in, I know. We need to talk more."

He ignores me completely, scanning the crowd like I'm not even here. Typical. The men in this family have always been champions at emotional exits.

"What the hell?" Thomas narrows his eyes, staring across the park.

I follow his gaze and nearly choke on my own spit.

There, in all his middle-aged glory, is David—Ass Hat extraordinaire—dancing with Suzanne and Amy. And not just any dancing. He's doing some unholy combination of the Boogaloo and what looks like an interpretive dance about a man being attacked by bees. His arms flail wildly as he spins between the two Fae women, their wings catching the sunlight as they twirl him around.

David stumbles, rights himself with a goofy grin, and attempts what might be a moonwalk but looks more like he's trying to scrape gum off his shoe. He's either drunk off his ass or high as a kite on Suzanne's special mushrooms.

Holy doodle. My ex-husband is tripping balls with Fairy women in front of the entire town.

Jessica bursts out laughing beside me, clutching her sides. "I don't think you're going anywhere, bro. Not today, from the looks of dear old Dad." She elbows Thomas, who stands frozen in horror. "You might want to stay and hear Mom out. It's actually pretty cool here."

I watch my son, still staring slack-jawed at his father's dance moves that would make even the most uncoordinated middle-schooler cringe. David spins again, nearly toppling into a group of tourists, before Amy catches him with surprising strength for someone her size.

"I think your dad found the special Fae brownies," I mutter, not sure whether to laugh or die of secondhand embarrassment.

Thomas stands up, still watching his father. "I could drive us, but it doesn't look like Dad wants to leave. This place really is..."

I rise quickly and wrap my arms around him before he can finish that thought with something like "insane" or "a cult." His body is stiff against mine, but he doesn't pull away. Well, that's progress, right?

"Give it a chance. Give me a chance, Thomas. Not everything is cut and dried, black and white; believe me." I squeeze him tighter. "All I'm asking is for you to keep an open mind. And to know I love you no matter what."

Jessica sidles up next to us, putting her head on her brother's shoulder as she joins our group hug. Her Riding Hood cape is still on, complete with glitter that's now transferring to Thomas's pristine button-down.

"I think I need to introduce you to Suzanne and Amy," she says with a mischievous grin. "Try a little of what they gave Dad."

Jessica grabs Thomas's hand to lead him away. My heart stutters—if Thomas gets dosed with Fae treats, I'll never hear the end of it. But before he steps away, he looks back at me with uncertainty swimming in those blue eyes.

"One night," he says firmly. "Then tomorrow I'm out of here. I don't know about magic or being a Witch, but you're still my mother. And Dad is having a good time, so..."

I smile and lean in to give him a kiss on the cheek. His skin is warm against my lips, and for a second, he's my little boy again.

"We'll figure it out. I'm glad you're staying the night."

Thomas shakes his head as Jessica drags him over to where people and Fae are dancing. I watch him leave, feeling a surprising sense of peace wash over me. It might be difficult, but that's usually the way when you choose the right course. I just hope Thomas will accept things and not make trouble.

I watch Thomas as Jessica leads him away, my heart a mix of relief and worry. At least he's staying the night. It's a start.

"That went well," Devon says, appearing at my side like he's got some magical teleportation power I haven't discovered yet.

I lean into him, wrapping my arms around his waist and burying my face in his shoulder. "Define 'well.' My son thinks I'm either delusional or having a breakdown."

Devon hugs me tight, his chest rumbling with laughter. "David and I got on much better than the first time I saw him. As I recall, I decked him then. Everything changed when I introduced him to Suzanne and Amy. Especially when they offered him some special brownies."

I pull back to look at him. "You're the reason he's out there dancing like a drunk octopus?"

"Guilty as charged." Devon's grin is absolutely shameless. "Figured he couldn't give you grief if he was too busy trying to count his fingers."

I peek over at the crowd where David is now attempting to limbo under Ida's outstretched arm. "That's... actually brilliant."

"I have my moments."

I scan the park, taking in the happy chaos we've created. The stage crew is breaking down the set while kids run around with fairy wings strapped to their backs. Reporters are interviewing Beth about her "brilliant marketing stunt," while she soaks up the attention like a sponge. Somehow, this ridiculous plan actually worked.

I catch Kara's eye across the lawn, and my new Witch friend gives me an A-OK sign. There's something reassuring about having an experienced Witch around—like finding a fellow survivor on a deserted island.

Libby joins us, her cheeks flushed from the excitement. "Kara kept everyone's attention on her when you were talking to Thomas," she says, bumping my shoulder with hers. "Did this weird sparkly hand thing. No one saw a thing."

I let out a sigh of relief. "Another crisis averted."

"For now." Libby adds, "But Thomas—"

"Is staying the night," I finish. "We'll deal with tomorrow when it comes."

Thirty-Four

Mary-Jane

I'm packing the last of the potato salad into a cooler when Ray's arm slides around my waist. The evening air has that perfect summer-is-coming feel—warm with just enough coolness to make you appreciate your sweater. Most of the crowd has cleared out, leaving only the truly dedicated partiers and those who couldn't walk straight if their lives depended on it.

"We actually pulled it off," I say, snapping the cooler lid shut. "The reporters were disappointed, but I think they still had a good time. Many said they're bringing their families next year."

Ray's eyes light up like slot machines hitting the jackpot. He gives me a thumbs up that screams *"Ka-ching!"* louder than words ever could.

"Think of the business, MJ," he says, his voice husky with capitalistic lust. "We could expand the restaurant. Maybe add that patio you've been nagging me about for years."

"I don't nag," I say, jabbing him with my elbow. "I suggest. Repeatedly. With increasing volume."

Jane floats over—literally, her wings giving her about two inches of air clearance—with Miguel trailing behind her like a lovesick puppy. The werewolf's nose twitches constantly, probably catching every scent in the park. God knows what that must smell like after a day of sweaty humans, mystical beings, and those "special" brownies.

"Need help with anything else?" Jane asks, looking suspiciously helpful. I'm still not used to this new, cooperative version of her.

"We're good," I tell her, then follow Ray's gaze to where the younger crowd is gathered by the pond.

Jack and Chloe sit close—too close—with their legs touching as they laugh with the other teens. My daughter throws her head back in a full-throated laugh at something Jack says, and from the corner of my eye, I see Ray's jaw tighten.

"They did well in the play," he says quietly, "but I think we need to keep an eye on Chloe around Jack. If he's anything like his brother and goes all Werewolf, then it could take their relationship to a level we won't want."

"You mean furry grandchildren?" I whisper, and Ray looks like he might pass out.

"Don't even joke about that," he hisses. "One minute they're holding hands, the next minute there's a litter of puppies running around our restaurant."

I glance over to where Shannon's son Thomas is sitting with Jessica. He's actually laughing, which is a miracle considering the enormous scowl he walked in with. Guess finding out your mom can control the weather is a hard pill to swallow, but Jessica seems to be making him see reason. Well, they are twins; so if there's someone he'd listen to, it would be her.

"Well, would you look at that," I nudge Ray. "Thomas isn't running for the hills yet."

Shannon and Devon sidle up beside us, both looking disgustingly happy despite the chaos of the day. Devon's got his arm wrapped around Shannon's waist like she might float away if he lets go. The man is smitten, and I'm here for it.

"Need help with cleanup?" Shannon asks, eyeing our mountain of coolers and picnic supplies.

"Sure. Looks like I've lost two of my helpers." I jerk my head toward Jane and Miguel, who are locked in an embrace that's bordering on public indecency. Her wings are fluttering so fast they're creating a small dust devil. "Those two need to get a room before they start a windstorm."

Ray makes a gagging sound. "I'm still trying to process how that happened. One minute she's obsessed with Duncan, the next she's playing tonsil hockey with a Werewolf."

"Speaking of unexpected pairings," I turn to Shannon, "I'm glad Thomas is staying, but what happened to David? Last I saw him, he was dancing with both feet pointing in different directions."

Devon chortles, his eyes crinkling with mischief. "Last I saw him, he was hitting on Mary, admiring her tats. I think Duncan set him straight, and he's moved on to Ivy and Suzanne again. Should we tell him he isn't their type?"

Shannon laughs, the sound light and carefree for the first time in days. "He'll find out soon enough. The only bed he's sharing with them is the bed of vegetables in the yard."

I nearly drop the cooler when I spot Jonas Silver and Beth James having what appears to be an intense conversation at the edge of the park. Beth looks like she's about to burst into tears, and Jonas has that self-righteous Werewolf sheriff stance going on—chest puffed out, hand hovering near his weapon. When he grabs her arm, something in me snaps.

"Hold this," I say, shoving the cooler at Ray before marching across the grass.

"Hang on, Sheriff! What's going on?" I step closer to Beth and shoot her a smile that I hope conveys both "I've got your back," and "Please don't make me regret this."

The sheriff shakes his head. "You know what's going on. She brought all this on the town. Sure, you covered for her, but it could have gone much worse. At the very least, we need to take care of her memories, make sure this doesn't happen again."

My eyes narrow looking at him. "She was a problem mainly for us, and we, the Witches in Wesley—specifically, Cynthia and I—took care of it. As I recall, you were obeying the blood-sucking mayor when he told you to stand down."

Jonas's face flushes red above his beard. "I was following orders—"

"Yeah, Nazi soldiers said the same thing," I snap, then immediately regret the comparison. "Look, I'm not saying Beth didn't cause problems, but we've handled it. The town's safe, the reporters think we're just theater geeks, and Beth was a tremendous help in all of that." I steal a look at Beth and back to Jonas. "And furthermore...if the Fae had been treated decently, none of this would have happened."

He makes a weak gesture, and I know that I have to give him a way out. Oh, the things we have to do to preserve the fragile male egos... "Look, Chief; Beth's learned some important lessons. Right, Beth?"

Beth nods frantically, mascara tracks streaking down her cheeks. "I swear I have. I'll never do this again."

I nod and squeeze her arm. "That's right! And if you need assurance that Beth has changed, I'll vouch for her personally. She made a mistake... just like you in trusting that old Vampire."

Jonas looks like I just farted in church. His nostrils flare—but I don't back down. I've dealt with enough alpha males in my restaurant to know you can't show fear.

"You're vouching for the woman who nearly exposed us all?" He growls, actually growls. "Did you hit your head during that play, or is this some witch solidarity thing?"

"It's a 'we've all screwed up' thing," I say, crossing my arms. "And frankly, I don't see you holding the Vampires to the same standard. They were literally snacking on tourists last night!"

Beth sniffles beside me, and I pat her shoulder without looking. God help me if she starts the waterworks again.

Jonas spears Beth with a look. "You better not try to cause trouble anymore, because it won't matter who vouches for you. We'll deal with you and your Fae friends."

Leading with my chin, I tap his chest with my finger. "That's another thing. The way the Fae are treated by you and Shifters and those blood-suckers. That ends. The Fae were angry, and they caused problems only because of how shitty they're treated. They did a hell of a lot more than you did to convince those reporters and outsiders that this was all just a publicity stunt."

I stare at Jonas, refusing to back down even as he towers over me. My inner voice is screaming, "What are you doing?!" but my mouth keeps right on going. Some days I think my mouth should file for independence from my brain.

"The Fae deserve better," I continue, feeling Beth trembling slightly beside me. "We all do. And frankly, this town needs leadership that doesn't see humans as juice boxes."

The sheriff puts his hands up. "Okay, okay. Maybe we all made some mistakes. And if you're so full of yourself and all the answers, why don't you run for mayor?"

I blink rapidly, my brain finally catching up with my mouth. Me? The Sheriff is suggesting I be Mayor? Of this supernatural circus?

"Hell ya!" Beth brightens, grabbing my arm with unexpected enthusiasm. "Can I be your campaign manager, MJ? I don't know who else would run against you, but I'm willing to work my ass off to get you elected."

The woman who nearly destroyed our town with a bunch of Facebook posts now wants to run my nonexistent political campaign? If that's not a perfect metaphor for how my life's going, I don't know what is.

I'm so gob-smacked by Beth and the Sheriff's suggestion that I don't notice Cynthia and Eric joining us until Eric speaks. "Did I just hear you offer to run a campaign for MJ? You actually want to be Mayor?" He looks at me as if it's absurd.

My spine straightens automatically. Nothing gets my competitive juices flowing like someone doubting me.

"I might! And if I do, then Beth will be at my side." I didn't add that it would be a great way to keep an eye on her. Just in case.

"I might just be the best damn Mayor this town has ever seen," I declare, putting my hands on my hips. "Which, considering our last mayor was a blood-sucking Vampire with impulse control issues, isn't exactly a high bar."

Beth's eyes light up like she just struck gold. She's practically vibrating with excitement next to me, and I'm wondering if I've made a terrible mistake. Having Beth as my campaign manager is like asking a pyromaniac to watch your matches, but maybe that's exactly what I need—someone who knows how to start fires.

Cynthia nods. "I thought it would be Shannon, but you might be a better candidate, MJ. With your gifts, you might be able to bring people together more easily."

I glance at Cynthia and grin. She's always been a little stand-offish with me up until now, and I appreciate the support. As I gaze at her, I realize for once she looks energized, holding her hands over her stomach. I step closer and place my hand on Cynthia's. The picture that comes through makes me smile. It's a girl, and from what I can pick up, the aura of the baby is so similar to Eric's that it's clear who the father is. Cynthia and I nod at each other. 'It's Eric's, not Steve's'. The thought ricochets between us.

The sheriff stalks off, tail between his legs (metaphorically speaking...for now). And I'm left standing with Beth and my newfound political ambitions. Wonderful. Add that to my list of things I never thought I'd say: "I'm a Witch," "My daughter is dating a potential Werewolf," and now "Vote for Mary-Jane Matthews for Mayor, the Witch who'll clean up this town!"

Beth smiles at Cynthia, her eyes softening in a way I've never seen before. She extends her hand toward Cynthia's stomach, her fingers trembling slightly. "May I?"

The request hangs in the air between them like a fragile soap bubble. These two have been at loggerheads ever since she and Eric became a couple, and now Beth wants to touch Cynthia's pregnant belly? I'm half expecting Cynthia to shoot lightning bolts from her eyes.

Cynthia glances at Eric, a silent conversation passing between them, and then she nods. I watch as Cynthia's sworn mortal enemy places her hand on her tummy, her eyes lighting up.

Beth pulls her hand back, and her smile fades. "I'm sorry for everything I did to you, Cynthia. I hope you'll forgive me."

Well, slap my ass and call me Sally. I didn't see that coming.

Cynthia stares at her and takes a deep breath. "We're family, right? Or at least we will be soon, so yeah. The past is the past. I forgive you." It's a surprise when Cynthia steps close and gives her a hug. Cynthia's never been the touchy-feely type, so that's a huge step. At any rate, I'm not complaining. This town's seen enough drama to last a lifetime.

I smile at the unlikely pair. "Yes. I think Beth's one of us now. Maybe not magical, but still one of us." And I know that it could have gone the other way if I hadn't been so understanding.

I spot Peter Bond's jeep backfiring down Main Street, leaving a trail of blue smoke that could choke a dragon. The ancient vehicle lurches to a stop near the park entrance, and out climbs the most antisocial Druid in three counties, looking like he just crawled out of a dumpster after a three-day bender.

"Sweet baby Jesus on a pogo stick," I mutter as Peter scratches his ass with one hand while adjusting his tinfoil-lined baseball cap with the other. "Even our local conspiracy theorist showed up."

Ray follows my gaze and snorts. "Five bucks says he's here to warn us about alien mind control or government surveillance through dental fillings."

"You're on. My money's on 'the Vampires are in cahoots with Big Pha rma.'"

Peter ambles over to where Stan, Libby, and Wayne Silver are chatting by the makeshift stage. He's gesturing wildly, probably explaining how his tracking technology saved the day. Wayne's expression is a masterclass in polite disinterest.

"Should we rescue them?" Ray asks.

"Nah. Wayne's dealt with worse, I'm sure."

I scan the crowd, taking in our bizarre little supernatural melting pot. It was just a year ago that I was just an overworked chef with a failing marriage and expanding waistline. Now I'm a witch with magical powers, possibly running for mayor, and actually happy with my life. Go figure.

My eyes find Shannon across the park, watching Thomas with that mixture of hope and terror only a mother can perfect. Devon stands beside her, solid as a rock, his hand resting protectively at the small of her back.

"Think Thomas will come around?" Ray asks, following my gaze.

"He will if he knows what's good for him," I say, feeling fiercely protective of my friend. "And if not, I'll slip him one of Suzanne's brownies and convince him it was all a beautiful dream."

THIRTY-FIVE

SHANNON

I'm up before the roosters, mixing pancake batter like my life depends on it. Maybe it does. My son's acceptance might hinge on these chocolate chip pancakes—his childhood favorite that I'm hoping will soften whatever emotional hangover he's nursing this morning.

"You sure you don't want me to stay?" Devon asks for the third time, hovering by the door.

"Positive." I gesture with my spatula. "This is mother-son territory. I need to handle it myself."

"Call me if—"

"I'll call if Thomas tries to have me committed or exorcised. Promise." I manage a smile that feels only slightly forced. "Now go help tear down that stage and whatever you construction types do."

After Devon leaves, I busy myself setting the table, arranging silverware with military precision. The knife and fork placement suddenly seems critically important, like the feng shui of cutlery might determine whether my son accepts me as a Witch or decides I've lost my mind.

The floorboards creak, and Thomas appears in the doorway. His hair is total bedhead, dark circles shadow his eyes, but there's something almost contrite in his expression.

"Morning," he mumbles, shuffling to the table.

"Hungry?" I slide a stack of chocolate chip pancakes onto a plate, trying to keep my hands from trembling. "I made your favorite."

Thomas stares at the pancakes, then at me. "You didn't, like... hex these or anything, right?"

I nearly drop the spatula. "What? No! I don't—that's not how—" I stop when I notice the corner of his mouth twitching upward.

"Mom, that was a joke."

"Oh." I exhale. "Right. Witch humor. Very funny."

He cuts into the pancakes, shoving a massive bite into his mouth. "These are good," he says around the mouthful. "Magic-free but still good."

I sit across from him, clutching my coffee mug like it's a lifeline.

"How was your evening with Jessica and the kids in town?"

Thomas shovels another forkful of pancakes, chewing thoughtfully. "Not terrible. Not sure about that Kevin though. He's obviously got a thing for Jess, so no accounting for taste, right?"

"I heard that, loser!" Jessica walks in and swats the back of Thomas's head. "Seems to me you were pretty interested in some young cheerleader type... Rachel? She's a bit young, bro. But maybe that's your attraction, the whole college man vibe."

I laugh seeing my twins tease each other like old times. The sound bubbles up from somewhere deep inside me, rusty but genuine. For a moment, we're just us—my kids bickering over breakfast, me playing referee. No witchcraft, no supernatural town drama, no ex-husband dancing with fairies.

"So, meeting the kids in town wasn't terrible. That's a start." I ruffle Thomas's hair as I set a glass of juice in front of him, something I haven't done in too long a time.

I plop down at the table across from Thomas, who's working on his third pancake. He looks up at me, and his smile is gone. "But they aren't my mother. A Witch, Mom? So where's your broom and cauldron?"

Rolling my eyes, I try to keep my voice light. "The broom is in the closet, and I use it for—wait for it—sweeping. Revolutionary, I know. And my cauldron is actually a Le Creuset Dutch oven that I got on clearance. Magic on a budget."

Thomas doesn't laugh. Tough crowd.

"Look," I say, leaning forward. "Does this mean you are starting to get your head around what I am now? Cause, I won't change. Doesn't mean I'll flaunt it, but I am what I am, to quote Popeye."

Jessica pauses in pouring juice and gawks at me. "Who?"

I shake my head. "An old Robin Williams movie. Never mind." Great, now I feel ancient on top of everything else. Nothing like your kids making you feel like you belong in a museum.

Turning back to Thomas, I watch him pour syrup on his pancakes till what's left sits in a small lake. Some things never change, Witch mom or not.

"Look, guys," I say, "When I came here, I didn't have much money and not many job prospects. I was lucky to inherit this place. A place that I loved when I was a teen. I had no idea what would happen, that I'd survive, let alone become a Witch. But I'm happy, Thomas. Aside from having you and Jessica, it's the happiest I've ever been."

Thomas takes a deep breath before looking over at me. "I'm glad you're happy, Mom. I mean, I'm not a complete asshole. But this Witch thing...it's a lot to process."

Jessica joins us at the table. "Not if you keep an open mind. Personally, I think it's tres cool." She looks over at me. "After I finish my exams..." Dipping her head to the side, she adds, "Yeah, number one son talked me into going back to Boston to finish the year. But I'm coming back for the summer. If MJ will still have me, I want that job in her restaurant. And... I also call dibs on the far cabin. No offense, but I've gotten used to my privacy."

I blink, totally gob smacked by that news. It's great that Jess is finishing her year and will return for the summer. And yeah, that cabin. Needs work, but why not?

Thomas continues, "Look, I can barely accept this Witch thing, but I'm trying. The only thing I ask is that you don't publicize that fact. At least not to any of my friends or the world at large."

I burst out laughing. "What the hell do you think we did last night? The last thing I want is to have my magic publicized!"

"What about Dad?" Jessica asks, licking syrup off her fork. "He saw the video and—"

I cut her off before she could finish. "Your father got wasted last night. I think he'd rather forget any of this happened." The image of David dancing with the Fae Women flashes through my mind. "Trust me, the special brownies and mushrooms Suzanne and Amy gave him will ensure he remembers nothing but a pleasant buzz and maybe some sparkly lights."

Thomas nods, his expression serious. "Well, I won't be trying to convince him the video was real. As far as he's concerned, this was just a huge publicity stunt for that play." He looks over at Jessica with a smirk. "Red Riding Hood? Seriously?"

Jessica swats him on the arm. "I nailed it! Admit it. You want my autograph, bro." She smirks while munching on a forkful of pancakes, syrup dripping down her chin.

I set my coffee mug down with a decisive thunk. Decision time. "I want to show you something after breakfast. How all this started."

Thomas eyes me warily, like I might suddenly sprout a third eye or turn him into a newt. "The source of your... powers?"

"The Witching Well," Jessica says with her mouth full. "It's epic. Grandma lives there now."

Thomas chokes on his orange juice. "I'm sorry, what? Grandma? As in, your mother? The one who died?"

"Yep," I say, popping the 'p' like I'm discussing the weather instead of my dead mother residing in a magical well. "She's kind of a pain in the ass about it too. Very particular about her offerings."

"Uh, okay, I guess?" Thomas rubs his temples. "After that, I should collect Dad from wherever he is."

I lead my kids through the forest, praying that this doesn't blow up in my face. Thomas walks beside me, glancing around as if the trees might suddenly grow arms and grab him. Jessica skips ahead, completely at ease in our magical wonderland.

"So, this well just... made you a Witch?" Thomas asks, ducking under a low-hanging branch.

"Not exactly. It's more like it awakened something that was already there." I step over a fallen log. "Family legacy stuff. Turns out great-great-grandma wasn't just making herbal tea for the neighbors."

"Wait till you meet Grandma Judith," Jessica calls back. "She's a bit cranky, but still pretty awesome."

Thomas stops walking. "I'm sorry, what? Cranky? As in she talks?"

"One revelation at a time, Jess," I mutter. "Let's not break his brain completely."

We reach the clearing, and it's like someone hit the mute button on nature. The forest goes eerily silent—no birds chirping, no insects buzzing, no leaves rustling. It's like the world is holding its breath.

And there, sitting beside the ancient stone well like he's posing for a calendar of "Mystical Creatures Monthly," is Robert, his one ear twitching as he watches us approach.

Thomas freezes mid-step, his body going rigid. "That's a bobcat, Mom!" His voice climbs an octave higher than I've heard since his voice changed at thirteen.

"No shit, Sherlock," Jessica says, rolling her eyes. She strolls over to Robert as if he's a house cat. "That's just Robert. He's Mom's familiar."

"He's Mom's WHAT?" Thomas squeaks, pressing himself against a tree trunk.

Robert tilts his head. "Your son lacks your daughter's adaptability, Shannon." His voice sounds like gravel being stirred with a stick.

Thomas's eyes bulge so wide I'm afraid they might pop out. "Watch out! He's growling really loud!"

I laugh. "No, he just told me that you need to lighten up."

"WHAT? Did that wild animal just say something? Don't tell me you talk to it!"

I shrug. "Maybe." I have to bite my lip to keep from laughing again at the expression on Thomas's face.

I pull my slouch bag off my shoulder and dig through the chaos inside. Past the wallet with no cash, a half-empty pack of gum, three lipsticks (all basically the same shade), and what might be the world's oldest protein bar, my fingers finally close around the wine bottle.

"You brought alcohol?" Thomas asks, his eyebrows practically touching his hairline.

"Family tradition," I say, working the cork out with a satisfying pop. "The spirit who used to reside in this well used to prefer Jack Daniels, but this one prefers wine... expensive wine, I might add." I wave the bottle of Cabernet that cost me forty bucks I couldn't really spare.

Thomas crosses his arms, looking exactly like his father when he's about to lecture me about something. "You're telling me there's something in that well. Something that helped you become... y'know... a Witch."

Jessica leans over the lip of the well, her hair dangling dangerously close to the dark depths below. Her voice is cheery as she calls out, "Not just anyone, bro. Our grandmother, Judith. I thought we covered this. Try to keep up, Tom."

I stare at the ancient well, feeling the familiar tingle of magic race up my spine. Robert gets up and rubs his side against my leg, his wild fur surprisingly soft.

"Go for it. This is who you are, and your son needs to know," he says, golden eyes fixed on mine.

I nod, drawing strength from his presence. "Yeah. I think so too."

Thomas's gaze pings between me and the bobcat like he's watching a tennis match played by aliens. His mouth opens and closes, but no sound comes out. Good. The kid who always has a smart comeback is finally speechless.

I raise my hands toward the sky, feeling the energy gather around my fingertips. The air shifts, responding to my call.

"By the air around us..." My voice carries on the breeze that suddenly swirls around us, lifting fallen leaves into a mini-cyclone.

I lower my hand to point at the ground beneath our feet. "The earth under our feet..."

The soil trembles slightly, and Thomas stumbles, grabbing the lip of the well for support.

I snap my fingers, and a flame ignites at my fingertips, dancing and flickering. "And the power of fire."

Thomas's eyes are now the size of basketballs. Jessica grins like she's at the best show on earth.

I blow out the flame and start emptying the wine into the well, watching the dark liquid disappear into the depths. "And water, although of a distilled variety."

The wine glugs out of the bottle, splashing against the ancient stones.

"I give thanks, and ask for blessings for me and my children." I take a deep breath, knowing what comes next might just send Thomas running for the hills. "Spirit of the well... Mom. Please honor us with your presence."

The well water starts bubbling like I've just dropped an industrial-sized Alka-Seltzer into it. I grab Jessica and Thomas by their shirts and yank them back just as a geyser erupts, shooting twenty feet into the air.

"Holy shit!" Thomas yelps, stumbling backward and landing on his ass.

"Language!" I scold automatically, then catch myself. "Actually, no, that's fair. Holy shit indeed."

The water settles, and a hollow voice echoes from the depths. "My daughter. You have brought both grandchildren this time. Come closer and let me see your faces."

Thomas's mouth hangs open so wide I could park my SUV in it. Jessica, meanwhile, is already leaning over the edge like she's about to dive in for a swim.

"Hi Grandma!" she chirps, waving down at the water.

I nudge Thomas with my elbow. "Go on. What's the worst that can happen? Another face full of water? It's your grandmother, Thomas."

He doesn't speak—I'm not sure he remembers how—but he inches forward like the well might sprout teeth and bite him. Finally, he leans over to peer into the water.

I join them, and my breath catches. There's my mother, her face shimmering in the water, smiling up at us. Not scowling. Not judging. Actually smiling. Will wonders never cease?

"Hey Mom. Finally, you meet both of them." I drape my arms over Jessica's and Thomas's shoulders, feeling something shift inside me. My kids. My mother. All together. It's like someone super-glued the broken pieces of my heart back together.

Judith's voice rises from the well. "You've done well. Not only averting the crisis which filled the town with outsiders, but it's an ill wind that doesn't blow some good. Thomas is here, and he knows." She addresses my son directly. "Be good to your mother. She's the only one you'll ever have, and a truer friend you'll never meet."

Thomas mumbles, "I can't believe this. Is this really happening?" He looks like his brain is about to melt and drip out of his ears.

Jessica ignores him, leaning dangerously far over the edge. "Grandma, I'm going back to school, but I'll be back in a couple of weeks. I want to learn, to become a strong Witch like you and Mom."

Judith smiles, her image wavering. "You will. My blessing goes with you."

Thomas starts to tear up, and I pull him closer. "It's okay, son. This will take some time to get your head around, but even if you don't, I'll still be here for you." Something in him must have broken, seeing magic, getting caught up in it, along with meeting his grandmother.

He turns and hugs me, openly crying. "I'm sorry for how I've treated you. Always judging and being so aloof."

I hug him back, my own tears falling. "It's okay. You're here now, and that's all that matters. Just don't be a stranger. I need to see you and be more in your life."

Jessica joins our hug, and we're a sobbing mess, clinging to each other like survivors of an emotional shipwreck.

Judith speaks one last time from the well. "All is well. Go in peace... for now."

My face tightens. What the hell does that mean? But Robert is already leading the way back through the forest, and we follow, arms still around each other.

I'll figure it out.

I always have, haven't I?

The End

Author's Note

I hope that you enjoyed reading the books of the Hex After 40 series as much as I've enjoyed writing them! It's been a couple of years since I completed Witch In Time, the fourth book in the series. To be honest, I thought that it would be the final book about Shannon and her gal pals.

But in the two years since I completed that book, some pretty crazy stuff's happened in my life.

For starters, in 2023, with all the COVID mania behind us, my family doctor wasn't too impressed with some lab tests and ordered a procedure.

"It's a simple one," he said.

"Ninety-nine percent of the people who have it done have no problems," he said.

"You'll be fiiine," he said.

I almost died.

And I'm not talking the 'Oh my gosh, I almost died' kind of hyperbole. No, I legitimately almost died. I'm talking graveyard dead almost died. Took me six months to recover. I kind of almost died.

So yeah, 2023 sucked...

But the wheel turns, people.

2024 started out 'Okay'. I wasn't dead (always a plus!), and I was on the mend. We got a new puppy to keep Suki company, I was moving around, and my sweet grand-daughter was turning one. I thought things were going fine, until I got an email last summer...

Oh boy.

What. An. Email... I can't believe it actually happened.

MGM STUDIOS BOUGHT THE FILM RIGHTS!

Yep, you read that right! **Hex After 40 is going to be on screen!**

Their concept was/is 'Desperate Housewives', but with Witches. After reading many books in the Paranormal Women's Fiction genre, their writer/producer felt my characters and plotlines were the best fit. They are currently creating the pilot, which if all goes well, will be released in 2026 or 2027.

Exciting? Yeah.

Every author's dream to see their book on-screen? Hell yeah!

And... during this period, I found myself missing my fictional friends, Shannon, Libby, Mary-Jane and Cynthia. So, I decided to do this book—Bewitched and Between. It was a totally new concept and an absolute blast to write. Jim and I conspire, plot and scheme, often while cooking dinner together. Yes, beer is often involved as well. Don't tell my kids.

But...it also made me miss my friends from the **Witch Way** series, Kara and Maren! And I thought, I'd like to have them pay a little visit to the mountain town of Wesley NY in their RV. I just knew all my Witches would become BFFs and even Maren's new love, Mike the Vampire would turn heads.

If you haven't read the Witch Way series with Kara and Maren, two middle-aged sisters on their RV adventure where they discover magic as well as the bonds of sisterhood, you would probably enjoy it. They're available on Amazon, right where you got this book from!

Readers have commented that the dynamic between the two sisters is familiar and very real (write what you know!). There's mystery, drama, lots of laughs and a host of quirky and fun characters they meet in their travels. Fans especially love Howie, the geriatric, wise, and amorous Werewolf!

So, dear readers, cherish your family and your time on this blue planet! Until next time...

For more updates on future books coming and on sales as well, please join my Newsletter group. No spam, promise. Our two pugs, Suki and Kerry ensure that doesn't happen, insisting on 'walksies' constantly, rather than sending out spam.

You can sign up at my website MichelleDorey.com

I also write ghostly fiction under my other pen name, Michelle Dorey, with an emphasis on eerie and not gore. You'll see them at my website! Enjoy!

As always, thank you for your readership. It means the world do me.

All the best, to you and those closest to your heart,

Shelley Dorey

The more light-hearted pen name of

Made in United States
North Haven, CT
02 November 2025